A Married Man

Piers Paul Read was born in 1941, brought up in Yorkshire and educated at Ampleforth and Cambridge. He spent two years in Germany, one in America and travelled extensively in the Far East and South America.

His other novels are *The Upstart*, *Polonaise*, *The Junkers*, *Monk Dawson*, *Game in Heaven with Tussy Marx* and *The Professor's Daughter*. He is the author of *Alive: The Story of the Andes Survivors* and *The Train Robbers*.

Piers Paul Read lives in Yorkshire with his wife and two children.

Also by Piers Paul Read
in Pan Books

Alive: The Story of the Andes Survivors
The Upstart
Polonaise
The Junkers
Monk Dawson
Game in Heaven with Tussy Marx
The Professor's Daughter

Piers Paul Read

A Married Man

Pan Books in association with
The Alison Press/Secker & Warburg

First published in Great Britain 1979 by
The Alison Press/Martin Secker & Warburg Ltd
This edition published 1981 by Pan Books Ltd,
Cavaye Place, London SW10 9PG
in association with The Alison Press/Martin Secker & Warburg Ltd
© Piers Paul Read 1979
ISBN 0 330 26369 2
Printed and bound in Great Britain by
Hunt Barnard Printing Ltd, Aylesbury, Bucks

author's note

To understand the story which follows, the reader should know
a little about the English legal profession. A man accused of a
crime must first see a solicitor who advises him on his legal rights
and draws up his defence. The solicitor himself is not allowed
to appear in a higher court so he calls upon the services of a barrister, whose office is called his chambers. The barrister, wearing
wig and gown, pleads the case (the brief) prepared by the solicitor before judge and jury. He may also, on occasions, be retained
to apply before magistrates for licences to open public houses,
gambling casinos and betting shops. This work is well paid; but
since a barrister should not seem to care about money lest he be
brought down in public estimation to the level of his customers,
he employs a clerk in his chambers who for ten per cent arranges
his appearance in court and negotiates his fee.

Part one

chapter one

On Friday 3 August 1973, three men sat in conference at one of the Inner London Crown Courts – one a fidgeting youth with a lean face; the second a plump, bespectacled man in a crumpled blue suit; and the third a tall, middle-aged barrister wearing a wig and gown. The case they were discussing was the same, but each wore a particular expression on his face. The young man appeared anxious – which, since he was the accused, was only to be expected; the second man, his solicitor, was nodding deferentially at everything said by the third who, while addressing them both, looked away into the middle distance as if someone more interesting might come in through the door.

If anything was unusual about this conference it was that the barrister, John Strickland, spoke more rapidly than was usual for someone paid by the day. Moreover his brow was creased with a petulant frown and there was an edge of irritation in his voice: for unknown to the other two he had told his clerk more than a month before that he had no wish to work during August, yet here he was on August the third appearing for this young mechanic charged with receiving stolen goods.

The case against him was weak, and the instructions from the seedy solicitor were to plead Not Guilty, but knowing that if he did so the case would last well into the following week John Strickland was now trying to persuade him that on the evidence his client might well be sentenced to six months in prison; whereas if they entered a plea of Guilty and saved the time of the Court, the sentence would almost certainly be suspended.

The youth seemed reluctant to accept this advice – as if he thought it was wrong to admit to something he had not done – but his solicitor was so impressed by John Strickland's reputation that he advised him to agree. The group broke up and a little later reassembled in the court. The mechanic pleaded Guilty: John was eloquent in mitigation, but the Judge did not act as he had predicted. The sentence was indeed six months' imprisonment, but it was not suspended, so while John Strickland made good his escape from the court in time to catch the five o'clock train to Norwich, the young mechanic was dragged down to the cells below.

Out in the street John hailed a taxi but absent-mindedly told the driver to take him to Paddington – the station from which he usually caught a train at weekends to go to his cottage in Wiltshire – and it was only the sight of some tourists wearing *Lederhosen* in Oxford Street which reminded him that he too was on holiday – that he was going to join his family at his parents'-in-law house in Norfolk and that the cab was therefore going in the wrong direction. As a result he arrived at Liverpool Street Station too late for the five o'clock train, and had to pay out more than three pounds to the contemptuous driver as well as a commensurate tip.

Having bought his ticket John went to a callbox to telephone his wife Clare. While he waited for her to answer he inhaled the sent of a drunkard's urine and studied the scratches on the beige enamel. Some contained names, some obscene messages, others football slogans, but more often they were gratuitous, meaningless defacements. There was no reply. He went to the station buffet and sat drinking milky tea from a plastic cup while waiting for the next train. The expression on his face was one of resigned melancholy, but he did not see his own expression: instead there appeared in his mind the lean face beneath close-cropped hair of the young mechanic as he had been sentenced – a mixture of misery and a kind of triumph, as if he had been expecting injustice and was glad to see his expectations fulfilled.

John was not pondering the injustice – he had long since established a detached attitude towards the fate of his clients. He wondered only if it had been apparent that his advice had been proffered for his own convenience – not to the mechanic, of course, who was patently stupid and probably a criminal anyway, but to the shifty solicitor. And though John knew that his reputation was sufficiently well-established for no damage to be done, it was all the same an added source of annoyance to the general discomfort of travelling out of London on a Friday evening.

John was also puzzled as to why he had been so determined to get away on a holiday he did not want to take in the first place. His wife's parents both irritated him, and it was said by some of his friends that he only went to stay with them in the summer to save himself the expense of taking his family elsewhere: or because Clare, who had a stronger character than was apparent in her inoffensive face, liked to return to the scenes of her childhood with her own children, leaving John to choose between joining them there or staying alone at the cottage in Wiltshire.

It was now established that the Stricklands went to Norfolk for the first two weeks of August, and John decided as he sat in the buffet that if he had been so determined not to return to London the following week it was because he was an orderly man who, having made arrangements, liked to keep them. It was this quality, after all, which had made him a successful barrister, and if the young mechanic had suffered as a result there were many others like him who would benefit in the end.

Aptly sacrificed in this way the youth was forgotten and John's eye focused on the squalor around him – the scruffy travellers and the listless slut serving tea behind the counter. It is a sign of a nation's decline, he thought to himself, that its people no longer take the trouble to dress themselves decently or keep themselves clean. He then reflected that sitting there on a grimy chair drinking insipid tea would dirty his pin-striped suit, and while musing over an action against British Rail for the cost of cleaning it he saw through the opaque plateglass window that a queue had formed for his train. He left the buffet and stood in its tail, shuffling forward every now and then to keep his place, wondering why he suffered this discomfort and indignity to reach an undesired destination, until finally he found a seat on the train and distracted himself with the trivia in the evening paper.

chapter two

He changed trains at Norwich, still in a sour mood. When he reached Cromer on the coast there was no one there to meet him, which changed his mood of self-pity into rage. He telephoned his mother-in-law from another public callbox and announced in clipped, uncivil tones that he was there. Half an hour later Clare drove up in their rusting Volvo station-wagon: John by then was so possessed by his anger that he barely embraced her but sat in the car with a white face and clenched jaw.

Clare Strickland was also tall, and had the confident gait of those who are tall and attractive. She had thick brown hair, blue eyes, and agreeable, even, slightly Slavic features which were delightful when she smiled and distinctive in repose. She was eight years younger than her husband but had borne two children, so though her legs remained long and her stomach slim her breasts were loose, there were bulging blue veins beneath her left knee and and a hard mass of bumpy flesh around her thighs. Just now, at the age of thirty-two, her complexion was beginning to lose its sheen, just as John, who looked so handsome and distinguished in court, was balding beneath his wig and had a white, flaccid stomach beneath his gown.

They had been married for twelve years. Driving him back to her parents' house Clare immediately recognized her husband's mood, and, with the nonchalance of someone raising an umbrella when it rains, asked: 'Why on earth didn't you tell me when you were coming?'

'I tried to telephone. There was no reply.'

'You can't expect us to hang around all the time.'

'You knew the time the train got in.'

'There are three trains on a Friday.'

'You might have known I'd be on this one.'

'You said you'd catch the earlier one.'

'Did you meet it?'

'I had to give the children their supper.'

'What about your mother?'

'She was having a drink with Mrs Sewell.'

'And your father?'

'He went too.'

'Of course they couldn't miss a drink with Mrs Sewell.'

'Why should they give up their own life just because we come to stay?'

They drove on in silence until they arrived at the Old Rectory, Busey, which was Clare Strickland's family home. They came into the house to find that her parents, Helen and Eustace Lough, had already gone to bed.

'Have you had any supper?' Clare asked her husband.

'No.'

'You should have had some on the train.'

'There wasn't a restaurant car.'

'Why not?'

'An unofficial strike.'

'We've finished the fish pie, I'm afraid. You'll have to have some scrambled eggs.'

They went through to the kitchen, where John sat at the table with his face so creased with self-pity that it bore more resemblance to the figure of Christ on the Cross than to a suave barrister at the London Bar: and even Clare, who was normally serene, was so fed up at having to return to the stove for the third time that her features were squeezed to look cross and pudgy.

She sat with him in silence as he ate, then cleared away his plate and went upstairs to take a bath. John followed twenty minutes later and washed himself in the same water – a habit left over from the early days of their marriage – and then joined his wife in the sagging double bed of the Loughs' spare room. They kissed and embraced under the blankets – another old formality – then switched off the lights and went to sleep.

chapter three

John did not wake in a better mood. From the moment he became conscious the next morning he was assailed by fresh irritations – first his son and daughter, Tom and Anna, bursting in on them, jumping on their bed, screaming and chasing one another around the room; and then, when they had been driven out, returning every four or five minutes to complain, quarrel or – with the fast change of mood that children can manage – to tease and tickle their comatose parents until gummed up, groaning and with taut bladders they staggered to the bathroom and then down to breakfast.

In the kitchen John came face to face with Clare's mother, Helen, who even now after twelve years could not conceal a look of disappointment whenever she saw him: she had hoped her daughter would do better. Then his father-in-law, the brigadier, came in from the garden and sat at the kitchen table, eager to talk about the news of the day which he had already read in the morning paper. Helen brought them toast, coffee and scrambled eggs – an act of solicitude which nevertheless irritated her son-in-law because there were grounds in the coffee, which she made in the same way as tea; there was no orange juice; and he had eaten scrambled eggs the night before and believed that too many eggs – particularly with coffee – were bad for his liver. The paper which she gave him to read was the *Guardian* and not *The Times,* and had already been crumpled by the brigadier, Eustace Lough, who while John tried to read it began a commentary of his own.

'Now, John boy,' he said. 'You're a lawyer. What do you think about the government bringing in the law to stop strikes?'

John, who disliked conversation at breakfast, and wished he was in his own home with a clean copy of *The Times,* said he had not given it much thought.

'In my opinion it's a damned stupid thing to do,' said the brigadier, whose appearance was what one might expect of a former army officer – tall, ascetic, correct, moustached – but whose opinions were quite unpredictable. 'I don't see the point of making laws if you can't enforce them, and they won't be able to enforce them, mark my words. They've run down the army anyway, and even if they hadn't, I can't see my old regiment running a coalmine.'

'You don't have to bring in the army,' said John. 'You could fine the unions or lift their immunity against civil actions.'

'I know, my boy, I know,' he said – warming to the argument. 'But when it comes down to it they'll come out on strike if they don't like what you're doing. And if you can't break the strike, you might as well leave them alone in the first place.'

'I dare say,' said John, trying to return to the paper.

'Because, in the last analysis, the working man is more loyal to his union than he is to his government. And who can blame him? The unions saw to him when he was down in the 1930s while all the different governments just washed their hands.'

Clare sat with the blank, bored look which always came on to her face when her father and husband discussed politics, money or motor-cars; and which John adopted when Clare and her mother discussed cooking, clothes, gardens or children, for while they both believed in the equality of men and women, they confined themselves to the conventional interests of their sex.

'All the same,' John said to the brigadier, 'how are the trades unions to be made to acknowledge their responsibilities if not through the framework of the law?' He did not want to continue the conversation, but it went against the grain to let a case go by default.

'I don't know,' said the brigadier, shaking his head with sincere anxiety as if the stability and prosperity of England depended upon the judgement of one retired army officer. 'You see, John . . . and I know you won't like this . . . but the whole system's been discredited by . . . by . . .' his hand searched for the words in the air above the kitchen table '. . . by the progress of history. The values we believed in – the king, the empire, a hierarchical society – they're all seen now not just as old-fashioned but as downright wrong. And I'm afraid that your profession is tarred with the same brush. The working man won't trust the law to give him justice, so perhaps the only thing is to give the unions their own courts, like the Church in the Middle Ages.'

'Don't listen to him, John,' said Helen. 'He's picked it all up from Guy.' She was referring to her son.

'I'm not senile yet, you know,' said the brigadier, with an angry look towards Helen which just fell short of meeting her eyes. Then, as if ashamed of having shown his annoyance at her remark, he left the kitchen and shuffled along the stone passage towards the garden door.

'Is Guy here?' John asked Clare.

'Yes,' she said.

'Where was he last night?'

'Over at the Mascalls'.'

'And he goes to the pub,' said Helen with a sigh.

She said this with a sigh not because she was a teetotaller who disapproved of drinking but because she was a snob who wished that her twenty-two-year-old son would drink in private, not public houses. It was often assumed by newcomers to the Lough family circle (and fourteen years before, John had been such a newcomer) that because the wife bore her husband's name she had somehow adopted his values, but before Clare's mother was Helen Lough she was Helen Dansie, which for those who do not know (as John once did not know) is the name of one of the oldest Catholic families in England – Catholics loyal to the Pope not through intellectual conviction or intermarriage with an Irishman but by hereditary right stretching back beyond the torture and persecution under Queen Elizabeth, beyond the Reformation itself, to the Middle Ages when all Englishmen were Catholic like the Dansies.

It was not that they were notably pious. A relation by marriage had been hanged, drawn and quartered, but the main line of the Dansie family was stubborn rather than holy, went occasionally to prison, and above all paid out heavy fines which reduced them over the generations from one of the richest families in England to the level of the minor gentry – all of which, for those outside the family, might seem rather obscure, but it explained why Clare's mother, much as she disliked her son drinking at the Malt Shovel Inn at Busey, would prefer him to drink there than at Chatsworth, Hatfield or any of those grand country houses built with the booty of the plundered monastries.

Some cynics said that should Guy Lough actually be invited to drink – or better still to stay – at Chatsworth or Hatfield or Burghley House, then Helen might relent, might forgive them their sins and in the ecumenical spirit of the age let bygones be bygones: for it was said that she was not just a subtle Catholic snob but also a simple social snob. Guy had not been taken up by these smart Protestant families, so the question did not arise, but it cannot be hard to imagine her reaction when Clare – her beautiful and intelligent daughter – introduced a young man into the family whose father was a provincial Presbyterian judge and mother an aspiring Anglican.

It had been particularly awkward that John's name was Strickland, since this was also the name of an eminent Norfolk family, and when the engagement was announced all Helen's friends had asked what relation John was to Lord N. The answer, of course, was none. Clare had hoped that because her mother had married an obscure young officer she would raise no objection to her marrying an obscure young barrister – not realizing that those who disappoint their own expectations usually double them for their children. She too had seen the expression on her mother's face, but she was tough and had rejected her parents' objections to John's modest means and his agnosticism. They had been married by a Jesuit in a Catholic church and Helen, after all, had Guy, whom she could dream of marrying to a Plowden, a Throckmorton or a Fitzalan-Howard.

Eustace was not a snob. He was happy, certainly, to have been born a gentleman, the second son of an East Anglican squire; to have gone to Harrow, and to have had a few hundred a year to supplement his army salary: but unlike his wife he seemed to realize that in marriage, as on a battlefield, a man's family did not matter but more fundamental qualities came to the fore. He had taken one look at John and had judged at once that a more or less decent fellow lay beneath the superficial charm. In the twelve years that had followed he had never had cause to doubt his judgement, and without the anxieties that troubled his relations with his own son, he tended to get on better with John than he did with Guy.

He was particularly pleased whenever he came to stay, because now that he had retired he was short of the company of men. The women – Helen and Clare – were no substitute for the camaraderie of the Officers' Mess. His marriage with Helen had been perfectly proper: the code of conduct of their class had seen them through the kind of crisis which often destroys a more modern marriage but, since he had retired, Helen seemed to have lost a certain respect for him, as if his authority had gone with the uniform. Frustrated, perhaps, after twenty years as an army officer's wife she had upon their retirement to Busey taken a course in Social Administration, and now held a post in the benevolent bureaucracy of the Norfolk County Council.

The effect on Eustace had been sad, for while he could not deny his wife the right to develop her own talents in the second half of her life, he saw mirrored in her career his own demotion.

He started to spend most of the day reading Russian novels and, almost as an affectation, to buy cheap, ill-fitting clothes at second-hand shops – he who had once had his suits made to measure in Savile Row and his shoes hand-made in Jermyn Street. He insisted that his old shirts would do, even when the collars and cuffs were frayed, and so began to look like a tramp: and the more he looked like one, the more he behaved like one, lunching off tins of sardines or the remains of dinner the night before.

The neighbours who had once been happy to invite him to dinner now became embarrassed by his appearance and his increasingly eccentric (that is radical) opinions. Those of his friends who remained alive began to avoid him; so during the long months of the winter he was obliged to invent imaginary ailments so that he could call on the local doctor as a private patient and chat to him at five guineas an hour.

These changes in Eustace, which may have been imperceptible to his immediate family, were noticed by John, who only saw him once or twice a year, but so saturated was he by his professional detachment that he returned no verdict of either innocence or guilt on his mother-in-law: he merely noted that her religious convictions did not seem to hamper her somewhat cruel treatment of the brigadier, just as he had noted before that Clare's contemporaries from her Catholic convent were the first to deceive their husbands.

This latent hypocrisy in Roman Catholics was yet another source of his grumbling irritability at Busey; nor is the list complete. Guy, who now sloped into the kitchen and sat in a cloud of adolescent odour eating his breakfast, was designed in every detail to annoy the middle-aged, middle-class man. His clothes were deliberately scruffy – not like his father's, haphazardly ill-fitting, but the product of many hours of bleaching and patching to match the fashion of the day. His body was handsome, gangling, slothful: blond whiskers glinted on his unshaven chin. He had a private education and a university degree, yet lived by selling icecream from a van in Hyde Park and when he chose to take a holiday went on the dole.

He was, all the same, good company, and it seemed to put Helen in a happy mood to have her two children sitting once again around the kitchen table. Here too, of course, there was a source of irritation: the more people there were in the house, the more work there was to do in the kitchen, and Helen Lough, who both as a child and as an officer's lady had been cooked for and waited upon as befitted her station in life, had found after Eustace's retirement that even with a small private income to supplement his pension and her salary from the Norfolk County Council they could not afford the staff which the armed forces had hitherto provided.

Then aged fifty-seven, her body may have been feeble but her heart had been strong, and in the spirit of the Blitz or the Black Hole of Calcutta she had marched into those areas of the house where she had hardly set foot before – learning how to peel a potato and roast a chicken until now, five years later, she could serve up a passable dinner. An old lady came in from the village two or three times a week to wash the floors and beat the carpets, but otherwise the housework was done by Helen Lough or more often by no one at all: for however competent she became at the domestic routine, Helen continued to behave as if she were helping out in a crisis which would one day come to an end.

Since Clare had left home before Eustace had retired, she too had been brought up with a nanny and servants: and even when they were without them she had never been encouraged to help in the house. Just as a mother in a famine will give her own share of gruel to her starving child, so Helen in this temporary crisis preferred to wash her daughter's clothes and make her bed rather than have her do these things for herself. It was almost as if she felt herself to blame for bringing a daughter into the world without servants, and it was part of her disappointment in John that Clare who was so pretty had not married a man who could provide them.

Of course Clare was more modern than her mother, but whenever she returned to Busey she relapsed into her childhood role and sat around while Helen did all the work. John, who had been brought up to help in the home, always rose from courteous reflex to help his ageing mother-in-law, only to find himself waiting upon his wife. If he told Clare to bestir herself, she would look sour and disappointed like a cat shoved away from the stove, and Helen would looked pained that her daughter had married a bully.

He had learned, after twelve years, to avoid such a conflict, so now, as soon as he had finished his coffee he rose from the table and left the kitchen. He went out into the garden, waiting upon his bowels, and here was confronted by another item in this long list of irritants – the state of the house and garden.

The Old Rectory at Busey was a charming, symmetrical house which expressed in brick and stone the late eighteenth-century conviction that a man of God could live both in comfort and good conscience. There were lawns, shrubs and flowers; and away from the house a walled vegetable garden, a green-house, outbuildings and paddocks, with a view beyond to a line of trees and a stream. All of it, however, was dilapidated and overgrown, and John, who had a Teutonic belief that everything should fulfil its allotted function, suffered to see the rotting window frames, the crumbling mortar, the broken panes of glass in the greenhouse and the tiles on the roof of the house dislodged by a storm the year before. In the herbaceous border thistles stood insolently side by side with the flowers, and bindweed rose like the folds of a gown to embrace and smother the shrubs. On the walls of the house creeper grew across the window panes and stretched its tendrils over the gutter onto the roof. Honey-suckle and clematis grew to the first storey, and then losing its grip on the wall entwined itself around its own branches and grew into dark, pendulous bundles. The lavender bushes planted along the terrace had long since left the narrow strip of earth and now reached halfway across the stone flags towards the lawn.

As John stood on this terrace in his dressing-gown studying fresh details of dilapidation, the brigadier was digging dande-lions out of the lawn with a silver teaspoon. It was his principal contribution to the upkeep of the garden – a labour of Hercules which never ended and left the lawn permanently pitted with little craters of black earth. John smiled in his direction, but afraid of being ensnared in another discussion which would make it awkward to return to the bathroom when the moment came, he turned and went back into the house.

The inside, like the outside, conformed to the pattern of elegance and gentility of the period in which it was built, but was now equally decayed. There was a slight aroma of dry rot in the stone-flagged passages. The paintwork in the drawing-room had been untouched since before the war. The loose covers had faded from many decades of oblique East Anglian sunlight filtering in through the unwashed windows. The tables and chairs, all of the period of the house itself, were chipped, broken, or too fragile to serve their purpose.

John sounded a chord on the piano. It remained out of tune. He looked up at one of the pictures – an Edwardian portrait of Eustace's mother – and saw that a fly had left its droppings on the tip of her nose. There was also a small Constable and a Turner watercolour, which Eustace had inherited from his father, and it added to John's frustration that one or other of these valuable paintings, rotting here and uninsured, would have paid to put everything right: but his parents-in-law, who otherwise had little money, either did not believe in or refused to consider the pecuniary value of their paintings; and John did not remind them of it because he hoped that one of them might pass to Clare.

The moment came. John went up the bathroom. The door was locked. He went to their bedroom where Clare was getting dressed.

'Who the hell's in the bathroom?' he asked.

'I don't know. Guy, I suppose.'

John sat on his bed in despair.

'Go to Mummy's,' said Clare. 'Or go downstairs.'

John made no answer, and she did not look as if she expected one, because they both knew that Helen would now be lying in the bath, and that the prevailing draught at Busey Rectory carried the stench from the downstairs lavatory straight down the passage into the rest of the house, to the discomfiture of whoever had been the last to use it. So John could do nothing but wait, and when Guy left the bathroom plunge into the polluted air and sit mournfully on the warm seat.

chapter four

When at last John was shaved and dressed his mood improved. He was, after all, on holiday in the country with his family. Tom, his ten-year-old son, and Anna, his seven-year-old daughter, met him halfway up the stairs and each caught hold of a sleeve. They dragged him out of the house, across the lawn and through a hole in the wall of the vegetable garden into the yard of the farm next door. There, together with the farmer's children, they had made a hideout in the upper storey of a barn, and had installed the farm cat with her litter of kittens. John followed them into the musty building, climbed over the plastic sacks of fertilizer and went up the ladder with half an eye open for rats. Spiders' webs brushed against his face but he had enough respect for the shining delight in the eyes of his children not to complain, nor to warn them that in a day or two the kittens would certainly be drowned.

When the women in Clare's family – her mother, her aunts and her cousins – sat in judgement on the men who had been so fortunate as to marry a Dansie (which they did whenever they met together), John was passed on his treatment of his children. His other qualities – his ability and his charm – were not what the family admired; but his affection for his children was so transparent that they could not deny him a good mark.

He returned with them now to the Rectory garden, where Anna insisted upon being swung round and round by her father until both of them were dizzy. The exertion producing a sharp pain in his back, he begged his son not to make him do the same, and being a decent boy Tom let him off. He and Anna now hung around to see if John would engender any fun, but he was not good at inventing games, so he paid them off with their pocket money, and while they went back to their hideout he drove with Clare into Cromer.

They parked near the church of St Peter and Paul, and, while Clare did the household shopping John went into a garage to inspect a model of a new car – a Triumph 2000 estate. He knew well enough that he had not the money to replace the rusting Volvo, but it helped pass the time to pretend that he had; and seeing a glass-fibre boat on his way back to meet Clare he wondered whether it would not be wiser to buy a cabin cruiser instead of spending this imaginary money on a new car. At least that would give him something to do each summer. He imagined himself in a peaked cap, and the children wearing life jackets, as they sailed along the Norfolk coast, and he continued the daydream until he met Clare, knowing all the time that not only did he not have the money but he hated the sea.

Many of those who knew John Strickland would not believe that he could not afford a new car. He specialized in licensing, a well-paid branch of his profession, and was generally thought to earn more at the Bar than most of his contemporaries. He had developed a knack – a righteous and reassuring manner – which outwitted the counsel for the residents' associations, and lulled magistrates into accepting nightclubs, betting shops and bingo halls in apparently unsuitable places. For the brewers, hoteliers and gambling entrepreneurs the fees asked by his clerk were money well spent, and by the early 1970s John was earning around fifteen thousand pounds a year.

If despite this he could not afford a new car it was because he was caught between the two conflicting ideals of the society in which he lived: on the one hand he led the kind of pseudo-aristocratic life that was commonly accepted as the style to which we should all aspire; on the other he was taxed by governments determined that if they were unable to make the poor any richer they could at least impoverish the rich – not of course the really rich, who always elude them, but the struggling bourgeois such as John Strickland. Thus the state was his greatest expense. His two houses came next: two thousand pounds went to the building society which had lent him fifteen thousand pounds to buy his house in London; a thousand to the insurance company which had provided a second mortgage for the cottage in Wiltshire. A thousand went on food, £500 on running the Volvo, £300 on heating the London house, £300 on a contributory pension, £450 on a holiday abroad, another £250 on his London club, £222 on electricity, £190 on the telephone, £180 on rates for the London house, £90 on rates for the cottage, £120 on National Insurance contributions, £200 on life insurance for the benefit of Clare should he die, £400 on policies for the children which could be used to pay their school fees; and though neither of them drank except in company, they spent £400 a year on alcohol – mostly gin and claret for their friends. Add to this the cost of restaurants in London, theatre and cinema tickets, and an occasional seat at the opera; the children's clothes, their own clothes, Christmas presents, birthday presents, and all the other things for which a man must put his hand in his pocket, and it will become clear why John Strickland could not afford a new car.

He met Clare in the market place and carried her shopping back to the car.

'I ran into some of the Mascalls,' she said referring to a neighbouring family who, like the Dansies, regrouped in North Norfolk each summer. 'They asked us to dinner.'

'When?'

'Tomorrow night.'

'Are Henry and Mary there?'

'They're all there.'

They reached the car.

'Do you remember Jilly?' Clare asked.

'Godfrey's daughter?'

'Yes. She's grown up with a vengeance.'

'How old is she now?'

'Sixteen or seventeen. Now I know why Guy's been going over there so often.'

They returned to the Rectory for lunch and sat around the kitchen table once again – the eccentric brigadier, his heroic wife, fashionable daughter, slobbish son, moody son-in-law and fidgeting grand-children. Food. Drink. Shepherd's pie. Cider. Stewed pums. Thoughts. And some conversation.

Then the longueur of the afternoon stretched before them. Eustace went to read and sleep in the drawing-room. Clare and her mother prepared to take the chidren to the beach. Guy set out to take his motor-bicycle to the garage, while John went into the library to smoke a Dutch cigar, re-read the *Guardian*, and wonder what the Mascalls would give them for dinner the next day. Twenty minutes later, when he had finished both the cigar and the paper, he decided to read a book. He rose from his chair, yawned, and staggered scratching his stomach towards the mahogany bookshelves. There a thousand books were set out at random, including uniform editions of Dickens, Scott, Dumas and Wilkie Collins, but there was no question now of embarking upon a fat work of fiction. In his last years at school, and throughout his time at university, John had been a periodic reader of French and Russian novels, but later his preoccupation with his work as a barrister, and the demands made upon him by marriage and family life, had led him to confine his reading to *The Times*, the *Economist*, the *Evening Standard*, a few Sunday newspapers and, of course, his briefs and law books. If he ever returned to fiction it was only when he was on holiday, and even then over the years he had developed a certain philistinism and was inclined to confine himself to biography and memoirs. He took the almost common view that no one reads novels any more, or that if they do it is only for distraction and never affects their lives.

His eye now was on the lookout for something new and it fell upon the spine of a book entitled *The Death of Ivan Ilych*. The name Ivan Ilych meant something to him: he thought perhaps that he was a Soviet dissident writer or a vegetarian guru in Mexico, so he pulled the volume from the shelf, looked at the front cover, and saw to his disappointment that it was the title story of a small collection by Leo Tolstoy.

He had read books by Tolstoy in his time – *War and Peace*, *Anna Karenina*, even *Resurrection* – and he had no intention now of re-reading a major work of Russian literature; but since these were only short stories, and it was some time since he had read any fiction, he thought he might as well look at one of them which would carry him through until tea.

The first in the collection was called 'Family Happiness' – an optimistic title which suited his present mood. He settled down in a brown, loose-covered armchair by the window and started to read. *We were in mourning for my mother, who had died in the autumn, and I spent all that winter alone in the country with Katya and Sonya* . . . It took him a certain time to get into the story. His mind kept wandering onto this and that – the shepherd's pie which they had eaten at lunch, the safety of the children on the beach – but he had covered thirty pages, and had reached the marriage of the narrator heroine to Sergey Mikhaylych, before faling asleep. He dozed contentedly, for while he could not quite see himself as the 'tall, robust, middle-aged' hero, he could well imagine Clare as the heroine. *In my heart there was happiness, happiness . . .*

He awoke after sleeping for half an hour or so and resumed reading the story. The sky had grown overcast, so the room darkened as the story darkened too. The marriage which had started so well turned sour. There were scenes between husband and wife which reminded John of unpleasant exchanges he had had with Clare – and he realized with growing annoyance that the title of the story was ironic. He felt almost angry with Tolstoy: he would never have started the story if he had known it was pessimistic.

On the other hand he had been brought up always to finish what he had started, so he hurried through the final pages – quite detached now from the narrative. Clare and he may have had their differences but there had never been any melodrama: nor did she resemble the heroine of the story. He could hardly imagine her trembling as a Frenchman whispered *je vous aime* in her ear, or being tempted to *throw herself headlong into the abyss of forbidden delights*. The ending, in which Marenchka declares *a new feeling of love for my children and the father of my children,* did nothing to redeem what he concluded to be an entirely disagreeable story

The women and children returned for tea. The family gathered yet again around the kitchen table. Eustace talked about cricket. Guy stirred four spoonfuls of sugar into each of his four cups of tea. The children bickered. Helen sighed. Family happiness.

It was only after a game of chess with Tom, and then racing demon with Anna, that John returned to the library and once again picked up his book. The next story in the collection was the title story, 'The Death of Ivan Ilych', and since this had a decidedly mournful sound to it John was about to shut the book and return it to the shelves when certain words jumped out from the first few lines which aroused his curiosity – *trial, Law Courts, Public Prosecutor.* It struck him that if this story was about barristers in Tsarist Russia then it might well be of some documentary interest, so he made up his mind to give it a try.

This novella, for those who have not read it, is about an amiable, intelligent young man – *le phénix de la famille* – who through the cultivation of the right people rises to the post of Public Prosecutor in a Russian provincial city. He leads a contented life. *The pleasures connected with his work were the pleasures of ambition; his social pleasures were those of vanity; but Ivan Ilych's greatest pleasure was playing bridge.* Then, at the age of forty-five, after an accident on a step-ladder during the decoration of his large new house, Ivan Ilych begins to have *a queer taste in his mouth* and *feels some discomfort in his left side.* The pain grows worse. Different doctors diagnose different conditions, but nothing they prescribe prevents his decline. Worse, however, than the deterioration of his body is the effect of the disease on his mind. *Ivan Ilych saw that he was dying and he was in continual despair.* He is terrified of death. He loathes his healthy family which while he is dying continues to live as before. Their life seems as futile as his own. *Life, a series of increasing sufferings, flies further and further towards its end – the most terrible suffering ... There is no explanation. Agony, death ... what for?*

By the time he had reached this point in the story, John Strickland was totally possessed by his fellow-lawyer, Ivan Ilych. He ceased to notice the room in which he was sitting or the passing of time. When he was called through to the drawing-room for a drink before dinner, and then to dinner itself, he obeyed automatically: he talked and listened as if some small tape-recorder were fixed in his larynx, playing pre-programmed replies to predictable questions – leaving his conscious mind in the suffering body of Ivan Ilych.

As soon as dinner was over John returned to the library to finish the story. The sufferings of Ivan Ilych increased: so too did his hatred for his bland, complacent wife. *Go away,* he shouts at her. *Go away and leave me alone. From that moment the screaming began that continued for three days, and was so terrible that one could not hear it through two closed doors without horror.*

By the time John had finished this story Clare and her parents, who had been watching television, were already in bed. John went upstairs still clutching the book and placed it on his bedside table. There was a curious expression in his eyes as he looked at Clare, but since she was absorbed by a Trollope novel she did not see it. She paid no attention to him as he took off his clothes, went to take his tepid bath, and returned to climb into bed in his pyjamas. It was only when he was lying beside her that she looked up from her book.

'Shall we sleep?' she asked.

'Yes.'

They switched off their bedside lamps and then embraced under the blankets as they had embraced every night since they had married – a gesture which served not just to express a residual affection for one another but to demonstrate by its intensity whether one or other or both were in the mood to make love. It had been evolved after those crises in the early years of their marriage when Clare, bored by the monotonous and mechanical expression of his so-called love, had refused his advances – leaving him baffled and humiliated. Later, of course, she had grown out of her illusions, and that night at Busey it was she who placed one of her long legs over his body and kissed him with soft lips and a half-open mouth. But still possessed by Ivan Ilych, John's body remained rigid beside hers. He gave her an abrupt kiss with pursed lips, so she turned to face away, wished him good night, and in a short time was asleep.

John was not so fortunate, for unlike the fictional Ivan Ilych who dies repentant on the last page of Tolstoy's story, John remained alive, awake, and in much the same state of terror and despair. The certainty of death now combined with the ache in his back to convince him that he too was dying; and even if a reasonable voice within him expressed the opinion that the pain came from a sprained muscle rather than cancer of the spine – even that sensible faculty could not deny that agony and death were as certainly the inevitable destiny of John Strickland as they had been of Ivan Ilych.

Looking forward to death in this way was only half of what led to his sleepless despair. To look back was worse. Like Ivan Ilych he asked himself: *Maybe I did not live as I ought to have done?* – and it was as inadequate for him as it had been for Ivan

Ilych to reply: *But how could that be when I did everything properly?* For lying in that sagging bed he could remember quite well the ambitions he had once had to dedicate his life to something more than his own material interests – to serve indeed, the old ideals of liberty, equality and fraternity in their new guise of socialism. At the age of twenty-five he had assumed that by forty he would be a Member of Parliament in the Labour interest – perhaps a Cabinet Minister – so how had it happened that he found himself instead the leading junior licensing counsel, pleading the interests of the very men who with beer and bingo take from the poor what little they possess? Why did he not defend the drunks, prostitutes, pimps and thieves whom he had once seen as the guiltless dross left after the harvesting of profit by impersonal capitalist combines?

For a moment the face of the young garage mechanic reappeared to torment him; then, as the clock of Busey Church struck one, he opened in his own defence. He specialized in licensing, he argued, because the clerks gave him the work; and they gave him the work because they knew that he was good at the job and needed the money. But why did he need the money? Others did with less. They lived quite happily in Ealing or Croydon, returning home each day to eat their tea, read their briefs, watch television and go to bed; while he had to have a house in Holland Park and dine with merchant bankers – or men with grotesque salaries as well as private means – or was obliged to invite them back to elaborate, expensive dinner parties in his own home. But why these friends? Why this way of life? Because he had married Clare.

It suddenly became quite clear to him that if his life had gone wrong it was from the moment he had married Clare, and for the first time in his life John felt that he hated his wife. Terror of disease and death was replaced by a venomous aversion for the woman lying beside him. Her regular, complacent breathing sounded to him like the grunts of a pig. She smelt like an old woman. The smiling, trembling girl he had married had imperceptibly disappeared like a smouldering log, and a hard middle-aged housewife had risen from the ashes – *le phénix de la famille!*

He smiled now into his pillow at the thought of the small revenge he had taken that night for the countless times when she had been the one to refuse to make love. Even now he suspected that she had only wanted to reassure herself that he still found her attractive – her whose body had borne two children and had become like a sucked-out grape. He now felt only repugnance and loathing for Clare, not just because she had spoilt his past life but for the role she would play in the future. He knew from statistics that she would outlive him, and he could well imagine how she who was so squeamish would detest his final suffering – retching at his incontinence, cowering from his pain. His children might be sorry, but their expectations would console them – just as the Constable or the Turner watercolour would console Clare. As with Ivan Ilych, John's family would watch him die, wishing that he would hurry up and praying to God to dispatch him.

The thought of their God as it pranced into his insomniac mind angered him so much that he ground his teeth together. Not only would Clare outlive him, but when she died she would believe she was going to Heaven whereas John, an agnostic, had no faith whatsoever in an afterlife; so while she could look forward to eternal bliss he lay dreading the empty unknown.

chapter five

The youthful idealism which tormented John that night was not an invention of his fantasy. It had come to him largely from his father, who although a judge on the Northern Circuit had a strong sympathy for those who in his day were called the poor and are now referred to as the working class. His father, John's grandfather, had managed a mill in Halifax, and although a strict Presbyterian had sent his son to the same Quaker school in York where John was later to be educated.

The Judge had been an early member of the Labour Party, and for many years had acted unpaid – or for token fees – for men against their masters. He had sympathy even for the guilty because he understood how poverty leads to temptation. 'Our law,' he once told John, 'is not given by God but made by man. Study the men who make it, and the purposes to which it is put – largely the protection of property by those who have it against those who do not.'

His wife, John's mother, a teacher's daughter, tolerated her husband's ideals but did not share them. When a Labour Chancellor offered him his appointment (itself an attempt to give political balance to the Bench), his first impulse had been to refuse: but she desired it and like all husbands since Adam he gave in. They bought an elegant house in a village outside York; were invited to dine by the local landowners; and for the rest of his life the Judge imposed a body of law in which he only half believed.

Without any express tutelage he passed on his ideals to his son John and his daughter Sarah as if they were all running in a relay race towards the betterment of mankind. Sarah became a schoolteacher, taught in slum schools, and then married another teacher and had three children. John had gone to Oxford, where his radical principles led him to join the Labour Club and speak for left-wing motions at Union debates. But he was also taken up by the sons of some of those Yorkshire landowners with whom his parents went to dine, and with his mother's blood also running in his veins he found in the course of time that his socialist colleagues became increasingly dreary while the boys from the Bullingden Club had wit and style. He went less and less to Labour meetings and applied, as it were, for membership of a club that was at once larger and more exclusive than the Bullingden – the British *haute bourgeoisie*. He learned the unwritten rules, was admitted, and went away from Oxford to country house weekends. He kept up with the same set when he left Oxford and was called to the Bar in London, and through them in due course he met Clare. If, all this time, he still called himself a socialist it was largely because it seemed to amuse his friends.

One of these friends from Oxford was Henry Mascall, whose father owned land around Cromer. Henry himself was just one of those Etonian merchant bankers who, in his insomnia, John had blamed for his way of life. It is difficult to see how he could have held Clare responsible for this connection, since it was

John who had first met Henry at Oxford. Certainly the two had become better friends since both men had married, because friends after a marriage are often changed to arrive at a common denominator. Others whom John liked more were too earnest for Clare; or had difficult wives; just as some of her friends were too stupid or plain to be welcomed by John. Both the Mascalls, however, suited both the Stricklands: each couple felt tacitly flattered by the companionship of the others – and that in their circle was often the basis for friendship. Both women were equally pretty; both wore elegant clothes. They came from similar backgrounds (although Mary was not a Catholic) and had similar personalities: both were quiet and almost shy in company, particularly beside their extrovert husbands, and each had an unusually stubborn personality.

Other practical factors drew them in from the outer circle of one another's acquaintance to the centre where they might ring one another up at the last moment to see if they were free for a film: their children were more or less the same age and both families went to Norfolk in the summer. The invitation to dinner which was made in the market place of Cromer was only the first of a series which would bounce back and forth between the two households – to lunch, to dinner and to picnics on the beach. Invariably Clare and John went more frequently to the Mascalls' than Henry and Mary came to the Loughs' because the Mascalls had a cook and a butler while the Loughs depended upon Helen to cook the food and the brigadier to pour the wine. And because of the butler and the cook John and Clare dressed up to dine at the Mascalls' while Henry and Mary 'came as they were' to the Loughs'.

chapter six

Throughout that second day of his holiday John was in a quiet, thoughtful mood. He went out for a long walk by himself in the morning, said little at lunch, and spent the afternoon alone in the library, standing at the window looking out at the trees.

After tea he announced that he was going for another walk. Clare warned him to be back in time to change for the Mascalls'.

Outside on the lawn the brigadier saw his son-in-law setting off down the lane, and by going through the farmyard he waylaid him.

'Do you mind if I join you?' he asked.

'Not at all.'

They walked for a while in silence: then Eustace asked if John and Clare were going out that night.

'Yes. To the Mascalls'.'

'You'll get some good food.'

'Should do.'

There was a further silence.

'And a Havana cigar,' said the brigadier.

'Shall I pocket one for you?'

'Never smoke them now,' said Eustace.

They walked for a while in silence.

'I saw you were reading Tolstoy,' said Eustace.

'Yes,' said John

'Those pessimistic stories . . .'

'Yes.'

'He was got down by married life.'

'Who?'

'Tolstoy. There's that scene in *War and Peace* when old Prince Bolkonsky says to his son: "It's a bad business, eh?" Prince Andrew asks him what he means. "The wife," says Bolkonsky. "It can't be helped. They're all like that. One can't unmarry."'

John blushed but said nothing. He watched a wood pigeon fly from the roadside high into the branches of a beech tree.

'The truth is,' said Eustace, 'that as you get older life often seems disappointing.'

'Did it to you?' asked John.

'Inevitably,' said Eustace shaking his head. 'I was a soldier.'

'Why should life disappoint a soldier more than anyone else?'

'Because after the last war we all knew that there would never be a war again. Not one between the great powers. Too dangerous. We'd all be blown to pieces. So all of us would-be Wellingtons had to settle down behind our desks and recruit scientists and technicians.'

'At least you remained alive,' said John.

'Alive, yes, but redundant. It wasn't just our skills that were out of date, but also the qualities we had been taught to admire. Honour. Courage. Discipline. They're as out of date as bayonets and revolvers.'

'I dare say,' said John. 'They're not words much used by my generation.'

'There have been two developments in my lifetime,' said Eustace, 'that'll change human nature. The soldier has lost his status – the heroic warrior is extinct . . .'

'And the other?'

'Birth control. The contraceptive pill.'

John laughed. 'It makes life easier . . .'

'But it changes things, doesn't it? It removes the necessary connection between physical love and procreation.'

John still smiled. 'Did people make love just to have children?'

'No, but they felt that wives should be faithful so that their husbands could be sure that their children weren't by other men. Now that doesn't apply. Fidelity's an abstract commitment. Makes it more difficult to stay in line.'

John turned away and looked towards the horizon. The smile had gone from his face. 'A man may stop loving his wife,' he said, 'but she remains the mother of his children.'

'That's right,' said Eustace. 'Love keeps a couple together for the first few years. Then they stay together for the children. And after that it's habit.'

'That's not much to look forward to.'

'On the contrary. The third phase is the best. No drama. No pressure. Companionship. Like being members of the same club.'

When they got back to the Rectory John found that Clare had already taken a bath. He followed her into the same water, submerged himself and closed his eyes. His back no longer hurt him – he was not going to die – but the insomnia of the night before had left him exhausted. As he lay in the bath he recalled with some embarrassment the thoughts and emotions which had kept him awake: he had got up that morning to find that the rancour like the backache had gone, and the loathing he had felt for Clare appeared part of a nightmare. He had blamed Tolstoy;

and before he had gone into breakfast that morning he had returned *The Death of Ivan Ilych* to the bookshelf in the library – pinioned between *Scott of the Antartic* and *The Oxford Book of Christian Names*.

And yet a mood of melancholy remained like the aftermath of an epileptic fit. Why, he wondered, when he had been so fortunate in life had he suffered this attack of discontent? He remembered his unfulfilled ideals, but reasoned now in the bath that either he no longer held them or, if he did, there was time enough left to serve them. But was it not possible, after all, that his socialist principles were an unsuccessful graft of those held by his father; and that the anxiety of the night before was only semi-conscious guilt at disappointing his dead father which, if he was analysed, would be explained away by the experiences of his early childhood?

He rose from the bath, wrapped himself in a towel, and once in his bedroom crossed to give Clare an unsolicited and unexpected kiss. At which she smiled – not perhaps with the sort of smile she had given as a girl, but with the smile one might wear when a dog is brought to heel. John, however, saw only the smile, not its meaning, and it was reflected first in his own expression and then in his face in the mirror as he tied his black bow-tie.

chapter seven

At dinner with the Mascalls that night John sat between Henry's mother and her grand-daughter, Jilly. The despair of the night before, and the melancholy of that afternoon, had been entirely superseded by a good mood. John enjoyed himself most, and felt he was at his best, exactly in these circumstances – ice-cold gin flowing in his blood, hock in one glass, claret in another: candlesticks, candlelight, black bow-ties, necks and bosoms – a witty woman to his left, a pretty girl to his right, and across the table the smiling, lovely face of Mary Mascall.

He talked first, of course, to Lady Mascall, who was famously bored in the country and pounced on any Londoner who strayed to North Norfolk. Brought up in a cultured liberal salon she was mystified by her husband's country pursuits – his shooting, hunting and coursing – and knowing that John did none of these things, she assumed it was because he too was above them. She liked to talk to him about the law, which when it came down to it meant that she liked to hear about gruesome cases in which John had acted for the defence. She always asked for details of the criminal's physical appearance as if storing it for a masochistic fantasy later that night.

The candlelight which flattered the older woman concealed the one advantage that Jilly Mascall had over her elders – the bloom of youth; and her conversation because of her age came out in awkward bursts. She laughed at her own jokes as if afraid that no one else would, but John did not listen to her wit. Rather he was fascinated by the change that had come over her since they had last met a year before. The child was now tall; and bosoms bulged beneath the bodice of her dress. Flirtatious looks came from under her eyelashes, which in itself was not new (since children can be flirtatious) but combined now with her adult body to confuse the older man.

He knew of course that she was over the age of consent: he even thought it quite likely that she had slept with a man – perhaps Guy – but it confused him nonetheless to consider with intent a girl who was so recently a child.

As the hock and claret joined the gin in his bloodstream, the very thought that he was too old to flirt with a girl of her age induced in him a kind of panic; and as he chatted to Jilly about the secretarial course she was going to take in the autumn he heard himself say: 'Well, you must let me take you out to lunch.'

'I'd love to,' she said.

'Where can I get hold of you?'

'I'm not sure yet. I'll probably be staying with Henry and Mary until I find a flat.'

'Then I'll ring you there except . . .' He hesitated deliberately – a court trick.

'What?'

'Well, they might disapprove.'

She giggled. 'I suppose they might.'

'Perhaps you could ring me at my chambers?'

'OK.'

'I'll give you a card . . .' And he reached into his breast pocket, fumbled in his wallet, and drew out a card which at once he concealed in his handkerchief. 'I'll pass it under the table,' he whispered – and while their mouths chatted on about this and that their fingers met under the linen tablecloth and the conspiratorial piece of cardboard was exchanged.

What they said could not be heard above the hubbub of the dinner (there were twelve at table – mostly cousins of the Mascalls), and John knew quite well that Henry and Mary would not have disapproved, but their conspiracy lifted the lunch which might otherwise have been tedious and banal into something exciting and illicit; and by the suggestion of sin had planted the idea of adultery into the mind of a possibly innocent girl.

John turned back to Lady Mascall – having remembered an incestuous rapist who had been defended by one of his colleagues. His assignation with Jilly went out of his mind, so that when she smiled at him as the ladies withdrew he had no idea what it signified.

The gentlemen stayed behind and, as the brigadier had promised, John was offered a Havana cigar. He cut off the end and sucked the thick smoke into his mouth, then gently released it into the air around his head.

Henry Mascall, who was John's exact contemporary and closest friend – a heavy, swarthy, handsome man with a curling, sneering mouth and a rich, caddish voice – was discoursing on politics – on the government's conflict with the unions.

'If you ask me,' he said, 'Heath will let things get a lot worse and then go to the nation.'

'But will he win?' asked John.

'Bound to,' said Henry.

'I'm not so sure.' John puffed at his cigar. This, after all, was his role – the devil's advocate at Tory dinner parties. 'Most people in this country feel greater loyalty to the unions than they do to the state.'

'But they don't want inflation,' said Henry.

'Quite. And if they thought about it they might concede that annual increases in their wages of twenty or thirty per cent will inevitably lead to inflation. But they don't think about it. Their left hand doesn't know what their right hand is doing . . . or rather the left side of their brain doesn't know what the right side is thinking: so while on the one hand they will say that increases should be limited, they will at the same time put pressure on their own union to demand exorbitant raises.'

'If you ask me,' said Guy – though no one had asked him – 'there's no reason why workers should cooperate with a Tory government to make capitalism work. The more chaos the better so far as they are concerned.'

It is a proof of the forbearance of the Engish upper classes that just as Guy was spluttering these revolutionary ideas, Sir George Mascall – who must have been worth several million pounds in land, securities and works of art – should pass him the decanter of vintage port without any outward sign of irony in the gesture. His eyelids did twitch, which might have been a sign of irritation, or just of old age, and he said to John and Henry: 'The mistake was to give up conscription.'

'We could bring it back,' said Henry, whose extreme ideas were currently in fashion among younger members of the Conservative Party.

'I'm not sure that it would help you,' said John. 'Conscription won't change a man's convictions. Eustace for one feels that you couldn't use the army we've got today to break a strike.'

'Eustace is out of touch,' said Sir George, who was one of those neighbours who now found Clare's father too unpredictable and eccentric to have him in the house.

'With any luck,' said Guy, 'the whole thing will collapse' – and he tossed back his glass of port.

'Up the Republic!' said Henry.

'What I think we'll see,' said John quickly – afraid that his drunk young brother-in-law might make some wild gesture and disgrace himself – 'is the incorporation of the trades unions into the state – the fourth estate, as Churchill put it . . .'

'I dare say,' said Sir George.

'Wonderful,' said Guy. 'You're back to Mussolini.'

'I agree with Guy,' said Henry. 'We can't have that. A corporate state. No, monetary self-discipline will do the trick. That's how the Germans and Japanese control inflation.'

And so on. The conversation continued while the women, slightly disgruntled, sat in the roseate drawing-room. Certainly nothing bored them more than talk about the economy, but they resented all the same this custom which separated the men from the women after dinner. 'They can't still be telling dirty jokes, can they?' Clare asked Mary after half an hour's segregation.

'Politics or money,' said Mary.

'Why is it,' Clare asked, 'that they're always sounding off about issues which they can't control, but when it comes to things they can do something about like tying up the raspberry canes or mending the Hoover they go all bored and blank?'

'Idle brutes,' said Mary. She laughed but said nothing more, and Clare said nothing to her: both were the passive partners in their respective marriages and they often sat in silence.

Jilly meanwhile left the pouf next to her grandmother and came to sit by Clare. 'I do hope you'll ask me round when I come to London,' she said.

'Of course,' said Clare, smiling coldly because she had seen the look in this adolescent's eye while she had been talking to John at table.

'I'm really rather nervous, I mean straight from boarding school to the big bad city.'

'Rubbish,' said Mary. 'From what I hear the city is not half as bad as your boarding school.'

Jilly grinned. 'Well what do you expect if girls are kept cooped up like that?'

'It wasn't like that in my day,' said Mary. She then hesitated, smiled and added: 'Well perhaps it was.'

The men now joined the women. John came to talk to Mary, whom he had only seen before on the other side of the table. They had all met recently in London, so there was nothing much to say, but the essence of friendship is that there need be no purpose in the presence of the friend.

In the middle of the night John suddenly found himself awake and anxious. He lay dreading the return of the previous night's insomnia and despair, and cautiously probed his mind for the source of his anxiety. He winced when he remembered that he had asked Jilly Mascall to ring him at his chambers. If she told the others they would gossip and laugh at him.

He lay wondering whether it was the coffee or the Havana cigar which had woken him. Sowly he moved his leg to feel the flank of his sleeping wife. It was warm and supine, which calmed him so that eventually he fell asleep.

chapter eight

The experience of many summers at Busey had taught John and Clare that two weeks was the right period of time to spend there. If they stayed longer Clare became irritated by her mother and the brigadier exasperated by his grandchildren. The feeding of the family was also a charge on the Loughs' physical and financial resources; so over the years 15 August had been established as the day of the drive home – or more exactly the day of the drive to their second home sixty miles west of London.

The cottage in Wiltshire was neither as large nor as pretty as Busey Rectory, and the countryside was within that singed ring which surrounds any great city. In Norfolk the land was farmed in earnest: every field was groomed for profit. The Wiltshire farms, on the other hand, because of their proximity to London, had been bought as weekend retreats by bankers and stockbrokers who being financiers rather than farmers knew that the value of their properties lay in where they were rather than in what was produced from their soil. It was therefore uneconomic to drain the marshy fields; the barns remained broken, the fences patched with barbed wire and only the tennis courts and swimming pools were kept in good order.

The Stricklands had neither a tennis court nor a swimming pool, for not being rich in the sense that people are rich in Wiltshire they were lucky to own a house in that area at all. Their first home was the house in London, and for the first seven years of their married life it was their only home. But then, on summer weekends when the children were young. Busey a long way from London, and half their friends away in their country cottages, John and Clare had longed for 'somewhere to go'. They had worked out that if they sold the few stocks and shares that Clare had been given by her father, and borrowed some money from an insurance company or a secondary bank, they could afford a modest place in the country; and they started to search the property columns of the Sunday newspapers and make expeditions in their then new Volvo out of London to the north, south, east and west. In the end they decided that the M4 motorway made it so much easier to get out of London on a Friday night that they would concentrate their search in Berkshire, Wiltshire and Oxfordshire, where, alas, the price of property was high because many of the same sort of people were looking for the same sort of thing.

They inspected a dozen different cottages – mostly built of antique rubble and roofed with rotting thatch. With his roots in the North of England, John expected houses to be built of brick or stone, and was repeatedly astounded that he should be asked to pay thousands of pounds for hovels which in his view should be razed to the ground. Clare, on her own admission, was looking for something like Busey – 'smaller, of course, but with the same sort of feel about it'. A cottage near Hungerford came on the market which more or less met her expectations: it was small and square with only four bedrooms, two living-rooms and a kitchen, but had been built of brick in the nineteenth century. They liked it, made an offer, and there followed a tense few weeks when the old hag who was selling it played them off against another young couple: they ended paying a thousand pounds above the asking price, but everyone assured them that it was a good investment and they had at last their country cottage.

It was a mile outside a village, with no other house in view. There was a garden, an orchard, a paddock, some sheds and a barn, all of which went with the house: otherwise the property was surrounded by rolling fields with huge elm trees growing in the hedgerows. When they moved in it was damp and dirty, but slowly over the years they had done it up as a duplicate home with even a second washing machine and tumble-drier ranged under the raw oak surfaces in the kitchen.

They ate in the kitchen. John had insisted, against mild resistance from Clare, that the cottage should be unpretentious – an expression in lifestyle of his open, egalitarian ideas. There were to be no candlelit dinners in a dining-room with phantom servants behind green baize doors. He saw himself as an exponent of 'Scandinavian man', and part of this philosophy was a faith in machines. They were, he liked to say, the domestic servants of the twentieth century: and while Clare had put in a quiet request for some cheap char from the village, John had spent hundreds of pounds on dish-washing and clothes-washing machines and a tumble-drier; as well as two different motor mowers (one for the lawn, another for the orchard); a rotovator (to grow their own vegetables); a chain-saw (to cut their own logs); as well as the usual domestic aids such as a vacuum cleaner, a liquidizer, egg-beater, coffeegrinder and lemonsqueezer – each powered by its own electric motor. If you counted the duplicate machines in their London house, the two gramophones, televisions and tape-decks, and the different motors in the Volvo, John and Clare had a staff of two dozen of these twentieth-century servants. But, just as live servants get ill, machines break down; and most Saturday mornings were spent struggling with an obstinate mower; and most Saturday afternoons taking a malingering machine to Marlborough or Hungerford.

The worst moment of the year was always the day they arrived from Busey – exhausted after the long drive – to be confronted by what nature can do if left alone for three weeks. The grass on the lawn had grown too thick for the lawnmower: the grass in the orchard too high for the orchard mower. The clean, weeded earth of the vegetable garden was a jungle; the seedlings of plants they wished to nurture – the peas, beans and courgettes – smothered by the healthy growth of those they had hoped to destroy. They went inside the house, dreading finding evidence of a burglary or a leaking roof; but on that Wednesday in August 1973 everything seemed in order. There was a sweet smell which they traced to the pool of black flies which lay – some dead, some still buzzing – on every window sill, but nothing worse than that: so silently, and without looking at one another, the two grown-ups set to work to clean up, feed the children, switch on the hot water, put sheet on the beds and air the rooms.

Although it was summer John lit a fire because the living-room looked desolate without one. By ten the children were in bed. John and Clare had a drink, ate some supper, watched television for a while and then went upstairs. The water was still tepid but from force of habit they took a bath.

'Is it worth it?' John asked Clare as they lay side by side in bed.

'I think so, don't you?'

'If we didn't have this, we could always rent a house in France.'

'I know.' She paused. 'But there are the weekends.'

'We could go to those country house hotels.'

'Perhaps when the children go away to school . . .' she began: but then stopped because that was a bone of contention between them. And John said nothing because he was too tired to think about his children's education. Instead he switched off his lamp. Clare did the same. They embraced as usual and then went to sleep.

chapter nine

The next morning John set to work to master the garden. He had always been determined that the cottage should never be overgrown and run down like Busey Rectory; and although increasingly bored by mowing and weeding, he still got some satisfaction by creating order out of disorder with a machine. He came in hungry at one o'clock, content with half a day's work.

He frowned to see that there were no knives and forks on the kitchen table.

'Isn't lunch ready?' he asked irritably.

'I'm a bit behind,' said Clare, pouring baked beans onto beige toast in front of the two children.

John sat down.

'Help yourself,' said Clare.

He stood up again and walked over to the stove. 'What is there?' he asked.

'Baked beans and baked potatoes,' she said, 'but you can have an egg as well, if you want.'

He broke two eggs into a saucepan and mixed them together with a wooden spoon. When they were cooked he took a baked potato out of the oven, slipped some baked beans onto his plate and took it back to the table. He put some salt over the potato and scrambled egg and started to eat.

'Is this recipe out of your *cordon bleu* cookbook?' he asked without smiling.

'Look,' said Clare. 'I've had to do the washing, and then go shopping, while you've been having fun in the garden.'

'I wasn't having fun,' he said.

'Well neither was I.'

She sat down beside him with her baked potato, which she had split open with a knife and anointed with butter, sour cream, chopped-up chives and some grated cheese. Beside it were some baked beans darkened with Worcester sauce and a dash of tabasco; and on a separate plate a sliced tomato, sprinkled with olive oil, lemon juice, salt, pepper and a little diced onion.

'You might have done me some of that,' said John.

'For God's sake,' said Clare. 'If you can't cut up a tomato for yourself . . . I mean, even Tommy can cut up a tomato.'

'But the baked beans . . .'

'John, really. *There's* the Worcester sauce. *There's* the tabasco. I said help yourself.'

'I hate that hot stuff,' said Anna.

'Can I have some beer?' asked Tom.

'Of course not,' said Clare. She looked down at the *Daily Mail* which she had bought out shopping, nudged it into alignment and then without further pretence started to read the front page. The children quarrelled about whether Anna should or should not have a second glass of orange squash, because her glass was smaller than Tommy's and if he had a second glass too she should have a third glass and if he had a million glasses she should have one million and one. John sat in silence – angry about his lunch yet reluctant to object lest by doing so he re-opened the whole question of women's relationships to men, which, like private education, was an unresolved issue between them.

*

'Have you asked anyone down?' he said that evening.

'Teddy and Tania might come down but I rather doubt it,' Clare replied without looking up from the paper.

'With all their children?'

'If they come they'll bring them.'

John sighed. Clare raised her eyes and looked at him. 'That's the trouble,' she said. 'There isn't really enough room to have people to stay.'

'What about the Mascalls? They could leave their children in London.'

'They'll still be in Norfolk. Anyway, people don't like leaving their children . . .'

'Henry doesn't mind.'

'How do you know?'

'He isn't very family minded.'

'I wouldn't say that.'

'He's always going off with other women.'

'That's only gossip. And it doesn't mean he doesn't like his children.'

There was a pause as John went to the stove to make some coffee. Then he said: 'Who else could we ask down?'

'There's no one I particularly want to have,' said Clare.

'What about those people we met with the Mascalls . . . the Grays?'

'We don't really know them well enough.'

'They might like to come for a weekend.'

'If we had another bathroom . . .' Clare began, raising another old issue.

'We can't afford another bathroom,' said John irritably.

'So let's not ask the Grays.'

'Why on earth can't they share our bathroom?'

'I hate sharing bathrooms,' said Clare.

'You are extraordinary. You don't mind a dirty bath, obviously, because you never clean it . . .'

'It's not the bath . . .'

'The Grays' excreta can't smell so different from the Mascalls'.'

'We know the Mascalls.'

'You contradict yourself,' he said again. 'On the one hand you purport to be so progressive; but on the other you behave like a prehistoric woman, disliking alien smells on your territory.'

'You're cross-examining again,' Clare said as he slipped into the pompous, sarcastic tone of voice that was so effective in court. 'Anyway,' she added, 'she may be pretty but he's a dreadful bore.'

'All right,' said John, 'but let's at least have someone to Sunday lunch.'

'Who?' she asked.

'Anyone. Try the Harts, the Frasers, or Sebbie Howard.'

She frowned and looked at the clock. 'What's on TV tonight?'

There's something at nine,' he said. Then he added: 'What about it?'

'What?'

'Someone for Sunday lunch.'

She sighed. 'Yes, well, you ask someone if you like.'

'It's usually the wife who does the ringing up.'

'*I* don't want anyone for Sunday lunch,' said Clare. '*I'm* not bored with my own family.' She did not say this angrily: she looked as if she was thinking of something else.

'I'm not bored but I like company.'

'So do I, at times. But you know all those people will be doing something else by now.'

'They may not be. You could try.'

'And anyway, I always feel a bit embarrassed having them here. I mean they can't swim or play tennis or anything . . .'

John scowled. 'So all you need now to make you happy is a swimming pool and a tennis court . . .' He stood up and took a cigar out of the packet by the toaster.

'I didn't say that,' said Clare. 'But there's a limit to eating and conversation and . . . well . . . why should they want to spend Sunday here instead of in their own houses?'

John looked at the clock: it was three minutes to nine. 'All right,' he said. 'Don't ask anyone,' and he stalked through to the living-room leaving Clare to clear up the dishes.

A little later she rang some other friends, the Jacksons, who did not have a tennis court or a swimming pool, and invited them over for Sunday lunch.

chapter ten

After two or three days' hard work the garden was tamed, some fresh vegetables were extracted from among the weeds, and the family settled in. When word got around that they were there the telephone rang two or three times a day, because the Stricklands were a popular couple who were part and parcel of the Wiltshire set. The children were invited out to tea and swam in their neighbours' swimming pools while John and Clare played tennis with the parents. Whenever they were invited out to dinner a farmer's wife came in to baby-sit, and in the last week they were there Clare herself organized two separate dinner parties and John was once again drawing corks from the claret bottles and decanting the vintage port.

To an outside eye the Stricklands were just the same as always – the children amiable and polite, Clare quiet and beautiful, John witty and disputatious. Indeed John, as he stood on the tennis court, or as he drew corks from the bottles of wine, looked at himself with an outside eye, thinking: 'This, surely, is what life is for – shouting, laughing friends: a pretty, intelligent wife. Stable children. A house in London. A cottage in the country. What more?'

There was nothing more he could think of: yet every now and then he felt a touch of what he now called Ivan Ilychitis. Like the tell-tale symptoms of a recurring disease, it sometimes came over him as a kind of philosophical vertigo: watching himself in white shorts on a neighbour's tennis court, he barely recognized himself. And even as he joked and argued at his own dinner table he slipped outside himself and listened to his own voice as if it was that of another person. 'But I'd never say that. That isn't me. It's one of them.' In other words, he felt he was playing a part in a play written by someone else: and when he woke up at night it was as if the curtain had fallen, the play was over, and he was alone behind the scenes in the dark with his own null personality.

It was then that he felt afraid of insanity or, in more modern terms, of a nervous breakdown; and the only comfort was the warm form of Clare beside him. In the morning – with daylight, movement and conversation – he felt back in his own skin again. With the children in particular, who looked at him with such direct, untroubled affection, there could be no doubt but that he was their father and nothing more.

Clare, who consoled him at night, was less reassuring during the day. It was not that she said or did anything to undermine him, but she behaved as if her mind was always on other things. She liked to doze in the morning while John went down and ate breakfast with the children, as if her dreams were more interesting than her real life. He could hardly be upset by that. It was only human. He might do the same. But even when she was dressed, and moving about the house and garden, she seemed removed from their everyday life.

John noticed this particularly in Wiltshire because the cottage itself obliged him to recall their earlier years together. The irregular alignment of the patterned wallpaper in their bedroom reminded him of how they had stood in old clothes decorating the room. Clare had sewn the crooked curtains: John had put up the curtain rail. The wardrobe had been found in a junk shop in Marlborough and both had spent days stripping the ugly varnish. Clare had smiled, in those days whenever their eyes had met. A picture came into his mind of the pink, embarrassed distortion of her features. Now neither sought to see the expression in the other's eyes, and if their eyes met, nothing disturbed the composure of Clare's features. At most her lips moved as if it was expected of them.

It occurred to John that perhaps she no longer loved him. He asked her once, in the kitchen, and she looked surprised. 'Of course I do,' she replied with a kind of absent-minded sincerity that convinced him. He wondered then whether it was he who no longer loved her: he remembered the loathing he had felt for her after reading Tolstoy's story, but now answered himself just as she had done – that of course he loved her, though not perhaps in the same way as before.

Part two

chapter one

Soon after their return to London in September, John and Clare went to dinner with Henry and Mary Mascall, where the conversation turned to adultery – a tricky topic because no one quite knew what was going on between the different husbands and wives. Micky Neill, a homosexual novelist who brought the subject up, may have done so for that very reason: 'Have you heard,' he said, 'that Sarah Cummings has run off with a travelling salesman?'

'He isn't a travelling salesman,' said Arabella Morrison, a plain, unmarried cousin of Mary's who because she was unlikely to give rise to gossip liked to be the first to hear it. 'He works for Hambros.'

'He's still a travelling salesman, isn't he, Henry?' asked Micky.

Henry Mascall drew together his thick black eyebrows in a comical frown. 'He travels, I suppose, and he sells the services of Hambros Bank. But then I do that sort of thing.'

'And no one could call *you* a travelling salesman,' said Clare with a sardonic laugh.

'He had it coming to him anyway,' said Arabella. 'Going away on business is one thing, but stopping off in Paris on your way back from the Gulf for a dirty weekend with Henrietta Jameson is quite another.'

'Tit for tat,' said Micky, flapping his hand like a puppy's paw in the way homosexuals mimic their own kind.

'It's nice to know,' said Mary Mascall, blushing in advance at her own boldness, 'that a deceived wife has *carte blanche*.'

'I can't help feeling that it's less serious for men than it is for women,' said Clare.

'I don't see why,' said Mary.

'It means less to them, doesn't it?' She glanced around the table for corroboration: but since Micky was a homosexual and John was her husband she could only turn to Henry.

'How do you mean?' he asked.

'Can't men have dirty weekends in Paris with Henrietta Jameson and then come home to be perfectly good husbands thereafter?'

'I should have thought so,' said Henry.

'And can't women?' asked Mary.

'A woman tends to love the man she sleeps with, doesn't she?' asked Clare. 'And if she loves him she wants to be with him. That's what breaks up the family.'

'I rather agree,' said Henry.

'You would,' said Arabella Morrison – confirming to Mary that her husband was thought to be unfaithful.

'You don't agree?' Henry asked Arabella.

'Of course I don't,' she said with a laugh. 'Clare's been brainwashed by the Catholic Church. It's the sort of argument men use in Catholic countries to keep their wives at heel.'

'You mean,' said Henry, 'that women are just as capable of a quick fuck with no questions asked?'

Arabella blushed. 'If you must put it that way.'

'Well you should know, I suppose,' said Henry in a tone of sincere intellectual humility.

'Oh shut up, Henry,' said Arabella, blushing with irritation at being caught between admitting to the bareness of her private life or sounding like a whore.

'Perhaps we would be if given the chance,' said Mary Mascall, returning to her husband's original question. 'After all, Jennifer Creeley had three daughters by three different men without causing a ripple in her family life.'

'So people say,' said John who, while the other two men wore open-necked shirts, was dressed in a suit and tie. 'I don't really believe it.'

'Oh, I'm sure it's true,' said Mary.

'As well as doing up other people's houses,' said Clare.

'They say,' said Micky, 'that if you remember whose house she was doing up nine months before the birth of each child, you know who the father was.'

'I wondered why she charged so much,' said Henry.

'I seem to remember,' said Mary, 'that you recommended her to your parents . . . Didn't she do up the flat in Eaton Square?'

'My goodness,' said Henry. 'Do you think I'm a half brother to one of those little Creeley girls?'

'More like father,' said Mary sourly.

'You overestimate me,' said Henry, filling the glasses of his guests with wine.

'It's all a mystery to me,' said Micky, who was sallow-skinned and feline, and spoke with a sing-song voice. '*I* would have thought that having found a wife or a husband you'd live happily ever after.'

'What balls,' said Henry. 'You fellows are as lecherous as cats.'

Micky winced, because although it was known that he was homosexual it was uncommon to refer to it so openly at table.

'Men are unfaithful to their wives,' Henry went on, 'because they get bored of sleeping with the same woman. It's as simple as that.' He spoke in a deep, emphatic tone of voice.

'And don't women get bored of sleeping with the same man?' asked Clare.

'I don't know,' said Henry. 'Do they?'

'Repetition makes anything monotonous,' said John.

'Who gets bored first?' asked Micky, turning to Arabella.

'How should I know?' she said.

'It's not so much a question of who gets bored first,' said John. 'It's more that sex isn't so important to women, or rather that it leads on to other things. That's why, I think, men sometimes feel double-crossed.'

'Why double-crossed?' asked Mary.

'Because when two people first sleep together sex is an end in itself: and for men it remains an end in itself, but for women it becomes a means to an end . . .'

'What end?'

'Children.'

'Don't men want children?'

'Not to start with,' said John. 'A man and a woman meet. They are attracted to one another. They fall in love and make love, or vice versa. They marry. There is a period of intoxicating copulation until the wife becomes pregnant. Then, almost at once, she loses interest in sex. She becomes introverted. She wants to be left alone at night to read her novel; to sleep. The husband is baffled and angry. If he's at the bottom of the social scale he beats her up: we have dozens of such cases in court. If

53

he's at the top he has the time and opportunity to look for other women.'

He paused, for effect, and took a sip of his wine. Like many men in middle age his professional persona had begun to obtrude into his private manner, and the slightly ponderous way in which he spoke made him sound like a judge summing up at the end of a case.

'So long as the wife is confident that the husband will not desert her,' he went on, 'she will put up with his infidelity. She has her baby. She suckles him with her secret, Mona Lisa smile. The father has fulfilled his function. So far as she is concerned he is redundant.'

'But then why do married women have affairs with men?' asked Arabella.

'That's the next phase,' said John. 'As soon as the children walk, talk and assert themselves they become demanding and tiresome. The mother now needs the father once again to exert authority; and the father, seeing his own features appear on the child's pudgy face, at last feels some pride in paternity. He abandons his mistress. She is too much trouble; she takes up too much time; above all she is too expensive. So instead of making assignations after work he hurries back from the office to see his children before they go to bed.'

'Children,' said Mary Mascall, 'who have been intolerable all day to their mothers, but are all charm to their Daddys for half an hour before bed.'

'Exactly,' said John. 'This is the moment when wives are at risk. They envy their husbands' careers. The home becomes a prison. Domesticity becomes penal servitude. They dream of a lover who will deliver them. They are an open city for any sexual buccaneer.'

John stopped and drank what wine was left in his glass.

Henry immediately filled it again. 'What do you think of that theory?' he asked Arabella.

'Male cynicism,' she replied.

'I really don't think it's as simple as that,' Clare said to her husband. 'Some married couples simply find they aren't compatible.'

'I don't agree,' said John. 'Look at the Grahams.' (He was re-

54

ferring to a couple they all knew who had both been married before.) 'Having gone through with a divorce, with all the suffering that involved for their children, they now realize that much of what they both put down to incompatibility is in fact endemic to the married state.'

'Perhaps,' said Clare.

'I have a different theory,' said Henry with a quick, malicious smile. 'It came to me in Norfolk as I was watching the chickens on the farm. There were two cocks and fourteen hens, and you'd think that it would have suited all concerned for the cocks to share the hens and the hens to share the cocks. But not at all. One cock which was admittedly bigger, brighter and more . . . upright than the other seemed to have all fourteen hens and the other cock – a droopy little fellow – had none. Nor was it the first cock who kept the second cock off the fluffy bums of the fourteen hens. It was the fourteen hens who would have nothing to do with him. They pecked at him whenever he came near. They wouldn't even let him share the corn. They treated him with contempt because they preferred one fourteenth part of the first cock to one seventh of the second.'

'That's a banal observation,' said Arabella. 'Kipling or someone said it all before.'

'And you can't really extrapolate from poultry to the human race,' said Micky.

'But I think you can,' said Henry. 'Sexual intercourse is an animal action. However much we may adorn it with poetry, music and *haute couture*, a fuck is a fuck. You can't disguise it. And I would suggest that women, like hens, prefer a share of the colourful cock to a dull cock all to themselves; to put it another way, to be screwed by an attractive man who runs several women than by a drab man who relies on the marriage vows for his piece of ass.'

'I do wish you wouldn't use American expressions,' said Mary.

'And what purpose is served by this preference?' asked John.

Henry shrugged his shoulders. 'It's the process of natural selection, isn't it? Survival of the fittest?'

'It's a most . . . corrupt philosophy,' said Clare.

'Don't blame me,' said Henry. 'I didn't design the human race.'

'Your case, then, is this,' said John, who liked to summarize the arguments of others. 'A man can be unfaithful to his wife because it conforms to nature. Whatever she may *think* she thinks it really enhances his attractiveness and as a result she loves him more. It thus strengthens the family bond. But if a wife is unfaithful to her husband she presents him with only one set of alternatives, each of which leads to a break-up of the family. Either he does not put up with it and they divorce; or he condones it – perhaps by pretending not to notice what is going on – and as a result is emasculated. The wife despises him and sooner or later goes off for good with cock number one.'

'Precisely,' said Henry. 'That's just what happened with the Farrels. He knew quite well what was going on, but he pretended not to notice. He even tried to disarm some of her boyfriends by befriending them. As a result she despised him more and more until finally she ran off . . .'

'You seem to be suggesting,' said John, 'that there is, whether we like it or not, an element of what is commonly called sado-masochism in the relationship between a man and a woman.'

'I am indeed,' said Henry. 'However delicate or gentle a man may be, he is inescapably assaulting a woman when he fucks her while she, lying there supine with her legs apart, invites him to do so.'

'You are disgusting,' said Mary – blushing, but not with outrage.

'Of course I'm disgusting,' Henry shouted, laughing. 'Sex is disgusting.' He turned to Clare with a mocking smile. 'It is disgusting, isn't it? That's why nuns and priests give it up. It's much more than simple copulation. It's the triumph of force!'

'What rubbish,' said Clare, meeting his mockery with a straight expression of no-nonsense. 'A lot of men and women love one another in a quiet, civilized way.'

'Don't pay any attention to him,' said Mary. 'He's only sounding off. I can assure you, he's not quite the cock number one that he makes himself out to be.'

'In fact over-aggressive, over-masculine types,' said Arabella, 'are usually compensating for fear of sexual inadequacy. You're probably really queer, Henry.'

'Henry dear,' said Micky. 'Is this your own, sweet, round-about way of making a proposition?'

As he drove back from the Boltons, where the Mascalls lived, to their own house in Holland Park, John brooded on what Henry had said. 'Do you think he believes in his own theories?' he asked Clare.

'No. I think he just says it to make conversation,' she replied. 'Like you and socialism.'

John said nothing and Clare, who was driving (because she had drunk less than John), glanced at him as if afraid that he might take offence at what she said. 'Don't you think?' she asked.

'No,' he said. 'I don't think my socialism is just a conversation piece.' There was a coldness in his tone.

'We don't exactly lead a socialist life,' said Clare.

'It's not a question of the life you lead. It's a question of the conviction you hold.'

'You can't entirely disassociate theory from practice.'

'There's no necessary connection.'

'Not in logic perhaps. But there is in life.'

They returned home and, both slightly drunk, they made love after which John lay awake, afraid again of another attack of Ivan Ilychitis. Instead of counting sheep he tried to remember when they had last made love when sober, but before he could recall an occasion he was asleep.

chapter two

The next morning John telephoned a journalist on the *New Statesman* called Gordon Pratt. They arranged to meet for lunch at Bertorelli's restaurant in Charlotte Street a few days later.

Gordon Pratt was now the only fellow-member of the Oxford University Labour Club whom John still thought of as a friend. They had shared a flat after moving to London but while Gordon, a Scot, had gone deeper into left-wing politics and journalism, John had been drawn – as if by some hidden hand – to see more of his rich right-wing friends and to date their debutante sisters. All the same a certain affinity and affection remained between them, and even after they had both married – John to a county Catholic, Gordon to a heavy-drinking, freethinking Ulster feminist – they continued to meet from time to time.

If either had been asked why he did not see more of the other, both would have replied at once that their wives could not stand one another – which was true: but had neither married, they would not necessarily have seen each other more; for even if they shared political convictions and cultural tastes, their other values were different. Sharing a flat had taught them that. John, for example, had been first astonished and then embarrassed that Gordon had removed his shoes in the living-room one evening when Clare was there: and he had noticed the same incredulity and embarrassment when soon after they had moved in he had decanted some sherry and placed it with glasses on a tray.

Twin souls in great things, they might like Herzen and Ogarev on the Sparrow Hills have dedicated their lives to liberty – and have overlooked the sherry decanter and the smelly socks – had not a fairly full measure of liberty already been there. In the absence of any great oppression to tighten those bonds of idealism which held them together, their paths diverged along the deeply rutted tracks leading from the two different childhoods and milieux until both fitted the role they played in life so well that anyone studying them in the restaurant would wonder what the sleek barrister in his tailor-made, pin-striped suit could have in common with the ill-shaven hung-over journalist wearing jeans and a leather jacket. Yet the conversation at their table went as fast as that on any other, without even touching upon nostalgic recollections of university days. After polite questions when they first sat down about one another's families they started on politics, the press and the law – all topics of interest to them both – which led quite quickly, and with no apparent design, to what John had had in mind in asking his friend to meet him for lunch. 'Do you think,' he asked Gordon, 'that's it's too late for a man of my age to go into politics?'

'It's never too late,' said Gordon quickly, as if fending off the question while he considered it.

'I'm forty, you know,' said John.

'So am I,' said his friend.

'I could hardly get a safe seat for the next election, so it might be as many as ten years before I could get into Parliament.'

Gordon looked at him and smiled. 'So when you say "a man of my age" you mean you?'

'Yes.' John felt that he was blushing. 'Do you think it's ridiculous?' he asked.

'Not ridiculous, no. But slightly surprising.'

'Why?'

'Because you haven't shown much more than a general interest in politics over the past ten years or so – and none at all in the Labour Party. I presume that you would still stand for the Labour Party?'

'Of course.'

'I'm also surprised that you should want to.'

'Why?'

'The House of Commons, so far as I can see, is a waste of a good man's time. You sweat your guts out to get elected, then hang around for ten or twenty years voting for bills you don't believe in, and if in the end you are given power it is, as Disraeli said, too little and too late.'

John paused for a moment and stared at his escalope *à la Milanese*.

'If I explain to you what I feel,' he said, 'will you tell me at the end what you think? An unbiased opinion?'

'Of course.'

John quickly cut up what was left of his escalope, and with his mouth half full of meat and potato, he started. 'First of all, you're quite right to say that I've been inactive as a socialist for the past ten years or so, and that may dish my chances as a candidate: but the truth is that I had to start my career and bring up my children, and there was little time or energy left over after that for the Party . . .'

He paused – arrested by the odd sound of that last word 'the Party', which he had liked so much when he was younger because it gave a touch of conspiratorial excitement as if he was a character in a novel by Sartre or Malraux.

'I still believe,' he said, 'that since the war the kind of socialism practised by the Labour Party has reduced poverty, injustice and, as a result, some human suffering. I believe that we should go on in the same way so that even if we can never build Heaven on Earth, we can gradually improve the material and cultural condition of most of our fellow citizens.'

'Yes, well,' said Gordon, 'if that's the kind of speech you'd make to an adoption meeting, it might do the trick; though in my experience the people who sit on constituency committees see selection of a candidate as a prize for knocking on more doors in the rain than a milk-man.'

'Would you vote for me?'

'Me?' He looked evasively over John's shoulder. 'Hey, let's have another bottle of wine.' He raised his hand to attract the attention of a waiter, saying at the same time: 'I'm not avoiding the question, John. It's just that I need fuel for heavy talk like this.'

The waiter came. Gordon ordered the wine, and when it was placed on the table a moment later, he filled both glasses. Finally he turned to John.

'There's no doubt at all,' he said, 'that you're an able barrister, and that the Labour Party should grab anyone they can lay their hands on of your calibre to set against the cunning bastards on the Tory benches. So if you ask me – and I could be wrong – a determined attempt to get a seat would succeed. If you could then face the grind of an election you could in a few years' time be a Member of Parliament. What I still can't understand is why you want to be a fucking Member of Parliament. Particularly now when the Party has lost most of its principles, and is really just the organized lobby for two or three of the big unions. It can't just be vanity, which is why most successful men want to go into Parliament . . . like owning a Rolls-Royce. There has to be some other motive and I can't figure it out.'

'You wouldn't accept,' John asked, 'that my motive might be a sincere desire to convert socialist principles into practical legislation?'

Gordon sighed and leant back in his chair as if a longer view would bring his friend into focus. 'I could only accept that,' he said, 'on the basis of the following hypothesis: that when we came down from Oxford twenty odd years ago, you buried your principles in peat; and that now you've dug them up again and found them perfectly preserved. That's the only explanation for their prime condition.'

John smiled. 'Would that disqualify me?'

'Nothing disqualifies you. It just staggers me to find you, aged forty, with the fresh ambition of a twenty-two-year-old.'

'Perhaps we're crossing paths again,' said John. 'I've spent the first half of my life building up private assets, while you've served the community . . .'

Gordon laughed. 'And now you want to serve the community, whereas I'd sell out to the *Daily Telegraph* if they offered me the right money.'

'But you wouldn't, would you?'

Gordon shook his head. 'No.'

'Because you're not as cynical as you make yourself out to be.'

'I'm cynical, yes,' he said. 'We'll never see the British Revolution because the bloody proletariat need the bourgeoisie to sneer at and torment. Class war is our national sport, and you couldn't have it without a capitalist class.'

'Then why don't you sell out?'

'I'm damned if I'll give any satisfaction to those rich, complacent bastards by giving up trying.' He emptied his glass and filled it again. 'I live for a dream, John, a dream that one day we'll wipe the collective smile off the face of the sodding upper classes.'

'And won't you accept that belatedly I feel the same way?'

'Of course I will,' said Gordon. 'Of course I will. Welcome home.' He looked at his friend with tears in his eyes and then drank what was left of the second bottle of wine.

chapter three

After lunch John went to his chambers in the Middle Temple to collect the brief for the following day. He sat down at his desk and the clerk brought him some tea. He picked up the brief, tied with red ribbon, and saw beneath it a message that he should call a Miss Mascall.

John had forgotten about Jilly Mascall: he had not even asked after her when they had dined with Henry and Mary the week before. But as he sat now at his desk, looking round in the fading light at the shelves of law books, the prints of London in the eighteenth century and the tin boxes where he and his colleagues kept their wigs and wing collars, he felt that her call was part of the new pattern to his life – his emancipation, as it were, from the domestic yoke. Nothing drives a man harder than the desire to confound those who doubt him, and just as he was determined to show Clare that he was not the impotent socialist she thought him to be, he now thought he would prove himself able to take a pretty girl out to lunch.

He picked up the telephone and dialled the number on the piece of paper in front of him. As it rang into his ear he heard another sound which beat a separate rhythm beside the ringing of the telephone. It was the beating of his heart. He was taken by a sudden panic. Perhaps he was making a fool of himself? Henry and Mary would get to hear of it and laugh at him. Clare would be embarrassed and ashamed. He hoped that no one would answer before he could reasonably return the telephone to its receiver (for there were others sitting in the same room) but suddenly a girlish voice said hello.

'Is that Jilly?' he asked.

'No. I'll get her.' There was a rustle, some murmuring, then the same voice said: 'Who is it?'

'John Strickland.'

There was another rustle, some more murmuring, and another voice said hello.

'Is that Jilly?'

'Yes. Sorry. I didn't know who you were.' Giggles.

'Quite right to be cautious. I might have been a heavy breather.' More giggles. Some heavy breathing.

'You'd better be careful,' said John. 'This telephone might be tapped.'

'Oh Gosh. Do they? I mean, tap lawyers' telephones?'

'Not yet. But it's coming.' A pause. 'Where are you living now?'

'In Warwick Square. I share a flat with a girl called Miranda. Do you know her? She's awfully nice.' More giggles.

'Is she there in the room?' asked John.

'Oh yes, but even if she wasn't I'd say she was awfully nice.'

'Well, are we going to meet for lunch?' asked John.

'I hope so.'

'How flexible are you?'

'Oh, I'm frightfully flexible.' More giggles.

'Well let's say next Wednesday week at one at Don Juan's in the King's Road.'

'Lovely.'

'Will you remember?'

'Don Juan's. Who'd forget?'

'I'll see you there.'

John put down the telephone, packed his briefcase and set off home.

chapter four

The area of London where John and Clare had bought their house varied street by street. On the higher ground of Holland Park and Campden Hill there were the spacious, elegant houses of the rich surrounding like covered wagons their exclusive communal gardens. Farther north, behind Notting Hill Gate, or at the northern end of Ladbroke Grove, the houses were semi-slums, packed with transient Irish or West Indians. Over the past decade there had been an ebb in the tide of these scruffy houses as energetic estate agents had evicted their improverished tenants and sold them off to their middle-class customers. The Stricklands' terrace house had, before they bought it, housed three families and because it was on the frontier of an unfashionable area had been bought cheap. They themselves had restored it to its original form with a kitchen in the basement and a drawing-room on the first floor, with a parents' bedroom beside it and the children's above.

They had chosen the area partly because it was both pleasant and smart; and partly because it was the area of town that John knew best. When he had first come to London he had shared a flat in Notting Hill Gate with Gordon Pratt which, it so happened, was in the same Parliamentary constituency as his present house in Holland Park. Nineteen years before, he had joined the branch Labour Party and had paid his subscription of two pounds a year by Banker's Order, an order he had never cancelled; so when now he returned to work as a Labour activist he found himself one of the most long-standing members of the branch Party. He started to attend meetings again; he organized a petition to the Council about play areas on unused building sites and within a month, was put forward as a candidate for the General Management Committee.

All this he kept secret from his friends. Clare, of course, had to be given an account of the evening he spent away from home, and he did not lie to her. 'I'm thinking of going into politics,' he said on one of the rare evenings when they dined alone, 'so I shall have to go to some meetings.'

She sighed. 'How often?'

'Only every week or so.'

She put on a plaintive face – the same she would wear when Tom told her that he wanted to join the Boy Scouts or a football club. Community activities were all very well but it was the mother who had to iron the uniform and wash the shirts.

The Labour Party, of course, had no uniform, and it was unlikely that John's shirts would be dirtied by his political work unless at some impassioned meeting he was to be pelted with rotten eggs; but she sighed nonetheless because John was older than Tom and should know better than to embark upon a Quixotic hobby when their social life was already so demanding. And sure enough, soon after the reawakening of John's political conscience, the Mascalls invited them to the opera on the same night as the Annual General Meeting of the branch Party.

'Can we go?' Clare asked John with her hand on the telephone.

'When?'

'Next Thursday.'

'No.'

'Why not?'

'I've got a meeting.'

'Can you cancel it?'

'No. I'm up for election to the GMC.'

She frowned. 'The GMC,' she repeated in a mixed tone of exasperation and contempt. 'Well, what shall I tell Mary?'

'Tell her what you like.'

Clare turned back to the telephone. 'Look,' she said. 'I'm afraid we can't because John's got something boring he's got to do . . .'

'Can't you come on your own?' asked Mary at the other end of the line.

'I could,' said Clare, 'but you'd probably prefer to get another couple . . .'

'Oh no,' said Mary. 'It's easy to find a spare man.'

Thus on the evening of John's first triumph in his political career Clare was at the opera with the Mascalls and Micky Neill: and while he returned early after a pint of beer with some comrades at the local pub, she returned late and tipsy after Dover sole and cold Rhine wine at Wheeler's in Old Compton Street.

'They all wanted to know about your meeting,' she said to John – giggling as she undressed. 'But I kept your secret.'

'It's not a secret,' said John.

'Oh isn't it?' Her face was flushed and puffed out with alcohol. 'Why should it be a secret?'

'I don't know. It's just slightly ridiculous, isn't it?'

He looked at her severely over his spectacles. 'Not to me.'

'Not to you, perhaps, but it will be to the others.' She tripped over her underclothes as she removed them and guffawed at her own clumsiness. 'One thing I can promise you,' she said. 'When Henry and Mary and Micky find out, they'll laugh.'

'I don't mind if they do,' said John quietly.

'Please yourself,' said Clare, struggling into her nightdress and then slumping into bed. 'But don't blame me if I laugh too.'

The next morning, as he sat in the Underground on his way to his chambers, John tried to analyse his wife's antagonism towards his convictions and stave off the slight resentment that he felt towards her. It was clear that she considered them insincere – that he had readopted them not because he believed in them but as a means of criticizing and demeaning her.

For a moment John wondered whether this was not true. Certainly it was her remark in the car which had stung him to telephone Gordon Pratt; and he remembered how when he had first met Clare he had argued with her – assaulting her conventional opinions about both politics and morality until her arguments had been defeated and the lips which had expressed them, with nothing more to say, waited passively to be kissed by the conqueror. Or, as Gordon had put it at the time: 'The cunt of that county girl is your bloody Bastille.'

But like the Barbarians who invaded Rome he had been seduced by her beliefs. Having won a battle he had lost the war. The life they had led since they married reflected her values, not his, so it was natural for Clare to assume that his renewed revolt implied some criticism of her. She went too far, however, if she thought that because what she had said in the car after dinner with the Mascalls had spurred him into action he had picked up the socialist stick to use against her. It was typical of a woman, he thought, to reduce the processes of the intellect to projections of personal conflict. When he now recalled that she had threatened to laugh at him for his socialist activism he was neither injured nor offended. In a sense he was even pleased, for it showed that he had indeed altered the course of his life away from those who cared only about Wimbledon and the Stock market.

On the other hand if he had (in his own eyes) redeemed the selfless and benevolent half of his personality, the snobbish side still shadowed him. He found his current comrades in the North Kensington Labour Party just as dull and unattractive as those in the Oxford University Labour Club twenty years before: and although no longer tempted by any smart set, he still regretted that socialist convictions seemed incompatible with physical beauty and a sense of humour. He therefore took an antidote, and the more deeply he was to become involved with the sober issues of public spending and incomes policy the more frequently he arranged to have lunch with Jilly Mascall.

chapter five

He had arrived on the first occasion at Don Juan's in the King's Road feeling nervous on two counts – first that they would be seen by friends and acquaintances and their meeting misconstrued; the second that his dull, conventional clothes, so normal in the Law Courts but out of place in Chelsea, would damn him in the girl's eyes before he had a chance to amuse her. He was shown to the table he had reserved, where he ordered a glass of Punt e Mes. He glanced at the menu, winced at the prices and started to eat one of the bread sticks placed in the basket before him.

His drink was brought by the waiter. Time passed. He felt self-conscious sitting alone at the table facing an empty seat, and so ordered another drink. At a quarter past one he was deliberating whether, if she did not turn up, to leave the restaurant or eat lunch on his own when Jilly Mascall came in through the door. She glanced around, saw John and marched towards him – smiling, opening her coat and brushing a basket of rolls off one of the tables in her path.

'I *am* sorry I'm late,' she said.

John rose from his seat. A waiter came up behind Jilly, picked the rolls up off the floor and took her coat.

They sat down facing one another. 'It's those bloody buses,' said Jilly. 'I mean you might as well not have them because you never know when they're going to come. I waited for hours and then had to take a taxi . . .'

'I'm sorry,' said John.

'Goodness, it's not your fault. I just hope you don't have to rush off anywhere.'

'No.'

They looked at the menu.

'The good thing about going out to lunch with an older man,' said Jilly, 'is that you don't have to worry about what things cost.'

John twitched. Jilly ordered an avocado pear with prawns and a fillet steak.

'What are you doing now?' John asked her.

'Oh, still that boring secretarial course,' she said. 'Then out with spotty youths in the evening. Really, I mean, I think London's a disappointment . . .'

'What were you expecting?'

'I don't know. More interesting people, I suppose. The spotty youths are boring but then so are the grown-ups. I stayed with Henry and Mary for the first week I was here and I thought I'd meet some interesting people there, but their friends are a pretty stodgy lot.'

'Like me.'

She stopped and looked at him under her eyelashes with a steady, measured look. 'It wasn't stodgy to ask me out to lunch.'

'Perhaps not.' John snapped another bread stick. 'And I dare say that if we're seen by my stodgy friends they'll be mildly shocked.'

'I could be *your* niece.'

For a moment John thought of his sister's daughter – an earnest pupil at a comprehensive school in Liverpool – and compared her to the glamorous girl in front of him. 'You couldn't,' he said, shaking his head.

'Your god-daughter, then.'

'Yes.'

'Talking of godfathers,' said Jilly. 'Do you know the Creeleys?'

'A little.'

'Is it true that Jennifer Creeley's daughters are by different men, and that their real fathers are their godfathers?'

'I heard a different story,' said John.

'What was it? Do tell me.'

'I was told that the fathers are the men whose houses she was decorating nine months before the babies were born.'

'Aha. I must tell Miranda.'

'Who's Miranda?'

'Miranda Creeley. The girl I share a flat with. She's the eldest daughter.'

'But does she know? About the different fathers?'

'Of course she does.'

'Who on earth told her?'

'She read it in *Private Eye*.'

'How dreadful.'

'I don't think she minds much. Anyway, she thinks that her father is her father because she was the first. But Laura, that's her sister – she doesn't look anything like her father, but she doesn't look much like her godfather either.'

'Who is he?'

'Grandpa.' Jilly burst out laughing, and since her glass of wine was under her nose as she did so some of it spluttered onto the tablecloth, leaving a rash of mauve spots. She did not seem to notice. 'It is funny, isn't it? I mean it means that Laura Creeley might be my aunt. But I'll tell her about the decorating theory.'

Jilly's avocado pear was placed before her and she started to eat it with a dainty greed. John watched her as she did so – her long, dark eyelashes were smudged with mascara; her haphazard brown hair fell over her face; her small, red tongue slipped out between perfect lips to lick a trickle of the dressing. Her nails, he noticed, were bitten to the quick.

'Does it shock you?' he asked.

'What?'

'All that about the Creeleys?'

Jilly shrugged her shoulders. 'Not really. But it makes me pretty cynical . . . It makes Miranda cynical, anyway.'

'Your generation won't have the same problem.'

'Why not?'

'Because of the pill.'

'No, I suppose not.' She scooped out the last sliver of avocado pulp and sat back with a sigh.

'Have you got a boyfriend?' John asked.

'No one specific.'

'Have you got one in mind?'

'Not really. They're all so boring.'

'Do you find Guy boring?'

She blushed. 'A bit.'

'Then you should look for an older man,' John said with a smile.

'Yes,' she said – staring at him for a third time with no smile on her plump little lips.

Their conversation now moved on to films and plays, to Henry and Mary, to Norfolk – and all the time John only half attended to what she said so distracted was he by her physical perfection.

It was not that he felt attracted to her: it was more the kind of astonishment he had felt at the birth of Tom, his first child – at his miniature fingers and toes. Jilly Mascall had nothing miniature, but despite her mascara and her gauche aggression she was an unspoilt specimen of a girl in bloom. He saw only her hands, her face, her neck, her hair. The rest of her body was shrouded in the scrappy, hanging clothes which were then in fashion. Had she been naked he might have marvelled in the same way at the pinkness of her pigmented bosom or the softness of her small stomach: as it was, when he thought of them, they could only be imagined and it was then that his fantasy first became infected and inflamed.

Over the coffee Jilly asked him quite casually whether Clare knew that they were having lunch together.

'Not yet,' said John as if he had been too busy to mention it.

'Are you going to tell her?'

'I don't see why not.'

'Nor do I,' said Jilly quickly. 'I just thought I ought to know in case Henry and Mary ask me anything . . .'

'Oh don't make a secret out of it,' said John.

'All right.'

'Unless . . .' He hesitated.

'What?'

'Well, it would be nice to have lunch again. That is, if you would like to.'

'Of course I would,' she said with deliberate deference. 'That's why I asked. I don't want to be a nuisance in any way.'

'In that case it might be better if we kept it to ourselves,' said John. 'We can show our hand when someone sees us.'

'OK,' she said. 'That's fine by me.'

chapter six

That Saturday morning at the cottage John was woken by the sound of his children quarrelling amicably in the kitchen below. He saw from the clock on his bedside table that it was eight o'clock. Tom and Anna, it seemed, were getting their own breakfast so John turned over in bed and closed his eyes again.

He could not sleep. He could rarely sleep again once he was awake, but because it was Saturday he felt some sort of obligation to lie in, as if the extra hour was a luxury he must enjoy like sun-bathing or stereophonic gramophone music. As a result his mind filled up neither with the nonsensical and irrational dreams which came to him when he was truly unconscious, nor with the incisive, systematized thoughts which when he was awake made him so good at the law: instead vague anxieties and fantasies flitted in and out of his mind, settling promiscuously on such subjects as income tax, the garden or a new car.

On this particular Saturday morning his semi-conscious mind went back over the week in London and settled – half-anxiously, half-pleasurably – on the thought of Jilly Mascall. And having remembered the past week it moved forward to the future: in anticipation of their new assignation he began to imagine how it would be. He smiled to himself as he saw her laugh at his amusing conversation: she directs more of those straight, sultry looks at him – and towards the end of their lunch she complains that the drain in her kitchen sink is blocked, and that although she has a plunger neither she nor Miranda is strong enough to dislodge the nugget of tea leaves and bacon fat or whatever it is . . .

John has nothing on that afternoon so he offers to return with her and see what he can do. He goes back to the flat. He clears the drain. She offers to make some coffee. They sit sipping, talking. He moves towards her. They kiss. Her passive, inexperienced lips press tentatively against his. He holds her. He touches her. Patiently, kindly, he removes her clothes. Desire and gratitude mingle in her eyes. He uncovers the pink, pigmented breasts with their tiny, child-like nipples. His hand stretches down to her stomach. He hesitates, remembering how young she is. 'Oh please,' she murmurs. They go ahead. With the care of an artist and the skill of a surgeon he makes love to her until, with an ecstatic whimper, then a cry, from her pink little mouth, she feels for the first time the consummation of sexual love.

Next to him in bed Clare shifted and sighed. There was a

muffled fart under the blankets. She raised herself on her elbow and leaned over her husband to look at the clock. The smell of her wind mingled with the liverish, early-morning odour from her mouth. She slumped back on her side of the bed, grunted, heaved around like an elephant and then was still. It was not yet time to get up.

In that his body had followed his mind so far in his imaginings but not all the way, John considered a move towards the passive haunch of his semi-slumbering wife: but since the contrast between the pink purity of Jilly Mascall and the heavy, smelly Clare Strickland was so great; and since the children might burst in upon them at any moment; and since his need to urinate was greater than his need to ejaculate, John rolled out of bed instead and stumbled through to the bathroom.

There followed a typical Saturday – a trip to Marlborough in the morning; raking up leaves into a bonfire in the afternoon. Tom followed his father like a puppy, insisting imperiously upon helping him to do every task – even if the rake was too large to be wielded effectively by a ten-year-old boy.

John as usual was torn between reducing the job to a game for his son or getting it done: he ended by letting Tom comb the grass with the rake while he picked up the leaves with his bare hands. Yet all the while – as his gumboots sank into the damp grass and his lungs blew mist into the cold air; while he laughed at his son, then shouted at him, then laughed again – all the while his mind was distracted by the image and idea of Jilly Mascall.

It grew dark. Clare called them in to tea. He sat in the kitchen eating buttered crumpets and drinking tea from a mug with his cheerful children and quiet, smiling wife. He too was content – in as much as he was there at the table: but just as in company he had stepped back from himself and failed to recognize the chatty host pouring wine for his friends, so now he stepped forward into set-pieces of romantic drama with Jilly Mascall as the juvenile lead. His conscious mind was like a pair of binoculars borrowed in turn by the different faculties of his brain – by his anxious sociability, by his hormone-sodden fantasy, by his paternal concern, his practical judgement, his stomach's appetite. They focused at random on the child, the leaves, Jilly, Clare, the crumpets. Without the conscious mind each faculty was blind, but it was not dead, for the ruminations of each proceeded unawares so that the combination of the different images, were it possible to see them, would be more like the fragmented pattern of a kaleidoscope than the precise, recognizable image of the binoculars.

Among these faculties there was his conscience. Although he was an agnostic John had some sense of right and wrong – indeed he believed that his ethics, based on decency and common sense, were more robust than Clare's Catholic morals, which included such dubious notions as sin and redemption. John liked to say that he had worked out his own morality, just as he had developed his own taste in art and music, and if it happened that he had come to the same conclusions as most other middle-aged, middle-class Englishmen that only confirmed in his own mind that he had reached the right conclusion.

His ethics, like English law, were based less on abstract principles than on each case as it arose; indeed they followed closely the morality of the law not only because John served the law and so had absorbed its values but because that law itself was framed by practical middle-class moralists of just his kind. A cynic would say that there was one simple principle behind it all: that it was right and reasonable to do what he and his friends would do but wrong and unreasonable to do what they would not do. Thus brawling and shop-lifting were punished while buggery and adultery were not, because many if not most of John's friends were either sodomites or adulterers but would never fight in a pub or steal from a chain store. In this way John Strickland differed from his father – and in this difference is reflected a change in the moral attitudes of a whole society.

John himself was not like Henry Mascall a habitual or enthusiastic adulterer. He had had one or two brief affairs with other women at times when Clare was sour and their marriage in crisis; but these had taught him that infidelity was more trouble than it was worth. And more expense. And since then – for the past seven years or eight years – he had been content enough to keep clear of any other attachmnts.

All this, however, had more to do with habit and convenience than with right and wrong; so when now Jilly Mascall lay panting voluptuously on his brain no qualms inhibited John from making love to her in his daydreams. The idea that 'whatsoever looketh on a woman to lust after her hath committed adultery with her already in his heart' seemed just the kind of silly notion that made Clare's convent friends feel that they had might as well be hung for a sheep as for a lamb and jump into bed with the first bidder.

John did not, then, feel ashamed that that Saturday night, rather than make love to his wife, he preferred to turn away from her and with a sweet, contented expression on his face imagine yet again his lunch with Jilly Mascall. She was, after all, more like the girl he had married than the thirty-two-year-old woman lying at his side.

chapter seven

Each time John saw Jilly Mascall he became more obsessed by this pretty but otherwise ordinary girl until everything she did or said only enhanced her charm. He studied her gauche gestures as if they were the graceful movements of a ballerina, and he listened with enraptured attention to her banal views and silly jokes. If anything prevented him from declaring his passion for her at one or other of their lunches together it was not any moral inhibition but the Englishman's terror of appearing a fool.

He therefore approached the position cautiously, through conversation – telling Jilly how pretty she was; how attractive he found her; how much he enjoyed her company; how fond of her he had become – all sentiments which could be ascribed to avuncular friendship as much as sexual passion if it became necessary to beat a retreat. He advanced only when he felt that his compliments were not only welcomed but returned – and they were returned, with innocent enthusiasm, for Jilly insisted that it was she who was fond of him: that it was she who benefited from his maturity; that it was he, the older man, who was attractive to the younger girl and flattered her by his attentions but in the end, sooner or later, was sure to find her boring.

What Jilly did not put into words she expressed in glances – by more of those long, sultry looks. On one occasion she even shifted her leg under the table and John sat with a pounding pulse trying to decide whether this was provoked by desire or cramp. He knew, of course, that the young were promiscuous and he was confident that if he became Jilly's lover he would not be the first. All the same it would burn his boats if he moved his leg against hers under the pink tablecloth, and anyway he did not care for such semi-public demonstrations of sexual attraction, so he did nothing but take hold of her hand while he was talking to her, as he might have held his daughter's.

One afternoon in mid-October they came out of the restaurant where they had eaten lunch into Frith Street and stood indecisively on the pavement as if both were loathe to part.

'Where are you going now?' John asked Jilly.

'Nowhere in particular,' she said.

'I've got to see a solicitor at four,' he said, 'but we might go for a walk in the park.'

'Except it's going to rain,' said Jilly looking up at the pale grey sky.

'Perhaps,' said John.

'Why don't you come and see the flat?' said Jilly.

'All right,' he said in a tone of voice that attempted to sound as if it was a natural invitation but was croaky all the same. He glanced at his watch. 'I'll have to be quite quick.'

They hailed a taxi and were driven down Shaftesbury Avenue towards Pimlico. In ten minutes they reached Warwick Square, where John paid off the driver and Jilly took her keys from her bag. John followed her up the stairs, watching the pretty calves of her legs where they emerged from her patent-leather boots. He felt the anxiety and excitement of a sixteen-year-old. 'This is it,' he thought to himself. 'She's made the position clear. There's no going back on it now.'

They reached the flat on the third floor. Jilly opened the door with her latch key and John came behind her into a small lobby. There they took off their coats and then passed through into the sitting-room. It was just what he might have expected: furnished and decorated impersonally with a bunch of copperplate invitations stuck on the mantel above the gas fire – some for Jilly Mascall and others for Miranda Creeley.

'I'll show you round,' said Jilly.

He followed her into the small kitchen which looked out over roofs and the backs of other houses. There were some unwashed cups and saucers in the sink and an open jar of powdered coffee on the sideboard.

They moved on. John glanced at the green bathroom and then was shown Miranda's bedroom – its double bed unmade and covered with heaps of crumpled clothes.

'And this is my room,' said Jilly.

Her bed was single and it was covered neatly by a patchwork quilt. Her blue nightdress lay folded on top of the pillow. There was a framed photograph of her parents on the chest of drawers, and on the dressing table next to a plastic carton of roll-on deodorant and a small box of mascara there was a group of glass animals – an elephant with a green trunk, a horse with pink legs, a monkey with a yellow tail. John picked up a book on her bedside table: it was called *The Breeding of Ponies*.

'Have you got a pony?' he asked.

Jilly blushed. 'Well, she's a horse really . . . a mare. I thought she might like a foal.'

She moved towards the door as if she wanted him to leave her bedroom. They went back into the living-room.

'What do you think of it, then?' Jilly asked John.

'What?'

'The flat.'

'I like it very much indeed. You're lucky to have found it.'

She may have sensed some hypocrisy in his tone of voice for she quickly said: 'We haven't done much to it, yet. We've only been here a month. But in the end I think we can make it nice.'

'It's nice already,' John said – thinking how precisely its lack of character fitted the unformed personality of the seventeen-year-old girl.

They stood side by side in front of the gas fire. 'Would you like some coffee?' she asked.

He turned and smiled. 'Not really, no.'

'Then . . .'

He put his hand on her shoulder and she swayed towards him

– arms rising timidly to embrace him. They kissed, but unlike the passive lips he had imagined Jilly's parted expertly and her tongue darted out from between her teeth to tickle and mingle with his.

Confused by contradictory impressions of both her innocence and her experience John might have stood back from what he was doing had he not been caught in the millstream of sexual motion. More obedient to nature than any serf to a Tsar his hands clasped her body, feeling her paltry bosom beneath the cashmere cardigan. Her hair tickled his face: she breathed furiously through her little nostrils and her small hands with bitten nails gripped the cloth of his jacket. They started to move towards the sofa but then both heard the sound of a key in the lock of the door to the flat.

They stood apart. 'It must be Miranda,' said Jilly. She looked flushed but unperturbed.

'Were you expecting her?' asked John irritably.

Jilly shrugged her shoulders, and at that moment a heavy, blonde girl came into the room – glancing curiously at the two who were already there.

'Miranda,' said Jilly with a look of some sort of triumph on her face. 'This is John Strickland.'

They shook hands. 'Don't you know my parents?' the blonde girl asked.

'Yes,' said John.

They sat down on the sofa and talked about friends in common while Jilly went to the kitchen to make some coffee. When she returned with cups on a tray John intercepted a glance she directed at her friend which expressed some sort of girlish feeling he could not understand. At twenty to four he rose to leave. Jilly went with him to the door.

'Thanks for the coffee,' he said, 'and for showing me the flat. I think you're very lucky to have found it.'

'We'll have a dinner party soon,' said Jilly. 'You'll have to come. And Clare too, of course.'

They kissed again – mouth to mouth – and again her tongue came out from between her teeth like a hamster from its hole.

'I'll see you soon,' John whispered.

'Yes,' she whimpered back. 'And thanks for lunch.'

chapter eight

John looked in on his chambers later that afternoon to pick up his brief for the next day. There he found a telephone message from his socialist friend, Gordon Pratt. With his mind half on the case he had been discussing with the solicitor and half on Jilly Mascall, John called him back and arranged to meet for a drink on his way home.

The pub at Notting Hill Gate had been their local when they had shared a flat together, but like everything else it had changed. The functional furnishing of the late 1950s had been replaced by the plush décor of a Mississippi steamboat; and whereas they had both drunk beer in the old days they now ordered double scotches – Gordon's straight, John's mixed with a little soda.

'I won't keep you,' Gordon said. 'We've both got the little wife waiting at home. But I wanted to know if you're still interested in being an MP.'

'Yes I am,' said John. 'I've become quite active around here.'

'I know,' said Gordon. 'I've made inquiries. Straight on to the GMC. I'm very impressed.'

'Anyone can do it who's prepared to find the time.'

'Do you think they would propose you as a candidate?'

'We've already got one.'

'I know. I don't mean for this constituency. But we've got to get you onto the B list at Transport House. That's the first step.'

John scratched his cheek. 'It shouldn't be too difficult.'

'Do you know who I mean by Jack Vaughn?'

'Yes. A small, dark chap on the GMC.'

'He says he'll propose you and find a seconder.'

'And what happens after that?'

'If both the GMC and Transport House approve you, which they will, then you go on the B list. You're eligible for selection anywhere in the country.'

'And I trudge around to selection conferences?'

'Normally, yes, but in your case we've got something cooking.'

John listened with some sense of excitement.

'Hackney and Haringey CP,' said Gordon.

'What about it?'

'It's a fairly safe Labour seat. Or it was until now. Bill O'Grady hase been MP for donkey's years. He's retiring at the next election.'

'I see.'

'Their GMC is in a real mess about a new candidate. It's packed with immigrants up there and the Tribune lot want an immigrant as a candidate. They say it's high time we had a black MP, so they've dug up some Pakistani Trotskyite.'

'What's wrong with that?'

'Everything. First he's a Trot, but that's nothing new. What's more serious is the colour of his skin; because while we're all for racial equality in the Labour Party, and a black or brown MP would look good, our good old working-class voters don't feel the same way. So not only will they vote Tory to a man, but even the fucking immigrants up there won't vote for him because they're all Cypriots. The Pakis all live in Brent.'

'So where do I come in?' asked John.

'Transport House expect a deadlock on the GMC between those who are determined to have a coloured candidate and the others who have put up some Irish gangster crony of O'Grady's. What they want down in Smith Square is someone of a different kind altogether to come forward . . .'

'But the Tribune people won't vote for me.'

'They'll vote for you before they vote for the Irishman. He's well to the right of Enoch Powell.'

John rose and fetched two more whiskies from the bar. 'I'm flattered that you should think I'm the man to do it,' he said as he returned.

'It'll be a good thing all round,' said Gordon. 'The Party want to hold the seat, and sure as hell they'll lose it with a Pakistani candidate. They also want good men of your age in the House of Commons. I was talking to one of the Shadow Cabinet yesterday. He thinks we're in for a really rough ride in the next few years. The increase in the oil prices means that everyone will have to take a cut in their standard of living. No one's going to like that – least of all the working classes. The TUC have already ditched Phase Two of the pay policy. There's a meeting of the miners next month, and from what I hear they're likely to vote for a ban on overtime – even a strike.'

'When will Hackney and Haringey choose their candidate?'

'Not until after Christmas. But it doesn't leave you much time to make yourself known. We'll have to move as fast as we can.' Gordon drank down his scotch.

'It's good of you to do this for me,' said John.

Gordon looked at him sharply. 'I'm not just doing it for you, John, much as I love you. I'm working for you because I think you could go far; and if I go even some of the way with you, I'll get further – a bloody sight further – than I would on my own.'

chapter nine

John returned home that evening in an excellent mood – flushed by Jilly Mascall's attraction to him as a man and Gordon Pratt's faith in his future as a politician. He came up behind Clare, who was writing letters at her desk, and kissed her on the neck as a son might kiss his mother after he had won a prize at school.

'Leave the bills for now,' he said, 'and come and have a drink.'

She followed him across the room. 'You sound as if you've had one already.'

'I met Gordon on the way home,' he said.

'Give me some vodka, then. I'll try and catch up.'

'Are we going out?' he asked his wife as he handed her her drink.

'Henry suggested going to see a film if we felt like it.'

'I don't mind going to a film,' said John, 'but I can't face a restaurant afterwards.'

'Why? Did you have lunch in a restaurant?'

'Yes. With a dull solicitor I knew at Oxford.'

'I can take some quiche out of the deep-freeze and leave it in the oven.'

'That sounds fine.' John sat down on an armchair facing his wife with his glass of whisky and soda. 'Down the hatch,' he said in an affected American accent which was so unlike his normal behaviour upon returning from work that Clare looked at him curiously and asked what he had done that day.

'Nothing much.'

'You look as if you've just won some difficult criminal case.'

John glanced at Clare and noticed something different about her. 'No,' he said. 'I wasn't in court. Just lunch with this solicitor, that's all.'

'Then why are you in such a good mood?'

'Well . . .' He hesitated, grinned at Clare, and said: 'It might not put *you* in a good mood.'

'Let me see if I can guess . . . You've been made a QC?'

John frowned. 'No.'

'You had lunch with a beautiful blonde?'

John looked sharply at Clare: she was straightening her skirt. 'I had lunch with the solicitor.'

'Oh yes, of course. Well I give up.'

'It seems possible that I'll be selected as a Parliamentary candidate.'

'Ah.'

'I thought you might not be pleased.'

'I am,' she said. 'For you.'

'It needn't involve you.'

'Won't I have to open fêtes?'

'Not nowadays. Not in the Labour Party. Certainly not in Hackney and Haringey, unless you can speak Greek, Urdu and Swahili .'

Clare smiled. 'Can't they find you an English seat?'

'I'll do my impersonation of Al Jolson. That should go down a treat.' He glanced down at the evening paper which lay on the sofa beside him. There was a faint rumble and the glasses on the drinks tray clinked against one another as a train on the Central Line passed underneath them. It was a disagreeable feature of their house in Holland Park: it was also why they had been able to afford it.

'I promised Tom you'd go up and say goodnight,' said Clare.

John sighed. 'All right.' He stood up and glanced again at Clare. 'There's something different about you,' he said.

'I had my hair done,' she said.

'That's it.' He moved towards the door. 'We haven't got anything on, have we?'

'No. Why?'

'You usually have your hair done before a party.'

Clare yawned. 'I know, but it was such a mess, and we aren't going to any parties, so I thought I'd better have it done anyway.'

'It looks very nice,' he said, 'and I like that skirt and blouse.'

'Thank you,' said Clare. 'Just right, don't you think, for the wife of an MP?'

chapter ten

John telephoned Jilly from his chambers the following afternoon and suggested meeting for a drink in the Ritz. Unfortunately Jilly 'simply had to go to a stupid cocktail party' with her mother. John then asked if she would like to have lunch with him again on the following Monday, which was the first day he was free.

'I'd *love* to,' said Jilly with a warmth in her reply which melted all the resentment he felt at being unable to see her that night.

They talked a little longer on the telephone. John would have liked to ask her whether they could count upon being undisturbed by Miranda in the flat on Monday afternoon; but not only did he think the question a little abrupt and indelicate but it might well be overheard by one of the other barristers in his chambers. He confined himself, as a result, to repeating their arrangement to meet on the following Monday at Don Juan's in the King's Road and expressing the hope that she would not 'have to hurry off afterwards'.

The disconnection of the line which carried her voice did not remove Jilly Mascall from his thoughts. He not only dwelt upon her in his romantic imaginings; he also schemed as to where he would uncover and enjoy that perfect body. If they could be sure that Miranda would not return to the flat then the flat would do – despite the constriction of the single bed and the pathos of the glass animals. If, on the other hand, they could not be sure of privacy then perhaps he should reserve a room at a hotel.

Would she find that exciting or seamy? Certainly London hotels were either squalid or expensive, and John was loath to pay for a room if the flat would be free, or start her off at Claridge's or the Ritz if he could not afford to go on seeing her in the same style.

On the Thursday night, just after he had returned home, he was telephoned by his clerk and asked if he would be prepared to go to Birmingham for an important licensing application on the following Monday. Some other barrister, it seemed, had fallen ill and the clerk felt sure that he could extract an enormous fee for John's services at such short notice. 'Lucky, sir, isn't it,' said the clerk, 'that nothing's been arranged for Monday?'

'I know,' said John, 'I know, but I had thought of . . .' He hesitated, knowing that nothing to the clerk could take precedence over a well-paid professional engagement on which he would collect ten per cent of the fee.

'Can't it be changed, sir?' asked the clerk.

'I suppose so,' said John. 'All right.'

He put down the telephone and for a while was depressed that he was to miss his lunch with Jilly. The only possible good to come out of it was the chance that she might be impressed by his busy life. But in the course of the evening (they were at dinner with some friends) he suddenly remembered how he had met one of his former mistresses in a provincial hotel on a licensing engagement. If Jilly could be persuaded to come up to Birmingham for a night, they could share a hotel bedroom with a good conscience and the cost could be set off against income tax.

The next morning – before going into court – John tried to telephone Jilly at her flat. There was no reply. He tried again at lunchtime from a callbox; but only got through to the number from his chambers at half past five in the afternoon.

It was Miranda who answered the telephone.

'Is Jilly there?' he asked.

'I'm afraid not.'

'Is that Miranda?'

'Yes.'

'This is John. John Strickland.'

'I know. I recognize your voice.'

83

'Do you know when Jilly will be back?'

'She's gone away for the weekend.'

'I see.' He paused. 'Do you know where?'

'To Norfolk. Her grandparents.'

'Good. All right. I'll try to get hold of her there.' He rang off and looked in his address book for the telephone number of the Mascalls in Norfolk. He was about to call them when he thought better of it. Jilly might not have arrived; Lady Mascall if she answered the telephone would recognize his voice. He sat at his desk, chewing a pencil, wondering how he could get hold of her – if only to postpone the lunch in London. He looked at his watch: it was not yet six. There was a good chance that a first class letter would get to Norfolk by the next morning. He therefore dashed off a quick note:

'Dearest Jilly – duty summons me to Birmingham on Monday so I can't make lunch at Don Juan's. Why not play truant and come up to Birmingham? We could check in at the Palace Hotel as Mr and Mrs S. and eat caviar in bed. Leave a message with the porter to say if you can come. Do try. I miss you terribly. John.'

He posted this letter on his way home.

He spent the weekend in London and after lunch on Saturday went for a walk in Kensington Gardens with Clare, Tom and Anna. Tom had a boat with an electric motor which he wanted to try on the round pond, and while he did so John sat on a bench some yards away watching the three other members of his family. Clare stooped over their son and as the sun caught her thick brown hair he was struck by how beautiful she looked in the weak light of that late October afternoon. The curve in her tall body, and the smile on her gentle features, contrasted so markedly with the turbulent idiocy of his own emotions that for a moment John felt that he was a fool and wished that he had never met Jilly Mascall.

But the sun went behind a cloud and they returned to tea. The children quarrelled over what to watch on television; Clare looked cross because John had forgotten to take the electric iron to be repaired; and John sulked because Clare had not emptied the kitchen bin. Each saw the bin as the responsibility of the other, and disposed of it alternately, but it always became too full for the plastic bag to be closed and sealed with the little white clips provided; now as John took it out to the dustbin the bag burst and chicken bones and coffee grounds fell onto the floor.

He retreated upstairs to the drawing-room. A train passed underneath. The glasses clinked on the drinks tray and he saw that they were dirty. He looked out of the window into the darkening street: people were hurrying past on their way to some Saturday evening entertainment. Of all the ten million Londoners they had nothing to do that night. He cursed his bondage to his family. He longed to be with Jilly in Birmingham. He turned and picked up the paper to see how he could blot out the rest of the day with the three channels of television.

On Sunday morning Clare took the children to church and John stayed in the kitchen in his dressing-gown reading the Sunday papers. Every now and then he would look up at the yellow plastic telephone fixed on to the wall. He itched to ring Jilly in Norfolk to see if she had got his letter: he even practised to himself the kind of pseudo-proletarian accent which would be common in a youth of her age. But much as he longed to hear her voice, he dreaded that of Lady Mascall or of Jilly's father, Godfrey Mascall. He therefore left the telephone alone and read the papers – saving the colour magazines until he was ready to go up to the lavatory. He half cleared the kitchen table before he went upstairs (in a good mood he cleared it all), and came down dressed just as the other three returned from church.

Clare frowned to see the crumbs on the table and the unwashed dishes, but with only a sigh set to work to load the washing-up machine and start on the Sunday lunch. John, as if to excuse himself for what he had not done, decided that he would mend the electric iron. He took it to pieces with a screwdriver; could find nothing wrong inside; but found it impossible to reassemble. When lunch was ready he swept the pieces into a plastic carrier-bag and told Clare she would have to take them to an electrician.

The roast beef and Yorkshire pudding was put on the table. John opened a bottle of beer. Clare drank water. The sound of their eating was interrupted largely by the children's prattle. John and Clare, after twelve years of marriage, could think of little to discuss together beyond the practicalities of domestic life.

'Guy's coming to supper on Tuesday,' said Clare. 'Is that all right?'

'Fine,' said John, 'but don't ask anyone else because I'll be exhausted after Birmingham.'

'He won't stay late,' said Clare.

'I dare say he'll be tired too,' said John sarcastically.

Clare said nothing.

'What's he doing,' asked John, 'now that the icecream season's over?'

Clare shrugged her shoulders. 'I don't know. We can ask him.' She glanced quickly at her husband as the expression of prosecuting Counsel came on to his face. 'Shall we go to a film this afternoon . . .?' she began.

It was too late. 'It really seems extraordinary to me,' said John, 'that after all the money that has been spent on his education your brother should end up as a tramp . . .'

Clare sighed, and for a moment it seemed that she was not going to reply: but then a look of determination came into her eyes. 'You judge everything superficially,' she said.

John sat up in his chair. 'How do you mean . . . superficially?' he asked – warming up for an argument.

'You call yourself a socialist, yet you're obsessed with things like qualifications and professional status.'

'Only because they signify that a man is going somewhere.'

'Exactly. Onward and upward. A career. You don't seem to see that there might be more to life than making it to the top of your profession.'

'I certainly think that there's more to life than selling ice-cream.'

'Of course there is. And there's more to Guy's life than selling icecream.'

'What?'

'Well, he thinks a lot, and he deliberately chose a simple job to leave his mind free to think. Like Spinoza becoming a lens-polisher.'

'So Guy's a new Spinoza?' said John scathingly.

'Not necessarily, but he does think . . .'

'What about?'

'About the sort of things you take for granted. A career. Or what he would call the rat race.'

'He'll have to start running some time.'

'Perhaps. Perhaps not. But at least he'll know the point of it all.'

John filled his mouth with food – meat, potato and cabbage – and he was chewing it as he said: 'You won't persuade me to spend thousands of pounds on sending Tom to a public school and university simply so that at the end of it all he can philosophize upon the obvious. He can do that at a comprehensive . . .'

'You don't understand what I'm trying to say,' said Clare.

'Then express yourself more clearly,' said John.

'I wish you wouldn't quarrel,' said Tom, their son, in exactly the tone of voice used by Clare to say the same thing to him.

'We're not quarrelling, darling,' said Clare. 'We're arguing. That's different.' She stood up to give the children their pudding. 'You're so bloody condescending,' she said to John in a quieter tone. 'We can't all be barristers.'

'I'm sorry,' he said. 'Please go on.'

'Guy has had a good education. Not only has he got A levels and a degree but his friends are intelligent. They may be lay-abouts at the moment but they talk about Marx and D. H. Law-rence, not football and pop songs. They're pausing, that's all, and when they decide what they want to do they'll be qualified to do it, not only by their degrees but by the fact they know their own minds.

'If he hadn't been to decent schools,' she went on, 'Guy wouldn't have the qualifications and he wouldn't have the intelligent friends. He might still be selling icecream but he'd be unqualified to work at anything else and all he'd think about would be sex, beer and football.'

'I see what you're trying to say,' said John in a patient,

reasonable tone of voice, 'but all it boils down to is the old middle-class terror that their sons won't have the mark of a superior caste.'

'Abusing my position doesn't answer my argument,' said Clare sharply.

'What evidence have you that boys from comprehensive schools don't talk about Hegel and D. H. Lawrence?'

'Forget Hegel and D. H. Lawrence. There's plenty of evidence that they don't pass their exams.'

'But that isn't the school. It's the environment they come from. If you put a hundred children from cultivated, educated middle-class homes into one school and a hundred children from cramped, deprived and cretinous working-class homes into another, and gave the two schools identical teachers and facilities, of course the middle-class children would pass more exams and the stupider working-class children would pass fewer. And put them all in the same school and the same middle-class children would still pass more exams because they're genetically more intelligent and their parents are pushing them whereas the working-class parents don't give a fuck whether their children pass their A levels or not.'

'But John darling,' said Clare as the children finished their icecream and ran upstairs, 'you can't have it both ways. You can't say on the one hand that middle-class children do better anyway because they're brought up in a favourable environment and then say that they'd do just as well packed into a huge school with the children of the deprived lumpen proletariat, because the school itself is an environment where the children scoff at what they don't understand – at Hegel, Lawrence, Mozart and Gauguin.'

'You're a snob,' said John. 'That's all there is to it. You're an old-fashioned, straightforward, élitist snob.'

'There you go again. Abuse rather than refutation. I mean you could argue that social polarization has gone too far, and that the sacrifice of our children's culture and intelligence, like death duties and surtax, is a price worth paying to keep the Bolsheviks at bay . . .' She stood up and started clearing away the plates. 'I mean you are a democratic socialist, aren't you?'

John frowned. Not only her body but also her mind had

changed since they had married. 'I don't know where you get all your right-wing ideas,' he said.

Clare blushed. 'Well anyway,' she said, 'we needn't decide until next year. Tom's down for Downside anyway.'

'You put him down. I had nothing to do with it.'

'Don't worry. I'll take all the blame.'

'It won't help me get a seat.'

'You should have one by then. Anyway, all the Labour leaders send their children to public schools.'

'Do you want some coffee?' asked John, standing and moving towards the stove.

'Why not?' said Clare with a smile.

Unlike the day before it was a dark wet afternoon. John wanted to take the children to the cinema but every film on in London seemed to be for adults only. They were driven back to the Sunday papers and the television.

'Why don't we see anyone at weekends?' John asked.

'We usually go down to the cottage,' said Clare.

'We should have gone down this weekend.'

'You said you wanted to stay here. Because of Birmingham.'

He sighed. 'I know.'

'You would have been just as bored.'

He sighed again. 'Perhaps.'

'What you need is a hobby,' said Clare.

He sucked at a piece of roast beef stuck between two teeth. 'What sort of hobby?'

'Carpentry? We need some new bookshelves.'

He grunted.

'I'll get you an electric saw for Christmas.'

'You can get an attachment for the electric drill.'

'Then I'll get you one of those.'

Later they ate supper because one always eats supper: an omelette joined the still undigested beef in their stomachs. At ten they went to bed: John had to be up at six to catch a train to Birmingham.

chapter eleven

John's application before the Birmingham magistrates was heard at ten and was over by four. He failed to persuade them that a gambling casino on the premises of a new hotel in the Edgbaston district of the city would benefit the community, so he arrived at the Palace Hotel with that slight feeling of dejection which inevitably came over him when he lost a case. He went to the reception and asked if there was a message from his wife. There was none. 'I'm expecting her to join me here,' he said to the girl behind the desk, 'so I should like to change my single room to a double.'

Sullen and spotty, she sighed and started to examine all the little pieces of paper that were slotted into a chart in front of her.

'I could let you have 526,' she said reluctantly.

'I'd like the best room you have available,' said John.

She looked at him blankly. 'We don't have best rooms,' she said in a semi-comprehensible Birmingham accent. 'It's either with a bathroom or without.'

'With a bathroom, then.'

'526 has got a bathroom.'

'Good. Has it got a double bed?'

She looked at him blankly again. 'Do you want a double bed?'

'Yes. If possible. We usually sleep in a double bed.'

'526 is a twin,' she said returning to her chart. She sighed again. 'I could let you have 432.'

'Has it got a double bed?'

'Yes. And a bathroom.'

'432 sounds fine.'

She looked up into his face, and for a moment John thought she might have divined the use he had in mind for the double bed, but her expression was the same indifference. She gave him a card with the room number and a porter appeared to carry his overnight suitcase. John could easily have carried it himself, but he did not like to look as if he was trying to do the man out of a tip, so they went up in the lift together, walked along a long corridor and eventually came to room 432. The porter unlocked the door, switched on the lights and drew the curtains. John put twenty pence into his ready palm and at last was left alone.

The room was dusty and impersonal. There was a slight smell of polish and cigarette smoke. He went into the bathroom, which had been carved out of the original bedroom and so had no window. The lavatory was covered with the paper *cordon sanitaire* that Americans were said to expect in bathrooms around the world, and the tooth glass was wrapped in plastic. It all looked clean and hygienic: John washed his face and hands.

He was not concerned that no message had been waiting for him at the desk. Although he knew quite well that Jilly might not have received the letter, other explanations suggested themselves to him. If she had got the letter but could not come she would certainly rather telephone the hotel in the evening when she could be sure of speaking to him than leave an impersonal apology with the receptionist; and if she was coming as he hoped she would probably prefer to make her arrival a surprise.

He sat down on the armchair in the bedroom and took off his shoes. They were wet, and had been hurting his feet all day. He began to massage his toes and felt his sodden socks, wondering whether his shoes leaked or this was cold sweat. He put his hand into one of his shoes to see if he could feel a hole: when he drew it out again there was a dank odour on his fingers.

He took off his socks, put on a clean pair and went back to the bathroom to wash his hands again. He had no other shoes with him, so he lay down on the bed in his stockinged feet and was about to drop off to sleep when he realized that Jilly, if she wanted to surprise him, might come straight up to his room: and remembering how shocked he had been many years ago to see Gordon in his socks he heaved himself off the bed, straightened the cover, put on his damp shoes and sat down in the armchair.

He dozed. He tried to conjure up Jilly Mascall to put him in a better mood and banish the recurring temptation to rush to New Street Station and catch the next train back to London and the comfort of his own home; but the image of her pink bosom or naked legs in that dreary room seemed so impossible that it would not come to life, so he decided to revive himself instead by taking tea in the lobby of the hotel.

It was filled with businessmen and commercial travellers

already drinking gin and whisky. John, all the same, managed to obtain some tea and hot buttered toast. He sat reading an evening paper, and when he had finished both the paper and his tea he rose and went to the desk to ask once again if his wife had sent a message. There was none.

He went back to his room and watched television. There was a moment while he was in the bathroom when he heard the telephone ring: he dashed to answer it but there was no one on the line. The sound had come from the television. The hotel operator asked him what number he wanted, so he asked her to put him through to Jilly's number in London. There was no reply.

By nine, however, he had given up hope and was hungry. His letter could not have arrived in Norfolk, and he wondered why he had ever thought it would. Low in spirits he went down in the lift to the lobby. He did not dare ask for a message but he loitered around the receptionist desk to give her a chance to alert him if Jilly had called while he was on his way down. She caught his eye but neither smiled nor called him over so he went out into the street.

It had stopped raining but the pavements remained wet. He stopped outside one or two restaurants to study the menus, but even when he was in a good humour he disliked eating alone in restaurants, and now he was afraid that the waiters, and those dining at other tables, would read in his melancholy expression the farcical absurdity of his being there at all. He hated to be scorned and pitied by waiters, so rather than return to the hotel restaurant, or order some food to be brought to his room, he went into a Wimpy Bar and ate a cheeseburger with a cup of coffee.

When he got back to the hotel at ten, the receptionist had gone off duty. The porter gave John his key. John asked to be woken at six the next morning, then went up to his bedroom and once again asked the operator to call Jilly's flat in London. There was still no reply. He took off his shoes and for a while watched television in his stockinged feet. At eleven he took a hot bath and went to bed.

chapter twelve

The case the next morning in London went better than expected, which put John in a better mood. He got to his chambers at four in the afternoon and prepared to ring Jilly, apprehensive because not only might she have waited for him in vain at Don Juan's restaurant the day before but a compromising letter could be lying at her grandparents' house like an unexploded bomb.

Miranda answered the telephone.

'This is John,' he said. 'Is Jilly there?'

'Er . . . no,' said Miranda.

'When do you think she'll get back?'

'She's still in Norfolk.' She spoke in a stilted way.

'You sound funny,' said John.

'Oh, sorry.' She giggled. 'I'm eating . . .'

'Isn't Jilly coming back today?'

'I'm not sure.'

'I see. Well. I'll try again tomorrow.'

'OK. Goodbye.' She rang off.

John took the Underground home, trying to work out what could have happened. If Jilly had not got the letter, and had stayed in Norfolk, then he would have been the one left waiting at Don Juan's. If she had got the letter, then she knew she had no engagement to bring her back to London on the Monday, but then why had she not left a message for him at the Grand Hotel?

He came into the house, put down his case and went down to the kitchen, where Clare was cooking supper.

'Hello,' she said as he kissed her. 'How was Birmingham?'

'Dreadful. We lost the case.'

'Poor you . . .'

'I won today.'

'Well done. What was it?'

'Nothing interesting.' He looked into a pot on the stove. 'Have we anything on tonight?'

'Guy's coming to supper.'

'Of course. I forgot.' He crossed to the refrigerator to take out some ice. 'Can I do anything?' he asked.

'We might have some wine.'

'I'll get some out.'

He went to the cupboard under the stairs and took out two bottles of ordinary claret from a case and stood them on the dresser in the kitchen. Then he went upstairs to the drawing-room and poured himself a glass of whisky.

By the time Guy arrived, the alcohol had put John in a benign mood, and because Guy was linked in his mind with Jilly Mascall John engaged him in an amicable conversation in the hope that he could steer it towards a discussion of their mutual friend. He was cautious because he knew from the practice of his profession how much can be inferred from unusual curiosity, but Guy was anyway so taciturn that he could not or would not be drawn to discuss Jilly, so John told him instead of his own political ambitions. 'Are you left or right these days?' he asked his young brother-in-law.

'I don't know, really,' said Guy.

'If there was an election would you vote Labour or Conservative?'

Guy hesitated. 'I'm not sure I'd vote at all.'

'If you *had* to vote,' said John.

'Liberal,' said Guy, 'or Socialist Workers Party.'

'But they're a lot of cranks, aren't they?'

'That's what people said about the Labour Party, once upon a time.'

'Yes,' said John who did not want to argue. 'I dare say they did.'

'You see,' said Guy, 'although there's a lot of argument between the two main parties, I don't really see much difference between them. You might get fifty pence more on an old age pension under Labour, and the Tories might sell off the steel industry to private enterprise, but that doesn't make any difference to the fundamental injustices of the system . . .' He went on talking in a slow monotone as they sat in the kitchen eating spaghetti. John stopped listening to him. He glanced at his watch. There was something he wanted to watch on television at nine and it was now two minutes to nine. Clare was arguing with her brother. John excused himself and went upstairs. He started to watch an American gangster drama. Anna appeared at the door, almost in tears, complaining that she had a tummy ache and could not sleep. John took her to the bathroom, prodded her stomach, took her temperature, gave her some cough medicine out of the bottle top and took her back to bed.

Clare and Guy came up to the drawing-room half-way through the drama. John explained to them not only what had happened but what would happen: it was a series in which the plot always followed the same pattern, and John took pride in identifying the killer before the first commercials.

At ten they watched the news, after which Guy rose to go. It was raining and there was nothing more worth watching on television, so John offered to run him to his flat in Fulham in the Volvo.

'Do you ever see Jilly Mascall in London?' John asked in a casual tone of voice as they set off down Holland Park Avenue.

'On and off,' said Guy. 'We don't really have the same sort of friends.'

'Hers are . . . what? Young guards officers?'

'Yes. And merchant bankers.'

'As a matter of fact,' said John, 'I took her out to lunch the other day.'

'Yes, I know,' said Guy.

'Did she tell you?'

'Yes.'

John paused as he drove the car around the roundabout at Shepherd's Bush. 'When did she tell you? What did she say?'

'At the weekend.'

'Last weekend?'

'Yes.'

'Were you staying with the Mascalls?'

'Yes . . . a whole lot of us.'

'I see. What . . . there was a house party?'

'You could call it that.'

Both men were silent until they drew up at the traffic lights at Kensington.

'You, er, I mean if I were you I'd take care,' said Guy – the confused composition of his sentence the only sign of embarrassment.

John glanced at him: he was looking straight ahead. 'Why?' John asked.

There was a long silence. The light changed to green. The Volvo moved forward again.

'She showed me your letter,' said Guy. 'I mean, she showed it to all of us.'

John was silent. 'Why did she do that?' he asked eventually.

'I don't know. For a laugh, I suppose.'

'Did you tell Clare?'

'No.' A further silence. The car stopped at another set of traffic lights.

'Is she back in London?' asked John.

'Yes. We all drove back on Sunday night.'

They started again. 'Did she show the letter to her parents?' asked John.

'Oh God, no,' said Guy. 'She's not nasty, really. Just young. You know.'

They reached Guy's flat. 'I'm sorry,' said John. 'It must have been awkward for you.'

'Oh no, not really, no. I was quite impressed, really. I didn't think you had it in you.'

'Will Clare get to know?'

'It's unlikely,' said Guy. 'I mean, we're all a different generation.'

'Yes,' said John. 'I suppose you are.'

After he had dropped Guy, John drove straight to Pimlico. Only rage kept him from tears. He parked his car in Warwick Square and rang the bell of Jilly's flat.

'Hello. Who is it?' came a voice from the small, aluminium box.

'It's John. I'd like to speak to Jilly.'

There was a pause; then the voice said: 'It's me.'

'Can I come up?'

'It's rather late.'

'I'd like to talk to you.'

'Can we have lunch tomorrow?'

'I'd like to talk to you now.'

'It's not a good idea, really, because Miranda's here and . . .'

There was a muffled splutter which John took to be laughter.

'You shouldn't have shown my letter to your friends,' he said into the box.

'But I didn't . . .'

'Guy told me.'

'Oh God. How awful. The pig.'

'Why did you do it?'

'I . . . I didn't really mean to.'

'Won't you let me in?'

'No, honestly, it's too late. And Miranda's gone to bed . . .' There were more splutters: more giggles. 'Can't you ring me and we can have lunch? I'll explain, I promise. At least I'll try . . .' A kind of gargle came out of the box: it was outright laughter.

'I think not,' said John. He turned away from the row of buttons and the aluminium box, and went back down the steps into the square. He stood for a moment looking up – not at the flat but at the orange London sky. Then, suddenly, every electric light in that section of the city was simultaneously extinguished and he saw above the black trees a muted yellow moon. He stood for some time watching the moon; then he went to his car and drove home through the chaos caused by the power cut.

Part three

chapter one

It is already difficult to remember the political passions which arose in England in the winter of 1973. The Conservative government had introduced a wages policy to control inflation – it was called Phase Three – and the trades unions would not accept it. The workers in the coalmines and the power stations refused to work overtime, so the supply of electricity dwindled and the Electricity Board was obliged to cut off whole blocks of their customers in turn. The aristocratic habit of dining by candlelight spread from necessity to all social classes, and on 13 November the government declared a State of Emergency.

On the evening of the 14th the Stricklands went to dine with some friends called Barclay, and arrived at their flat in Belgravia to find it in semi-darkness. The host – a publisher – gave them a drink by the light of a candle and explained that since their oven was electric they would have to wait for the supply to be reconnected before the food they had prepared would be ready. Other guests arrived – among them the Mascalls – but the warmth of their bodies did not make up for the breakdown of the central heating which, like the oven, depended upon electricity. Tired, hungry, cold and increasingly drunk, the men began to talk about politics: and since most of those present were of the same persuasion, their conversation quickly degenerated into abuse of all socialists and trades unionists.

Like St Peter at the judgement of Christ, John kept quiet: he sat in a corner away from this political discussion talking to Mary Mascall about a trip to Venice both couples might make together in the spring. No one seemed to notice his presence. Then at ten the lights went on: Eva Barclay brought in some biscuits spread with pâté to palliate their hunger, and half an hour later they were at table eating undercooked vegetables and rare meat.

At one end of the table a stockbroker called Tim Potts, slurring his speech from drunkenness, was continuing the conversation which the others had abandoned some time before. 'What *fucking* excuse have they got . . . excuse me, Eva, but it's the only word to use . . . what fucking excuse have they got, now tell me, for holding the country to ransom to get *their* pay rise and sabotage the whole policy of the government which, damn it all, was *democratically elected . . .'*

This final phrase led to a lull in the conversation not because of what was said but because the man's body seemed to have slumped forward, and all were interested to see if his face was in his food. 'For God's sake, Timmy, sober up,' his wife said from the other end of the table.

'It's an interesting point, though, isn't it?' said Henry Mascall, addressing John, who sat opposite him on the other side of Eva Barclay, but in a voice loud enough to be heard by the whole table. 'Tell us, John. How will you deal with that one at the hustings?'

'Are you standing for Parliament?' asked the black-eyed, ambitious Eva Barclay.

'Possibly,' said John.

'But as a Tory, surely?' she said.

'No.'

'Haven't you heard?' asked Henry. 'John's weighed in as champion of the downtrodden poor. He's taken the brief of Joe Gormley and Mick McGahey . . .'

'Hardly,' said John.

There was an awkward silence.

'Go on, then. Tell us,' said Henry. 'What "fucking" excuse have they got?'

'For what?'

'For trying to bust Phase Three?'

'The excuse,' said John, 'that this particular government promised never to introduce an incomes policy . . .'

'That may be so,' said Henry. 'And that may be why the ignorant workers feel double-crossed by Mr Heath. But you're not an ignorant worker. You know that the House of Commons is not a delegate body: it is sovereign, and as such has the right to change its mind.'

'Don't talk about politics *now*,' said Mary Mascall.

'No *do*,' said Eva Barclay. 'I don't think I've ever met anyone before who actually *defends* the unions.'

'I think they have a case,' said John reluctantly.

'What is it?' asked Simon Barclay.

'That it is unjust if some members of society are allowed to sell their services to the highest bidder and others are not.'

At the other end of the table Mary and Clare started a separate conversation in which their host was obliged to join.

'The coalminers are not selling their services to the highest bidder,' said Henry. 'They're operating a cartel, which in business is forbidden by law – law we all expect the businessmen to obey. But trades unionists are somehow above the law . . .'

'You expect too much of the law,' said John.

'That's very modest, coming from a barrister.' There was a hardness in Henry's tone of voice.

'There must always be some sort of consensus that law is just, and that to break the law is wrong.'

'And isn't there a consensus?' asked Eva Barclay. 'Surely everyone is against inflation?'

'Yes,' said John doubtfully, 'but you cannot expect coalminers or power workers to accept that they should always be paid less than barristers and merchant bankers . . . They have, over the past hundred years or so, improved their relative position and I can see no reason why they should not continue to do so.'

'And when will enough be enough?' asked Henry.

John laughed. 'When a coal-face worker earns as much as you.'

Henry did not laugh: he scowled, and his face went dark and pink – almost to the colour of his velvet suit. 'There's no law to prevent a coalminer becoming a merchant banker,' he said.

'No law, no,' said John, 'but I don't see you giving him a job.'

'Because he wouldn't be able to do it.'

'There you are,' said John – turning to Eva Barclay as he would to a jury. 'He assumes that coalminers are stupider than merchant bankers, when there is no evidence whatsoever that that is true. He also assumes that the merchant banker's financial cunning should bring a greater reward than the courage and endurance of the coalminer . . .'

'I have to admit,' said their hostess, 'that I wouldn't be a coalminer for anything . . .'

'It's not surprising,' John went on in an amused tone of voice, 'that those on the top of any given hierarchy should see it as the natural order of things, but it is equally predictable that those on the bottom – be they helots, plebeians, serfs, slaves, or

British workers – should take a different view . . .'

'What confuses your equation,' said Henry in his deep, throaty, fruity voice, 'is your own position. Why do you, well on your way to the top of the pile – indeed already there to all intents and purposes – side with those at the bottom?'

John smiled. 'It's a barrister's job to plead . . .'

'Don't avoid the question.'

'Why do I plead for them and not for you?'

'Yes.'

'Because you don't need me.'

'But they do?'

John hesitated. 'Yes.'

'Were you asked by any of these working-class serfs to stand for Parliament?'

'No.'

'You put yourself forward?'

'I was put forward.'

'By friends?'

John hesitated again. 'By friends of friends.'

'Who knew that you wanted to stand?'

'Yes.'

'Because you told them?'

'Yes.'

'So in effect you put yourself forward?'

'I suppose so.'

There was a pause in the conversation at the other end of the table: Clare, Mary and Simon Barclay turned to listen to John and Henry.

'And why, I wonder?' asked Henry.

'Why not?'

'You're not doing yourself justice, John. You're hiding your finest quality – your conscience, your idealism . . .'

'I see it more as common sense.'

'Common sense? To stand for Parliament in the Labour interest? Think of the fees you will lose in return for a paltry Parliamentary salary. It can't be common sense for you to give up a large part of a lucrative practice at the Bar to answer tedious letters from old widows who have lost their pension books . . .'

'It could be enlightened self-interest.'

'How?'

'To reconcile the rich and poor before the country falls apart.'

'What . . . a revolution?'

'Perhaps. At any rate, grumbling revolt.'

'So you ride into battle on your white charger not to destroy the bourgeoisie but to save it?'

John frowned. 'That's certainly what a Marxist would say of me.'

Henry gave an affected sigh. 'You are underrating yourself again,' he said. 'It's as if you're ashamed of your idealism . . .'

'Im not ashamed of it.'

'It does exist?'

'Yes.'

'I thought so.'

'Why?'

'Because the biggest blunders are always perpetrated by those with an inner voice.'

'It's not an inner voice,' said John irritably.

A cold smile came onto Henry's face. 'Perhaps that's the wrong phrase,' he said. 'Is vanity a better word? That's what inspires you, isn't it? Neurotic vanity? You think you're cleverer than the rest of us, and to prove it you have to take a contrary view – wading into politics, waving the banner of common sense and infecting others with your idiocy.'

There was silence around the table, for although the surface sound of Henry's voice gave a jocular tone to this abuse, it was apparent from the tight control of his facial expression that he meant what he said.

'You haven't established that it is idiocy,' said John, reluctant to go on with the conversation.

'Of course it is,' said Henry. 'From the beginning of time the strong have been rich and the weak poor. The poor only get richer if the rich get richer still, because bigger crumbs fall from their table. What have you socialists ever achieved? Poverty all round. Drab, dull, universal penury imposed by a dictatorship and justified by the out-of-date ideology of a German Jew.'

There was an embarrassed rustle around the table because some suspected that Eva Barclay had Jewish blood – but if she did, she did not seem upset that Henry had laid down the racial origins of Karl Marx as if it was a trump card. She appeared more concerned as to whether this almost acrimonious argument between two friends who knew each other better than they knew her reflected well or badly on her dinner party.

'I'm not a Marxist,' said John, 'and it's a cheap trick to tar all socialists with the Marxist brush.'

'That is the irony and the tragedy,' said Henry. 'An intellectual . . .' – he pronounced the word with the greatest distaste – 'thinks himself too clever to be a Conservative and too noble to work for his own interest; and to satisfy this vanity offers his services to the Mick McGaheys of this world – open, card-carrying members of the British Communist Party – and thereby helps the tyrants to take over.'

'On the contrary . . .' John began.

'And when they do,' Henry interrupted, 'I may be the first to go – to disappear into some re-educational establishment which is, I believe, the term you socialists use now for concentration camps; but you, John, you'll be the second. You'll go just as certainly as I will, and your children will have to struggle on as best they can with a government which practises "positive discrimination" – socialist cant, I believe, for keeping clever children out of decent schools. Our children, with their bourgeois origins, will be barred from the universities as they are in Czechoslovakia: they'll be forced to take jobs as janitors and lavatory cleaners. The working class you helped to "liberate" will become the new bourgeoisie while Tom and Anna will be condemned to the new class of slaves.'

There was a silence at table. They all waited for John to reply.

'You're unduly pessimistic,' he said.

'And you're unduly insincere,' said Henry – his words now quiet and steady like the movement of a snake. 'It must be something to do with being a barrister. You can plead either way with equal conviction and you cease to question whether one side might be right and the other wrong. And if you did you would know I was right, because you're not a fool, but to work out some chippy little complex of yours you have to take the other side. That is insincere, isn't it? It's rather your speciality these days.'

Again the whole table awaited the barrister's expert repartee – but nothing came. John drew air into his lungs to answer; his eyes flashed in advance as if to warn of what he was going to say – but before he opened his mouth he caught a look in Henry's eye across the candlelit table – a gloating, knowing look – the look of a poker player with a royal flush. In the fraction of a second before he spoke John realized that Henry had something up his sleeve, that perhaps it was the letter – his letter to Jilly Mascall – so he slowly let the air out of his lungs and said, at the very end of this long sigh: 'Maybe. I don't know,' and took a gulp of his wine. Henry laughed. Clare blushed. Mary looked annoyed, Eva Barclay baffled; and then, all at once, they started up a different topic of conversation.

chapter two

The disagreeable emotions aroused by this argument between the two friends did not last for long. Even before the evening was over, when food, drink and the central heating had put him in a better mood, Henry chatted amiably to John about the holiday in Venice as if trying to make up for what he had said before. There was no mention of Jilly or the letter, and John concluded that if Henry knew he did not care. They parted that evening on the usual friendly terms.

And yet when John awoke in the middle of the night – as he so often did after a dinner party – it was the political conversation that was turning round in his mind – the charges of vanity, idiocy and insincerity; and he felt wholly sad that this friend, almost his best friend, had abused him in this way. Had England become like Spain before the outbreak of the Civil War, when a friend became an enemy because in his opinion he was thought to betray his class?

He lay for some time in this anxious, melancholy insomnia listening to the occasional roar of an accelerating car, the ticking of his clock and Clare's guttural breathing. Her presence in the bed did not comfort him as it had done before, because she too ridiculed his political aspirations – thought them silly, disingenuous and vain. Not content with enslaving his body to work for her social pretensions, she wanted also to shackle his mind to her pseudo-aristocratic values. She was on Henry's side. John was alone.

The thought of this heroic, existentialist solitude gave him some strength – enough, at any rate, to think of Jilly Mascall, whose image he had recently censored from his mind. It was now more than a month since he had been turned away from her flat in Warwick Square, and in that time he had shed the conflicting emotions she had inspired in him – not just the love and desire but also the hatred and anger. He now saw what she was – a gauche seventeen-year-old girl who had treated his advances in a predictable if not proper way. The reason he still winced when he thought of her was because she embodied the humiliation he had brought upon himself. Nothing had survived the fiasco – not even a momentary longing for her fluttering tongue – to justify his aberrant behaviour: he therefore doubted the stability of his emotions and wondered now if Henry was right – that his political convictions were as fickle as his lust: for while science, agriculture, banking or business had objective values upon which all men were agreed, politics – like art and love – depended upon the subjective judgements of different individuals, each encased in his own egoism. Henry Mascall's attack on socialism that night had not been inspired by an abstract, intellectual assessment but by his anger that his privileges were threatened, and his dinner delayed, by the striking coalminers. Were this not so, he might have admired John for his disinterested idealism – just as Jilly Mascall, had she been more confident and less naïve, might have seen him as a romantic figure like Byron rather than a prurient old man like Humbert Humbert.

John shifted his position in bed. The question he could not answer was whether his own excursion into politics was based upon sound or fallacious principles; for if history is made by impersonal forces and is unaffected by the convictions and actions of an individual, he was not only wasting his time but was confounding a natural process by acting against his own interests. But if events were more like a clay which – within the limits of the medium – individuals can mould into a shape of their creation, then he had a right to put himself forward as a sculptor of his country's future. Were there not, throughout history, a few men – mostly educated idealists from the middle classes – who went against their own material interests to pursue an ideal? He thought of the imperial ambition of Bonaparte; the belief in the destiny of a people which inspired Mazzini and Garibaldi; the convictions of Lenin and Mao Tse-tung that they must nurture and harvest history itself.

Had not all these men seemed absurd at the start? It was not hard to imagine Henry Mascall as a Venetian banker, scoffing at the ideas of Mazzini; yet it was Mazzini's idealism which, in the end, united Italy. Venice, a power which had once dominated the world with its mercantile empire, had become, after its decline, one part of a larger nation. But what was Venice now? A museum, a resort waiting for tourists like the Stricklands and the Mascalls to come and admire what remained of its past. If this was the future for England, could he then blame Henry, Mary and Clare – the Venetian oligarchs – for defying history and fighting a Quixotic battle against the decline of their civilization? Were the swank, the snobbery, the drawling accents, the public schools, the country houses, shooting parties and fox hunting – everything he hated about the English upper classes the true taste of England? What would be left if these disappeared? The Tower of London, like the Rialto Bridge, and red double-decker buses instead of gondolas? Would socialism, in its pursuit of justice and equality, destroy what was unique in a living culture just as Ataturk, in the name of progress, had obliged the Turks to wear Western jackets and trousers instead of flowing robes and the fez – thereby changing a majestic nation, once the terror of the civilized world, into a nondescript mass of swarthy tramps?

With these thoughts running through his mind John eventually fell asleep.

chapter three

At the Central Criminal Courts at the Old Bailey there is a large concourse where barristers, solicitors, journalists, probation officers and prisoners on bail mingle with one another as they go about the business of Justice. It was in this hall, late in November, that John Strickland was stopped on his way out to lunch by a young woman who asked if she could talk to him. She was elegantly dressed and spoke not just with an educated accent but with a reassuring upper-class drawl, so John agreed to listen to her and they went out into the street.

'What can I do for you?' he asked, raising the collar of his coat against the wind.

'Can we go to a pub or something?' she asked.

John looked at his watch. 'I'm due back in court at two,' he said, 'and I was hoping to have some lunch.'

'Are you meeting someone?'

'No.'

'Could we talk over lunch, then? It'd be much easier.' She suggested this with an unaffected confidence.

'All right,' said John, and they set off together towards St Paul's.

'Are you a journalist?' he asked.

She shook her head. 'No.'

'What are you?'

'I'll tell you in a minute,' she said. 'It's all part of what I want to talk about.' She dodged a pedestrian walking along the pavement in the opposite direction.

'What's your name?' asked John, 'or must I wait for that too?'

She smiled as if to apologize. 'Paula Gerrard.'

They reached the Brasserie Benoit, which was not the restaurant where John had intended to have lunch but was better suited to conversation. Once inside the girl took off her coat and John noticed that she wore a skirt and jacket cut from the same blue tweed as the coat – something rare in a girl of her age, because suits of that kind were slightly old-fashioned and very expensive.

They were shown to a table: ordered their food. John was

brought a carafe of wine and the girl a bottle of mineral water.

'It's about Terry Pike,' she said at last.

John looked into her face as if her expression might explain who it was she was talking about. She had sharp, pretty features and dark hair – the face of a girl in her early twenties.

'You don't know who I mean, do you?'

'I'm afraid not.'

'I didn't think you would.' She seemed satisfied.

'Should I?'

'Not really. You once defended him, that's all.'

'Quite likely,' said John. 'Half my clients seem to be called Terry.' He was puzzled by her manner, which was that of an older woman.

'This one, Terry Pike, was in Wandsworth Prison, where I'm a probation officer . . .'

'Are you really a probation officer?' John asked in surprise. 'You don't look like one.'

She blushed. 'I'm not actually a probation officer. I'm a voluntary social worker and it was part of my job to help Terry Pike.'

'Is that part of a course?' asked John.

She blushed again. 'It qualifies you to take the course.' She frowned. 'But I don't want to talk about my life.'

'I'm sure you're more interesting than Terry Pike,' said John.

Her eyes which had been moving nervously around the wall of the restaurant behind John's head suddenly focused on him with an angry stare. 'I'm not,' she said.

John turned down his mouth in mock apology for his gaffe. 'I'm sorry,' he said. 'Go on.'

'You probably know the sort of work we do for prisoners . . .'

'Yes.'

'I ran errands for Terry – to his mother. That sort of thing. And I tried to find him a job to come out to . . .'

'What sort of job?'

'He wanted to "do the knowledge" – that's Cockney for learning the streets of London to become a taxi driver.'

'Would he get paid to do that?'

'No, but I got him a sort of grant.'

'Are there scholarships for taxi drivers now?' John asked – the wine making him feel flippant.

'No,' said Paula, 'but I arranged something through a company.'

'You seem very efficient,' he said.

'I try my best.' She looked at him severely and pointedly.

'So do I,' said John.

She stared at him. 'Terry,' she said, 'or Pike as you would call him, was only on a six months' sentence. He came out on probation last month. He's already been rearrested for robbery, conspiracy to rob and causing grievous bodily harm to a security guard.'

John shook his head and looked down at his onion soup as the waitress placed it before him. 'Not a way to repay your care and attention,' he said, picking up his spoon.

Another frown distorted her brow. 'That's not the point,' she said, ignoring her potted shrimps. 'And anyway,' she added, 'he says he didn't do it.'

'Of course,' said John, digging through the crust of bread and melted cheese which covered his soup.

'But he has been committed and he wants you to defend him.'

'How flattering,' said John. 'Tell him to tell his solicitor . . .' He looked up into the large angry eyes of the girl facing him. 'And eat up,' he said. 'We haven't got that much time.'

She started to eat her shrimps. 'Will you do it?'

'I will if I can,' said John, 'but it has to go through the solicitor and the clerk.'

'If you agree to do it, I'm sure it can be arranged.'

'Why is this Terry Pike so keen for me to defend him?'

'He thinks you'll try harder.'

'In what way?'

'He's convinced that barristers do deals with the prosecution. Favour for favour.'

John laughed. 'I hope you explained that it doesn't work like that.'

'I told him he was optimistic.'

'And why does he think that I'd try harder and do this sort of deal for him?'

'Because he thinks it's all your fault.'

For a moment John paused: then he scooped up the last of his soup.

'Why my fault?'

'He was sent down last August for receiving stolen goods. You defended him. He didn't do it but you advised him to plead guilty. You said he'd get a suspended sentence.'

'Yes, I remember the case,' said John – his flippancy gone.

'In prison, you see, he made some friends – some older men. Real criminals. And it was because he was seen with them afterwards that they pulled him in for robbing the van.'

'And did he do it?'

'He says he didn't.'

'Obviously. I wouldn't expect him to admit it. But what do you think?'

Paula Gerrard hesitated before she spoke. 'I think, perhaps,' she said, 'that he did have something to do with robbing the van, but I know he didn't receive the stolen goods; and if he hadn't gone to prison for that he would never have got involved with serious criminals.'

John filled his glass with wine. 'No. Perhaps not.'

This concession seemed to soften Paula's manner towards him. 'It's horrible and terrifying inside a prison,' she said. 'And what's so sad is that Terry boasts about it now as if it made a man of him. He met professional killers in there – men who would kill anyone for five thousand pounds. And these other villains – this firm that's been pulled in for the wages snatch – they're dangerous people.' Her eyes widened as she spoke but she pronounced the underworld jargon with her usual genteel drawl.

'Have you met them?' asked John.

'No, but Terry's told me about them.'

'You seem to have won his confidence, at any rate.'

'To some extent, I think, but it hasn't helped.'

'Why not?'

She sighed and paused while the waitress brought their second course. 'You see,' she said (while John started his *boeuf à la mode*), 'one amateur social worker isn't really enough to pull a boy like that out of a criminal environment however hard you try.' She had an earnest, agonized expression on her face, and she forced her knuckles together as she searched for the words to express her felings. 'You see he comes, anyway, from a poor, working-class background. His father left his mother when he was a boy and he's been brought up by his mother, aunts and uncles. At least one of his uncles is "at it", as they say, and drives around in a silver-grey Mercedes. Another's "in the print", which means . . .'

'I know,' said John, his mouth half-full. 'Where?'

'At *The Times*. And a third's a porter at Smithfield. Terry worked as a mechanic for a while, but the uncle he likes and admires is the thief, and I can't say I really blame him.'

'Eat up,' said John.

She picked up her fork and put a morsel of chicken into her mouth. 'From his point of view, you see, the whole system's loaded against him. Do you remember what Romeo said to the apothecary? –

Need and oppression starveth in thy eyes,
Contempt and beggary hang upon thy back,
The world is not thy friend, nor the world's law;
The world affords no law to make thee rich;
Then be not poor, but break it . . .

Well if I was honest I'd say the same to him.'

'Do need and oppression starve in his eyes?' asked John, glancing to see how much wine was left in the decanter.

'In a way, yes,' she said. 'Don't you remember what he looks like?'

'Not really,' John began but then hesitated; because as he spoke the young mechanic's image came vividly into his mind – the thin face with skin stretched over the bone; the baffled, angry eyes. 'As a matter of fact,' he said, 'I do remember Terry Pike and he did have rather "a lean and hungry look".'

'I don't think he is undernourished in a literal sense,' said Paula, 'although the diet of people like that – chips, crisps and beer – isn't particularly healthy; but in a wider sense, a cultural sense, he is critically undernourished . . .'

'He can't quote Shakespeare?'

Paula scowled. 'It's not a question of quoting Shakespeare. It's a question of . . . I don't know . . . feeling that you don't be-

114

long to society, that you hate society . . . in fact you belong to a different society altogether.'

'The Wandsworth Old Boys' Association.'

'Exactly.' She smiled at him. 'You see before he went to prison he was straight and in spite of his uncle with the grey Mercedes he might have stayed straight – particularly if he had got some sort of job that made him a decent living. But three months in Wandsworth was enough to tip the scales the other way. It's a dreadful place. They're under such pressure – emotional pressure. The screws are the enemy: the cons are the good guys, so when they get out they project the same values onto society at large. Old Bill – that's what they call the police – is the enemy, and going straight somehow seems like an admission of defeat, or surrender.'

'I'm sure you're right,' said John, watching the *suprême de volaille* which she had hardly touched grow cold on her plate. 'But I don't see what can be done about it.'

'What can be done in general?' she asked, 'or what I can do for Terry Pike?'

'Both.'

'They're separate questions. I agree that individually there is very little we can do. When Terry came out of prison I got him this grant to do the knowledge and . . .' She stopped and blushed. 'Well, you'll laugh, but I gave a cocktail party to introduce him to some of my friends.'

John smiled. 'How did it go?'

'It was a disaster. Awful. I mean they all treated him like an animal out of a zoo and he was so shy he could hardly talk. And when he did they only understood half of what he said.'

'I can imagine it.'

'The gap is too wide to be bridged just like that. And then, well, seeing my friends through his eyes I thought: why should he want to cross from his society into ours? There's something friendly and lively about the criminal fraternity and something false and cold about the upper classes.'

'I quite agree with you,' said John. 'Would you like some pudding or some coffee?'

'Just coffee, please.' She looked down at her plate. 'I'm sorry

I haven't eaten much. I wasn't actually very hungry.'

They returned to their discussion of crime and punishment. 'So it would seem,' said John, 'that there's nothing much to be done for Terry Pike.'

'I think if you would defend him he'd feel that at least someone was trying to do something.'

'I will,' said John; and then added in a slightly pompous tone of voice: 'But I think it ought to be made clear that I do not accept the responsibility for his earlier conviction. On a charge of receiving stolen goods the prosecution do not have to prove that the goods were stolen, just that the accused must have known that they were stolen; and so far as I can remember the amount of money Terry Pike admitted paying for the goods was so small that he would probably have been convicted anyway.'

'I'm sure you're right,' she said. 'One of the saddest things about boys like Terry is that they see everything as a conspiracy. That's why he wants you to defend him. He's convinced that you could do some sort of deal.'

'I hope *you* realize that I can't.'

'Of course,' she said with a smile. 'I'm not a convert to the criminal classes.'

Coffee was brought to them. Paula took out a packet of French cigarettes and as she put one to her lips John leaned forward with a match to light it for her.

'And in a more general sense,' he asked, 'can anything be done?'

'*I* think it can.'

'How?'

'Have you read *Sybil* by Disraeli?'

'Some time ago.'

'Do you remember the "two nations"? The rich and the poor? How they should be one?'

'Yes.'

'They aren't, are they? Despite the Welfare State.'

'I'm sure Terry Pike's uncle who's a printer at *The Times* earns more money than many a law-abiding schoolteacher or civil servant.'

'It's not just a question of cash,' said Paula, leaning forward on the table and looking at John with an urgency which now that his stomach was full he noticed gave a great charm and animation to her face. 'You see we're brought up to believe that the nation is the natural unit of society – that a group of people living in the same geographical area and speaking the same language have rights and obligations towards one another which they do not have towards citizens of a different nation. In other words it was right and proper for British soldiers acting for the British government to seize different chunks of the world, sub-due the "natives" and then oblige them to sell their silks and spices in a monopolistic buyers' market . . . or even seize the natives and sell them as slaves in America.'

'I'm very impressed,' said John, 'that not only can you quote Shakespeare but you know about buyers' markets.'

'It's not so impressive,' she said. 'I read English at Cambridge and my father's a banker.'

'What sort of banker?'

'He's called Sir Christopher Gerrard.' She spoke this name of one of the richest men in England with no apparent desire either to impress or dissemble. 'If you look into how *he* makes his money you might find some moral riddles: and if you go on right back to the source of the money that made the money in the seventeenth and eighteenth centuries there is no riddle about it: piracy, slavery, opium . . . That sort of thing.'

'Times have changed,' said John, still surprised that the social worker sitting opposite him was the daughter of Sir Christopher Gerrard.

'Yet while that was considered OK because they were only stealing off foreigners, an Englishman who stole a sheep from my ancestor's estate was hanged, however hungry he may have been.'

'I see the paradox,' said John – a new note of respect in his voice. 'But surely one should try and expand the scope of morality into international relations rather than remove it from those areas of human relations where it already exists?'

She sighed. 'Yes, I suppose so. I mean for you and me that's obvious in a sort of theoretical way: but emotionally, subjectively, I'm the same as Terry Pike. I feel instinctively secure with my own kind, by which I don't mean Englishmen like Terry. I mean the rich. The upper classes. The bourgeoisie. I should think you do too.'

'I . . .'

'And in my case it's complicated by the fact that my mother is American.'

'So are you loyal to the Americans or the English?'

'What I'm trying to explain,' she said with a touch of exasperation in her voice, 'is that people's loyalties are based more on class than nationality. An Italian landowner, for example, feels more at ease and has more in common with an English landowner than with a worker in the Fiat factory in Turin. I know. I've seen them together. My father is much closer to his fellow-bankers and businessmen in Frankfurt and New York than he is to the likes of Terry Pike. His loyalty is to his capital, not his country . . .'

'You sound as if you and your father don't get on.'

Paula looked at John severely as if he had overstepped the mark. 'We get on extremely well,' she said.

'Does he agree with you about the two nations?'

'I've never discussed it with him.'

'Is he pleased you're a social worker?'

'He doesn't mind so long as I'm happy.' She relaxed and smiled. 'My mother is appalled. The idea of my mixing with murderers . . . She longs for me to be safely married to a stock-broker.'

'And you?'

'What?'

'Do you long to be married to a stockbroker?'

'I'm hardly likely to find one in Wandsworth Prison, am I?'

'No.'

'I don't want to marry a stockbroker, anyway, but I dare say it's time I got married.'

'Why?'

'I'll soon be on the shelf.'

'How old are you?'

'How old do you think?'

'Twenty-four or five.'

'I'm twenty-eight.'

'That's not too old.'

'How old were you when you got married?'

'Twenty-eight.'

'And your wife?'

'Twenty.'

'There you are. I'm on the shelf.'

'I think Clare wishes she'd waited a little.'

'Is Clare your wife?'

'Yes.'

Paula laughed. 'I'm certainly glad I didn't marry at twenty.'

'Why?'

'I'd have married someone ghastly.'

'What sort of person?'

'I don't know.' She laughed again. 'A stockbroker.'

It was ten minutes to two. John called for the bill and wondered, as it was handed to him, whether, since she had asked herself and was the daughter of Sir Christopher Gerrard, Paula would offer to pay her share. The thought did not seem to occur to her: she sat waiting as he drew out two five-pound notes.

'Can I tell Terry that you'll defend him?' she asked as they went up to the street.

'It has to go through the solicitors and the clerks,' said John. 'But tell him that I will if I can.'

'Good,' she said: and without thanking John for the lunch she parted from him and walked away towards Ludgate Circus.

chapter four

There are conversations which run on in the mind: one thinks of new arguments or wittier replies than those made at the time. John returned to his chambers to fetch the brief for the next day and finally arrived home at six – all the time rerunning the discussion he had had with Paula Gerrard.

It was her voice, not her face, which remained in his mind – a strong sound which he could now ascribe to her American blood. Her body had made no impression on him at all: he remembered only spindly legs and a paltry bosom. He recalled her eyes as they flitted nervously around him, then settled seriously upon him to emphasize the importance of what she had said –

large eyes with light brown irises and unclouded corneas.

'Do you know who I mean by Sir Christopher Gerrard?' he asked Clare as they sat together in the drawing-room before going to the theatre.

'A banker or something, isn't he?' Clare was sewing a button on to their son's shirt.

'That's right. Well I met his daughter today.'

'In court?'

'At the Bailey. She's a social worker and wants me to defend a protégé of hers.'

'What's she like?'

'Quite nice. We had lunch together.'

'I hope she paid,' said Clare – biting the thread.

'Rich girls never pay,' said John.

'Stick to poor ones, then,' she said, standing. 'Or better still, avoid them altogether.'

For a moment John wondered whether this meant that Clare had heard something about Jilly Mascall, but she went on: 'It's slightly unfair that you've made me make supper here tonight to save the expense of a restaurant and then you swan off and have lunch in a restaurant with some social worker . . .'

'I've got to have lunch somewhere,' said John.

'You could have gone to a pub.'

'I was going to . . .'

'But thought it wouldn't be good enough for whatever-her-name-was Gerrard.' She sniffed. 'Come on. We'd better go.'

'Where's the baby-sitter?'

'In the kitchen.'

They set off in the Volvo for the Royal Court, where they met Micky Neill, Arabella Morrison and the Mascalls. The play, David Storey's *Life Class,* had a naked woman on the stage which, Micky said afterwards, quite spoilt it for him. Henry complained about the 'whining working classes' but the women all professed to have enjoyed it.

'What about you, John?' asked Henry as they sat around the Stricklands' kitchen table. 'Rather up your street, wasn't it? The working-class lad educated above his station?'

'For God's sake don't start on that again,' Mary Mascall said to her husband.

Henry cowered in mock terror as John poured out the wine.
'I preferred the other one,' said John, 'about rugby players.'

'So did I,' said Micky.

'Was that the one with a lot of bare boys' bums?' asked Henry.

'Oh do shut up, darling,' said Mary. 'Can't you quieten down a bit?'

'What have I said?' Henry asked.

'Nudity,' said Clare, 'seems to have become the indispensable element in the modern play.'

'Where else?' asked Arabella.

'Didn't Diana Rigg do a strip in *Jumpers?*' asked Clare.

'It's called the Theatre of Flash,' said Henry.

'You can't expect suburban couples to come all the way into London just for a *play*,' said Micky.

'Do you think it excites them? asked Henry. 'Do you think that many a middle-aged couple will have gone home tonight to a rekindled sex life?'

'I dare say,' said John.

'I hope it did something for you, old boy,' said Henry. 'For Clare's sake, of course.'

Clare blushed and looked away.

'Really, Henry,' said Mary.

'That's the trouble with the theatre these days,' said Arabella. 'The audience expects stunts and the playwrights provide them.'

'Of course they do, darling,' said Micky. 'That *is* theatre, isn't it? Even old Shakespeare had his fair share of stunts.'

'But Chekhov didn't . . .'

As she spoke the house began to tremble as an Underground train passed underneath.

'Thank God,' said Henry. 'Saved from an inty conversation by the eleven seventeen.' 'Inty' was his abusive abbreviation of intellectual.

Clare gave a weak smile: she preferred her guests to ignore the Central Line. 'The conversation's going above Henry's head,' she said to Arabella. 'Bring it down a peg or two.'

'I'll bring it down,' said John turning to Henry. 'Tell me what you know about Sir Christopher Gerrard.'

For a moment Henry looked serious: his face changed to the expression he wore at the bank. 'Why on earth do you want to know about Sir Christopher Gerrard?'

'He had lunch with his daughter,' said Clare.

'Ouch,' said Henry. 'The formidable Paula.'

'Do you know her?'

'Quite enough, dear boy, and I advise you, if you intend to make a pass at her, to wear gloves.'

John laughed. 'I don't intend to make a pass,' he said, 'but if I did . . .' – he glanced at Clare: she was pushing the salad bowl towards Arabella – 'why the gloves?'

'Because she has poisoned points to her tits and tiny teeth . . . sharp little teeth . . . in her . . .'

'We know where,' Mary interrupted. 'No need to spell it out.'

'At least so I'm told,' said Henry quickly.

'Haven't you tried?' asked Mary. 'If I was a man I'd give it a go, just out of curiosity.'

'Have you ever seen me come home with bleeding fingers? Are my knuckles scarred?' Henry Mascall held up his hands for his wife's inspection: she pushed them away.

'I dare say *you* were wearing gloves,' she said.

'*I* can tell you about Sir Christopher,' said Micky, who as a novelist collected information about disparate and unexpected people. 'He inherited around a million pounds himself, married an American worth twice as much, and must have trebled their joint fortune in banking. Paula's their only child.'

'Worth the risk?' Henry asked with a wink, wiggling his fingers at John.

'He left his wife once, about six years ago,' Micky went on, 'with a girl called Sandra something or other. Common and sexy. I've met her. He wanted a divorce but old Lady Gerrard wouldn't give him one. She threatened to take her money out of the bank and refused to budge from Prinnet Park, which has been in the Gerrard family for three hundred years. Given this choice between his floosie and his ancestral acres, Sir Christopher came to heel, but from what I hear he's been pretty washed out since then.'

'And what about the daughter?' asked Clare

'She's said to be neurotic, but then she can afford to be, can't she?'

'Is she married?'

'No,' said Micky, 'and I've never heard her name linked with anyone else's.'

'Didn't she go out with Johnny Teddington?' asked Arabella.

'Only for a week,' said Micky.

'He's the one who told me about the teeth,' said Henry.

'She's become a do-gooder, hasn't she?' asked Mary.

'She's a social worker,' said John. 'That's how I came across her.'

'I was at school with her,' said Mary.

'Impossible,' said Micky.

'Why?' asked Mary.

'She's too young.'

'You mean I'm too old.'

'Paula can't be more than twenty-five.'

'She's twenty-eight,' said John.

'There you are,' said Mary. 'She was in her first year when I was in my last.'

'And can you remember her?' asked John.

'Clear as crystal.'

'What was she like?'

'Pure poison.'

chapter five

Mary Mascall's judgement on Paula Gerrard as a young girl did not prevent John musing over their lunch together with retrospective pleasure. It was not that he summoned into his mind any of the concupiscent fantasies in which he had appeared with Jilly Mascall: quite the contrary, he felt himself to be effectively inoculated against that kind of infatuation; but he hoped that she might somehow be brought into his circle of friends so that her intelligence and idealism could act as an antidote to the reactionary philistinism of the others.

The conversation they had had in the Brasserie Benoit encouraged him to pursue his political career, and he only wished that he had mentioned his ambitions to Paula Gerrard. He was afraid that he had appeared complacent, pedantic and flippant: if she had known that every week or so he gave up an evening to travel to north London on the Underground and sit for long hours in a pub with some dull but influential member of the Hackney and Haringey Constituency Labour Party she might have respected him more.

The days passed. Her image grew fainter. John was distracted not just by his work in the courts, his political activities, his family and social life, but also by increasing anxiety over money. He had, some months before, applied for his 'silk' – that is he had submitted a claim to the Lord Chancellor to be made a Queen's Counsel. The advantages in this lay not just in the honour which would come to him if he was accepted – particularly at such an early age – nor in the eligibility it conferred for high appointments in his profession, but also in the higher fees his clerk could then charge for his services.

It was known, however, that shortly after a barrister's abilities had been recognized in this way his income might drop for a time: a Queen's Counsel was obliged to employ another barrister as Junior to assist him, normally at two thirds of his fee. Clients were therefore likely to avoid his services if equal abilities could be found in one less esteemed: and it would be only when John Strickland QC had established himself in these higher echelons that his income would at first equal and then exceed its present level.

In normal circumstances the initials QC went well with the initials MP after a man's name because the duties of a Member of Parliament left less time anyway for the practice of law: but John's standard of living, as we have seen, was wholly dependent upon his income. If fees did not come in, how else could he feed his family and repay the loans with which he had bought his two houses? Little economies like eating at home after the theatre were neither here nor there: it seemed much more likely that if he was made a QC they would have to sell the cottage in Wiltshire.

A further distraction was the worsening atmosphere in politics. The train drivers followed the coalminers and power workers in refusing to work overtime, so the supply of what coal there was at the pitheads to the power stations was disrupted and power cuts increased. Commuter trains were cancelled, so barristers from Surrey and Kent often failed to turn up in court. They might have come to town in their cars, but petrol was still in short supply because of the oil embargo by the Arab nations. There was much talk among the Stricklands' friends of a Communist conspiracy.

Towards the end of November the papers on Terry Pike arrived at John's chambers and were passed on to him by the clerk. There seemed to be strong evidence against him. The police, 'acting upon information received', had gone to the flat in Balham which Terry had shared with another youth called Jimmy Stott. There, it was alleged, they had found two knotted stockings, a cosh and £450 in £5 notes all traceable by their serial numbers to the security van. Stott when charged was said to have said: 'Yes, well, we should have changed it up.' Pike: 'Who grassed?'

Pike's defence, as laid out in the solicitor's brief, was that the stocking, the cosh and the money were all planted by the police, and that the alleged statements were invented. John sighed as he read it: he knew from experience that however probable these counter-allegations might be they were rarely believed by juries. As the evidence stood Pike would go down for at least seven years.

He decided that he should telephone Paula Gerrard to tell her this, and was wondering whether her number was in the directory when his telephone rang and he heard her voice on the line.

'Did you get the papers?' she asked.

'Yes,' he said. 'I've just been reading them.'

'What do you think?'

'It doesn't look good.'

There was a pause. 'Has he had it then?'

It was John's turn to hesitate. 'Is Pike . . . Terry, that is . . .is he out on bail?'

'Yes. We got him bail. Why?'

'Can we talk about it?'

'Come round for a drink.'

'When?'

'Now. Whenever you're free.'

'All right. Where do you live?'

'Twenty-three Purves Mews. It's off Victoria Road.'

'I know.'

'Good. I'll see you in about half an hour.'

It was misty and wet. As John walked to Holborn Underground station the passing cars and buses threw up their spray into the orange fog, splashing his trousers beneath the knee. It became apparent that if he travelled west by Underground and walked from Gloucester Road station to Purves Mews he would arrive wet through. John did not mind this in itself, but wet hair, he knew, looks dirty: moreover he was wearing the same shoes he had worn in Birmingham – the shoes which leaked – and a heavy old suit which when it was wet smelt like a damp dog. He therefore turned and hailed a taxi. 'Damn the expense,' he thought as he sat back in the comfortable seat. 'And anyway, the cost of a taxi is neither here nor there.'

Paula Gerrard opened the door of her mews house soon after John had rung the bell: the diesel engine of his taxi still clanked on the wet cobbles as she shut out the noise and the rain. As John took off his macintosh he found himself standing in a large, open kitchen from which a spiral staircase led to the second floor. Paula, who was wearing jeans and a jersey, had gone straight from the door to the refrigerator. 'I'm just getting some ice,' she said, 'and then we can go upstairs.'

John threw his macintosh and briefcase on to a kitchen chair. 'It's wretched weather,' he said.

'I haven't been out all day.'

'Didn't you go to Wandsworth?'

'No. In fact I've given that up.' She put the ice into a bowl on a tray and then looked for some glasses in a cupboard.

'Why?'

'My father got jumpy. He thought I might get kidnapped.'

'Did the prisoners know who you were?'

'It was beginning to get around.'

She put glasses on the tray and then picked it up. 'Let's go upstairs,' she said.

'Let me carry that.'

'All right.'

She passed the tray to John, took a packet of Gauloises from

126

the kitchen table and started up the spiral staircase. John followed, his eyes unavoidably at the level of her compact backside, and once at the top found himself in the living-room. It was large – taking up most of the second storey. Three low-slung, beige-coloured sofas were placed around a fireplace in which a log fire burned in the grate. There was a Kelim carpet on the floor, some modern pictures on the wall and a disparate collection of books – some vellum-bound, some paperbacks – in the bookshelves.

Paula crossed to a table and pointed to where John should put the tray: already on the table were a dozen bottles, none with the sticky, dusty look which invariably appeared on the bottles at John's house in Holland Park.

'Help yourself,' said Paula.

'What would you like?' asked John.

'I'll have some scotch and water,' she said. 'Oh fuck, I forgot the water.'

'Shall I get some?'

'Don't worry.'

She jumped up from the sofa where she had already sat down, went out of a door towards what John assumed must be her bedroom, and reappeared a moment later with a pretty painted mug filled with water. 'It saves going downstairs again,' she said.

John poured her a whisky and water; dithered over what he wanted to drink himself; and eventually sat down opposite Paula with a glass full of gin and tonic.

'So what are you doing now?' he asked her.

'Nothing.' She frowned as if he had asked a tedious question.

'Don't you get bored?' he asked.

'No.' She scowled again, so John did not ask her any further questions about herself.

'I've looked at the papers on Terry,' he said, 'and of course I'm prepared to defend him, but I don't hold out much hope of getting him off.'

'But don't you see how unfair it is?' she said in a tone of exasperation rather than anguish. 'The police *planted* those things in the flat.'

'So Terry says.'

'He wouldn't lie to me.'

'Has he denied that he did it?'

She hesitated. 'No. As I told you before, I think he may have had something to do with the robbery, but a very small part. He certainly didn't cosh the driver. He isn't in that league.' She drank some of her whisky, then lit a cigarette.

'How do you think he became involved?' John asked.

'He met Jimmy in prison,' said Paula.

'That's Stott?'

'Yes. Jimmy was only on remand for something small, and in fact he was acquitted . . .'

'Can you remember what it was?'

'I think it was robbing a sweet shop.'

'Go on.'

'They came out at the same time and shared a flat. Jimmy knew this firm which was planning the wages snatch and they were both brought in.'

'Jimmy involved Terry?'

'Yes.'

'Has Jimmy any previous convictions?'

'I don't think so. Why?'

'I'll tell you in a minute.'

'Someone certainly tipped off the police,' said Paula, 'and it must have been someone in the gang because how else would they have known that Jimmy and Terry were involved?'

'Has anyone turned Queen's evidence?'

'No. They wouldn't dare.' Her eyes widened as she said this.

'And Terry says that the police planted the cosh, the stockings and the money – is that right?'

'Yes. And I believe him. He wouldn't be such a fool as to leave them lying around.'

'What about Jimmy?'

'I don't know. I've never met him.'

'Terry didn't give a cocktail party for you to meet *his* friends?'

She blushed. 'No.'

'Do you mind if I ask if you are . . . emotionally involved with Terry?'

She stood up to pour herself another drink. 'What do you mean by emotionally involved?'

'Are you in love with him?'

'No. Of course not. He's seven years younger than I am. But I'm emotionally involved in that I don't want to see him rot in gaol.'

'Even if he did rob the van?'

'I don't think he did . . . actually rob it.' She sat down again with her drink and curled up on the sofa.

John sighed. 'I don't doubt that the police, particularly the Flying Squad, are capable of planting evidence,' he said, 'but first of all it's unusual to do it with such small fry as these two boys . . .'

'I know.'

'And second, I don't see how they could have got hold of stolen, numbered notes to introduce as evidence unless the banks were also part of the conspiracy . . .'

'They didn't take all the money.'

'Who didn't?'

'The thieves.'

'Why not?'

'They were in such a rush that they left one of the boxes.'

'But according to the brief all the boxes were stolen.'

'Of course. The last box was nicked by the police. You don't expect them to hand back a couple of thousand quid in cash, do you?'

'I see. You mean the police stole what the thieves had left behind, but took out £450 to incriminate Jimmy and Terry?'

'And the others.'

'Expensive evidence,' said John. 'They could have planted £50 or even £10.'

'I know,' said Paula and suddenly she started to cry. 'I'm sorry,' she said, brushing the tears off her cheeks: then, in a loud, angry voice she said: 'I hate myself when I'm like this.'

John crossed over to sit next to her on the sofa but like all Englishmen he was embarrassed by this breakdown in Paula's self-control, and even though he felt inclined to comfort her he was too inhibited to touch her body. 'Cheer up,' he said.

'Well it's such a bloody mess,' said Paula. 'I worked so hard to help Terry and I *thought* he trusted me and told me the truth but now I don't know . . . I don't know what to believe, but I don't want him to go to prison.'

'There is a possible way out,' said John.

'What?' She sniffed and stopped her tears while John crossed to pour himself another glass of gin and tonic.

'As things stand at present,' he said, 'no jury will believe Terry and Jimmy rather than the police. They'll both be convicted and would be better advised to plead guilty.'

'Like the last time,' said Paula.

John blushed. 'As a general rule, after a plea, the sentences are less severe.'

'Is that the way out?' asked Paula.

'No. The way out is for Terry to persuade Jimmy to carry the can. If Jimmy pleads guilty now, or changes his plea in the course of the trial, and then appears as a witness and admits under examination by me that the cosh, the stocking and the money belonged to him, then – as a first offender – he should get a shorter sentence than Terry, and Terry would probably go free.'

Paula bit her lower lip. 'But how could we persuade Jimmy to do that?'

'It's up to Terry. He might either try to make Jimmy feel responsible for involving him in the whole fiasco; or he could bribe him with his share of the £40,000.'

'Or I could pay him off,' said Paula.

'Not, if I were you.'

'Why not?'

'You mustn't get so deeply involved with people like that.'

'Perhaps not.'

'All you must do is convince your two friends that as things stand at present they'll both go down – Terry for at least five years. Probably more. But if Jimmy takes the blame he may only get a sentence of three years, which means just over a year in prison.'

'Good,' said Paula. 'At least we know where we stand. Now let's talk about something else.' She stood and crossed the room to put on a record of Fats Waller.

'What can we talk about?' asked John. 'You won't talk about yourself.'

'Only because I'm not interesting.' She returned to her place on the sofa opposite her guest. 'Let's talk about you.'

'I'm not that interesting either.'

'Oh yes you are.' She gave a smile which because her prevalent mood was sulky had the effect of sudden sunshine on a dull day.

'How?' asked John.

'You aren't what you seem.'

'What do I seem?'

'A good-looking but otherwise ordinary lawyer.'

'Is that a compliment or an insult?'

'Neither.'

'And what is it that doesn't appear on the surface?'

'Your political principles.'

'Where did you hear about that?'

'At a dinner party. I won't tell you whose it was, but you were being discussed.'

'And what was the general view?'

'There wasn't a general view. That was what made you seem interesting. One of the people there said you were a sham – a "drawing-room lefty" were the words he used. Another was very complimentary. He said you would end up in the Cabinet and that it was good for democracy if people of your calibre went into politics.'

'And didn't anyone say I was a traitor to my class?'

Paula laughed and stood to take his empty glass. 'Oh yes,' she said 'There was a lot of that sort of talk. Why couldn't you be a Tory, or at least a *Liberal* . . .'

'And did you defend me?'

Their eyes met as she took his glass. 'Should I have done?' she asked.

John shrugged his shoulders. 'I thought we had some principles in common.'

'We do,' said Paula from where she was filling John's glass.

'Then you might have put in a word in my favour.'

'I've given up talking about politics at dinner parties,' said Paula. 'Men hate women with radical views. They feel emasculated. It's tedious. The number of men who've made passes at me just to prove their point about Free Enterprise and Nationalization.'

She came back to the sofa, handed John his glass and returned to her corner.

'It's not much easier for me,' said John. 'Unless you're a duke or a duke's son they think you're being chippy.'

Paula laughed. 'You can't win. If you're poor you're chippy: if you're rich you're a hypocrite. That's why I keep quiet. It seems to enrage people that someone as rich as I am should also be left-wing.'

'I dare say.'

'And above all I don't argue with people like that because they aren't worth it. If you did open their closed minds you'd find nothing inside.'

'Then why do you go out to dinner with them?'

She shrugged her shoulders. 'I've got to go out to dinner somewhere, and that's the circle I've been plonked in, isn't it? I tried to diversify with Terry and that hasn't got me very far.'

'There must be some middle ground between upper-class oafs and working-class crooks.'

'Yes,' she said with another unusual smile. 'You're the middle ground. I'm relying on you to introduce me to a whole lot of new, intelligent, enlightened people. That is, if you're prepared to consider me as a friend and not just a pesty social worker. You and . . . what was her name? Your wife? Clare?'

'Of course,' said John with exaggerated enthusiasm for which the gin in his blood was half to blame. 'You must come to dinner. But I'd be hard pressed to find many enlightened, intelligent people for you to meet.'

'Haven't you any Labour Party friends?'

'I've got one,' he said.

'Isn't he enlightened and intelligent?'

John hesitated. 'Yes, I suppose so, but . . .'

'But what? No, I know. He's enlightened, intelligent, alcoholic and scruffy.'

'More or less.'

'It's the hallmark of the Labour Party politician. They all have greasy hair and dandruff, and they wear nylon shirts with their grammar school Old Boys' tie.'

'I'm not quite as bad as that, am I?' asked John.

'Not quite. Not yet.' She crossed and sat next to him on the sofa. 'But we could work on it,' she said looking at the label on his tie. 'Liberty's? That won't do.'

The alcohol in his blood led John to accept her proximity – and the smell of her scent – as if it was quite ordinary. Her unnaturally youthful face with its snub nose was suddenly a foot from his and her wide, brown eyes looked into his with an expression of ironic detachment.

'Tut, tut,' she said. 'You haven't even got dandruff.'

'I can sprinkle some Readybrek over my hair before the selection conference.'

'What's Readybrek?'

'A children's cereal. Like porridge.'

The expression in her eyes hardened for a moment. 'Of course, you've got children.'

'Readybrek and Brylcreem should do the trick,' John went on. He had barely noticed the change in her manner.

'No,' she said standing and returning to the opposite sofa. 'You mustn't change your appearance. You're neither a reactionary lawyer nor a seedy politician.'

'So what am I?' He spoke with a slight slur.

'Well you might become a statesman.'

'Isn't that the same as a politician?'

'Oh no. For a politician power is an end in itself. For a statesman power is only a means to an end – the means to achieve some sort of vision. You have a vision, don't you?'

He hesitated. 'Yes.'

'Describe it.'

John wished he was not drunk. 'Of Disraeli's one nation.'

'Good,' she said. 'So do I.'

'I'm not a dreamer,' said John. 'Some inequality and injustice may be unavoidable, but in no other country in the world, except perhaps India, is there so much unnecessary and purposeless differentiation as there is in England. And, what's more . . .' – he suddenly felt eloquent – 'it's all in the mind. The more we level people through taxation the more they retreat into the kind of petty privileges whose only purpose is to insult those who haven't got them – directors' dining-rooms, executive washrooms, private schools. It's a kind of obsessive fetish which will drag the country down.'

'I agree,' said Paula quietly.

'I don't know how much can be done in Parliament,' John said.

133

'You'll do a lot, I'm sure,' she said. 'They're such a bunch of mediocrities. You'll go through them like a knife through butter.'

'Well . . .' he began modestly.

'God, I wish I was a man,' she said vehemently.

'Why?'

'Because then I'd do the same as you.'

'Can't you as a woman?'

'No.'

'Why not . . . these days?'

'I'm an anti-feminist, really. It's what I said before. Men feel threatened by bossy women and other women feel patronized. My only hope is to hitch myself to . . .' She hesitated, blushed but went on: 'To some rising star.'

'What a pity I'm married,' said John with a smile.

'What a pity. Yes.' She laughed.

John looked at his watch. 'Talking of which . . .' he began.

'Of course,' she said.

They stood. John put his glass down on a small, glass-topped table and swaying slightly made his way towards the spiral staircase. 'We ought to meet again when you've seen Terry,' he said.

'All right,' she said.

'And I'll try to dig up some intelligent, enlightened friends.' He went down the stairs, gripping the wrought-iron balustrade to keep his balance.

'You don't want to meet Terry, do you?' she asked.

'No,' he said. 'It would be . . . unethical.'

'Quite.'

'Anyway,' he said as he reached the bottom and turned to smile at her, 'it's nice having you as a go-between.'

They kissed one another on the cheek as they parted, which in their circle did not mean much more than that a certain affinity had been established. As he walked down the mews towards Victoria Road, John passed a white Ford Escort in which a youth sat in the driver's seat smoking a cigarette. He had a thin, familiar face.

chapter six

When John reached home at twenty past eight he found Clare in a bad temper. 'Where the hell have you been?' she asked

'I was held up. Why?'

'You asked that man Sanderson for a drink.'

'I'm sorry,' said John. 'I'd quite forgotten.' Sanderson was the secretary of the local residents' association.

'And Anna's ill so I had to go to and fro filling his glass with sherry and emptying her bowl of sick.'

'I'm very sorry.' John took off his coat.

'Where were you, anyway? Your clerk said you left at six.'

'I had to look in on Paula Gerrard about that case of hers.'

'She obviously gave you a stiff drink. Your breath stinks of gin.' She turned and went towards the stairs which led down to the basement.

'Is Sanderson still here?' asked John

'No. He left at eight.' She stopped and turned to her husband. 'Also,' she said, 'Henry phoned to see if we wanted to go to a film. I said we would because I've been stuck in the house all day and I thought you'd be back so I got Mrs Powell in to baby-sit, but now it's too late. Henry just phoned again and I told them to go without us.'

'We could catch them, couldn't we? What are they going to see?'

'I don't know, and anyway I've sent Mrs Powell home.'

Clare went down to the kitchen while John went up to see his daughter, who lay in bed with an expression of pious self-pity on her face. There was a smell of vomit and disinfectant but it was clear from her enjoyment of her invalid status that Anna was not seriously ill. He sat on her bed and read her a story: she told him that his breath smelt of something horrid. He then switched off the lights and kissed her good night, but she had forgotten to say her prayers so the light had to be switched on again while she knelt up in bed to say a 'Hail Mary' and an 'Our Father' and a 'please God make me better' with an air of self-conscious devotion.

In the next room Tom was sticking mug shots of football

players into an album. 'I've got the whole Arsenal team now, Dad,' he said, 'and half of Leeds United.'

The electric trains which John had bought him the Christmas before lay unused: so too did the 'Action men' which had once been the craze. Now Tom only thought of football: like some contagious disease or fanatic religion it had swept him up six months before. He would recite to his father banal details about the private lives of the Arsenal team: and while John longed to share in his son's enthusiasm he found it impossible to bring himself to care whether a leather ball was kicked into a net by a group of youths wearing red shirts or by a group of youths wearing blue. Thus father and son remained fond of one another but now went their own way – Tom to his football album and John to the evening paper.

'You'll go to bed at half past eight, won't you?' he shouted up from halfway down the stairs.

'Yes, Dad,' Tom replied in a weary voice.

'Quiet. I'm ill,' came a muffled shout from Anna.

Still feeling hazy from Paula's gin John went into his bedroom to change out of his wet shoes and put on a jersey instead of his jacket. He then went through to the drawing-room and was about to sit down with the evening paper when another muffled shout reached him from the basement, which was Clare calling him to supper. He got up and went down to the kitchen to find Clare already sipping some soup.

'It's all tinned,' she said aggressively.

'Would you like some wine?' he asked meekly.

'Not for me,' she said. 'And you look as if you've had enough.'

He sat down and started his soup.

'So it's drinks with Paula Gerrard, is it?' asked Clare. 'Where does she live?'

'In a mews off Victoria Road.'

'She would. Well, I hope it's not going to become a habit.'

'You won't let me ask her out to lunch.'

'She should ask you out to lunch.'

'It never works that way. In fact, I thought we might ask her to dinner here.'

'What? Just her?'

'No. Give a dinner party.'

'Who on earth would we ask with her?'

'Anyone. The Mascalls . . .'

'Mary hates her!'

'She hasn't seen her since she was at school.'

'I bet she hasn't changed.'

'I don't know why you're so determined to dislike her.'

'She doesn't sound my type.'

'Why not?'

'I don't like rich people.'

'The Mascalls are rich.'

'Not as rich as that.'

'It's not her fault.'

'I'm sure it's not, but it's corrupting . . .'

Restored by the soup John felt less defensive. 'I'm glad you think that money's corrupting, because we've more or less run out of it.'

'You're always saying that.'

'We're two thousand pounds overdrawn at the bank and I've yet to pay last year's tax.'

'Everyone has an overdraft.'

'They usually have assets to secure it, whereas all we have is this house, the cottage and my income. If I'm made a QC and then take time off to stand for Parliament, our income will drop quite a bit . . .'

'Huh.' Clare sniffed. 'Well what do you want me to do about it? Shall I get a job?'

'I don't see how you can, with the children. But we may have to sell the cottage.'

'Why?'

'Because anyway if I'm elected I'll have to spend weekends on constituency business, and if we sell the cottage we'll not only be relieved of the second mortgage but there should be plenty of money over to pay off the overdraft, pay off some of the mortgage on this house and buy a few things like a new car . . .'

Clare stood up, went to the sink and flung down her soup bowl with a crash. Then in total silence she put a plate in front of her husband and dolloped onto it some tinned ravioli which she had heated up in a saucepan.

'What do you think?' asked John.

'Help yourself to peas if you want some,' she said.

John stood and went to the stove. 'It will certainly be sad,' he said, 'because we've put a lot into the cottage, but I really don't see any alternative . . .'

'And where are we meant to go in the holidays?' asked Clare. 'Hackney Marsh?' She hissed her words in an ominous way.

'No,' said John. 'Of course not. But there's Busey . . .'

'You know I can't stand it there for more than a week. We're going back to exactly where we were ten years ago.'

'We can go on holidays abroad . . . rent houses in Tuscany or the Dordogne.'

'That's what you say now, but when the time comes you'll say we can't afford it. You always do.' He soft face, so lovely when she smiled or in repose, was now flat with her angry exasperation.

'And what should I say,' asked John, 'if we haven't got the money?'

'Say what you like.' She squinted at a strand of her lank hair as if wondering if she should wash it.

'If you showed any kind of financial restraint . . .'

'Oh, so it's my fault, is it? It's my extravagance? All the St Laurent dresses and weekends in St Moritz that have dragged us down . . .' Her eyes had left her hair and looked at John with real scorn. 'And of course the staff costs us a lot, doesn't it? The cook and the nanny and the housekeeper . . .'

'That's not what I mean.'

'What do you mean, then? How am I extravagant?'

'By insisting upon two houses when we can barely afford one.'

'We could afford two houses if we wanted to – if you gave up buying lunch in restaurants or belonging to a club. What does the Garrick cost you? £150 a year? And you never go there.'

'It's a small luxury which given that I earn the living . . .'

'So that entitles you to small luxuries, does it? Well why don't we swap? You stay cooped up in this little house all day with a bored, sick child and the secretary of the fucking residents' association grinding on about conservation areas, and then have *me* lurch in drunk from some young man's mews house saying how *you* have got to cut down because I want to be a QC and an MP so that everyone will think I'm wonderful . . .'

'Is that what you think? That I want everyone to think I'm wonderful?' John had turned pale.

Clare stopped herself, pondered, then said: 'Yes. That's *just* what I think. Your whole life is one big ego trip. You're addicted to your own self-importance and like a real junkie you need bigger and bigger doses to keep going. Onward and upwards is your motto. It always has been. You don't care a damn about me. You don't really care about the children. You just like us around to adorn your life – a reliable source of sex, food and affection – while you continue on your heroic progress towards the greater glory of John Strickland.'

Turning paler still, John pushed away what was left on his plate of the tinned ravioli. 'Do you really think,' he asked, 'that I come running home for the kind of sex, food and affection I get in this house?' He stood up and took an apple from a bowl on the dresser. 'Or the conversation?'

'Oh go to hell.'

He left the room and went upstairs. There was the sound of sobbing in the kitchen behind him, but it was half past nine and there was something he wanted to watch on television. Clare came up later; he did not look to see if there were marks of tears on her face. They sat staring at the animated, illuminated screen like two bored bloodhounds in front of a dying fire. At half past ten – earlier than usual – Clare took a bath and went to bed. John waited until the very end of the evening's broadcasting and when he joined her she was lying with her lamp off facing towards the wall. He made no move to give her the customary embrace and there was enough gin still in his blood to send him straight to sleep.

chapter seven

John arose neither angry nor forgiving. He neither looked at Clare nor spoke to her, but behaved as if she was a piece of moving furniture for which he must wait as it passed through the bathroom door. He read the papers over breakfast and kissed

his son when he left for school as if he was in an ordinary benevolent mood: but as soon as Tom had gone his eyes went back to
The Times and Clare's to the *Daily Mail*. Had they met they
would have seen identical expressions mirrored in the eyes of the
other – not anger and resentment but boredom and distaste.

The Times like the television distracted John until he was
seated on the Central Line travelling to court: it was only then
that he thought about his feelings and realized that the Ivan
Ilyichitis he had suffered as an insomniac in the summer was now
his permanent condition as a waking man. He knew that the first
half of his life had been largely futile; that he had reached a turning point; that his wife blocked the way to fulfilment. The creature he had married to complement his personality now con-
founded it: the women who had first demoralized his body was
now strangling his soul.

Nothing in his manner in court that morning gave away his
inner agony as he contemplated the proposition that his marriage
had failed. That very phrase made him cringe: he used to read
it with contempt in feature articles in the *Guardian*. He had
always despised those who thought of marriage as something
which succeeded or failed like a chemical experiment or an
assault on the Matterhorn; or broke down like a car or a washing
machine. The bond between husband and wife might have some
choice in its inception, but once formed it was of the same nature
as the bond with a mother or a daughter whom one might like
or dislike but could not divorce.

Yet it was patently clear that John could not become a politician if Clare remained his wife. She had no sympathy with his
principles and so was not prepared to make any sacrifices for
them; nor did she believe in his qualities as a man. There were
men and women he barely knew in the Hackney and Haringey
Labour Party who had faith in his future, yet his own wife
thought it more important that he should work to pay the mortgage on a country cottage than dedicate his energies to the
common good. He felt that morning like Prometheus chained to
the rock of his marriage, with Clare the vulture gnawing at his
liver: if only he had foreseen how his life would change he would
have married quite a different woman.

When he got to his chambers at half past four there was a

message to say that Paula Gerrard had called and had asked him to ring her. He did so at once. She said she had spoken to Terry Pike and would like to see John again. He promised to look in on his way home.

He went once again by taxi and Paula opened the door as to an old friend. She fetched ice from the refrigerator, and John carried up the tray: it already seemed part of an established ritual.

'Terry saw Jimmy this morning,' she said as they sat down on either side of the fireplace as before.

'And what did he say?'

'He said he'd think about it.'

'How did Terry put it?'

'I don't know.'

'Has any money changed hands?'

'I dare say Jimmy was offered a "drink" of some sort.'

'Not by you, I hope.'

She smiled. 'No. Not by me.' She stood to put on a record. 'They want to know if they should say anything about a deal to their solicitors.'

'No. Better not.'

She returned, but not to where she had been sitting before: instead she stood facing him, her back to the fire. John rested his head on the sofa and looked up at her tall figure dressed that evening in a black skirt and blue blouse.

'It's very kind of you to do this,' said Paula. 'I'm a little worried that I've persuaded you to behave . . . What was the word you used . . . Unethically?'

John shook his head. 'No,' he said. 'There may not be many barristers who would go quite so far, but the odds are so heavily against the Pikes and Stotts of this world that it does no harm to tilt the scales of Justice in their favour. After all, the police break the rules by inventing verbal statements and planting evidence . . .'

'I know.'

'Under our adversary system of justice the object of a court case is not to arrive at the truth but to play out a skilled and subtle game according to certain rules. The evidence is the hand you are dealt at the outset and false evidence is a kind of

141

accepted cheating that has crept into the system.'

'Most people don't realize that.'

John laughed. 'Of course they don't. They're not expected to. The suspension of disbelief is as necessary for justice as it is for politics or the theatre. If people thought Hamlet was not the Prince of Denmark but some homosexual actor living in a bed-sitting-room in Cricklewood they wouldn't go to see the play.'

'Are politicians actors too?'

'Up to a point.'

'I thought you had principles.'

'I do, but I'm not under any illusions. People only want social justice if it means they'll get more than they've got already.'

'So why do you – or for that matter why do I – work for a change in society which would leave us worse off?'

'Clare would say it was vanity.'

'Isn't she a socialist?'

'No. Quite the opposite.' He drained his glass of whisky.

'That's funny.' Paula moved forward to take his glass and re-fill it: again, as on the day before, their hands almost met on the glass. John felt her proximity, smelt her scent and without pre-meditation, as she stooped, he moved his head forward and brushed his lips against hers in a kiss. She seemed to blush beneath the hair that had fallen forward around her face and she raised her head again not in any gesture of rejection but to con-tinue the sequence of movements which made up her progres-sion from the fireplace to the table upon which stood the bottles of alcoholic drink.

'Is she a Conservative then?' she asked as if the kiss had not taken place.

'By instinct, yes, but not by conviction.'

'Will she open garden parties?'

'I hope she won't have to in Hackney and Haringey.'

'It probably won't make much difference. Socialists are meant to encourage women to have independent opinions.' She came back towards the fireplace and in passing handed John his drink.

'It's more complicated than that,' he said.

'How?' she asked, standing once again with her back to the fire and looking down at him.

'It's all to do with money,' he said, 'but it can't be of much interest to you.'

'Anything about you interests me,' said Paula, 'but I don't want to pry into your private affairs.'

'It isn't that. There isn't much to pry into. The problem is that if I become an MP my income will drop and we'll have to cut down our standard of living. Clare doesn't want to. She doesn't think it's worth it.'

'How strange,' said Paula quietly, looking down into her glass. 'One would have thought she'd be proud of you.'

She said this with such exceptional modesty that her appearance – her strong, dark features and small, thin body – seemed to soften in his eyes into a shape of irresistible gentleness and attraction. He put down his glass, stood up and took two paces towards her. With his hands holding her shoulders he asked: 'Would you be proud of me?'

She was still looking down into her glass as if a flea was floating on the surface of the whisky. Now she looked up into his eyes with a look of yearning and apprehension. 'Yes,' she said. 'I would be proud of you.'

They kissed. His arms went over her shoulders to clasp her back; hers came up politely – one hand still holding her glass – as if she was his partner in a dance. No tongue protruded from her lips: she merely pressed them to his for half a minute or so until they moved apart.

'Paula,' John said – but he did not go on because he could not think of what to say.

'It's funny, isn't it?' she said, almost in a whisper. 'We've only met twice before.'

'I would have kissed you the first time,' he said.

'So would I.' She gave a mock grimace. 'But you'd have thought me an awful flirt.'

He kissed her again. 'And what would you have thought of me?'

'Oh, nothing different.' She laughed. 'I'm sure I'm just one among many anyway.'

'Many what?'

She blushed and smiled. 'Well . . . women.'

'You're not.'

She gave a quizzical look. 'Don't say you've never kissed any-one other than your wife?'

'Not quite.'

'I thought not.'

'But I'm not . . .' He balked at the word promiscuous. 'I'm not particularly unfaithful.'

'Nor particularly faithful from what I've heard.'

'What have you heard?'

'About Jennifer Creeley.'

'What?' He frowned. 'Am I meant to have had an affair with Jennifer Creeley?'

'Haven't you? Everyone else has.'

'I haven't.'

'I'm sorry.' Now she kissed him: a short, sharp kiss.

'I don't care what people think,' said John, 'but I do care what you think and I don't want you to see me as some middle-aged Casanova . . .'

She stopped his mouth with another kiss. 'I don't,' she said. 'And *I* don't care what people think except perhaps . . .' She hesitated.

'Who?'

'Well, your wife.'

'She won't know,' he said quickly. 'Anyway,' he added, 'our marriage is pretty unsatisfactory.'

A faraway look came into her eyes. 'Don't ever let me come between you and Clare,' she said. 'I don't want to break up your marriage.'

'No,' said John. 'You can't break up what's smashed already.'

They sat down together side by side on the sofa, hand in hand, and started to talk with that ease and urgency which follows the discovery of a sudden affinity. There were moments when John felt physically uncomfortable and would have moved to adjust his position had he not been afraid that Paula might mistake the movement as a gesture of rejection. Only when he could wait no longer did he rise to go to her bathroom.

As he stood at the lavatory he noticed with approval the cleanliness of the bath and the exotic oils and unctions ranged along the painted tiles which surrounded it. The room con-trasted so markedly with the bathroom in his own home, where several grimy lines always circled the tub, and old tubes of squeezed-out toothpaste lay stuck to the shelf by dried-up pools of spilt cough mixture. On his way back down the passage he passed Paula's bedroom, and saw that her large bed was unmade: but instead of a tangled mess of sheets and blankets there was the neat imprint of her body up against the very edge of the mattress. It left no doubt but that she slept alone.

'Are you going out tonight?' he asked as he returned to the living-room.

She hesitated. 'Not really.'

'Shall we have supper somewhere?'

'Don't you have to go home?'

'I'll ring Clare and tell her I have to go to Hackney.'

'Don't feel you have to,' said Paula.

'I don't,' said John. He went to the telephone and dialled the number of his home. It was answered by Tom.

'Can I speak to Mummy?' John asked.

'She's upstairs washing Anna's hair.'

'Is she better then?'

'Yes. She's going to school tomorrow.'

'Well tell Mummy that I won't be home for supper.'

'All right.'

'Tell her I had to go to Hackney.'

'All right.'

'Tell her not to wait up.'

'OK, Dad, I'll tell her.'

John rang off and for a moment felt a twinge of remorse because it was usually he who washed his daughter's hair, but he took hold of his emotions and turned to Paula with a smile. 'Where would you like to go?' he asked.

She chose a Russian restaurant in Soho and they drove there in her car – a Lancia. They ate caviar and blinis and drank vodka; then wine with shashliks, rice and salad. This was followed by blackcurrant sorbet and coffee, and the bill when it arrived was grotesque, but John barely noticed the sum as he scribbled out a cheque: he was intoxicated not so much by the vodka and wine as by Paula Gerrard's beauty and charm. Indeed he drank less than he might have done for fear that he become too befuddled to hear what she said or, when they returned to Purves Mews, to enjoy what she would offer. There was no doubt in his mind but that she would offer him the other unused side of her unmade bed: she was not, after all, an over-grown schoolgirl like Jilly Mascall. Everything they talked about at table seemed tacitly to assume that later they should become lovers.

They returned to Kensington in her Lancia and when they reached the top of Gloucester Road she asked: 'Should I drive you home or what?'

'No,' said John. 'Let's go back to your house.'

'All right,' she said and she turned into Victoria Road.

He followed her into the house and up the spiral staircase. The fire had died down and Paula crossed to put another log and stir the ashes with a poker. This view of her stooping body incited John's senses and when she turned back into the room, brushing some soot from her fingers, he was waiting there to embrace her. He grasped her body and kissed her lips with some fervour and once again her arms came up in a reciprocal gesture. Entwined like this they moved towards the sofa and collapsed together on the cushions. John removed one hand from her shoulder and with it touched her leg just above the knee and beneath the skirt. She lurched away: they broke apart.

'I can't,' she said.

'Why not?'

She sat with her knees together chewing the knuckle of her thumb. John moved to sit beside her: his arm went over her shoulder but she did not move to face him.

'You do . . . care for me, don't you?' he asked.

'Yes I do. It's not that.'

He sat baffled, imagining a string of gynaecological complications which Paula might not like to explain.

'There are things you don't know,' she said, almost choking as she spoke.

'Can't you tell me?'

'No. Not now.'

'I love you very much,' said John, 'so the . . . sexual side of things isn't everything, but you ought to tell me if for some reason we can never sleep together.'

She turned and looked at him: there were tears in her eyes. 'I hope we will,' she said. 'If I didn't think that we would . . . that we'd be together . . .' She did not finish this sentence. 'Only please, don't ask me why. Not now.'

He smiled at her and kissed her cheek as he might have kissed Anna's. 'When can we see each other again?'

'Whenever you like.'

'Let's have lunch on Friday. I've a case that should finish in the morning so after lunch we could go for a walk in the park.'

'Good,' she said. 'I'd love that. We'll meet at the Brasserie Benoit, shall we? I liked it there.'

Out in the mews it was silent. John walked over the cobbles feeling sober, sad and relieved. It was past midnight when he got home and Clare had gone to bed but she stirred when he got in beside her and drowsily hugged him when he gave her the customary embrace.

chapter eight

Terry Pike, Jimmy Stott and the three men said to have robbed the security van of £40,000 came up for trial at the Old Bailey early in December. By this time John had met Paula two or three times more – for lunch, or for a drink on his way home – and when not confessing their still unconsummated love for one another, they discussed the case against Terry Pike.

Jimmy Stott was unwilling, at first, to sacrifice himself for his friends. Even though his own counsel concurred with John – that he was sure to be convicted on the evidence and should therefore plead guilty – he retained the irrational optimism of many a thief who, having seen his friends acquitted on legal technicalities he does not understand, hopes that some such arbitrary advantage may turn up for himself.

On the eighth day of the trial, however, after the two detectives in charge of the case had given their evidence, this pudgy, cunning-looking youth suddenly changed his plea to guilty and was removed from the dock. Either he had sensed that things were not going his way, or he had received an offer of more money from Terry Pike: the precise reasons for his change of heart were not given, but John was told that Stott was prepared to appear as a witness in his friend's defence. In due course, on the tenth day of the trial, Jimmy went into the witness box. John, conscious that Paula was watching him from the public gallery, rose in his wig and gown.

'Mr Stott,' he said. 'I am defending Mr Pike.'

'Yer . . . I know.'

'Mr Pike is a friend of yours, is he not?'

'Yer.'

'Of long standing?'

'Nah. We met . . .'

'I don't want to know where you met, Mr Stott, just how long you have know each other.'

'Six months. Yer, around six months.'

'Do you know any of the other defendants in this case?'

'Nah. Never met 'em before.'

'None of them?'

'Nah.'

'Now Detective Inspector Green has given evidence that when he came to your flat that Saturday morning he found one cosh, two knotted nylon stockings and a bundle of five pound notes with the same serial numbers as some stolen from the van. Can you tell us to whom these belonged?'

'Yer. They was mine.'

'The cosh?'

'Yer.'

'The stockings?'

'Yer.'

'Both stockings?'

'Yer.'

'And all the five pound notes?'

'Yer.'

'They were your property, or rather you were the one who brought them into the flat?'

'Yer.'

'Had Terry Pike ever seen them?'

'Nah. They was locked away, wasn't they?'

'Did he know anything about them?'

'Nah.'

'Did Terry Pike have anything to do with this robbery?'

'Nothink at all.'

'Did he know before the robbery that you intended to rob the van?'

'Nah.'

'Did he know after the robbery that you had robbed the van?'

'Nah. I tell you, he didn't know nothink abaht it.'

'Thank you, Mr Stott,' said John. 'I have no further questions.'

John sat down and the prosecuting counsel got to his feet. His expression was bland and imperturbable as a barrister's should be, yet John tried to read in the subtle nuances of this blandness and imperturbability whether his colleague was glad to have the opportunity to cross-examine a witness who had pleaded guilty to the crime, or was irritated to see that one of the accused might now slip between his fingers.

'Mr Stott,' he began. 'I am delighted, as I am sure His Lordship is, that you have seen fit, even at this late hour, to save the time of the court by admitting your guilt. Perhaps you will be good enough to save even more of its time by telling us who, if not your fellow defendants, did help you rob the van?'

'I dunno who they was. I never met 'em before.'

'You went to rob a van with people you had never met before?'

'I was only the driver. I met this geezer in a pub and he said he needed a driver . . .'

'Which pub was that?'

'I can't remember.'

'Would you now help the police identify this man?'

'I wouldn't remember who he was, honest I wouldn't.'

'I dare say. Yet you are quite sure – despite the other evidence against them, that it was none of the other accused?'

'The geezer in the pub wasn't any of them lot. On the blag, I don't know. They was all sitting behind me and wearing masks . . .'

'Because you were the driver?'

'That's right. I didn't do any of the 'eavy business.'

'That wasn't your style?'

'No.'

'Yet you told my learned colleague a moment ago that the cosh found in your flat belonged to you?'

'Yer, well, of course I 'ad to 'ave one, didn't I, just in case . . .'

'In case of what?'

'In case things got really 'eavy.'

'I see. If things had, as it were, got out of control you might have had to use your cosh?'

'Nah. Not really. I'm not like that.'

'Yet it was your cosh?'

'Yer.'

'And the money came from the security van?'

'Yer, but I only got a monkey . . .'

'Five hundred pounds?'

'Yer. I wasn't on a full whack.'

'And Terry Pike. Was he on a full whack?'

Jimmy Stott grinned. 'He wasn't on it at all, was he?'

'So you say,' said the prosecuting counsel, his voice rising a tone or two. 'Yet Detective Inspector Green has given evidence that he found *two* knotted stockings in your flat.'

'They come in pairs, don't they?'

'One for you and one for Pike?'

'The other was a spare.'

'You have a spare mask?'

'Yer, o'course.'

'But not a spare cosh?'

'Nah.'

'Could you tell us why you have a spare mask but not a spare cosh?'

'Well, what you meant to do with the other stocking? I ain't got a one-legged girlfriend.'

There was some laughter in the court and the prosecuting counsel, with no more questions to ask, sat down. The case was then adjourned for the day.

The trial itself lasted for another week. In his final submission John argued that since Stott had admitted that the incriminating articles found in the flat belonged to him there was no evidence against Terry Pike. The judge, in his summing-up – like the prosecuting counsel before him – made it clear to the jury that in his opinion Stott was a worthless witness, and that his evidence should be taken with a pinch of salt; yet when the jury returned their verdict three days before Christmas all the defendants were found guilty except for Terry Pike, who was acquitted on all counts.

As this verdict was announced in court, John looked for Paula in the public gallery. He found her face and she smiled at him; then her wide, excited eyes looked over his head to the dock. John turned in time to see his client give a cursory nod in Paula's direction then slowly lower his head to look straight at John with an expression of triumph and sneering contempt.

Part four

chapter one

Every year at Christmas the Stricklands went either to Clare's parents at Busey or to John's mother outside York. They then moved on to celebrate the New Year in whichever household had not had them at Christmas. This was done in strict rotation and in 1973 it was 'Granny Strickland's turn to receive them first. On 23 December they all piled into the old Volvo and set off up the M1.

Her simple, rectangular house in the village of Stainton had once belonged to the doctor: it was more than a cottage or farmhouse but less than a manor, for in Yorkshire even bricks and mortar know their place, and The Garth (as John's mother had named her house) stood firmly in third place after the Hall and the Rectory. It was still too large for a widow, but when alone Alice Strickland used only three of the ten or eleven rooms – the kitchen, a small sitting-room and her bedroom – which she heated with electric fires. The rest of the house – the drawing-room, dining-room and the spare bedrooms – was kept neat and clean for when she entertained or when her children and grandchildren came to stay: then the shutters would be opened, her china ornaments dusted and the central heating switched on.

This arrangement suited her well: for as she grew older and away from the influence of her dead husband Alice returned to the pattern of her childhood home in Halifax where the front parlour had been preserved in just this way as a sacrosanct tableau of gentility. Indeed life as the wife of a County Court Judge had carried her beyond the point where she felt at ease; yet she could not sell The Garth and move to the kind of semi-detached suburban house in which she had been brought up because that would be to lose all that she had worked for; and she continued to dine with her county neighbours not from any real pleasure in their company but to remind herself every now and then just how far she had succeeded in her social ambitions.

When it came to returning their hospitality she preferred to wait until either her son or daughter came to stay. Clare, because of her background, she thought particularly suitable to help entertain the most recalcitrant dullards of the locality; and soon after they had arrived that Christmas – exhausted after their long drive – Alice began to outline the programme she had prepared for them. 'The Taylors are coming to dinner tonight, darling, and the Frampton-Dussets. Now I *know* you say you don't like the Taylors but he *is* a JP and always likes to talk to you about the law: and the Frampton-Dussets have a boy at Stoneyhurst which is where your brother went, isn't it, Clare? They're longing to talk to you about *that*. And tomorrow evening I've asked one or two people in for a drink – don't sigh like that, John darling – in fact I want you to make some of that mulled claret of yours, except you'll have to use some Italian wine because the French is too expensive these days, unless of course there's a power cut in which case they'll have to drink sherry. Sarah and Graham are coming tomorrow so they'll be able to help, but you're the ones I rely on. You're so good with my old friends.'

John escaped to fetch the luggage from the car and carry it upstairs. Clare followed and they settled in to one of the spare bedrooms, which because the central heating had only been switched on that afternoon remained a little damp. Clare smiled at her husband as they unpacked their suitcases. 'Business as usual,' she said.

'I can't wait to talk to old Gervase Taylor about the law for the tenth time,' said John.

'Nor I to discuss the Jesuits at Stoneyhurst for the third year running.'

Clare left the room to see to the children's clothes while John searched around for somewhere to put down his brush and comb. As always every surface was occupied by some knick-knack from his mother's collection of china statuettes. In the end, as Clare returned, he pushed aside a Little Bo Peep and seven sheep.

'There are more of these bloody gnomes,' he said to her. 'They breed like rabbits.'

'You should see the bathroom. It's like a china shop.'

Of the many things at Stainton which irritated John, this collection of china statuettes irritated him the most, not just because they occupied the top of every table and chest of drawers in the spare bedroom but because they embodied the bad taste which seemed to him to betray his mother's social origins; for while good breeding, as Clare would call it, did not guarantee good taste there often went with it a certain unconscious culture which told a man whether a china figurine of Little Bo Peep was a delicate masterpiece or a piece of worthless rubbish. At Busey, for example, everything might be shabby but the atmosphere in the house was of faded elegance; whereas everything at The Garth, from the name Alice had given to the house to the tasselled covers on the lavatory seats, was neat, tidy and vulgar.

Clare was amused by this genteel vulgarity; John was more often ashamed. It had been part of his mother's character for so long that he and his sister Sarah had at times teased her about it, but they had never managed to alter their mother's taste. While the Judge had been living his austere aesthetic sense had kept her kitsch at bay: the china ornaments were rationed in the drawing-room and forbidden in his study altogether – even the statuette of a dragoon guard she had once bought him for his birthday. He had placed it on the sill of the downstairs lavatory. But soon after he had died Alice had started to collect 'in earnest' pronouncing it her hobby – and there was rarely a visit to York, the West Country or the Lake District from which she did not return with one or two cardboard boxes containing delicate, expensive statuettes in the worst possible taste.

John's shame had many layers. He felt humiliated first and foremost because his mother's bad taste betrayed not only her origins but also her pretensions, for she believed that her collection, although not quite equal to the treasures of Castle Howard, was a step in that direction: and nothing gave her more pleasure than to show off her ornaments to those who affected to admire them. But John was also ashamed of his own embarrassment; for while there were many aspects of his mother's character for which he might hold her to account, how could he blame her for having no taste? If taste could be taught, it was too late to teach her; and if he did not believe in an aesthetic faculty comparable to conscience on the moral plane, how could he castigate her for the sin of bad taste? Nor was it, he knew, the ugliness of the objects which offended him; nor the money she spent on them, which he knew she could ill afford: it was the social connotations which he minded most – as if she had spoken with a regional accent or had smelt of sweat because she never took a bath. His objections to her china ornaments were snobbish objections and he knew it.

Happily the Mascalls never came to Yorkshire and the local landowners who had taken up the Judge and his wife either had no taste themselves or had long since come to accept Alice Strickland for what she was. The only other person to be irritated by the china ornaments was John's sister Sarah, and her objections were rooted not in social prejudice but in the strict functionalist principles of the Bauhaus, which she had espoused with her husband Graham and had held ever since with the fervour and fanaticism of one converted to a new religion.

Like John she had inherited radical instincts from their father, but in spite of this Sarah irritated her brother as much as Alice did; and she got off to a bad start that Christmas by arriving the next day with her husband and three children in a brand-new Citroën station-wagon. John's annoyance at beholding this shining vehicle was not a matter of simple envy, nor chagrin that the headmaster of a comprehensive school in Liverpool should be able to afford a new car when he, a successful London barrister, could not. He knew, for example, that his sister earned a considerable amount of money teaching at home those pupils who could not go to school – pregnant or criminal twelve-year-olds – while her youngest child went for nothing to a nursery school. He also knew that Graham and Sarah rarely went to a restaurant and never entertained; that they had only a small mortgage on their house; that they took out no life insurance, had no intentions of ever paying school fees, and had their contributions towards a pension paid for by the state. What irritated John was not just that they were so expert at exploiting the free facilities provided by the municipal and central governments, nor that they could afford a new car, but that despite their relative prosperity they still exuded an air of poverty and deprivation so that Alice, for example, would always repay her daughter for the cost of the petrol they had used to drive from Liverpool to York.

It was also that he could clearly remember the time when Sarah had despised all those who bought imported station-wagons. Ideologically she had always cut her coat according to her cloth: when they first married and lived in a rented flat she and Graham poured scorn on the little bourgeois who struggled to buy a house on a mortgage. Then, when they had paid a deposit on a house with money given to them by Alice, yet still travelled by bus, they despised only the private motorists who cluttered up the streets and polluted the atmosphere. A year later they had bought a Mini, and it was then that the purchasers of foreign cars came in for abuse: this was just after John and Clare had first bought the Volvo.

Sarah looked like John. She was tall and lanky with thick black hair but her face was plumper and she had a fierce look in her eye. Her husband, Graham, was an inch or two shorter than she was and since 1968 had worn a droopy moustache. They both invariably dressed in denim – indeed Graham boasted that he no longer owned a suit or a tie. As a concession to his mother-in-law he put on a blue silk polo-necked sweatshirt for her drinks party, and a denim jacket which matched his denim trousers; but he was not amused when Clare referred to this as his dress suit – he frowned as if one of his pupils had gone a little too far.

He spoke in the nasal sing-song accent of the city where he taught, and this together with his appearance and his opinions confirmed the worst fears of Alice Strickland's neighbours who came to her party about the corruption of youth in the state schools. At heart, however, Graham was not unconventional: he had been educated at the same grammar school in Newark as Sir Isaac Newton, had attended University College, London, and was as instinctively conservative as his father, who was a chemist; but he was also ambitious and he had realized early on that a man who was superficially modern but fundamentally old-fashioned would go far. He saw the denim and the Liverpool accent as advanced professional qualifications and with matching attitudes in education (anti-streaming, and so on) he had indeed gone far to be headmaster of a comprehensive school under the age of forty.

On Christmas Eve, once the guests had gone, they cleared up the glasses, put the younger children to bed, ate supper, put the older children to bed and then watched television until half past ten, when there was a power cut. Alice lit the candles which she had placed ready at strategic points around the house, and then left with Clare to go to midnight mass in York. She was, of course, an Anglican and would go again next morning to the service at Stainton Church: but she liked the midnight ceremony and thought it only polite that her daughter-in-law should have company. John, Graham and Sarah sat drinking, still facing the television in the little sitting-room.

'Does Clare go to mass every Sunday?' Graham asked John – dropping for a while the Liverpool accent.

'Yes,' said John.

'And does she take the children?'

'Yes.'

'Don't you object to them being brainwashed to believe in all that superstitious nonsense?'

'Not particularly.'

'Does Clare really believe it?' asked Sarah.

'Yes. I think so.'

'It's funny, isn't it?' she said. 'She seems quite intelligent otherwise.'

'It's in her family,' said John.

'She doesn't have to believe it because of that, does she?' asked Graham.

'No, of course not.' John rose to refill his glass with port even though a miasma of festive indigestion had already settled upon his stomach.

'So does she believe in it?'

'She must do. I've never really talked to her about it.'

'Does she try and convert you?' asked Sarah.

'No.'

'And do you try and convert her?' asked Graham.

'To what?'

'To whatever you believe in.'

'We argue about politics.'

'I would have thought you'd agree on that,' said Sarah.

'Why?'

'Aren't you both Tories?'

'I'm not.'

'What are you, then?'

'Labour. I've always been Labour.'

Graham guffawed. 'Come off it,' he said.

'In fact I might well be standing for Parliament.'

'For Labour?' asked Sarah incredulously.

'Of course.'

'How extraordinary.'

They sat in silence for a moment.

'Where for?' asked Sarah.

'Hackney and Haringey.'

'Have you been selected?' asked Graham.

'Not yet. The selection conference isn't until the end of January.'

'But are you a socialist?' asked Sarah.

'As much as you are.'

'You don't *live* like a socialist.'

'How does a socialist live?'

'He doesn't have two houses for a start.'

'Half the Shadow Cabinet have two houses.'

'They aren't socialists.'

'Well I'm as socialist as they are. Will that do?'

There was a further silence caused by irritation on both sides.

'Anyway,' said Graham, still evidently baffled by the news that his brother-in-law had just imparted, 'Parliament's a waste of time.'

'Perhaps,' said John. 'What isn't a waste of time?'

'No, well, it may be of some use,' said Graham. 'I mean you've got to have laws, haven't you? But they're pretty blunt instruments, really . . .'

'So what do you do? Leave things as they are?'

'No, but you've got to go deeper.'

'How?'

'Into the minds of people. Catch them when they're young. By the time they've grown up their minds are closed. It's all prejudice.'

'You may be right,' said John sarcastically, 'but some people change their minds, don't they? That's why we have different governments from time to time.'

'But they aren't really different, are they? I mean so far as I can see the front benches of the two parties are more or less identical. The only way to change society is to change people and the only way to change people is in the schools.'

'By brainwashing them?'

'Call it what you like,' said Graham. 'I certainly see it as part of my job to try and overcome the prejudices my kids bring from their home environments and open their minds to more liberated attitudes of which socialism would be one.'

John yawned. 'Good. Perhaps they'll vote for me in 1990.'

'If they voted for you I'd feel I'd failed,' said Graham earnestly: then he laughed as if to pass off what he had just said as a joke.

John was about to reply when the power was suddenly restored. They blew out the candles and returned to the television.

Graham and Sarah went to bed at half·past twelve; John waited up for Alice and Clare. He fell asleep in his armchair but was awoken at one by the sound of the front door opening and a quick, cold draught which blew into the small sitting-room. He stood and staggered out into the hall. Clare, still in her coat, looked at him with a beaming face.

'You should have come,' she said. 'It was lovely.'

John yawned again.

'What have you been doing?'

'Watching television. Arguing about politics . . .'

'Not on Christmas Eve . . .'

He shrugged his shoulders. 'I'm going up.'

'I'll be up in a minute. Your mother's just making a hot drink.'

John climbed the stairs and went to his children's room. They lay asleep – Tom on his back, his face in repose like that of the stone effigy on a crusader's tomb. Anna had kicked off her sheets and blankets and lay twisted like a gargoyle – her mouth open, her limbs abandoned. He covered her, and then took the large woollen socks from the end of both their beds. In his own room he started to pack Tom's stocking – putting a tangerine in the toe; a book, chocolates and nuts in the foot and a bright red apple in the heel. Clare came in behind him and filled Anna's stocking: then together they returned to the children's room and on tiptoe placed the bulging socks back on their beds.

They whispered good night to Alice; took a quick bath to warm themselves up and then shut the door to their room. In the dark John gave an account of his dispute with Graham. Clare giggled. '*He's* your socialist man,' she whispered as they kissed one another good night; but after she had said it her cool lips lingered, and in spite of the late hour they made love under the blankets. Then Clare sighed and went to sleep, while John lay savouring the image of Paula Gerrard until he too fell asleep.

chapter two

They awoke on Christmas morning to find that a ground frost had settled during the night leaving a white edge on everything they could see from their bedroom window. The children squealed as they played with the toys from their stockings, and the smell of coffee and bacon wafted up from the kitchen. John and Clare went down in their dressing-gowns and slippers.

After breakfast Alice and Clare took all the children to the morning service at the village church. Graham and Sarah went back to bed. John, once shaved and dressed, decided to go for a walk. He put on his overcoat, picked up a blackthorn stick that had belonged to his father, and set off down the village on his own.

There were two walks he had taken as a child – 'up and round' and 'down and round'. The lower walk was shorter and gave a view of Stainton Hall, but such was the glory of the day that he decided to take the longer walk 'up and round', and so walked to the end of the village and set off over the fields.

The heavy frost had lined everything with minute crystals of frozen moisture – the spiders' webs among the bushes, the sheep-wire in the fencing, the stem and leaf of every plant. The brittle grass on which he walked reflected the sun like a carpet embroidered with white and silver thread, and John felt sad to spoil this artistry of nature with his footprints. He climbed a gate into a second field which had been ploughed, but so hard was the frozen ground that John could walk over the furrows as if they were tight-packed logs. The third field was grass again and led to the top of the hill where the land fell away to give him a clear view north.

At this point he stopped, for the vale spread out before him was covered by a thick but shallow mist. Only the patches of higher ground in this undulating countryside were visible above it like islands in an ethereal sea. To the east a line of upright, regimented poles carried electric cables towards misty oblivion; and here and there a giant tree stood out from the whiteness. In the distance, nine or ten miles away, the escarpment of the Howardian Hills rose suddenly like the far bank of Lethe, the river of forgetfulness.

John stood motionless in the cold, affected by the beauty of what he saw. The real and visual silence brought calm to his confused emotions – and for a moment he longed for permanent peace like that of the landscape before him. He realized that since the summer – since that afternoon when he had read Tolstoy's story – he had been split in two, one half of him leading his old life as barrister and married man, the other setting off in a different direction towards another woman and a new career. In London conflict was so common that he had barely remarked upon this inner contradiction: it had seemed that friction was necessary to life itself. But this misty view seemed to promise that a man could be at peace within himself. Why then could he not attain that same serenity? He had attractive, affectionate children; good health; interesting work; an adequate income; amusing friends. He had been through it all before and could find no grounds for an action against fate. Clare might not sympathize with his political aspirations but she was an agreeable companion in life, and even her anti-socialist scepticism would not prove to be, as he had once thought, an insuperable obstacle to his future; for like her mother Clare had great reserves of dutiful self-sacrifice. Nor was John himself without doubts. His conversation with Graham and Sarah the night before had made him most pessimistic about his ideals; for his sister and her husband seemed to exemplify a new bourgeoisie which had expropriated and exploited the Welfare State. Instead of scrambling to save money to send their children to private schools they schemed to get them into some chosen comprehensive which, because word had gone around among like-minded members of the state-employed élite, was then packed with the progeny of up-and-coming couples while the children of the working classes were relegated as before to the second-class schools.

He saw quite clearly too how, having captured the best

schools, and set their children on a clear course to 'O' levels, 'A' levels and university degrees, they then, in the name of progress, made the best-paid positions in the gift of the state accessible only to those with those very qualifications. As each area of endeavour was brought under the community's control so a man had to demonstrate not just that he could do his job but that he also possessed the hallmark of a good education. It was not enough for a painter to be able to paint a picture if he wished to study at an art school: he must also have his 'A' levels in Biology or Mathematics. Understanding and experience were insufficient for a social worker without a diploma: and an architect might build a cathedral like the Minster at York but without the requisite qualifications he could never be employed by the borough council.

Many of John's fellow-socialists wished to nationalize the land, and in principle he thought it right that it should be taken from the kind of complacent snobs whom his mother asked to dinner; but then he remembered the farmer who lived next to The Garth, a tenant of Stainton Hall: he could barely read or write yet his fields and cows were better tended and yielded a greater return than those of the most highly qualified agronomist. If the Labour Party nationalized the land would his son be excluded from running the farm because he could not pass two 'A' levels? Would the management of it be handed over to some son of the urban middle classes with a Diploma in Agriculture from a polytechnic?

The cold penetrated his clothes: he walked on thinking that he might well withdraw from his political career did he not dread the disappointment it would cause to Paula Gerrard, for even there in the fields, amidst the calm of nature, he felt a total, irrevocable love for the slight, dark girl he had left in London. She possessed a good half of his waking affection. He was walking now in the woods and fields of North Yorkshire; yet he was also three hundred miles away in Prinnet Park – the home of the Gerrards – receiving imagined smiles from Paula's pretty lips; holding conjectural conversations; feeling her phantom, tentative embraces.

Asleep he did not dream of her but each morning he awoke aware that something fierce and wonderful lay in his life – as if the day before a leopard had crept into the house and produced its litter in the laundry basket. And if at times during the day he became preoccupied with his real, ordinary life – playing with his children or reading the newspaper – then the part of him that loved Paula Gerrard would lie in wait. He might open *The Times* and feel a sudden acceleration of his pulse only because his eye had seen – before his mind had comprehended – an advertisement in the financial section for her father's bank. Again, the day before on Christmas Eve he had been sitting drinking tea in the kitchen with all the children and the sons of the farmer next door when something said by one of these Yorkshire boys churned his insides like a sudden attack of wind. He played back in his mind what he had not consciously listened to a moment before: 'Paul an' me's goin' to't panto on Sunday.' So inflamed was some part of his brain that the first two syllables of that sentence had been enough to send a message down his spine to the network of nerves in his stomach.

Doubtless if he had been with Paula at Prinnet Park, spending Christmas with the Gerrards, half his attention would have been equally absent with his wife and children in Yorkshire; and the sound of a boy or girl playing in the garden would have provoked the same spasm in his stomach. But since he was bodily present at Stainton he took what he had there for granted and thought all the more of Paula whose absence caused him suffering. He imagined her mostly talking to him, smiling at him or kissing him with affection. He went over the occasions when they had met in London restaurants, remembering little phrases of conversation; and he pictured what it would be like when they met again in London. It was now only five days since he had parted from her in the concourse at the Old Bailey, but the distance in space had stretched the time to seem much longer, and already the real characteristics of her face and personality were softening into an idealized image. The unattractive features which a dispassionate observer might mention – her bossiness, say, or her curiously unformed face – were forgotten, and already as he walked back towards the village on Christmas Day John wondered how he could endure being parted from her until after the New Year.

He returned to The Garth, uncorked four bottles of burgundy

and then sat alone in the empty drawing-room. Clare looked in, licking rum butter off her fingers. 'Graham's gone to the pub,' she said. 'He said you should join him there if you want to.'

'I think I'll stay here.'

'Are you all right?'

'Yes. Why?'

'You seem rather . . . removed.'

He smiled. 'Christmas has a funny effect on people.'

'You're not unhappy?'

'Oh no.'

She stooped and kissed him, and then went back to the kitchen.

chapter three

On 28 December they moved to Busey, where John became still more withdrawn. That was the only outward sign of his inward preoccupation. He had to be questioned twice if anyone wanted an answer, so among the Loughs where Eustace and Guy were always clamouring to speak at the same time he was generally left out of the conversation.

The children barely noticed his distraction: they were delighted to be in the larger house where they could run around without fear of smashing a china statuette. Clare was aware of it, but as we know she was used to his moods and this one, at least, was not a bad mood. He sat quietly with that empty look which comes into the eyes when they are doing no work for the brain. Helen Lough assumed that his distant behaviour was due to their old antagonism and the brigadier took it that John shared his dislike of the Christmas season.

The cause of John's reticence was not just that his mind was on other things than the conversation at table: a less careful man – or a man less experienced than John in watching his words – might well have betrayed his thoughts by steering the talk towards Paula Gerrard, or something linked to her, like banking or the probation service, for he longed to discuss her or anything associated with her which would keep her alive in his mind; but twenty years in the law had taught him not to say anything which when fed into the computer of an intuitive feminine mind would give away the thoughts that were passing through his own. He loved Clare enough not to wish to hurt or humiliate her. He recognized that all love is possessive and there is always pain when it takes in another party – when a mother meets the girl her son intends to marry or a son his baby brother: he also had conscience enough to concede that in these two instances nature exacts this suffering as a price for the survival of the species, while for the introduction of a mistress there is no such justification. He was also shrewd – calculating that the longer his love remained secret the longer it could be enjoyed without precipitating a crisis. He had not resolved the contradiction implicit in loving two women at once or considered any contingency solution to the crisis should it arise, and he made no particular attempt to do so other than wishing at times that he was a Muslim and imagining at others that Clare suffered unknowingly from leukaemia and was soon to die.

This fantasy of Clare's death was not the expression of any hatred for her: he loved her as he felt it was proper to love a wife. Nor did he blame her for being the only obstacle to his marrying Paula Gerrard, but it did not escape him that if Clare should happen to die, and he then married Paula, it would not only enable him to live with her, but would also provide him with a partner who believed in his political future, could resolve his doubts, and could back her faith with her money. Gone would be his anxieties about life insurance premiums and school fees. He could then give up all practice of the law – except, perhaps, for some notable cases which would bring him renown – and concentrate his energies on public affairs. He therefore imagined Clare in a fatal car crash (which would dispose of the Volvo as well) and himself, after genuine and appropriate grief, going to Prinnet Park to claim Paula. There was only one snag: Clare rarely drove the Volvo without one or other of the children, and not even in his most far-fetched, speculative daydreams did John contemplate the death and extinction of Tom and Anna.

Henry and Mary Mascall were not in Norfolk for the New Year:

they had gone to stay with some friends in Scotland. John and Clare went over for a drink with Henry's parents before lunch on New Year's Day and to John's relief Jilly was not there either: nor from Lady Mascall's hospitable manner did it seem as if the family knew anything about the letter. Guy was at Busey, but he never alluded to what he knew about his brother-in-law's erstwhile passion. Indeed the second half of the holiday was as unassuming as the first: they went for walks, ate a goose, played games and watched television.

Late in the afternoon of New Year's Day, when it was already dark outside, John went to the drawing-room to escape from the children who were playing Monopoly in the library with Guy. He sat down quietly with a book – an old Ian Fleming thriller – which he had found in their bedroom. He saw that the brigadier was lying asleep on the sofa with an open book on his chest – the way in which he habitually spent the dark, winter afternoons. Then suddenly there was a grunt from the recumbent figure. 'What y' reading?'

'I though I'd look at this.' John held up his book.

'What is it?'

'*Thunderball*.'

'Ian Fleming?'

'Yes.'

'Huh. Well, safer than Tolstoy.'

The brigadier picked up his own book.

'What are you reading?' John asked.

'Jung.'

'Ah.'

'Ever read him?'

'Er . . . no.'

'Should do. Good on the problems of the middle-aged.'

John laughed. 'Is that why you're reading him?'

'I'm not middle-aged. I'm old.'

'Then perhaps I'm the one who should read him.'

'Perhaps you should.'

'What does he say?'

'About what?'

'About the middle-aged?'

His father-in-law hauled himself up to a sitting position. 'His theory is that a man, from when he's born until the age of thirty-five or forty, is as it were on a voyage of exploration; he is discovering and conquering the world. Anything's possible. But there comes a point in middle age when he reaches the horizon and sees down the other side.'

'To what?'

'To the rest of his life and, in the distance, death.'

'Even children know that we all must die,' said John.

'They may know it,' said Eustace, 'but they don't take it in. Even young men of twenty live as if death is an old wives' tale. I've seen them in the army . . .'

'But how does it affect your life – this awareness of death – in the gospel according to Jung?' There was a note of scorn in John's voice because he had a long-standing suspicion of psychoanalysis.

'You have to come to terms with it.'

'I can see that if, like you, one believes in an afterlife one might make a reservation in heaven and start to pack one's bag for the journey; but if, like me, one does not believe in an afterlife, then surely one must just go on living as before – eating, drinking and being merry . . .?'

'On the contrary. You're the one Jung's worried about. If there's life after death then even the most miserable little clerical lance-corporal has something to hope for; but if there isn't, then this life is all you've got; and the man who always dreamt of being a general suddenly realizes that he'll never be anything more than a company commander. Younger men are promoted over his head. His wife is disappointed and despises him. He finds her unattractive anyway. His children take his money and lead their own lives. His health fails. His mind decays. No wonder so many go gaga in middle age.'

'But you're not gaga.'

Eustace gave a curt smile. 'Don't you think so?'

John blushed. 'No. Not really. Not at all.'

'And you're not gaga?'

'Me? Do I seem gaga?'

'You're damned silent these days.'

'Yes, well I'm preoccupied. This business of standing for Parliament . . .'

'I heard about that.'

'Would Jung have approved?'

'I doubt it.'

'Why not?'

'He didn't have much time for abstractions like "mankind" or "society" or "the working class".'

'Or the regiment?' asked John with a smile.

'Or the regiment,' Eustace repeated.

John rose from his chair and went to stand with his back to the fire – the way Paula had stood in the living-room of her mews house. 'I haven't sold my soul to the Labour Party,' he said. 'At least I hope I haven't.'

'I'm sure you haven't,' said Eustace, 'and I'm not saying you shouldn't go in for politics. They need good men, particularly in times like these.'

'So why do you . . . or rather why would Jung worry about me?'

Eustace pulled himself up and swung his feet on to the floor. 'It's a question of tactics,' he said. 'You should only advance if you're sure of your home ground.'

'Which is what?'

'Yourself. Your stability and happiness. Otherwise you might just be a blind man leading the blind.'

'I fee reasonably stable and reasonably happy. Of course it's difficult to know what's the norm.'

'Jung had a list of five or six things which made for human happiness.'

'What were they?'

'Good health . . .'

'I've got that.'

'Appreciation of beauty in art and nature.'

Remembering his walk on Christmas Day John said: 'In nature, anyway.'

'A reasonable standard of living.'

'It seems reasonable to me.'

'And satisfactory work.'

'Yes.'

'Some sort of philosophy or religion which can cope with life's vicissitudes . . .'

'I'm afraid I fall down on that,' John said with a laugh.

'And a happy marriage.'

Involuntarily his laugh ceased. 'Yes, well, of course I've got a happy marriage.'

Later that night, as they were about to go to bed, John remarked to Clare that her father seemed in a strange mood.

'That's just what he said about you.'

'I think he thinks I'm going off my head.'

'He's the one who's going loony.'

'He's reading Jung.'

'A great mistake. It's like reading a medical dictionary. You imediately feel all the symptoms of the worst diseases.'

She got into bed and pulled the covers up to her chin. Her face, framed by her brown hair, looked up at John with an amiable but uncertain expression. 'Do *you* think you're going off your head?' she asked.

'No. Why? Do you?'

'No. You're a bit quiet, that's all.'

'I know. I'm sorry. There's a lot on my mind and I'm never much good at Christmas.' John got into bed beside her. They switched off their lights, kissed one another and went to sleep.

chapter four

On 2 January 1974, they returned to London at fifty miles per hour. Since the beginning of the year this speed limit had been imposed by the government to conserve fuel. Moreover electricity was now only supplied to industry on three days a week, and no television was broadcast after half past ten at night.

They reached the house in Holland Park at four in the afternoon. It was already almost dark, and because of a power cut the whole street was illuminated only by the grey twilight. John entered the house and searched in the gloom for candles. Down in the kitchen he found one or two stumps in saucers standing where he had left them before the Christmas holidays, but there were no matches by the stove.

Clare and the children came in behind him struggling with bags and suitcases. Clare had no matches either, so John went up into the drawing-room, which was in a state of complete disorder. He cursed his wife for leaving the house in such a mess, and finding no matches there either he went into their bedroom. There he saw that all the drawers had been removed from the chest of drawers and emptied on to the floor. The house had not been left in a mess: it had been robbed while they were away.

John found some matches – a small wallet with the name of the Russian restaurant where he had taken Paula. It would have given him a twinge of longing for her if he had not been thinking of her already – indeed so determined was he to see her that the burglary of his house left him unmoved.

He went downstairs again to where Clare and the two children were waiting in the cold hallway. 'I've found some matches,' he said – and then added: 'I think we've been burgled.'

'Oh no,' said Clare. 'What have they taken?'

'I don't know. If you'd left the matches by the stove I might have found out by now . . .' He went down to the kitchen.

'How do you know they didn't steal the matches?' Clare shouted after him – her voice wobbling on the edge of tears. Behind her Anna started to sniff quietly in the dark.

'Perhaps they're still in the house,' said Tom.

'They'll have run away by now,' said Clare without much conviction.

Anna's tears became sobs.

John came up again with four candles on a tray. 'Go down to the kitchen,' he said. 'I've lit the stove and opened the oven so it should warm up quite soon.' While his family did as he suggested he put two candles on the hall table and carried the other two up into the drawing-room. Their wavering light revealed the clutter caused by the thieves who had emptied every cupboard on to the floor. He knelt at the fireplace and crumpled up a newspaper to light a fire. There were twigs and logs in the basket (it was a smokeless zone but like most members of the middle classes John disobeyed those little laws which inconvenienced him) and soon they were alight.

173

Clare came in. 'What a lousy thing to come back to,' she said.

'What?'

'Well this.' She waved at the photographs, cards and the contents of her sewing basket which were among those things scattered over the floor.

'Something like this always happens when we go away,' said John. 'Last year it was a burst pipe.'

Clare looked quizzically at John: it was quite unlike her husband to take such things so calmly. 'Have you found out what they've taken?' she asked.

'All the silver from the kitchen,' said John.

'Including the teapot?'

'Yes.'

'Was it insured?'

'I think so.'

'And from here?'

'All the ornaments . . . and I'm afraid they must have got your jewellery.'

Clare sat down: now she started to sob. 'It's so unfair,' she said. 'It's not as if any of it was worth much . . .'

'I know,' said John, who saw in her tears the links of a chain which would prevent his escape to see Paula.

'The mean little shits,' said Clare. 'God how I hate them.'

'Just think how much worse it would have been if we'd had an accident on the way down.'

Clare wiped the tears from her cheeks. 'I know. One shouldn't mind so much about possessions, but it's horrid all the same.' She stood up. 'I know what we'll do,' she said with a forced smile. 'We'll have a nice cup o' tea.' She went up to her husband: he kissed her; and then together they went down to the kitchen.

At five the electricity came on, and with it the central heating. The children cheered up and when a policeman came to inspect the evidence of the burglary they followed him around the house at a respectful distance, solemn with excitement and awe.

Seeing their spirits restored John escaped to his chambers. There he found a message to ring Gordon Pratt as soon as possible, but politics at that moment was not foremost in his mind.

Instead he dialled the number of Paula Gerrard. 'Paula?' he asked.

'John?'

'Yes.'

'When did you get back?'

'This afternoon. When did you?'

'I've been back for ages. I didn't stay for New Year.'

A pang of jealousy twisted in him. 'Where were you?'

'In London.'

'What did you do?'

'Nothing.'

'Weren't you lonely?'

There was a silence over the line. 'I pretended you were there.'

His voice became hoarse: he cleared his throat. 'Can I come now?'

'I wish you would.'

'You've nothing else?'

'No.'

'I'll be there in half an hour.'

He rang off and was about to leave his chambers with his brief for the following day when he saw the message from Gordon Pratt. He looked reluctantly at the black handle of the telephone which he had just returned to its cradle, and then with a sigh picked it up again.

'Thank God you're back,' Gordon said. 'Things are starting to move among our friends in North London.'

'How?'

'They've brought the selection conference forward to mid-February . . . the fifteenth.'

'Does that affect our position?'

'Not as such, but that old bugger O'Grady has announced that in view of the crisis he's willing to carry on.'

'But he's seventy-five years old.'

'I know, I know. But if he persists he'll hurt us more than the Tribune lot. We've got to have a confab. Are you free tonight?'

'No, alas, I've got something on.'

'Can't you change it?'

'Not really.'

'Then we'll have to meet later in the week. A pity, though, because the others were all set to meet tonight.'

'I can't get out of it,' said John. 'It's a dinner with a Judge which was arranged months ago.'

'OK. Not to worry. What about Thursday? Are you free Thursday evening?'

'Yes.'

'Good. I'll try and fix something up for Thursday.'

He rang off. John put down the telephone and then picked it up again to make a final call. 'Clare?' he said when he reached his wife. 'Is everything all right?'

'Yes,' she said. 'The Bobby's gone. He says the CID will come round in the morning.'

'Good. Look, there's a crisis up at Hackney. They've brought forward the selection conference to the fifteenth of February because they think there might be an election and old O'Grady now wants to stand again.'

'What a bore. Can he do that?'

'Yes. There's no reason why not, but it means I've got to go up there this evening.'

'Oh. All right.'

'Will you manage?'

'Yes. But come back quickly. The burglary has made me a bit nervous.'

'I'll get away as soon as I can, but don't wait up for me.'

'Have you got your key?'

'Yes.'

'I'll see you later, then.'

chapter five

John had driven to his chambers in the Volvo and he used it now to go to Purves Mews. He parked outside Paula's house and rang the bell. A moment later Paula opened the door and stood back to let him in. He glanced at her face and then went on into the kitchen while his mind worked fast to match her real face to the idealized image he had formed in his memory. He turned to find that she had closed the door and come up behind him. They kissed, and her scent and substance were also different to what he had been savouring over the past two weeks in his imagination: but in their reality they were more powerful, and in a minute had driven out the dreams. The only Paula he knew now was the girl whose slightly dry lips were pressed to his, and whose tongue tasting of cosmetics moved sleepily against his own.

Still she had not said anything, but the way she clung to the fabric of his crumpled coat with the half-clenched fist of a baby expressed her feelings. When their faces drew apart he saw that she was crying.

'What is it?' he asked.

She smiled and shook her head. 'Nothing. I'm just happy to see you.'

She crossed as usual to fetch ice from the refrigerator and as usual he carried the tray up to the studio room where a log fire burned in the grate. He sank back on the deep sofa with a long sigh and she came and curled up beside him.

'I have missed you very much,' said John.

She hugged his chest.

'Did you miss me?' he asked.

'Huh.'

'Well?'

She raised her head and looked into his eyes. 'Do you know,' she said, 'that I missed you so much that I couldn't bear it . . . I couldn't bear being with other people. I came back to London the day after Boxing Day – my mother and father were furious. They'd asked a lot of people for New Year's Eve, but I said I had a party I'd promised to go to here . . .' Her words, now, tumbled out of her mouth.

'And was there a party here?'

She smiled. 'A little one. Very intimate.'

He looked away to hide his pang of jealousy.

She put her hand to his cheek and brought his face round again to look into his eyes. 'Just me,' she said. 'I saw the New Year in alone.'

'I wish I'd known.'

'What would you have done?'

He hesitated. 'I'd have telephoned.'

'Yes,' she said in a tone of voice which might or might not nave been ironical. 'That would have been nice.' Then she stood and went to pour two glasses of whisky. 'It's very strange, you know,' she said. 'I haven't spoken to anyone for a week. No one at all except the girl at the supermarket.' She handed John his drink and sat down again beside him. 'But I wasn't lonely. I pretended you were here living with me. We quarrelled rather a lot, I'm afraid. You were rather sloppy. You left your clothes lying all over the floor . . . Are you sloppy, by the way?'

'No. I'm fairly tidy.'

'Then we'll have to quarrel about something else.' She smiled.

'Is that all we did together – quarrel?'

'I have to admit – though I say it myself – that I cooked you some rather delicious little suppers. I may even have put on some weight.' She looked down at her body, which was shrouded anyway by a loose silk dress.

'I didn't know you could cook.'

'There's a lot you don't know about me,' she said with a brief expression of perplexity. Then she smiled again. 'Shall I cook something tonight? Would you like that? Or do you have to rush off?'

'No. I'd love it if you did.'

'It'd be nicer than a restaurant, wouldn't it?'

'Much nicer.'

She leaned forward and kissed John's cheek. 'Are you hungry?'

'I am quite.'

'Have you driven down from Yorkshire today?'

'Yes.'

'You must be exhausted.'

'Not really.'

'Would you like a bath? I can lend you a towel and you can put on your Christmas present.'

She jumped up off the sofa and crossed the room and so did not see the look of embarrassment that came on to John's face both at the mention of a bath and a Christmas present; because a bath seemed something more personal than was warranted by the present unconsummated state of their love affair, and it had never occured to him to buy a present for Paula.

She came back with a parcel and stood watching him while he opened it. He unwrapped a blue silk shirt.

'Do you like it?' Paula asked, her dark eyes glancing at him with some uncertainty. 'I had to guess your collar size. Is fifteen about it?'

'Perfect. It's a beautiful shirt.' He stood and kissed her. 'There's only one thing wrong with it.'

'What?' She looked upset and held her breath like an apprehensive child.

'I haven't got a present for you.'

She exhaled with relief – a pleasant little puff of air which smelt as her tongue had tasted – of *eau de toilette* and lipstick. 'Oh men don't buy presents. Daddy never does – except for me. And anyway, you've got your children and so on to think about. I only had my parents and you.'

'What did you get from them?'

'Oh, lots of things. Mummy gave me a pretty necklace thing – gold and those blue stones. What are they called?'

'Sapphires.'

'No. Lapis something.'

'Lapis lazuli.'

'That's right.'

'And what did your father give you?'

'He gave me that.' She pointed to a small pastel on the wall by the fireplace. John stood up and crossed to look at it.

'Is it a Renoir?'

'Yes. I think it's his son Jean.' She was walking away towards her bedroom.

'It's very nice.'

'Yes,' she said doubtfully. 'But it was less a Christmas present than a shift of resources to avoid death duties.' She left the room.

John remained for a moment studying the picture and wondering what it had cost; then he went back to the sofa. Paula returned a moment later with a huge white towel.

'Here you are,' she said. 'You know where the bathroom is, don't you?'

'Yes.'

'I've started running the bath so don't let it overflow.' She went to the top of the spiral staircase. 'I'll go down and start cooking.'

John emptied his glass of whisky down his throat and walked through to the bathroom. Steam rose from the tub and with it the aroma of some essence. He shut the door, locked it and began to remove his clothes. His body longed for a bath; his limbs ached to be immersed in hot, sweet-smelling water: yet the act of standing naked in her bathroom, of lying in water drawn by her, seemed one of irrevocable intimacy, and he trembled as if he had at last come to the moment when he must make love to her.

He sank slowly in the scalding water and as its heat reached his nerves the trembling stopped. He sighed as he relaxed and rested his head against the enamelled edge of the tub. Everything around him was elegant and luxurious: a green dish with a china frog crouching on its edge held a huge oval of matching soap. The drops of moisture on the ceramic tiles bulged like precious stones. The water of the bath itself had the greenish tinge of the essence but was clean, hot and pure: how long was it, he wondered, since he had taken a bath without hair and scum floating on the surface?

John washed himself, then lay submerged. He studied his body and wondered how it would look to Paula if ever she chose to take him as her lover. He had grown thinner since the summer and had taken some exercise, so his bosom was more manly and his stomach flat. He doubted all the same whether Paula would feel a physical passion for his lanky limbs and pallid skin, and rather than think further about his age and her youth he rose from the water and stepped out of the bath into the huge white towel which wrapped around him like a Roman toga. He opened the door of the bathroom to let out some of the steam and heard music from the living-room. He stepped out into the short passage and saw Paula sitting on the sofa next to the fire.

'Hurry up,' she said. 'I want you to open a bottle.'

He walked forward wrapped in the towel. 'I'll open it now.' She pointed to a bottle of champagne on the tray. 'It's to celebrate your triumphs in court,' she said.

'Ah yes,' said John. 'I'd forgotten that.'

'You should have been dressed like that,' said Paula. 'You look just like Cicero.'

John took the foil off the cork and untwisted the wire which held it to the bottle. 'I'm not sure the Judge would have liked it.' The cork popped off and he filled two glasses. 'Here's to . . .' He hesitated.

'To what?' she asked.

'To a girl who is . . . lovely, body and soul.'

'Is that meant to be me?'

'Yes.'

'I can't drink if you're toasting me.'

John raised his glass and took a sip of the fizzing wine.

'And here's to . . .' She laughed. 'Well, the next Prime Minister . . .'

'Is that meant to be me?'

'Why not?'

'Aren't you a little unambitious?'

'All right. To the first President of Europe.' She drank from her glass of champagne.

'Can't we drink together?' John asked.

'Yes. Here's to love and politics'

They both drained their glasses and then John went back to the bathroom to put on the blue silk shirt.

He wore it open at the neck and discovered, sitting opposite Paula, that she could indeed cook – or at any rate that she could grill lamb cutlets, bake potatoes and mix a salad dressing. The pâté which preceded the lamb came out of a tin from Harrods and the claret they drank once they had finished the champagne came from the vineyards of the Château Latour.

'Do you always live like this?' John asked her.

'Like what?'

'Like this.' He waved at the food and drink on the table.

'Not all the time, no. But I believe that if you can afford the best you might as well have it.'

'So do I.' He stuffed his mouth with chocolate mousse.

'People always assume that if you have left-wing principles you want to bring down everybody's standard of living to the lowest common denominator rather than raise it to the highest.'

'Can you have a highest common denominator?'

'I don't see why not. Cars used to be luxuries for the super-rich. Now everyone has one.'

181

'But would *pâté de foie gras* taste the same if every working man had it for breakfast?'

She sipped her wine. 'I don't see why it should taste different.'

'If beer was twice the price of wine you might be drinking lager rather than Château Latour.'

'I hate lager.'

John tapped his head. 'It's all in the mind. For example women used to think it was unattractive to have sun-tanned skin. Girls would shelter under parasols to protect their complexions from the sun. Why? Because a brown skin came from labouring in the sun. It betrayed your peasant background. Only the rich were pink and pale. Now, however, in our urban society it signifies the opposite: a tan betrays the leisure class who ski in the winter and lie idly on beaches in the summer, while a pale skin means that you work in an office or a factory and take your holiday in Blackpool or Torquay.'

'If that's the case,' said Paula, 'then our socialism is a chimera.'

'Why?'

'Because it implies that people are not made happy by equal shares but only if they have more than others.'

'It's certainly a chimera if we think that the state's ownership of everything will somehow end all human discontent. But the exaggerated expectations of some socialists shouldn't be allowed to discredit a belief in pragmatic reform.' He slowed his pace and gesticulated as if addressing a jury or a political meeting. 'It shouldn't follow that because you can never build paradise in Rochdale or Bradford you shouldn't try to improve the cultural and material conditions of the poor. Look back, after all, and compare the lives of most of us today with what it was one or two hundred years ago. There are no slaves, no child labourers, reasonable working conditions, a free health service. No one should ever belittle these achievements . . .'

Paula yawned.

'I didn't tell you,' said John, 'that the sitting member at Hackney wants to stand again.'

Paula frowned. 'No, you didn't. Does that present a problem?'

'It makes it more difficult.'

'Then we must stop him.'

'We're meeting on Thursday to see what can be done.'

She stood to put the kettle on for coffee. 'I might be able to help,' she said from the other side of the kitchen.

'How?'

She hesitated as if preoccupied with turning on the tap. 'I have contacts in that part of the world,' she said.

'In the Labour Party?'

She turned and gave John an odd look. 'Not the Labour Party, exactly, but impeccably working-class.'

'Are they friends of Terry Pike by any chance?'

'More acquaintances.' She put the kettle on to boil. 'But some of them are what he'd call "faces". They have considerable influence . . .'

'I'd rather do without their help.'

'Why?'

'Because people like that always expect favours in return.'

'Not if you pay them; and anyway, they owe you a favour. At least Terry does.'

'I'd rather call it quits.'

Paula returned to the table with an expression of mild irritation on her face as if she had just discovered that the lamb was overdone. 'All right,' she said, 'it was only a suggestion. But you know you won't get very far in politics if you're too fastidious.'

'What do you mean by fastidious?'

'Gentlemanly. Playing the game according to the rules.'

'At least I won't end up in prison.'

'Nor did Churchill or Lloyd George, but they were unscrupulous when they had to be. The trouble with people like us is that we're brought up to believe that life is less savage than it really is. It's a luxury – like a yacht or a Rolls-Royce – this belief in fair play.'

'I thought that that was what we meant by civilization.'

A fierce look came onto her face and a strong colour into her cheeks. 'Civilization is a charade,' she said. 'That at least I learned from working in Wandsworth. Life is just as much a struggle among human beings as it is among animals . . .'

John found her impassioned manner poignant and endearing. 'With the survival of the fittest?' he asked, smiling.

'Yes.' She seemed annoyed that John was amused by her views.

183

The kettle was boiling: she went back to the stove to make the coffee. 'I know it's natural to assume that if you're rich it's part of the natural order,' she said caustically, 'and to feel mildly irritated if the poor don't see it in the same way. That's certainly my father's point of view. But if you look at society through the eyes of someone like Terry, you see the way in which it is organized to protect the property of those who have it against those who don't.'

'Perhaps civilized values are based on injustice,' said John in a more serious tone of voice. 'And perhaps they're a luxury, but they are still preferable to uncivilized values.'

'I'm not sure I even agree with that,' said Paula, putting the coffee on a tray. 'Let's go upstairs,' she interjected, setting off across the room towards the spiral staircase.

'Why don't you agree?' asked John, following her up the stairs.

'Because what you mean by civilization, which is a well regulated Welfare State, makes people flabby and dull like the Swiss.' She reached the top and walked towards the fireplace. 'You certainly can't claim that art flourishes in a law-abiding society. They were always murdering one another in Renaissance Italy or in Shakespeare's England.' She sat down on a sofa and poured out two cups of black coffee.

'You're optimistic,' said John, sitting down beside her, 'if you think that Terry Pike will write a *Hamlet*.'

'He won't write *Hamlet*,' said Paula, 'because culture has been poisoned for him by its middle-class connotations; but he certainly has more of Hamlet's qualities than the kind of youth you meet at a dinner party or a debutante dance. If he thought his uncle had murdered his father he wouldn't just report it to the local police.'

'And you approve of that?'

She hesitated. 'Yes. I admire the way they solve their own problems and don't go whining to social workers and marriage guidance counsellors.'

'Solve them, you mean, with sawn-off shotguns?'

She laughed. 'Do you expect them to use swords?'

'I don't expect them to use violence at all.'

'That's what you say. That's what we all say, yet the men we hold up as heroes in history and literature are more like London gangsters than lawyers and businessmen. Look at the siege of Troy. Paris pinched another man's wife so Menelaus got his friends together and went to take her back by force. Alexander the Great, Julius Caesar, Napoleon – they're all men who used force to get what they wanted, and we admire them. Othello smothered his wife because he thought she was unfaithful, and the tragedy is not that he smothered her but that she wasn't unfaithful. Force, blood, love, friendship are all mixed up together and even today, in our careful little bureaucrats' paradise, those who live dangerously live intensely . . .'

'Like Terry Pike?'

She flushed. 'Yes. Like Terry and Jimmy and some of their friends. They despise the safe world of annual increments and contributory pensions. They refuse to be tamed and emasculated by the law. Friendship, honour, loyalty and love aren't just words to them as they are to us: they are often a matter of life and death. What we enjoy vicariously through books and films, they actually *do:* they may be outcasts and outlaws and spend half their lives in prison, but at least they'll have lived real lives in the other half whereas we'll have had a full spell of watching it all on television.'

A little taken aback by this waterfall of words, John just grinned and said: 'You make them sound irresistibly attractive' – whereupon Paula, still flushed from her defiance, looked at him straight in the eyes and with an angry expression asked: 'Do you love me?'

'Yes,' he said. 'I do.'

'Do you really love me?'

'Yes. I really love you.'

She sighed and looked away.

'Do you doubt it?' he asked.

'No, but it would be easier if you didn't,' she said.

'I know.'

'And it would be easier for me if I didn't love you.'

'You do love me, don't you?'

She looked at him. 'Yes.'

He smiled and took her hand. 'Don't look so tragic.'

'But it *is* tragic, for a dozen reasons, because I love you and want to sleep with you but you're married . . .'

185

'That doesn't mean anything any more,' he said.

She paused as if to absorb this; then shook her head and said: 'I'd hate to destroy your marriage.'

'It wouldn't be you. What's wrong was wrong already.'

'Are you sure? Do you promise?'

'Yes.'

'And if there was something on my side . . .' She looked away as if afraid of what he might see in her eyes. 'The reason I couldn't sleep with you before – which if I didn't love you I could hide from you but since I do I can't?'

'You must tell me.'

'But if I do you won't want me.'

'You don't trust me much.'

She turned, gripped his hand and said in a flat, breathless voice: 'I lied to you before.'

'About what?'

'I did sleep with him.'

'With whom? With Pike?'

'Yes.'

John removed his hand from hers and looked away.

'It was after that cocktail party I gave for him. Do you remember? I told you about it. He was so humiliated. I had to . . . to prove . . . I don't know . . . to prove that I understood him.'

'Was that the only time?' John asked in the cold, dispassionate tone of the cross-examining barrister.

'No,' she said sadly. 'It's no use pretending. I had an affair with him.'

'Until when?'

'I didn't love him,' she said.

'Until when?' he repeated.

'Until the trial. After the trial we came back here. That was the last time. I had to stay with him until then. But it's finished now. He knows. I haven't seen him since.'

'But before Christmas, before the trial, while you were seeing me, you were also seeing him.'

'I didn't love him. I only loved you. But he relied on me. I felt I couldn't just dump him. But I couldn't sleep with him and you. I thought of it, but I couldn't do it, even though you were the one I cared about.'

'Yes, I do see,' said John sarcastically. 'Indeed I'm most grateful to you for being so honest . . .'

She was silent; then spoke in a low, dejected tone of voice. 'I thought it would put you off, but I couldn't go on unless you knew.'

They sat there side by side like two strangers on a park bench – neither looking at the other, both waiting for their emotions to subside like the cramps of a rumbling stomach. 'I suppose,' John said at last, 'that after all I had Clare . . . I mean we both when we met had . . . prior commitments.'

She turned to him and gripped the fabric of the sofa just by his hand. 'I shall never see Terry again,' she said. 'I have no one now but you, and if you don't want me then I shall be alone.'

'I do want you,' he whispered.

She filled her lungs with air. 'Well here I am.'

He kissed her: she clung to him. They tilted and then fell side by side on the sofa and in due course made love for the first time.

chapter six

In the weeks which followed John rarely returned home before midnight and Clare seemed to accept that she must sacrifice her husband's company for the sake of his political career. Every now and then she would offer to go with him to Hackney or Haringey but always seemed relieved that he declined her offer, preferring (he said) to keep her in reserve for the election itself.

For every evening he spent in North London, John spent two in Purves Mews: in a short space of time it had become almost a habit for him to go there from his chambers, take a bath under the eye of the green frog on the soap dish, change into some jeans, a silk shirt and a jersey; eat in or out, according to Paula's mood; return, make love, and at midnight change back into his cotton shirt and suit, creep out on to the cobbles and take a taxi home.

This double life worked well. Politics was his alibi for his family and his family his alibi for his supporters in Hackney. Only Gordon Pratt seemed to suspect that there was something in between the two, for whenever now he engaged John on a political topic (and as the coalminers had now voted for an all-out strike there was much to talk about), a vague, semi-beatific smile came on to his friend's face.

'You seem to be somewhere else,' Gordon said to John one evening in a pub. 'Here's Heath trying to do a Franco on us and introduce a corporate state and all you do is smile.'

John shook his head as if the physical gesture would dislodge the ever-present image of his mistress. 'I'm sorry,' he said.

'Have you lost interest?'

'No.'

'Or your nerve?'

'No.'

'Things are getting ugly.'

'I know. Don't worry. I won't let you down.'

Gordon looked uncertain. 'You aren't having trouble with Clare, are you?'

'A little. She thinks it's all a waste of time.'

Gordon waited but John did not enlarge so he said: 'Well, I won't pry,' and returned to talking about those members of the General Management Committee who were wavering between John and O'Grady. 'It seems ridiculous,' he said, 'that the whole thing isn't sewn up when your only opponents are a Pakistani Trot and an octogenarian fascist. But several comrades are suspicious of you. You talk too well. You went to Oxford and a public school. You make too much money and you've been active for too short a time.'

'You can't blame them,' said John.

'You can't blame them,' said Gordon, 'but they must be made to realize that they're choosing a Member of Parliament, not awarding a bloody prize . . .' And he talked on in his unrelenting Scottish accent while John retired behind his fixed smile to think about Paula.

Her body which was beautiful when wearing clothes was less attractive naked on the bed. The fresh, plump, youthful beauty which Renoir depicts in his paintings was unfashionable at the time, but a thin, lanky girl like Paula, however well suited to a contemporary couturier, was when undressed marred by the hard protuberance of her hips, the skeletal structure of her ribs beneath the skin, her disproportionately small bosom and disproportionately large mass of pubic hair.

As a lover she was more nervous and less lethargic than Clare, and she sighed as if satisfied: yet there was something in her approach to their sexual encounters which was mechanical and conscientious, as if she did it because that was what was done by grown-up people in love. She seemed to like the liberty of a love affair – moving around her house in front of John wearing no clothes at all – but when actually on the bed beneath him she seemed as it were to grit her teeth and behave as expected until it was all over.

John sensed this but was not perturbed. Although his inner complaints against his wife had often included her passivity and indifference as a sexual partner, and although he had often imagined a more tumultuous delight in Paula's body, what he now enjoyed was the symbolic possession of her person. As with the *pâté de foie gras* and the champagne, it was not so much the taste he enjoyed as the rarity and luxury of Paula Gerrard: in John as in most men the venereal urge acted in obedience to a psychological compulsion, and it was to satisfy his brain rather than his loins that he established his domain over this scraggy heiress by intermittently ejaculating into the deepest recesses of her body.

One evening, as she sat opposite him in a candlelit restaurant, Paula complained to John that it was some time since she had seen him in daylight. He suggested that they meet the next day for lunch but she asked instead whether it would not be possible to meet on a Saturday morning.

John frowned. 'I usually do something with the children . . .'

'Bring them along. I'd like to meet them.'

The frown had not left his brow.

'Would Clare be with you?' asked Paula.

'It's not that. She'd be only too glad to get rid of them. But if I brought them here . . .'

'You needn't do that. We could meet somewhere else. Accidentally on purpose. In Knightsbridge, say, and then we can all have a cup of coffee or something.'

189

On the following Saturday morning John offered to take the children into town and leave Clare free to do some shopping on her own. His offer was accepted by all three members of his family and he set off at ten o'clock and met Paula as arranged outside Harrods. John introduced Tom and Anna to Paula and she said hello to them with an energetic, radiant charm which John had not seen in her before and which, he decided, must come from her American mother.

They went into the large department store and sat down in the coffee shop. The children sucked at Coca-Cola through straws while the two grown-ups sipped coffee. John attempted some oblique conversation with Paula but she barely attended to him – chatting all the time to the children about their schools, their Christmas presents, displaying (to Tom) an unusual knowledge of football and (to Anna) an equal familiarity with the position on the charts of the currently popular songs.

The children responded well. They always enjoyed a trip to the West End, and this elegant woman who was so kind to them seemed like a fairy godmother who had stepped out from the mannequins displaying the pretty women's clothes in the window. John too saw her in this role and after he had paid for the drinks and they had left the coffee shop he saw as he had feared that Paula was leading his children towards the toy department. As they moved among the loaded shelves he wondered whether he could ask them not to tell their mother that a strange lady had bought them some presents, or how he could explain to Clare why Paula should have done so, when Paula came up with the solution. She lowered her body to the level of the children, put an arm around each of their shoulders and said: 'Now you choose any toy you want and I'll persuade your Daddy to buy it for you.'

Tom and Anna wandered off to search and to choose while Paula waited for John. 'You don't mind, do you?' she asked.

'It's spoiling them so soon after Christmas.'

'I'd like them to like me.'

'They'd like you anyway.'

'You just don't like paying,' she said with a smile.

'No,' he said. 'It's better that I should pay.'

'That's what I thought,' she said, 'but I'll pay you back.'

'You don't have to.'

'I will but I can't now. I haven't got any cash.'

'I'd rather you didn't.' He looked a little irritated. Paula was about to say something more when Anna came back with a doll which cried real tears and wet its nappies; and then Tom with a new coach for his electric trains.

'Who was the "nice lady" you met out shopping?' Clare asked John as they changed to go out to dinner that Saturday night.

'Paula Gerrard.'

'I'd like to meet her some time,' she said. 'I thought you were going to ask her to dinner.'

'You said all our friends would hate her.'

'The children seem to have liked her, so she can't be as bad as all that.'

'You trust their judgement more than mine.'

She smiled with slight embarrassment, then took off the dressing-gown she had worn since washing her hair. Seeing her naked body John was struck by how much he preferred her figure to Paula Gerrard's.

'I loved your children,' Paula said when John lay beside her on the following Tuesday night.

'They liked you.'

'I felt so sorry for them.'

'Why?'

'It's always awful for the children when a marriage breaks up.'

John was suddenly still, as if, out of the corner of his eye, he had glimpsed a poisonous spider on the ceiling above the bed.

'They seemed so confident and optimistic,' she said.

'They are,' he said.

'It would be best, wouldn't it, if I gradually got to know them so they thought of me first as a friend rather than a rival to their mother?'

John sat up in bed. 'I hope that doesn't mean that every time we meet they're to be given a free rein in the Harrods toy department.'

'No,' said Paula earnestly. 'I don't want to bribe them to like me. What would be nice if the four of us could go away for the odd weekend . . . perhaps to Prinnet.'

'What would your parents think?'

'About my bringing home a married man and his two children?' She laughed. 'A year ago they'd have been appalled but now, quite honestly, they'd be rather relieved.'

'Why?'

'They'd rather see me as the second wife of a distinguished barrister than the first wife of a petty crook.'

'Did they know about Terry?'

'They got wind of it.'

'I can see why it might have worried them.'

Paula got up out of bed and went towards the bathroom. 'I must try and do a biggy,' she said. 'I haven't been for days.'

John blushed. It was not the term they used at home.

chapter seven

It was now more than two months since John had suffered an attack of Ivan Ilychitis. His political activities seemed to have cured him of the despair and self-doubt which had afflicted him in the summer, yet that night, after creeping into bed beside Clare, he found that he could not sleep but lay the victim of ill-defined anxiety. Paula, Clare and the children moved in and out of his mind repeating phrases which sometimes made sense and sometimes did not, so that he wondered if he was really awake or was rather asleep and dreaming. Little images from the recent past flashed on and off like a slide show in a darkened room – Paula's fevered friendliness to his children; Clare's volte-face about asking her to dinner; then Paula again, straining on the lavatory and asking: 'Do you love me? Do you really love me?' And suddenly Gordon Pratt was also on the lavatory saying: 'Have you lost interest? Have you lost your nerve?'

He slept and then woke again, uncertain where he was or which woman lay beside him. When he realized that it was Clare he wanted to hug her and weep into her flank, but how could he – a grown man? And what could he say if he woke her up? And why should she comfort him?

He moved his body to lie on his back, looking with open eyes into the darkness, listening to the ticking of his clock. Once again he probed into his mind to discover what it was that made him feel so miserable. Suddenly his breathing faltered: while the clock continued to tick he paused with his lungs half-full of air as he remembered what Paula had said that afternoon about his children – about how they would suffer from a broken marriage. He remembered too the remarks which followed and he flinched as he realized what it all implied – that she took for granted that he would leave Clare and marry her.

Now he breathed again but with rapid, panting inhalations as if extra oxygen was required by his brain to work out first how it had happened that she had made this assumption and secondly how he could extricate himself from such an awkward misunderstanding. Had he said to Paula that he was considering divorce or separation? It seemed inconceivable that he had done so because the idea had never come into his head. He might have had daydreams of Clare's demise but he had never thought of leaving her, with or without the children. What had he said on the night of his return to London? Had he, in passion, implied that he would leave Clare? He tried to remember just what he had said to Paula but the words would not come back to him. She had said, he recalled, that she did not want to destroy his marriage and he had replied . . . He could not remember. What had he meant to say? That loving Paula would not destroy his marriage: that sleeping with her would not affect it one way or the other because his love for Clare was no longer exclusive, romantic or inspired by sexual desire: but it existed all the same. She was his wife. He had not meant to deny it nor to suggest that he might ever abandon her.

He turned over on to his side again, calmer now that he had isolated the cause of his anxiety. When he saw Paula the next day he would explain that while he loved her now, and would love her always, he could never leave Clare. With that thought in his mind he gave a final sigh like a child who has just stopped sobbing and fell asleep.

The resolutions which we make like that at night are not always easy to implement when we wake the next morning. As soon as he was conscious John remembered what had to be done that evening, but as he sat at breakfast watching his two children cheerfully stuff cereal into their mouths as if in imitation of some television advertisement, he was confirmed in his determination to make it quite clear to Paula that he would never leave his family. Although he could see quite clearly all the advantages that would accrue to him as the husband of Paula Gerrard, he was more certain still that he could never bring himself to tell either Tom or Anna that he and Clare 'were going to live in different houses' – or whatever euphemism people used to explain divorce; that he would not be there to watch them eat their breakfast but would see them only on Saturday afternoons, at half-term or during the holidays. Were Paula Helen of Troy he could not bring himself to do that: better, he thought, remembering a phrase of the Bible from his childhood, better tie a millstone around one's neck and throw oneself into the sea than destroy the happiness and innocence of a child.

Clare staggered into the kitchen looking bleary-eyed and sheepish that she was still wearing her dressing-gown. She made the children put boots on before setting off for school because it was raining outside and she gave each an old supermarket carrier-bag for their indoor shoes. After they had left she took a cup of coffee from the pot on the stove and sat down opposite John at the kitchen table.

'What are you doing today?' she asked.

'I hope to finish a case at the Old Bailey.'

'Will you be in this evening?'

'I'm afraid not. I'll have to go straight up to Hackney.'

She sighed. 'I hardly see you these days.'

He glanced at the paper. 'It'll soon be over, one way or the other.'

'I hope you're not selected,' she muttered into her coffee like a defiant child.

'So do I,' said John without looking up from the paper. 'But it's too late to get out of it now. I'll have to see it through.'

chapter eight

John had by now seen Paula in quite different moods. There had been evenings when for no apparent reason she had been so sour and silent that it had taxed his good temper to suffer her for three or four hours; and there were others when she was so funny and vivacious that like Cinderella he dreaded the approach of midnight. This contrast in her moods was part of Paula's charm: he could not deny the 'pure poison' that Mary Mascall had seen in her, but like the ice-cold winds in Yorkshire it made her amiable temper all the more welcome when the wind died down and the sun shone from a clear sky.

This unpredictability made him a little frightened of her, and although twelve years older than she was he tended to let her make the decisions which affected them both. For example when it came to the question of whether to eat in or out, John had a strong interest in eating in: taking her to restaurants where the quality of the food, the skill in the cooking of it and the maturity of the wine approached those standards she had established at home was costing him a great deal of money; yet though he knew her well enough to borrow her toothbrush or chat to her while she sat on the lavatory, he did not feel able to confess that the thought of a grotesque bill at the end of each excursion to a restaurant not only spoilt his appetite but destroyed much of the pleasure of an evening out.

The only advantage of eating in a restaurant was that it was more likely to put Paula in a good mood. She was not a gourmet: she usually chose, and then picked at, an expensive dish on the menu while gossiping gaily about this and that. The danger of eating in was that something might go wrong with what she was cooking: a joint would be overdone or a sauce would curdle, and that would ensure a sour mood for the rest of the evening. If John assured her that he liked meat well done, or that a Hollandaise sauce tasted the same curdled or uncurdled, it only made her more sullen still: indifference to her failures implied an equal indifference to her triumphs.

Thus when he let himself into her house that evening (he now had his own key) and saw her standing at the stove, he was in one way relieved that they were not going to a restaurant and in another apprehensive that some culinary disaster would make it more difficult for him to discuss the nature of their liaison.

Paula turned as he entered, smiled, and came towards him licking the tips of her fingers. 'How was it?' she asked, referring to the case at the Old Bailey. 'Did you win?'

'Yes. By the skin of my teeth.'

'Congratulations.' She kissed him, and then turned to go back to the stove. 'Don't be long in the bath,' she said. 'I'm trying quenelles and I don't want them to get all dry.'

As he lay staring at the green frog, with the hot water lapping at his chin, John considered what tactics he should follow – whether he should bring up the subject of Clare before dinner, after dinner or when lying in bed. He was determined not to leave that night without making his statement of intent; he was equally determined not to rupture his affair; yet it was difficult to think of a way of expressing what he had to say without making it seem that he was somehow rejecting Paula and preferring Clare to her.

He rose from the water, dried himself in his huge white towel, changed into his casual clothes and came out into the living-room. He called to Paula that he was out of the bath and hearing her steps on the stairs he decided to bring it all up at once rather than have it hanging over him all evening. He handed her a drink and they both stood arm in arm with their backs to the fire.

'I had lunch with my father today,' she said. 'He says Heath's going to call an election.'

'When?'

'He'll announce it tomorrow.'

'That would mean a poll in February.'

'The twenty-eighth.'

'Has he been told?'

'Not officially, but he knows someone in the Cabinet.'

John turned down his mouth and sucked at the inside of his cheek.

'You don't look very excited,' said Paula.

'I am . . .' he began but did not go on. He sounded half-hearted, even to himself.

'What will it mean up at Hackney?'

'I don't know. It may strengthen O'Grady's claim to stand again.'

'Is that why you're worried?'

'No. It's just that if I'm to fight an election, I'd rather do so in a less emotional atmosphere, without a coal strike or a three-day week. The only issue will be the power of the unions, which is a social phenomenon, not a political issue at all.' He sighed and gulped down his drink.

Paula took his glass and crossed to the bottles to fill it up again. 'I see what you mean,' she said, 'but I feel quite excited all the same. I'm sure you'll be selected; and I'm sure you'll win the seat. I don't think it matters much if Labour win or lose because you can make a name for yourself in opposition . . .' She came back with the drink.

John took it. 'I suppose you're right.'

She put her arm around him again. 'What's the matter? You look awfully portentous this evening.'

'I couldn't sleep last night. I lay awake worrying about things.'

'What things?'

'About whether I'm really cut out to be a politician . . .'

'If you aren't,' said Paula, 'I don't know who is.'

'And wondering what would become of you and me.'

'We'll grow old together, won't we, like any other couple?' She spoke quickly and casually as if it was an ordinary question with an obvious answer.

'What about Clare?'

'She'll marry again.'

'She can't.'

'Why not?'

'She's a Catholic.'

'No one pays any attention to that any more, do they?'

'She does.'

They were silent for a moment – a silence like darkness or cold.

'Are you trying to dump me?' Paula asked quietly.

'God forbid.' He turned, kissed her lips and hugged her until she whimpered. Still holding her he said: 'I'm old enough to know that I shall never go back on anything I have ever felt and . . . affirmed. I love you now and I shall always love you. If I hadn't got a wife I would beg you to marry me; and if you refused I would die of despair. Even with a wife I feel that I belong to you and you to me – that we were destined to meet and are doomed to love one another. But there she is, back in my house in Holland Park, giving my children a bath, ironing my shirts and then watching television on her own. I doubt that if I left her she would find another husband. Other men don't seem to find her attractive, or if they do they are put off by her cold manner. I am all she has. She married me when she was twenty. She went straight from one home to another. If I left her, divorced her and married you she'd either marry again – which in her church is a sin, a mortal sin – or I would be condemning her to premature widowhood – the extra woman at the odd dinner party to match a faggot; an easy lay for the odd husband of a friend who gets drunk and takes pity on her. And even if I could do that to her – whose only offence, after all, is that I'm bored of her – I couldn't condemn Tom and Anna to a broken home. You said it yourself; they would suffer. I've seen the children of divorced parents – shoved off to boarding schools and then posted back and forth in the holidays between two strange houses, neither of which is a home. If I did that to Tom and Anna for your sake I would, in the end, loathe you for it . . .'

She gripped him. 'That mustn't happen. You must never loathe me.'

'I trust I never will.'

'You would marry me, wouldn't you, if Clare wasn't there? There's no one else, is there? I'm not just one of your girls?'

He smiled. 'And when would I fit them in?'

'Perhaps there's a secretary in your chambers or a Labour Party girl in Hackney . . .'

'No. There's no one else. There never will be. If Clare died, or if she ran off with someone else, then we would be married and I would never look at another woman. But I'm afraid that she won't die, and she won't run off, so we must think of what we should do.'

'Yes.' She broke away from him and went to sit on the sofa, her legs apart, her body bent forward, her eyes on the floor as if she was someone who had just fainted. 'You see,' she said, 'everything you said about her . . . a divorced woman . . . you could say about me. The easy lay. The queer's escort. I mean however much you love me now, and however much you go on loving me, there just isn't time, is there, to be with two women as much as they's want to be with you?'

'It'll be easier,' said John, 'if I go into Parliament. I'll be away from home most evenings anyway.'

'Yes, of course. I could buy a house within the sound of the division bell – in Lord North Street or Smith Square. And you'll have excuses, won't you, for trips abroad? I mean it would be nice to go on holiday together some time . . .'

She looked up at him wistfully.

'Of course.' He knelt at her feet and took her hands into his. They were cold.

'And in twenty years people will point to me at parties and say: "That's Paula Gerrard. She's the Foreign Secretary's girl-friend. It's been going on for years." ' Her eyes were wet at the corners as if two tears had almost squeezed out of them, but there was also a trace of mischief in their expression and her voice as she went on took a harder tone. 'I won't be unique, will I? After all half the Labour leaders have mistresses who run their private offices. I'm sure the Tories do too, or is it just the sons of provincial noncomformists on the Labour side? At least that would put you in a good tradition.'

'How?'

'Wasn't your father a provincial noncomformist?'

'Yes. I suppose he was.'

'It's a good thing I'm rich,' she said, 'and don't need a husband to support me. Perhaps you'll give me a job? You'll need a secretary.'

'Of course,' said John. 'We can work out something like that so that in the end I'll spend more time with you than with any-one else.'

She smiled; then sighed. 'It's a pity, all the same, that we can't marry. I'd make such a good politician's wife.'

'I'd be sure to disappoint you. I don't have enough ambition to succeed.'

'I'll provide the ambition. I won't let you give up. You're exceptional – at least I think you are . . .' She spoke now in a high-pitched, slightly hysterical voice. 'I believe in you, perhaps because I love you; or I love you because I believe in you. It's so unfair.' She looked down at the floor again. 'You and Claire said some silly words to one another twelve years ago and signed some silly paper so you're hers and I can't have you: yet in my heart, as the poets say, I've said those words. I've signed more than a piece of paper. I told you, didn't I, that I'd never been in love before? Well it was true. I'd never loved anyone. I'd slept with people to see if all that pumping down here . . .' – she pointed to her groin – 'would somehow inflate the emotion but it didn't. So I decided that if I couldn't love one man I might as well love mankind and be a do-gooder in the prisons. You know where that got me. Nowhere. Nowhere at all. A little crook who thought I was kinky for rough trade.' She looked up at him. 'And then you. Distinguished, decent, a little pompous, but with good innocent ideals.' She put the palms of her hands onto his cheeks. 'You can't blame me for loving you. You're much, much nicer than the people I'd met before – rich or poor. Perhaps because you're neither. What a pity there's Clare. Never mind. We'll think about it later. Let's eat, now, or the quenelles will be spoiled. In fact they're probably ruined already.'

She stood up and they both went down to eat supper. Later they made love. Later still John went home to Clare. In the course of the evening there was no further mention of his marriage and John went quickly to sleep, pleased that he had managed things so well.

chapter nine

Paula's political intelligence proved accurate: the Prime Minister announced on 7 February that he would advise the Queen to dissolve Parliament. There would be a General Election three weeks later.

This news caused panic in Hackney and Haringey Labour Party. An emergency meeting was called of the Executive Committee to decide whether the Selection Conference, already brought forward to mid-February, should be brought forward again. All agreed that a candidate must be chosen at once; that the conference should be held that Saturday: but there was some disagreement as to whether the Executive Committee had the authority to do this, or whether it should summon a special meeting of the General Management Committee which would then authorize the new date for the Selection Conference. O'Grady's supporters argued that since the General Management Committee was the same as the Selection Committee it was absurd to summon it simply to have it summon itself. The Tribune Group saw the logic of this argument, but since it was put forward by O'Grady 's men and was supported by John's, they sniffed a fascist plot and insisted that it must all be done strictly according to the rules.

After three hours of argument they were outvoted, and the General Management Committee was summoned to select a candidate two days later at two o'clock in the afternoon on Saturday 9 February 1974. John, with Gordon's help, immediately started to draft his speech. This was not difficult to do because his own appreciation of the current crisis not only matched the advice from Transport House, it also suited the balanced tone he must strike if he was to win over delegates from both Left and Right. Only fanatic Conservatives, he argued, believed that the current industrial unrest was the fruit of a Communist conspiracy to subvert society. We socialists knew, from the 'bitter experience' of history, that the strike was the only weapon that the working man could use to better his material condition: that with it he had improved both his relative and absolute wealth. Certainly we were all against inflation; certainly we were all in favour of the law. But Parliament had no right, through a wages policy, to enslave the working classes by denying them the right to sell their labour for what they could get. It was against all natural justice to extend the liberty of the market place to the businessman and then deny it to the worker. 'If you select me,' he would conclude, 'I shall pursue to the best of my abilities those social, economic and political reforms which are proposed in our Party's manifesto. I do not ask to be your candidate as a favour, a privilege or a reward for anything I may or may not have done for the Labour Party in the past: I offer what convictions and abilities I possess so that our movement towards socialism in Great Britain may flourish in the future.'

Having typed out his speech with two fingers on a machine in his chambers, John had it approved by Gordon and then showed it to Clare, who ran her eyes over the text and said: 'Very good, darling,' as if it was Tom who was showing her his homework. The next day he asked Paula for her opinion. She read the speech three times before she made any comment and then went through it line by line. 'You don't want to seem too sanguine about strikes,' she said, 'because even people in the Labour Party are worried about the power of the unions.'

'I know,' said John, 'but they'll be voting for O'Grady anyway.'

'Shouldn't you be trying to win them over to your side?'

'Gordon divides the delegates into four groups. There are the old Tammany Hall Right; then the younger, Social Democratic Right; the reasonable Left; and the bigoted Left. My support is almost exclusively in the second group, so I've got to win over one of the other groups. To try and outdo O'Grady would be fatal; and suddenly to espouse Leon Trotsky might carry no conviction. It's the reasonable Left I have to go for . . .'

'Then perhaps you should say something about the National Enterprise Board. Isn't that a pet project of theirs?'

They went on like this long into the night – sitting at the kitchen table, not lying in bed. Paula had some knowledge of politics but little feel for the kind of people who made up the Labour Party. John was obliged to justify many nuances in his speech to which Paula made some objection, for in her new role as his political adviser she let nothing through. By the end of the evening, however, the speech was little changed and as John returned home exhausted he wondered if, in the end, he would not prefer Clare's indifference to Paula's committed interest.

Clare would not be deflected from doing her duty on the day itself. She had planned to go down to the cottage that weekend to make sure that there were no burst pipes after the cold weather, but she changed her plans and prepared to appear with her two children at her husband's side.

'What shall we wear?' she asked at breakfast. 'I mean should it be our Sunday best or rags?'

'Something in between,' said John. 'I'm wearing a corduroy suit.'

'Tweeds?'

'A bit county for the East End.'

'I've got a rather common skirt I bought at a sale. I'll wear that and a blouse and a jersey. And the children can wear jeans. I feel it's rather American, being a candidate's wife and children.'

After an early lunch they set off in the Volvo for Hackney. Tom sat silent and slightly sad because he too had wanted to go down to the cottage to try out a model aeroplane; but as they drove along the Marylebone Road both he and Anna cheered up and started to imitate their father practising his speech in front of the bathroom mirror.

Their high spirits calmed John's nerves; for although during the week he had doubted his whole venture into politics, now that it was upon him he was determined to succeed. He liked the feeling of dread and excitement in his stomach; and he liked the way that Gordon and a small group of supporters were waiting for him outside the Town Hall.

Gordon stepped forward to open his door.

'Can I leave the car here?' asked John.

'It should be OK,' said Gordon.

'I hope the rust will make up for it not being British,' said John.

'Don't worry,' said Gordon. 'Volvo components come from the Midlands.'

They went into the building and walked down a corridor towards the conference chamber. It was a little like acting in a film – some powerful, political drama. As he listened to the sound of their heels on the floor John almost heard martial music superimposed on the soundtrack and almost imagined a camera silently trailing him on rubber wheels. Clare and the children walked beside him – neat, attractive, a copywriter's dream. Tom and Anna were quiet now, in this strange place, and Clare wore a fixed bland smile. While Gordon and the others went into the meeting they sat with John as if all were waiting to see the dentist. Then Gordon came out again and took Clare and the children up to a public gallery.

John made his address to the Selection Conference, and so far as he could judge it was well received. He looked at no one in particular because each of the delegates' faces seemed in its own way alien to him – ugly, envious or dull. He smiled up at his wife and children, but even then it was a weak smile for fear that the delegates would intercept it and judge such a demonstration of affection as opportunistic electioneering. When he had finished, during the applause, he looked for Gordon's face in the audience to see if he could judge his success or failure from its expression: but he was not next to Clare in the gallery, and as he looked down towards the back of the hall instead of Gordon he saw Paula. Her black hair and dark eyes immediately distinguished her among the other dour faces. Again John gave a weak smile of recognition and she half-waved in return. John then began to wonder first how she had managed to get in to the conference, which was not a public meeting, and then whether her presence would prove awkward afterwards.

He was distracted from these thoughts by a question from the floor. A seedy-looking man with a Lenin/Ulbricht beard was on his feet. 'You offer your abilities and convictions to the socialist movement,' he said in a sneering tone of voice. 'I just wondered what these abilities and convictions are.'

John stood. 'My convictions are socialist convictions,' he began.

'But what are they?' the man shouted from his seat.

'I don't believe,' said John, 'that the state should own everything, as they do in the Soviet Union, but I do believe that the necessities of life should not be left to market forces; that the community should own or control enterprises upon which we all depend.'

'Including the banks?' a woman shouted from the back of the hall.

'I don't see why not. The French government, after all, owns banks. The question one should always ask is whether the nationalization of any particular concern will benefit the nation or not. I am not an ideological fanatic. I do not believe we should nationalize for the sake of it down to every grocer and fish and chip shop: but where there is a good case for nationalization – as there was in the past for toll roads, electricity, water, then health, then coal and steel, then parts of the motor industry, and now the aircraft industry, and possibly some drug companies – then I am in favour of it.'

He sat down. There was applause. He glanced up at Clare: she smiled. Then down at Paula beneath Clare. She smiled too. There was another question. He made another answer. There was an angry shout from the back: then the man with the Lenin/Ulbricht beard stood up again and said: 'You didn't tell us about your abilities, comrade.'

John stood again. 'My abilities are quite simply those of a barrister. I am trained to plead a case and I would like to plead the socialist case in the House of Commons. I do not overestimate my talents – or indeed the importance of any individual to our movement. All the same it is with laws that we shall improve our society, and a man with a legal training is better equipped than many others to frame those laws and take them through the House of Commons.'

There were murmurs of 'hear, hear' from the floor.

The *barbu* stood again. 'You wouldn't argue that the bourgeois members of the Labour Party have always acted to frustrate the socialist intentions of the working class . . .'

There were protests at this from different sides of the hall.

'I do not agree,' John shouted above the hubbub. 'All too often the socialist intentions of the Labour movement have been frustrated because our people in Parliament have been outwitted by the cunning of civil servants. Let me remind you, comrade, that Marx, Engels, Lenin and Fidel Castro all came from the middle classes, while Ramsay McDonald was the son of a crofter. What is more, this great movement of ours is doomed if it becomes the mouthpiece for bigoted working-class chauvinism, and I for one will never be a party to it.'

Applause, uproar, and the hammering of the chairman's gavel on the table. 'I think,' he said, 'that John's time is up, so if he will kindly step down and someone call Brother Patel.'

John left the platform and went out through the anteroom into the corridor. Gordon came out after him. 'That was good,' he said. 'You may have put up the backs of some of the Tribune people but you made a strong impression. You couldn't have done better.'

As he was speaking Paula came out through the same door just as Clare and the children came down the stairs from the gallery. Seeing them approach Paula quickly held out her hand to shake John's as if she was a casual admirer. 'Congratulations,' she said. 'I'm sure they'll choose you. I certainly would.' She smiled and moved on down the corridor. John opened his mouth to reply but at that moment Anna tugged at his sleeve saying: 'Weren't they rude, Daddy, shouting like that?'

They went out into the street. 'There's a café over there,' said Gordon. 'Not too posh, I'm afraid, but if you buy the kids an ice-cream and yourselves a cup of coffee, I'll bring you the news when it's all over.'

John did as he was told. Looking left and right as if afraid of a passing car he searched for Paula but she was not to be seen. They went into the café and ordered coffee and icecream. Clare sat at the yellow plastic table in an odd, upright position – she seemed afraid that the chair would dirty her clothes. When she came to drink her coffee she turned the cup so that the handle faced away from her and her lips would not have to touch that part of the china from which other customers had drunk before. Tom and Anna, on the other hand, attacked their icecream quite oblivious to their surroundings.

The Indian or Pakistani behind the counter looked at them mournfully. Does he know, John wondered, that I am the rival to his fellow-countryman, Patel? Or is it just that we look out of place?

'I suppose we'll have to come here quite a lot, will we, if you're selected?' asked Clare.

'*You* won't,' said John.

She smiled. 'I'm quite prepared to play my role,' she said. 'In fact I might get to like it. But I can't pretend that Hackney is my favourite part of the world.'

'I wouldn't have chosen it myself.'

'It's funny, isn't it? The poor parts of Paris or Rome have a certain charm, but in London they're just squalid. It's not just the dirt . . .' She squinted at the rim of her cup. 'It's more the

ugliness of everything. The excruciating bad taste . . .' She took
another sip. 'And in France the coffee at least is coffee. Not this
kind of indescribable liquid.' She shuddered.

John said nothing.

'Even the Americans have decent coffee, don't they?'

'You should have had tea.'

'Perhaps I should.'

They sat in silence.

'Who was that woman who came up to shake hands?' asked
Clare.

'One of the delegates.'

'Why didn't she wait to vote?'

'I don't know. Perhaps she wasn't a delegate.'

'She was very pretty, didn't you think?'

'I didn't notice.'

'And very well dressed.'

'I didn't see what she was wearing.'

'St Laurent. There can't be many women wearing St Laurent
creations in Hackney.'

'On the contrary,' said John. 'Most of my clients live in Hackney and their wives always dress in *haute couture.*'

'Perhaps that's what she was. A gangster's moll. She certainly
gave me a nasty look.'

John said nothing. The children finished their icecream. He
went to the counter and ordered two more dishes and another
cup of coffee for himself: as he went back to the table he saw
Gordon's beaming face at the door.

'You've done it, lad. Well done.' He took John by the hand.
'You're the official Labour Party candidate for the constituency
of Hackney and Haringey. Come back to the hall. They're all
waiting for you.'

chapter ten

Such is the pleasure of power and adulation that from the
moment he heard this news to the moment he returned home at

seven that evening John did not think of Paula: and when he did it was like suddenly remembering some irksome duty that was left undone.

He had half-promised, the day before, to go round to Purves Mews after the conference, but now he was so tired that he only wanted to lie on the sofa at home and watch gangster films on television. It was also difficult to think of an excuse for Clare: since he had just returned from Hackney and Haringey, and had given Gordon a lift to Bayswater, he could hardly pretend that he had a political engagement. He therefore muttered to Clare about going to an off-licence for some whisky and once on Holland Park Avenue went to a telephone box and called Paula.

'I'm sorry about this afternoon,' he said.

'About what?'

'Passing like strangers . . .'

'It wasn't your fault. I knew she'd be there. Anyway, what happened?'

'I won. I was selected.'

'Wonderful. Brilliant. I knew you would be. Are you coming round? I've got the champagne on ice.'

'Look I don't think I can. For one thing, I'm totally exhausted. For another I can't think of an excuse to get away.'

'No. I see. Anyway, you should celebrate with her. She's your wife.'

'I'm not going to celebrate with anyone. Certainly not with Clare. She'd much rather I hadn't won. I'm going to watch television and go to bed.'

'You must be tired,' she said in an ambiguous tone of voice. 'Those sort of things are very tiring. They strain your nerves. And you've got a lot ahead of you.'

'You don't mind if I don't come?'

'Not at all. I'll do the same as you. Watch TV and go early to bed.'

'I'll ring you tomorrow while Clare's at church.'

'All right.'

'And we'll meet on Monday evening.'

'Good. I'll keep the champagne. We can celebrate then.'

Later that evening Clare reminded John that the children's half-term began on the following Friday. 'What I thought,' she said, 'is that we'd send them up to Busey on Saturday with Guy.'

'Is he going up?'

'He will if I pay his fare.'

'What about you? Wouldn't you like to go?'

'Won't you need me here?'

'Not really, no. You've done your bit for the time being. Your next engagement's on election night.'

She looked away. 'In that case what I'll do is go down to the cottage on Saturday and see it's all OK, and then go straight up to Norfolk on Sunday.'

'You won't mind being on your own?'

'No. Not for a night. There are one or two things I want to do in the garden before spring starts. I'll be all right.'

On the following Monday morning John told his senior clerk that he had been selected to stand for Parliament and would like to cancel what engagements he could. He saw on the old man's face the contradictory emotions the news aroused in him – pride that someone from his chambers would soon be a Member of Parliament fighting confusion and embarrassment that it would not be as a representative of the Conservative interest. John's colleagues took much the same attitude. In calmer times they might have seen his socialism as a racy sop to intellectual fashion, but in February of 1974 they all shared the view that the Communists would use the Labour Party over the country.

He looked in at Purves Mews on his way home and told Paula about his family's plans for the weekend.

'I didn't know you had a cottage,' she said. 'Where is it?'

'In Wiltshire.'

'Whereabouts?'

'Near Hungerford.'

'I know that part quite well. I sometimes stay down there.'

'Who with?'

'The Templetons.'

'We're about half a mile from their front gate.'

'It's very nice round there . . .'

She took the champagne from the refrigerator and they drank to his triumph at Hackney, but neither could muster a jubilant mood: John had indigestion and Paula appeared unduly pensive. 'Does that mean,' she asked – referring back to Clare's trip to the cottage – 'that you'll be free at the weekend?'

'Both weekends and all through the week.'

'Will you spend the odd night here?'

'If you'd like me to, I don't see why I shouldn't. I can take the telephone off the hook at home and pretend it's out of order.'

'What would be nice,' said Paula, 'would be to go down to Prinnet for a short weekend.'

'I'd love to,' said John with somewhat artificial politeness.

'We could go down on Saturday afternoon and come back after lunch on Sunday. I'd like you to see it and meet my parents because somehow, until you do, I feel you don't know me properly.'

The week went quickly. On the Tuesday morning John went before the magistrates in Harrow to obtain a licence for a betting shop: it was granted, and with that case completed he was free until after the election. He drove across London to the Labour Party Committee Rooms in Hackney, ate a late lunch with the agent in a pub and spent the afternoon with him and other constituency workers planning the campaign. They decided upon a heavy canvass as well as a sequence of public meeting in schools and community centres.

He returned to the West End at nine, spent an hour with Paula and then went home. On Wednesday he was back in Hackney by nine in the morning, canvassed all day and spoke to a crowd of twenty-three people in the evening. On Thursday he had hoped to get back in time to dine with the Mascalls but he telephoned Clare at five to say she would have to go alone: another meeting had been arranged, and while it was unlikely to draw more than a dozen people it would be demoralizing for those who were working for his election if he cancelled it for a dinner party.

On the Friday he came home at teatime to see something of Tom and Anna before they left on their half-term holiday. Then as they went up to bed he felt a twinge of advance remorse as he thought of Clare in the cold cottage and himself with Paula in the sumptuous luxury of Prinnet Park. He therefore suggested that they go out to a film and then dine at a cheap local restaurant. Clare looked surprised at the suggestion but telephoned the baby-sitter and then went to fetch her coat.

The evening was not a success. There was a power cut at the cinema in the middle of the film; and because they arrived at the restaurant an hour before the time they had booked a table they had to wait on a cramped sofa by a so-called bar drinking unwanted aperitifs. When at length they were seated at a table John ordered *scampi à la provençale*, regretted it almost at once, and watched with ill-disguised envy as Clare ate a grilled sole. Nor could either think of much to say to one another: John's mind was on the election, which was of no interest to Clare, and Clare seemed equally preoccupied with something she appeared to think of just as little interest to John.

They went home, paid off the baby-sitter, looked at the children and went to bed. John made a dutiful gesture towards making love to his wife, but from her abrupt kiss it was apparent that she was not in the mood so they rolled away from one another and went to sleep.

chapter eleven

Prinnet Park bore little resemblance to the elegant, comfortable mansion of John's imagination; and Sir Christopher and Lady Gerrard were both quite unlike the urbane and charming people he had assumed Paula's parents to be. Certainly the house was large; it was at the end of a long drive; and there was a butler to open the door and take the suitcases out of the boot of Paula's car: but the neo-Gothic hallway and cold passages brought to John's mind a public school or a provincial art gallery – particularly the latter, since the walls were hung with Victorian paintings.

He followed Paula down one of the passages into a small living-room where an old man sat on a sofa with a piece of toast in his hand. When they entered he looked up, then down again at the toast, which he quickly crammed into his mouth. A woman rose from an armchair on the other side of the room and came towards John and Paula to greet them. It was immediately apparent that this was Paula's mother and that it was from her that Paula inherited her physical appearance.

'Mummy, this is John Strickland,' said Paula.

Lady Gerrard shook John by the hand, gave him a weak smile without actually looking into his eyes and then glanced over his shoulder towards the old man on the sofa. John turned to see the last morsel of toast disappear between his thin, wrinkled lips. He too rose to his feet and greeted his daughter's friend with a little curiosity in his eyes.

Lady Gerrard offered John some tea and when, out of politeness, he accepted seemed thrown into confusion. She rang a bell on the wall but remained standing next to it, saying with the trace of an American accent: 'He's sure to be upstairs now doing the rooms.'

'I'll get some cups,' said Paula.

'No, no,' said Lady Gerrard. 'You mustn't go into the kitchen just now.'

'Why not?'

'Mrs Greaves has a nap . . .'

'Don't be so ridiculous,' said Paula. She stalked out of the room with a black look on her face.

'Do you have . . . er . . . staff?' Sir Christopher asked John while wiping his fingers on his corduroy trousers.

'No,' said John. Sir Christopher was an old man – older than he had imagined.

'They're much more trouble than they're worth, really, but you can't live in a house like this without them.'

The room was cold. It seemed to be heated by only the single bar of an electric fire. The lights too were dim and the walls were hung with the same kind of large, dark Victorian paintings that John had seen in the hall.

'Do you like art?' asked Sir Christopher.

'Very much,' said John. 'Paula showed me the delightful little Renoir that you gave her for Christmas.'

'Rather nice, wasn't it? We used to have several of those Impressionist chaps – Renoir, Manet, Cézanne. Sold the lot in '66. Thought the market had reached its peak. Been proved wrong, of course, but you pay those fellows for advice so you might as well take it, what? They told me to go into this Victorian stuff. I bought almost anything that came on the market for two or three years but they haven't done very well since. One or two have gone up – that Tissot, for instance. I've a Leighton and an Albert Moore that are quite firm, but on the whole I'd have been better off in equities.'

'They still add up to an . . . impressive collection,' said John.

'Do you think so? I'm blind to that sort of thing. But one's got to hang something on the wall.'

Paula returned with two teacups and a silver pot filled with hot water. 'I don't know why you don't sack that old bag,' she said to her mother.

'I hope you didn't upset her, darling . . .'

'I didn't upset her. I just woke her up, that's all.'

'She's entitled to have a nap . . .'

Paula sat down and poured out two cups of tea. She gave John a forced smile as she handed one of them to him as if to conceal her ill-humour. 'It's weak and tepid, I'm afraid,' she said, 'but it's the best we can do.'

At six o'clock the butler came in to take away the tea tray. A moment later he returned with another tray laden with glasses, bottles and ice. Sir Christopher gave a glass of sherry to his wife, whisky to John and Paula, and then poured half a tumbler of pink gin for himself. 'You're standing for Parliament, aren't you?' he said to John.

John blushed. 'Yes,' he said.

'For the Labour Party?'

'Yes.'

'You're probably right. If you can't beat 'em, join 'em.' He sat down and looked sadly into his glass.

'Is anyone coming to dinner?' Paula asked her mother.

'No, dear. Not tonight.'

'Are you going to change?'

'We will, but you needn't.'

'We might as well.' Paula turned to John. 'Do you mind?'

'Not at all.'

Paula showed him to his room, where the butler had unpacked his suitcase and had laid out his evening clothes. 'I'm miles away at the other end of the house,' she said. 'But don't worry about later. I'll creep along when the coast's clear.'

She left him to take a bath and change. The room was non-descript and cold. John felt the radiators. They were tepid, so he switched on the small electric fire. It surprised him that such a rich family as the Gerrards should live in such discomfort: he had assumed that because Paula's house was warm and comfortable her parents' home would demonstrate the same qualities magnified by their greater age and importance; but he realized now that the rich are often mean, and so are the old; and that children's habits are often in reaction to those of their parents.

He lay in the bath. Why, he wondered, had Paula wanted him to meet her parents and see her home when both were so singularly dull? Had she hoped that this drab mansion would impress him? Or had she thought to draw him closer to her by exposing the loneliness and poignancy of her home life? How extraordinarily different some things are, he thought to himself, from what we imagine. Six weeks before, while in his mother's house in Yorkshire, he would have sold his soul to the Devil to spend a weekend with Paula in Prinnet Park. Now he longed only to be back in his own home in Holland Park with the Underground thundering beneath the foundations and the children squabbling in the kitchen. The very thought of his family produced a pang of homesickness like that in a twelve-year-old boy on his first day at boarding school; and just as that boy looks forward to the last day of term, John fixed his mind on the Sunday in eight days' time when he would see them all again.

He went downstairs wearing his evening clothes. Sir Christopher was waiting for him wearing a moth-eaten green smoking jacket. Later Lady Gerrard came in wearing a dress which seemed to John like an original creation of Dior's 1947 New Look. Paula appeared last in a long woollen skirt and a blue blouse. 'Christ this house is cold,' she said, shivering as she came in the door.

'Only the government can keep themselves warm these days,' her father muttered with an apologetic look towards John.

'I dare say it's expensive to heat a house this size,' said John.

'The truth is,' said Paula, helping herself to a glass of whisky,

214

'that my father hates to spend money when he could invest it. Isn't that true, Daddy?'

Sir Christopher smiled uneasily but did not reply.

The food at dinner was cool and bad. Perhaps the cook was punishing Paula for disturbing her afternoon sleep. The wine, however, was good, and every now and then, when the butler was out of the room, Sir Christopher would leap up from his seat and fill everyone's glass. Lady Gerrard, who drank as much as her husband or daughter, seemed unaffected by the alcohol. She made stilted, formal conversation throughout the evening, and when John asked her about her childhood in America she drew herself up as if this was a gaffe – as if she had hoped to conceal her transatlantic origins and pass herself off as the daughter of an English duke.

At the end of dinner the ladies withdrew. John and Sir Christopher remained behind in the dining-room and drank a decanter of port. It was as good as the wine that had gone before: Sir Christopher seemed prepared to spend his money on this variety of fuel and he talked about the different wines he had stored in his cellar with more affection and discernment than had been apparent earlier in his talk about art. By the time they went through to sit with the two women in the drawing-room both men were drunk. Sir Christopher had to lean on the jamb of each doorway as he passed through, and he crossed the passages as if staggering on stepping-stones over a swollen torrent. John found it hard to control the muscles of his face and so slurred his speech.

Paula and her mother were watching show-jumping on television, and when the men returned showed no inclination to turn it off. John and Sir Christopher therefore turned two arm-chairs to face the set, and in a few moments the older man was asleep and the younger one hard pressed to keep his eyes open. At half past ten the parents went to bed: half an hour after that John and Paula followed.

With a great effort of will John brushed his teeth and, fumbling with the buttons, took off his clothes and changed into his pyjamas. He then got into bed but left the lamp on, waiting for Paula. His head was still swirling from the wine and port: he found it impossible to keep his eyes open and so was half-asleep when he heard the door open and then shut again. He saw Paula's hand switch off the lamp. He tried to raise himself from the bed but the same hand moved to his shoulder and pushed him down. She got into bed under the blankets. She was naked and cold. He felt her hand unbutton his pyjamas and take them from his body like a nurse with a sick patient. He tried to rise again but again she pushed him down. She lay on top of him, her legs astride his loins. In the gloom from the moon outside he could just make out her face and dark, wide-open eyes. He felt her breath on his face. She groaned and bit the skin on his neck. When he fell asleep she still lay like a leech on top of him.

chapter twelve

They returned to London after lunch on Sunday. John dropped Paula at Purves Mews, then drove on in her Lancia to his own house in Holland Park. Paula had advised him to stay there that night in case Clare telephoned from Busey. He therefore put the telephone back on its receiver. Some time later, he was telephoned by his mother-in-law, Helen Lough.

'John. Is that you?'

'Yes.'

'There's something wrong with your telephone. It sounds engaged but it isn't.'

'The children had left it off the hook upstairs.'

'I see. Well, is Clare there?'

'No. Isn't she with you?'

'She said she was going to leave the car in London for you and catch the train that leaves about twelve, but she wasn't on it and she wasn't on the next one either.'

'Did you ring the cottage?'

'Yes. There's no reply.'

'And she didn't ring you?'

'No. And Eustace has been in all day.'

'Perhaps your telephone is out of order.'

'No it isn't. Joyce Sewell rang twice this afternoon.'

'It's a mystery. The Volvo isn't here, so perhaps she decided to drive all the way.'

'She told me you'd need the car in London.'

'We certainly agreed that she'd leave it here.'

'I hope she hasn't had an accident.'

'I'll look into it,' said John, 'and ring you later on.'

John put down the telephone and immediately picked it up again to ring the Thames Valley Police. He asked if there had been any accident that day involving a yellow Volvo station-wagon. When told that there had been none he became anxious that Clare might have fallen down the stairs or electrocuted herself at the cottage. He tried to think of friends or neighbours who might be down in Wiltshire on a Sunday night in February, but eventually made up his mind that it would be simpler if he drove down himself in the Lancia to set his mind at rest.

He left at seven and reached the cottage a little more than an hour later. There were two cars parked in the courtyard – the yellow Volvo and a blue Ford Cortina. Lights shone from the sitting-room windows and from the windows of their bedroom upstairs. John parked the Lancia next to the Volvo and went to the back door. It was not locked so he walked in, calling Clare's name. No one answered. He went through to the living-room. The lights were on but the fire was dead. He called again, and again no one answered. He was about to leave the room when he noticed that one of the curtains in front of the French windows was half torn from its runner. He went towards the door and saw framed by the curtains a naked figure leaning motionless against the glass as if staring out into the garden. There was a black hole the size of a grapefruit beneath the right shoulder and a black line of blood led down to the thigh. It was Clare, dead, her buttocks resting on her heels, her breasts flat like limpets against the panes of glass. Both arms dangled at her side.

He stood quite still with no immediate emotion but fear. He listened and then with speed and lightness of a ballet dancer he darted towards the door; but before he reached it he realized that the blood was black and dry. She had been there for some time. He therefore went back to look at her body. He could not bring himself to touch it and since her forehead leant against the glass door he was unable to see the expression on her face. He studied the wound in her back: there were pellets and fragments of white bone amidst the red flesh. It seemed clear that she had been killed by a shotgun at close range.

John left Clare's body propped against the door and went to the foot of the stairs. Light shone down from the bedroom. He went up to find evidence of what had happened and saw first that the blankets had been dragged from the bed, and that the sheets were rumpled, as if a struggle had taken place there; then he noticed clothes scattered on the floor – a man's and a woman's mixed together. The man's clothes were not his, nor did he recognize the clean silk underclothes edged with expensive lace as any of those which had belonged to Clare. For a moment he felt that he had been mistaken – that it was not Clare's body down below – but then, beside a new silk petticoat, he recognized a dark blue blouse and a black skirt, both of which were hers. He moved farther into the room, and now his eye fell upon another figure, also naked, lying on the floor between the bed and the wall. He went closer. The body was that of a man but the head was half blown away and John looked at the black hair on the chest, and then at the grizzled genitals, as if they would somehow identify the corpse. He thought at first that it was someone he did not know, and only when he looked back at the head and saw the snarl on what was left of the lips did he recognize the body of Henry Mascall.

He looked around the room. Everything else was as they had left it last time they were there. He fixed his eyes on the wallpaper, studying the joints where years before he had failed to match the pattern. Then, as his brain began to make sense of the things his eyes had seen, he started to sway. He staggered back towards the stairs, giddy with anger, fear, sadness and jealousy, and sat down on the first step. He did not want to see again the body that had betrayed him: the thought that her cold thighs had been seen and caressed by another man led jealousy to triumph over grief and he thought of the dead man on the floor with an expression of momentary delight.

But then from legal reflex he realized that if a woman is found murdered with her lover the husband is usually the murderer. Fear now usurped revenge, and John started to consider if he could account for his time between Clare's departure from London and his arrival at the cottage in sufficient detail to remove all suspicion that he had killed them. He could rely upon Paula and her parents to confirm that he was at Prinnet Park until after lunch on Sunday; and his mother-in-law would vouch for his presence at Holland Park when she telephoned him that evening: but what if they had died in the middle of the afternoon when, by driving fast, he could have killed them? Or that very evening, shortly he arrived? He had seen so many alibis destroyed in court that he suddenly doubted his own. He must go to Paula. She would swear that she had never left him – that they had been together all week-end. He went downstairs, and leaving the house just as he found it, set off back to London.

As he was driving on the motorway past Heathrow Airport John remembered when he and Clare had last flown to France and he burst into tears. Then, because fear was still his dominant emotion, he became afraid that if Paula saw he was sorry about Clare she might not provide an alibi for the hours since they had parted that afternoon. When he reached Purves Mews he parked her car behind a white Ford Escort a short way from her house and waited in the dark until he had regained his self-possession.

It was after ten at night, but there was still a light in the upstairs sitting-room, so John let himself into the kitchen and crossed in the dark to the spiral staircase. When he reached the top he was dazzled for a moment by the light. Paula stood when she saw him, but another figure of a younger man remained sitting on the sofa.

'I'm sorry,' John said, 'I didn't know . . .'

'Come in,' she said. 'It's only Terry. He was passing . . .'

Struck now with this evidence that not only had his wife betrayed him and been murdered with her lover, but his mistress was now entertaining the former lover she had sworn never to see again, John staggered like a ham actor acting out such a melodrama on the stage. He put one hand on the familiar drinks table to prop up his body and prevent it from falling.

Terry Pike stood up. His face was without expression. 'Evening, guv',' he said.

'I'd better go,' said John.

'Don't be silly,' said Paula.

'I'm the one that's got to scarper,' said Terry. His lips moved slightly – a flickering smile.

John's knees felt funny: he sat on the arm of the sofa.

'Where's m'bag?' asked Terry.

'Here,' said Paula. She handed him a blue canvas hold-all.

'Be seeing you,' said Terry.

Paula did not reply. John noticed Terry wink at her before he disappeared down the stairs.

'You promised . . .' he croaked.

'You look awful,' said Paula. 'Come and sit down by the fire.'

'You promised you'd never see him again.'

'He was passing. That was all.'

'Then why did he bring in his things?'

'What things?'

'He had an overnight bag.'

She shrugged her shoulders. 'Oh I dare say he hoped to stay the night. I dare say he hoped for a quick fuck for old times' sake.' She smiled. 'But I'd have thrown him out whether you'd turned up or not. Now tell me what's happened and I'll get you a drink.'

Part five

chapter one

When John awoke the next morning to the scent of coffee he wondered first why Clare had got up before him; then why the children were not bouncing on his bed. He looked for the clock on his bedside table, and only when he saw the unfamiliar lampstand did he remember where he was and all that had happened the day before. He shut his eyes again and plunged his face back into the pillow as if he could go back to sleep and there bring his nightmare to a different ending.

He could not sleep. The ugly image of Clare's corpse propped against the French windows made his heart thump in his own ears; the thought of Henry Mascall's naked body on their bed twisted the nerves in his stomach. He then remembered his children, Clare's parents, Paula and Terry Pike and the Hackney and Haringey Labour Party and he thrust his face still deeper into the pillow as if to suffocate himself and obliterate all conscious thoughts.

He heard a sound next to the bed. He imagined at once that it was the police, but he heard Paula gently call his name. He turned and opened his eyes.

'Are you awake?' she asked.

'Yes,' he said, sitting up in bed, 'but I wish to God I wasn't.'

She was carrying a tray upon which coffee and milk, toast, marmalade, butter and a boiled egg were laid out on a white tablecloth. 'I've brought you some breakfast,' she said.

'I'm not sure I can eat anything.'

'You must,' she said. 'And I'll give you another Valium. It'll calm you down.'

He took the tray on to his knee and she went to her dressing-table for the pill she had promised. She watched him like a nurse as he swallowed it with his coffee, then sat down at the end of the bed.

'Listen,' she said. 'You were in such a state of shock last night that there was nothing to be done, but this morning we must make some quick decisions . . .'

'I know,' said John.

'The first thing is to ring the police. Tell them what's happened; tell them that you were down there last night; and arrange to meet them there today.'

'You said last night that you'd support my alibi.'

'I will if you really want me to, but I'm convinced it would be a mistake to lie. First Terry knows that for an hour, anyway, we weren't together and I dread to think what use he might make of that. Secondly someone might have seen the Lancia at your cottage.'

'Perhaps you're right.'

'Above all I think it's stupid to lie when there's no need.'

'But they must suspect me . . .'

'Nonsense. You said the blood was dry. That means that they must have been killed some time before you got there.'

'Yes.'

'Well you were at Prinnet until after lunch on Sunday. Then I was with you until four. You couldn't have got to your cottage more than an hour before you did.'

'No. But they might think that you had conspired with me . . .'

'No. I've thought of that. You might conspire with a mistress to kill a wife, but not a wife and lover. Anyway the Greaves live above the garage at Prinnet. They'd have heard you start the car.'

John sighed. 'I hope you're right.'

'Now do you have a solicitor?'

'I know quite a few but I don't have one in particular.'

'Good, because I rang Sir Peter Craxton, who is Daddy's solicitor, and he's coming here on his way to the office.'

'I'd better get dressed.'

'He'll be here in about half an hour.'

'Shall I ring the police now?'

'No. Wait until he gets here.'

John put the tray on to the bedside table. 'It's very good of you to see to all these things. 'I'm not sure I'd be up to it myself.'

She looked at him with a fierce affection. 'You've had a most awful shock. It would knock anyone out for a month in normal circumstances, but we don't have a month because there's the election in a fortnight's time and we mustn't let this horrible . . . accident get in the way of that.'

'But I'll have to withdraw.'

'No. You mustn't. If you do, not only will it look as if you did kill your wife. You will also never get another chance. As it is you're lucky to get a safe seat . . .'

'But no one will vote for a murder suspect.'

'You're not a murder suspect and you never will be. When the police know where you were, and who can provide your alibi, they won't suspect you; and if you're not a suspect you become an object of sympathy – that is, if the news gets out before the election.'

'It must get out.'

'Perhaps, but Sir Peter is very good at that sort of thing.'

'What?'

'Stopping things getting into the papers.'

'I can't see how I can make speeches . . .'

'You must,' said Paula vehemently, 'not just for the sake of your career but for the sake of your sanity. If you don't you'll turn into a morose vegetable. Think of your children. You must do it for them.'

'You don't really understand.'

She stood, came forward, and sat again next to him. She took his hand into hers and stroked the wrinkled skin and bumpy, protruding veins. 'I know I'm young,' she said, 'and that I am what you would call an interested party, but I do understand much more than you think. I know that you loved Clare and that it has hurt you very badly not just that she was murdered in such a dreadful way but that she died with a lover . . . I won't pretend that I'm glad you loved her, and that now you're jealous and sorry, but that has never stopped me loving you, and because I love you I'm determined to help you until you're over it, or over it enough to manage yourself. Then, if you like, I'll go away and you can live alone or marry someone else; but now I think you need me and I can help you so please, please let me.'

He looked up into her youthful, beatific face and hard, innocent eyes. 'Of course,' he said. 'Of course. I couldn't cope . . . just now . . . alone.'

chapter two

Sir Peter Craxton, the Gerrards' family solicitor, drove John down in his Daimler to the cottage where five or six men were already at work like a team of energetic decorators – dusting down the door handles and taking photographs of the bodies. Clare's corpse looked less terrible in daylight: afraid that it would seem prurient if he studied closely, John glanced at it out of the corner of his eye. There were black patches on her buttocks where the heels dug in to support them, and her hair had been parted and swept forward over her shoulders to reveal a small black hole in the back of the neck. One hand was covered with dried blood, and there was blood beneath it on the floor – a small, sticky pool, and beside it two streaks at right-angles to one another.

On the other side of the room his suave solicitor was talking to two other men. They came towards him. 'John,' said Sir Peter (who seemed to assume that he must be on Christian-name terms with any friend of the Gerrards), 'this is Detective Inspector Thompson and this is Detective Sergeant Simms – both of the Wiltshire CID.'

John shook hands with each of the policemen.

'I've told them,' Sir Peter went on, 'that you're quite prepared to answer any questions in my presence.'

'Of course,' said John.

'We have to warn you, sir,' said Thompson – a plump, pink-faced man more like a farmer than a policeman – 'that anything you say may be used in evidence . . .'

'Mr Strickland is a barrister,' said Sir Peter. 'He knows the Judges' Rules.'

The four men went through to the kitchen and sat down at the table. It was still covered with the debris of an intimate dinner for two – two candles, two plates with the peel of tangerines, two wineglasses, one still half-full; a third glass with a bottle of brandy beside it and the butt of a thick cigar stubbed out in an ashtray. The Detective Sergeant made a space for his notebook, and while Thompson asked questions both he and Sir Peter took notes – the latter on the pages of his pocket diary.

It was straightforward interrogation to establish that this was John's cottage; that Clare was his wife; that she had come there (to his knowledge) alone while he had gone to Prinnet Park with Miss Paula Gerrard; that he had been in Miss Gerrard's company from midday on Saturday until four o'clock on Sunday afternoon; that he had been telephoned at home by his mother-in-law; as a result of this call he had become anxious; had telephoned the Thames Valley Police to inquire about accidents; had driven to the cottage in Miss Gerrard's car; had found his wife murdered; had driven back to London.

'Can you tell me, sir,' asked the Detective Inspector, 'why you did not call us in last night?'

John blushed and glanced at Sir Peter, who nodded as if to say: 'Tell the truth.'

'I was shocked and . . . frightened.'

'Of the murderer?'

'No. I realized that he must have gone but I thought . . . I thought that you might think that I had killed them.'

The Sergeant wrote down this reply.

'Why did you think that?'

John shrugged his shoulders. 'I couldn't think who else would have a motive.'

'Did you kill them?'

'No.'

Thompson now made a gesture to Simms not to write down what he was about to say. 'It may reassure you to know, sir, that your wife and the gentleman upstairs were killed between ten and twelve on Saturday night.'

'So if you can establish, as of course you can,' said Sir Peter, 'that you were with the Gerrards on Saturday night, you can hardly be considered a suspect.'

'You were at Prinnet Park, were you?' asked the Inspector. His Sergeant was taking notes again.

'Yes.'

'All night?'

'Yes.'

'What time did you go to bed?'

'At about eleven.'

'Did anyone see you between the time you went to bed and the next morning?'

John felt himself blush again. 'Paula . . . that is, Miss Gerrard . . . we spent the night in the same bed.'

Sir Peter nodded at this satisfactory reply, and Detective Inspector Thompson seemed content for the time being. He asked John if he would formally identify the bodies. The four of them went first to the bedroom, where a blanket had been put over Henry's corpse.

Thompson drew it back from the face blasted by the shotgun. 'That is Henry Mascall, is it?' he asked.

'Yes,' said John.'

'Are you sure? There isn't much left of the face.'

'I'm quite sure.'

'Do you happen to know his home address and next of kin?'

'His wife is called Mary Mascall.' John gave her address in the Boltons and then her telephone number. The Sergeant wrote down what he said in his notebook.

'You knew him quite well, then?' said Thompson.

'Yes,' said John. 'He was one of my closest friends.'

'Will you inform his wife?'

'I'd rather not.'

The four men now went downstairs. 'That's blood,' said the Detective Sergeant, Simms, to John – pointing to black stains on the staircarpet.

'It looks as if your wife was shot in the bedroom,' said Thompson. 'I would have said that the gentleman was shot first, then your wife seems to have dodged them but got the second barrel here on the stairs. She then must have tried to escape through the garden door, but whoever it was caught up with her and shot her in the back of the neck with a revolver.'

They came into the sitting-room.

'How did they get into the house?' asked Sir Peter.

'We think through that window.' Thompson pointed across the room. 'There are footprints in the flowerbed outside.'

'Of how many men?'

'Only one, but he might have let another in the back door.' He turned to John. 'Can you tell me, offhand, if anything's been stolen, sir?'

'Not that I've noticed.'

'You didn't have any silver or valuable paintings?'

'No. Just the gramophone and television, which are still there.'

Thompson nodded and crossed to Clare's body, removed a sheet which covered it, and pulled it gently back from the door. It was like a statue and John saw for the first time how her eyes had rolled round to stare into her skull.

'Is this your wife?' asked Thompson.

'Yes.'

The Inspector propped the body back against the door.

'Who can have done it?' asked John.

Thompson shrugged his shoulders. 'Probably thieves, sir. It isn't likely to have been Mrs Mascall, is it?'

John shook his head. 'No. She wasn't jealous.'

'It looks to me as if thieves broke in, thinking it was empty, and then panicked when they found your wife and Mr Mascall.'

'But petty thieves don't carry shotguns and revolvers,' said John.

'On the up and up,' said Simms.

'Especially Londoners,' said Thompson.

'But here,' said John. 'A naked man and woman. They could have just run away. And to pursue Clare down the stairs like that and shoot her in the back of the neck . . .'

'I agree with you, sir,' said Thompson. 'It is a little strange. We thought at first that your wife might have recognized the killer.'

'Why?'

'Well look at her finger, and the mark in blood on the floor.' He stepped forward and pointed to the two smears of dried blood which crossed one another on the polished wood. 'It looks as if she was starting to write something.'

'It's like half an H, isn't it?' said Sir Peter.

'Or a T,' said Thompson.

'Or a J,' said Simms.

'If she knew she was going to die,' said John, 'it may be the sign of the Cross. She was . . . religious.'

Behind him the Sergeant guffawed.

chapter three

Later that morning John returned to London with Sir Peter Craxton and then took the train for Norwich and Cromer. When he arrived at Busey in a taxi the children were already asleep in bed. He sat in the kitchen and told Eustace and Helen about their daughter's death – explaining too how Henry had been found dead in her bed and how he had been at Prinnet Park with Paula Gerrard.

True to his legal training he gave them the facts and made no special pleading either for Clare's behaviour or his own. Yet as he spoke he saw on Helen's face that the information about her daughter's adultery came as a far greater shock than the news of the death itself. Her expression, which at first had been one of grief and resignation – as 'if hearing what every parent fears yet half-expects to hear – then turned to one of utter horror and despair. She turned to Eustace, who took her hand as if to stem the breach in her self-possession: then he asked John to go on, and John, with a sudden understanding of what meant most to his mother-in-law, described the cross of blood on the floor.

'And you say she was kneeling?' asked Helen in a hoarse, impatient whisper.

'Yes. She was kneeling beside a sign of the Cross.'

It was easier, the next morning, to tell Tom and Anna that their mother was dead – first because John felt he need only say that she had been killed by 'bad men'; and second because children take the gravity and significance of news they cannot quite comprehend from the mood of the adult who imparts it, and John – drugged on Paula's Valium – was calm and carefree.

After breakfast – before he returned to London – Eustace came to him like Joseph of Arimathea to ask if Clare could be buried in the churchyard at Busey. 'I think it would make Helen happy,' he said, 'to have her near at hand.'

'Of course,' said John. 'Of course. In fact I'd be grateful if you could arrange the funeral. I must get back to the election.'

'Will you still stand?'

'Yes. I think I must.'

Eustace nodded. 'I suppose you're right. Life must go on.

He spoke this last phrase in an ambiguous tone: John looked to see how he meant it but his father-in-law was already shuffling towards the door of his bedroom.

At Norwich station John bought all the morning papers, and on the train back to London looked through their columns for some mention of the murders. There was none. At Liverpool Street Station he telephoned Gordon. They met twenty minutes later in the lobby of the Great Eastern Hotel, where John explained to his friend what had happened. It was clear, though left unsaid, that Gordon had never cared for Clare, so he was brief in his expression of sympathy: if he then leant forward in his chair and rubbed his face in his hands it was more a mannerism to help him think than any gesture of condolence or grief.

'Should I withdraw?' asked John.

'I don't know. Let me think.' He paused. 'You're sure you're not a suspect?'

'Fairly sure. I was in Sussex.'

'Reliable witnesses?'

'Yes.'

'In which case it becomes a private tragedy which might win you some sympathy votes.'

'It's too squalid for that.'

Gordon nodded. 'I suppose it is. The *News of the World* will have a field day.'

'It may be kept out of the press.'

'How?'

'The Gerrards' solicitor is acting for me. He evidently has some influence.'

'Who is he?'

'Sir Peter Craxton.'

Gordon laughed. 'Yes. He also acts for several newspapers.'

'What do you think, then? Should I withdraw or go on?'

'I think you should go on. The posters have been printed. They've advertised the meetings. It would be a disaster for the constituency if you withdrew now. Yes. I should go on. When all is said and done, it's a private affair. It's none of their business.'

'I may be a little off form . . .'

'You seem very much in control,' said Gordon, 'for a man

231

whose wife was murdered two days ago: but then I always knew you had guts behind that smooth barrister banter. That's why I backed you in the first place.'

From the Great Eastern Hotel John went straight to Hackney, where he told the agent only that his wife had been killed and that he did not want it known until after the election. 'I want to fight it on the issues,' he said, 'and not have them muddied by tragedy in my private life.' He spoke that night at a meeting where he was heckled by members of the National Front. Paula met him afterwards and drove him back to Purves Mews in the Lancia.

It was not until the Wednesday afternoon that John went back to his own home in Holland Park to fetch some clothes. In the green light of the late afternoon he hurried upstairs to his bedroom, looking neither to right nor left, as if running the gauntlet of tormenting poltergeists. In the bedroom he paused. It was unduly still. He went to the wardrobe to fetch a suitcase and saw on the chair a heap of Clare's clothes – a skirt, two blouses and a pair of faded underpants and tights which she had peeled off in one piece. He took out a suitcase and then sat on the bed and wept.

After crying like this he felt it less urgent to leave the house again. He went down to the kitchen, turned up the heating and made himself some tea. He felt hungry. There was some stale, sliced bread in the bin which he made into toast. The butter in the refrigerator was a little rancid but he smothered it with honey. When he had eaten one slice and was about to start another the telephone rang and he answered it.

'John?' It was a woman's voice he did not recognize.

'Yes?'

There was a pause. 'I want to see you.'

'Who is it?'

'Mary.'

Now he hesitated. 'All right. When?'

'Now.'

'Come round. I'll be here.'

She rang off and John returned the telephone to its cradle on the wall. He was then about to return to his tea and toast when there was a knock on the basement door. He opened it and Guy entered.

'I was passing,' he said. 'I saw you were in.'

'Come and have some tea.'

Guy went to sit at the table while John filled the teapot with hot water and put some more bread in the toaster.

'I'm sorry about Clare,' said Guy.

'Did Helen tell you?'

'Dad, actually. He rang up. I knew it was something big. He never usually uses the phone.'

John returned to the table and poured his brother-in-law a cup of tea.

'Who did it? Do they know?' asked Guy.

John shrugged his shoulders. 'It must have been burglars . . .'

'A bit heavy for burglars, wasn't it?'

'I would have thought so.'

'What about Mary? Perhaps she went berserk?'

'She's coming round in a minute.'

'She could handle a shotgun.'

John shook his head. 'Whoever did it gave Clare a *coup de grâce* with a revolver. I can't see Mary doing that . . . or having a revolver in the first place.'

'No.'

John looked at Guy, who now reminded him of Clare. 'We weren't as unhappy as it must seem,' he said.

'I know,' said Guy. 'I guess marriage isn't easy.'

Although Guy said 'I guess' like an American, and was dressed in the usual scrupulously scuffed denim, John was not irritated by his presence; indeed he felt an unusual affection for him. 'In all this,' he said to him, 'the only thing I regret . . . Well, I regret it all, but much of it's my own fault. I wasn't faithful to Clare, as you know, so I shouldn't be upset that she was unfaithful to me, but I am. I shouldn't be upset that it was Henry because I knew what he was like -- he never pretended to be otherwise – but I am. But what is almost the worst thing about it all is that Clare was killed with him, because Helen must think that she's in Hell.'

'She doesn't,' said Guy, 'because of that story about the sign of the Cross in blood.'

'It wasn't a story,' said John.

'I though you'd made it up.'

'It might not have been a sign of the Cross. The police thought she was trying to write a name . . .'

'It's given Mum something to hang on to.'

'Let her believe it, then.'

'I'd like to believe it too.'

John looked at him in surprise. 'I was never sure how seriously you or Clare took your religion.'

Guy shrugged his shoulders. 'It varies. She went to mass on Sundays, didn't she?'

'Only after we had children . . .' The doorbell rang upstairs. 'That'll be Mary.'

'Do you want me to go away?' asked Guy.

'I'd rather you stayed.'

Guy remained sitting at the kitchen table while John went up to the front door. He opened it and Mary stalked in out of the dark. 'You might have told me yourself,' she said without looking at him.

'I couldn't face it.'

'It wasn't very nice, coming from a policeman who obviously thought I'd done it.'

'I'm sure he didn't.'

She turned and in the light of the hall John could see from her blotched face and red eyes that she had been crying.

'I'm sorry,' he said. 'I should have come.'

Mary started sniffing. 'Oh don't let's quarrel. It's all so squalid already without that.' She looked towards the stairs. 'Can we go up?'

'Come down to the kitchen. Guy's there.'

She sniffed again. 'Guy? Oh yes. I don't mind him. What's so hellish about this sort of thing is the way people come hanging around. Mummy won't leave the house. She thinks I'm going to kill myself.'

She went down to the kitchen, greeted Guy with a sniff and a smile, and sat down next to him at the kitchen table.

'Do you want some tea?' asked John.

'No. Scotch.'

'I'll get it,' said Guy.

He left the room and John stood propped against the kitchen sink. 'Did you know they were having an affair?' he asked.

She gave a short, nervous burst of laughter. 'I knew he was interested. I think it was mainly to get at you. Your standing for Parliament annoyed him . . .' She waved her hand dismissively.

'I had no idea.'

'I knew he was going to see someone. Whenever he said he was coming back from Frankfurt or Jedda on a Monday I knew he'd be stopping off with some tart for the weekend.' She saw John wince. 'I'm sorry. Clare wasn't a tart. It was probably her first time, wasn't it?'

'I don't know. I never thought she'd be unfaithful.'

Mary laughed again: another neurotic bark. 'I never thought she'd sleep with Henry.'

'Nor did I.'

'Friendship doesn't count for much these days.'

'No.'

Guy returned with the bottle of whisky. John poured a double measure into three glasses and added water from the kitchen tap.

'What have you told your children?' Mary asked.

'Just that she's been killed.'

'Same here, but they're bound to find out sooner or later. In fact I can't understand why it hasn't been in the papers. I've been waiting to see "Socialist's wife shot in love-nest with merchant banker" since it happened.'

'I hope it won't get into the papers.'

'But what do we tell our friends?'

'The truth.'

'Then it's bound to get out.'

'In the end.'

'But not until after the election. Is that it?'

'Yes.'

'Well I can't say I blame you. Life must go on. The only thing is I don't quite see how mine will go on . . .'

'Well . . .' John could think of nothing to say.

'Henry was a swine,' said Mary, 'but I relied on him.'

'I know,' said John.

'Perhaps you'll take me out now and then?'

'Of course.'

'Except you've got that bitch Paula Gerrard, haven't you?'

'Yes.'

She gulped down her whisky. 'There's always Micky,' she said, standing. 'I must get back. Children's bath-time. I just wanted to see you. What are you doing tonight?'

'I . . .'

'Of course. You mustn't neglect your alibi.'

'I didn't kill them.'

'No, I know. Nor did I. What about you?' She turned to Guy.

'What?'

'Are you free tonight?'

'Sure.'

'Let's go to a film.'

'OK.'

'Come round later . . . at about eight.'

Looking happier she left the kitchen. John followed her up the stairs to the front door. 'It's boring, isn't it,' she said, 'being a cuckold like that for everyone to see? If he'd been killed in a plane crash, that would be one thing. But this is just squalid. I'm sorry. It's just as bad for you. Except you've got that bitch. Well, I'll see you later. No I won't. I'll see Guy. Don't worry, I won't eat him.' She leaned forward and kissed John on the cheek. 'Don't forget about me, will you?'

'No.'

'We can still be friends.' She put her hand on the handle of the front door. 'By the way, do we go to one another's funerals? What's the form, I wonder? I might write to an agony column. Tricky etiquette.'

'Don't come to Clare's.'

'No. All right. Where's she being buried?'

'At Busey.'

'Henry's being buried in Norfolk too. The family plot. So they'll be almost side by side. Only four or five miles between them. So near and yet so far. Ha, ha. Did you see his body? I had to identify it. Horrible. Never mind. It'll all taste the same to the worms.' She opened the door. 'Oh dear, I wish he was here to tell me to shut up. Bye-bye.' She went out without looking at him again and closed the door.

chapter four

Only the immediate family were asked to Clare's funeral that
Saturday afternoon, but many worthy Norfolk neighbours came
all the same. It was conducted in the Anglican churchyard next
to the Rectory garden by a Catholic priest who in his address
told the story of the Cross in blood on the floorboards without
mentioning the lover upstairs.

John stood at the graveside with his two children. His face
was without expression for he had no thoughts to inspire his
features. Tom, to his right, looked solemn as if solemnity was
expected of him: Anna, to his left, fought hard to control the
excitement she felt at the occasion. Both had been told that their
mother lay in the polished wooden box but neither seemed to
take it in. 'Is *that* going to be buried?' Anna whispered to her
father – incredulous that something with such shiny handles
should be consigned to the damp earth.

Eustace stood erect with Helen leaning on his arm. He was
wearing a dark-grey suit from earlier days which because it had
been carefully preserved in mothballs gave him an unusually
elegant appearance. His head was raised as if he was on parade,
or perhaps because his gaze was directed over the heads of the
other mourners to the white clouds in the sky.

Helen's face was half hidden by a grey veil. John noticed that
though she smiled occasionally at the children she did not lift
her eyes to his: perhaps, he thought, she blamed him for what
had happened or was afraid that he would go back on the story
of the Cross, for when the priest mentioned it in his address she
nodded vigorously as if Clare – shot dead in adultery – was already to be counted among those Dansies who had died for their
Faith.

There was a reception afterwards at the Rectory – a funeral
wake. Although the neighbours had not been invited they were
clearly expected, because glasses had been laid out in the faded
drawing-room and one of the women who helped in the house
stood in an apron filling them with sherry. As the guests entered
the room they shook hands with Eustace and Helen, and expressed their sorrow and regret, but they avoided John as if his

presence embarrassed them. Only his own mother – who had come down from Yorkshire – kissed him melodramatically as she entered the room and then went on, with tragic mien, to chat to the Loughs' neighbours as if they were her own – as indeed they might have been: they were the same breed.

John, who at first barely noticed that the other mourners were avoiding him, moved around the room after his two children; but when they had run off to the kitchen to fetch the dishes of sandwiches and sausage rolls he approached one group of people and then another but sensed (or imagined) a reserve and disapproval in the way they talked to him. This made him irritated and angry. Who were these people? Why had they come? How dare they make him feel unwelcome and ill at ease at the funeral of his own wife? Did they know about Paula? Had Eustace and Helen maligned him? Or was it because he was standing as a Labour candidate? Or did they think that adultery and socialism went together and that he embodied them both?

He left the drawing-room and went into the library, where two logs smouldered in the grate. He crouched and tried to blow up a flame with the bellows. When they blazed again he stood and went to the window and stared out at the damp, dead garden. How hard it was to believe that the black trees and shrubs would ever again flourish with leaves and flowers. Would he come to Busey next summer? Probably not. It was Clare's home, not his, and if the Loughs were going to hold him responsible for her murder – perhaps even for her infidelity – then he would rather not see them. The children could come up on their own, or with a nanny. He would have to hire a nanny to look after them, but he was damned if he would come up to Busey simply to suffer the Loughs' reproach.

From the passage outside he heard sounds of the guests departing. He turned and went back to the fire. He glanced at his watch: he had made the election his excuse for an immediate return to London but there were still two hours before the train left Cromer. He stood warming the backs of his legs, running his eyes along the bookshelves. They settled on *The Death of Ivan Ilych*. He stepped forward and took it out from where he had left it the summer before, between *Scott of the Antarctic* and *The Oxford Book of Christian Names*. To think that only a few months ago a little story like that had upset him so much, when real life . . . He opened it, glanced at the pages and remembered how he had gone to bed that night, disgusted with life, loathing Clare, convinced that he was dying while she would live for ever. Whereas now . . . How had the story ended? He looked at the last page. *He tried to add 'forgive me', but said 'forgo' and waved his hand, knowing that He whose understanding mattered would understand.* Of course the chap had died repentant. Like Clare. He snapped the book shut and put it back on the shelf.

chapter five

The general election was held on 28 February. By midnight the votes had been counted in the Hackney and Harringay constituency and the result announced in Hackney Town Hall. John Strickland had been elected with a majority of 8,328. There were cheers from his supporters and John made a short speech. After that there was a party in the committee rooms arranged by the agent and Gordon Pratt, to which John took Paula without explaining who she was.

His majority was much the same as O'Grady's had been in the election of 1970, but already by the time his result was declared it was apparent that the Conservatives had not got the support they expected – that a slight preference for the Labour and Liberal parties had been expressed throughout the country. A television had been set up on a trestle table and John's happy comrades gave increasingly drunken cheers every time a favourable result was declared, or whenever the Labour leader, Harold Wilson, appeared on the screen: but the cheers were those of football fans whose team had won the game, not the blood-curdling cries of vengeful revolutionaries, and John felt, beyond the exhilaration of victory, a sense of professional satisfaction that his calm analysis of the public mood had proved more accurate than the hysterical fears of his middle-class friends.

The children had stayed at Busey, so John went back that

night with Paula to her house in Purves Mews. When he awoke at ten the next morning he knew quite well where he was: once again Paula was already up – the smell of coffee wafted up the spiral stairs – and when he went down in his dressing-gown John found all the morning's newspapers laid out on the kitchen table.

'We haven't got an overall majority,' said Paula, 'and Heath won't resign.'

'He'll have to.'

'It depends on the Liberals . . .' She put a plate of bacon and egg in front of him. 'Celebration breakfast,' she said, sitting down next to him. 'You were wonderful last night,' she went on as John began to eat and read the papers. 'I really felt proud of you. A lot of people thought that they were seeing the start of something important. There was a man next to me in the hall who said. "He'll go far, that one." '

John smiled. 'Don't expect too much.'

'I don't expect anything. Be just what you are. I talked to that friend of yours at the party. What's his name? The journalist with the Irish wife?'

'Gordon.'

'Yes. He said he'd known you since Oxford . . .'

'We shared a flat when we came down.'

'He believes in you as much as I do. He was enormously impressed by the way you didn't let Clare's death get you down; the way you carried on in spite of it.'

'It was you . . .'

'It wasn't really. He said – and I think he's quite perceptive, really – that what you've lacked until now is a kind of inner self-confidence. He say that the English public schools make you feel that external things are important – the right school, the right university, the right accent, the right wife – and that the law with its emphasis on precedent and legal technicalities does the same; that you've been smothered by what he calls "class culture" but that now your real feelings and ideals are breaking through and are making you more convincing to yourself. Do you see what he means?'

'Yes,' said John with his mouth full of bacon and egg.

'He also said . . .' She hesitated. 'He wouldn't have said it if he wasn't drunk so perhaps I shouldn't repeat it.'

'Go on,' he said – half listening to Paula and half reading the paper.

'He also said that Clare had held you back.' She paused as if to see whether it would upset him to discuss his dead wife.

'How?'

'He said that she didn't share your ideals, that she didn't really appreciate your potential.'

'She wasn't a socialist . . .'

'He didn't just mean your political potential, though he used a lot of political jargon. He said that he knew you quite well when you first met Clare, and that he thinks you fell in love with her and married her . . . The phrase he used was "to secure a home base in the elistist bourgeois subculture".'

John smiled. 'He must have been very drunk.'

'He meant what he said all the same. He thought you were kept going afterwards by mutual interests like your house and your children, but that underneath it all you were working at cross-purposes, and repressing one another's true personalities. He said it was as if Danton had been married to Marie-Antoinette.'

'He should have been a marriage guidance counsellor,' said John, turning the page of the paper.

'There's a short piece about the murders,' said Paula.

'Where?'

'On page three, at the bottom.'

It was a brief statement that Henry Mascall, a merchant banker, had been found murdered along with a woman in Wiltshire.

'I suppose it had to break some time,' said John.

'And today is a good day, really. Everyone will be reading about the election.'

'They don't mention Clare by name.'

'Not in *The Times*. They do in the *Telegraph*. There's a nastier piece in the *Mail*. I shouldn't read it if I were you.'

'What does it say?'

'It's more what it doesn't say.'

'Does it name Clare?'

'Yes.'

'What about the *Guardian?*' he asked, thinking of Eustace and Helen.

'Nothing.'

'Good.'

'By the way,' said Paula, 'I've bought you a present to celebrate the victory.'

John looked up from the paper: he disliked both giving and receiving gifts. 'What sort of present?'

'I hope you won't mind . . .'

'Why should I mind?'

'You might.' She smiled timidly.

'Give it to me and we'll see.'

'I can't actually give it to you.'

'Why not?'

'It's a bit heavy.'

'Then tell me.'

'Come and see.'

They both got up from the kitchen table and Paula led him to the window which looked out into the mews. 'There,' she said.

He looked out and saw parked on the cobbles immediately next to the house a sparkling, dark-blue Volvo estate car. 'Is that the present?' he asked.

'Yes. Do you mind?'

'Of course I don't mind. It's wonderful . . .'

'I thought that the police were being so boring about hanging on to your old one, and that anyway it was past its best . . .'

'But they cost the earth.'

'Not really. But perhaps you'd rather have had something else? I thought that with the children . . .'

'It's perfect.'

'Do you like the colour? We can always change it . . .'

He turned and kissed her. 'You're very kind to me,' he said.

'It's not kind to be kind to someone you love.'

'Not kind, then, but generous.'

'It isn't generous either. How can I give you anything when everything I am is yours already?'

*

Although Paula had by now vacated one of her fitted wardrobes for the increasing number of clothes that John kept at Purves Mews, both had enough sense of propriety to realize that some months should elapse before they could openly live together, so when the children returned from Busey John went back to live in his house in Holland Park. Paula, however, took over the running of it. She hired a Norland nanny for the children and an efficient daily char who cleaned the house and washed and ironed the clothes. She made sure that Tom took the dinner money to school on a Monday morning; that he took his bathing trunks every other Thursday; that Anna went from school to her ballet class on Tuesday afternoons and to her piano lesson on Saturday mornings. All this made it possible for John not only to pursue his new career as a Member of Parliament but to resume his practice at the Bar.

The only flaw in this efficient organization of his life was the mood of his children. It was only when they returned home and found two strange women in their mother's place that they seemed to take in for the first time that Clare was dead for ever. They said nothing, but all their gaiety vanished. They looked pale, sad and ill at ease, John too found it odd to see them so well-groomed and unnaturally polite, and he was inhibited in front of Paula and the nanny from tickling and teasing them as he had done before. Whenever he could he came home at teatime, but when he did they all seemed conscious that he had, at some inconvenience, set aside this time to be with them. On Sundays it was the same. He was determined to keep the day free for family life, but so many other matters were pressing on his mind that it was inevitably frustrating to spend idle hours watching Tom on his bicycle in Holland Park or Anna on the swing.

It was frustrating, too, in a different way to live apart from Paula – even in just this formal sense. They would dine together in the House of Commons, or in restaurants near to Westminster; and two or three times a week he would look in at Purves Mews on his way home. But he was often now exhausted after a hard legal and political day; and he found himself increasingly loath to break away from Paula's soft, warm and scented body at one in the morning, put on his old clothes and drive back to

Holland Park. Nor did he like to see the beaky face of the Norland nanny across the table at breakfast, so he and Paula agreed that they would give propriety six months from the day Clare had died, and that on Saturday 3 August they would live together or rather, since it would make things simpler still, they would be married from Prinnet Park.

chapter six

Shortly after the opening of Parliament, Detective Inspector Thompson and Detective Sergeant Simms came to see John at the House of Commons. With them there was a third policeman in plain clothes whom they introduced as Detective Inspector Blackett of Scotland Yard's Murder Squad. 'We've had to call in the Yard, sir,' said Thompson, 'because quite frankly we've got nowhere at all on our own.'

Blackett was the kind of London detective with whom John was already familiar: he had cross-examined them many times on the witness stand. If Thompson looked like a farmer, Blackett, with a heavy, pock-marked face, looked like a criminal; and when he spoke to John it was with that sneer of pseudo-deference which hard-bitten detectives use towards members of the Bar. 'It's a baffling case, isn't it, sir?' he said to John.

'Yes,' said John. 'It's certainly baffling if it isn't fortuitous.'

'Fortuitous?' Blackett repeated. 'Yes, that's a good word. A "one-off job" is how we'd put it. As you must know, sir, from your experience in the courts, crimes usually conform to a pattern: you get a little firm doing country houses or post offices, sometimes using shooters, sometimes not. Now we have had some fairly heavy villains doing the country houses – and there's even been a bit of GBH when they've been disturbed – but they've always had good information. They've never gone in when there's nothing to take. So why your cottage?'

John shook his head. 'I don't know. It doesn't make sense.'

'You have some wealthy neighbours,' said Thompson. 'It's possible that they mistook your house for another one, stumbled on your wife and Mr Mascall, panicked, and ran away.'

'Yes . . . but wouldn't they have seen the cars?'

'There is an alternative theory,' said Blackett.

'What is that?'

'That the murders were deliberate.'

'But who would want to kill them, apart from me or Mary?'

'I agree, sir, and we've ruled you both out of our inquiries. But what if someone wanted to kill *you* and murdered Mr Mascal instead?'

John swallowed. 'Why should anyone want to kill me?'

'You tell us,' said Blackett.

'I can't think of any reason . . .'

'Take your time. Is there anyone you've prosecuted who might have the hump?'

John shook his head. 'No.'

'Or someone you defended. Felt you hadn't done your best?'

For a moment John thought of Terry Pike. 'No,' he said. 'I don't think so. You see I don't do much criminal work. It's mostly licensing.'

'I know, sir,' said Thompson. 'It was just a theory. We don't want to leave any stone unturned.'

'Perhaps you could go over your cases for the past year or so,' said Blackett, 'to see if you can turn up some nutter who might have taken against you.'

'I will, certainly,' said John, 'but I don't think it will help.'

'And you can't think of anyone who might have wanted to kill Mr Mascall?' asked Blacket.

'For himself?'

'Yes.'

'No.'

'Not one of his women? He seems to have had quite a few . . . besides your wife, that is.'

'I shouldn't have thought so. They weren't the type to . . .'

'I agree, sir,' said Blackett. 'These society birds don't go in for much *crime passionel*. Not in my experience, anyway.' He got to his feet. 'Sorry to have taken up your time, sir.'

John crossed the room to see them to the door. 'I'd like to help in any way I can,' he said. 'I'm very keen that you should find the murderer.'

'We'll do our best,' said Thompson.

'I could be wrong,' said Blackett. 'It could just be . . . what was the word for it sir? Fortuitous? A couple of cowboys down from the smoke. Chose a place at random – nice and lonely at the end of a lane. But it's like catching VD from a toilet seat. Very unusual. Very unusual indeed. If my wife tried that one on me, sir . . .' He shook his head and went out.

That evening, as he lay beside her on her bed, John asked Paula if she thought Terry could have murdered Henry and Clare. Her face was pressed into his chest and for a moment she did not answer: then, shifting her head to talk but without looking at him, she said: 'Why on earth would Terry want them dead?'

'He might have meant to kill me, and got Henry by mistake.'

'Why should he want to kill you?'

'Because of you.'

She laughed. 'No, I promise you. He didn't love me like that. He'd feel humiliated if a woman meant as much as that to him.'

'You don't think I ought to say something about him to the police?'

'I shouldn't.'

'Perhaps you're right.'

'The danger is that if you do, and they can't find the real murderer, they'll try and pin it on him just to close the case. They're quite capable of that . . .'

'I know.'

chapter seven

Although Paula now saw to the practical side of his domestic life there was one task which John could not delegate to her and for which she did not volunteer – the disposal of Clare's clothes and private possessions. At first John had simply stuffed the things she had left piled on the chair into a drawer and her shoes and slippers into the bottom of the cupboard. Then, one Sunday morning, while the children were at church with the nanny, he had gone through the drawers of her dressing-table to see what pieces of jewellery should be kept for Anna when she was grown up. Seeing and touching these articles that had belonged to Clare he found he remembered her so clearly that she seemed to be there beside him in the room. It was not a psychic presence, but just as a dream can be so vivid that you believe it to have been real experience some time after waking, so John's long life with Clare made his memories of her seem more real than the everyday coming and going of the past week. It was not that he remembered particular incidents, but rather that he seemed to see her moving about the room; to smell her body beside him on the bed; and to hear her calling from the kitchen that lunch was ready. The house was silent and John fell into a nostalgic trance, feeling the emotions he had felt when Clare was alive, but because he knew that she was dead – that she was not down in the kitchen making lunch – those very feelings which at the time had been so deep that he had taken them for granted now tried to surface in his conscious mind, but were kept submerged by the crust of his current passions. Beneath the crust past and present acted upon one another to stir the dregs: for a time John remembered Clare with a real hatred – he narrowed his eyes and clenched his teeth – because the woman he now sensed and remembered had betrayed him with Henry Mascall. He repeated in a soundless whisper her words of casual deceit – 'I'll go down to the cottage to see that everything's OK . . . there are one or two things I want to do in the garden before the spring' – phrases which he now heard quite clearly in her tone of voice though he had hardly listened to them at the time. He went on to savour images of her body entwined with Henry Mascall's – his wife with his best friend – and thought with satisfaction of the vengeance that had befallen them by some unknown hand. Then the jealousy subsided and he was left with a powerful, inarticulate, animal feeling for Clare which made him feel so sad that when the children came back from church a little later on they found him crying with one of her seed-pearl necklaces held in his hand.

It was because Clare's presence lingered like this in her belongings that John had shut them away and put off the question of how to dispose of them. The problem, nonetheless, preyed on his mind because there were many decent skirts and pairs of shoes which he might well have given to some jumble sale had he been able to bear the idea of some other woman wearing Clare's clothes. Nor could he bring himself to put them into the dustbin. He decided he would rather burn them all on a pyre, but that was not easy either in the small back garden of a London house.

At the end of May, Paula bought a long lease on an elegant terrace house in Lord North Street – a five-minute walk from the House of Commons. On the morning of 1 June, a Saturday, she suggested to John that he and his two children come and inspect what was to be their new home. The former owners had left the house clean and in good condition but it was unfurnished: the floors were bare boards and there were dark rectangular patches on the walls where pictures had shaded the paintwork from the light.

The rooms were arranged in much the same way as the house in Holland Park, with a kitchen in the basement and a drawing-room on the first floor. The chief difference was a panelled dining-room on the ground floor with a service lift from the kitchen. It was this contraption which most impressed the children, and while John admired the proportions of the room they played with the ropes and pulleys.

On the second floor, above the drawing-room, there was a bedroom with an adjacent bathroom; and at the top of the house three attic bedrooms and a bathroom for the children and their nanny. 'You'll have to decide which of you wants which room,' said Paula as she showed Tom and Anna their quarters, 'and Nanny can have the one you don't want.'

'Does Nanny have to live with us?' asked Anna plaintively. 'Can't she come every day like Mrs Giles?'

'No,' said John. 'It's best if she lives with us.'

'We'll get rid of her when Tom goes away to school,' said Paula.

'I thought I was going to a day school, Dad?' said Tom, turning to his father.

'It isn't decided yet,' said John.

As they were going downstairs again Anna asked where the playrooms would be. 'There are plenty of rooms,' said John

'There's that nice little room opposite the dining-room. Perhaps you could use that?'

'I rather thought that would be your study,' said Paula. 'You'll certainly need one.'

'Yes. I suppose I will. Then what about that back room in the basement?' he said to Anna.

'I thought that might do for a Filipino,' said Paula.

John frowned. 'Do we really need a Filipino? Aren't a nanny and a daily enough?'

'Not if I'm to be any use to you as a politician's wife. We'll have to entertain a certain amount, and I'd like to help on the political side . . .'

'Of course.'

'Those Filipino women are frightfully good. You hardly notice they're there.'

'I'm sure they're good, but it doesn't really leave anywhere for the children.'

'Can't they play in their rooms?'

'I suppose so.'

'But where will we watch TV?' asked Tom.

'I'll tell you what,' said Paula in the gushing, enthusiastic tone of voice that she used with John's children. 'Each of you can have your own little colour television in your bedroom. How about that?'

'One each?' asked Tom.

'One each,' said Paula.

'What about Nanny?'

'She can have one too.'

'Isn't that a little excessive?' said John.

'I don't see why. They don't cost much. Cheaper than building on a new room, anyway.'

'What about a bed?' asked Anna with a sombre, timid face. 'I'll need a bed.'

John smiled, crouched and kissed her. 'Of course,' he said. 'You'll have the bed you have now. And your desk. And your chest of drawers.'

'But what about my room at home? It'll have to have a bed.'

'But when we live here we won't be living there. We'll sell that house. Someone else will be living there.'

'You mean we won't live at home any more?' asked Anna.

'This will be our home,' said John.

They all ate lunch together in a restaurant, which because it was now so frequent was less of a treat for the children than it had been before. They therefore fidgeted and quarrelled while they waited for their food: Paula's face took on an expression of suppressed irritation, and so John grew angry and smacked Anna who then cried quietly into her thick linen napkin.

After lunch they dropped Paula in Knightsbridge and then drove back to Holland Park. The nanny was away for the week-end so the three of them were alone. The children went down to watch a film on the old black-and-white television in the play-room while John went up to the drawing-room to read some Parliamentary reports. His mood had changed for the better. He felt calm and unusually cheerful. At five he came down to the kitchen to make the children's tea. He put on the old butcher's apron he wore when cooking and put on a bowl of water for the spaghetti which he knew was Tom's favourite dish.

Hearing their father at the stove, and hungry because they had eaten little of the rich food at the restaurant, the children came into the kitchen. Anna climbed on a stool to fetch a tin of tomatoes from the cupboard while Tom set the table. They laughed, jumped about and chased one another around the table. When at last they were both seated in front of bowls of spaghetti with grated cheese and tomato sauce – and John with a cup of tea – Anna looked up and said: 'Can't we stay in *this* house, Daddy?'

'Not really,' said John, looking down into his cup.

'I mean I know the other one's posher,' said Tom, 'or it will be when it's all painted and got furniture and things, but I like this one better, really, don't you?'

John looked up at his two children's intent faces. 'The new one's much nearer to where I work. It'll make it easier for me to come home to tea.'

'I know,' said Tom, 'but this house has got all our things in it and we've always lived here and Mummy lived here . . .'

'It wouldn't really be big enough . . .'

'Why not? It's big enough now.' Tom argued amiably but was insistent, and Anna watched with wide-open eyes.

'It wouldn't really be big enough when I'm married to Paula.'

Tom looked down at his plate. 'No, I suppose not,' he conceded.

'Are you really getting married to Paula?' asked Anna.

'Yes.'

'But you're married to Mummy, aren't you?'

'Not now.'

'Because she's dead?'

'Yes.'

'Do you stop being married to people when they die?'

'Yes.'

She nodded as if she understood.

'Do you have to marry her, Dad?' asked Tom. 'I mean couldn't we just go on – us three – without Paula or Nanny or the Philip woman . . .'

'Not really, no,' said John. 'If I'm doing this important job in Parliament I really need someone to look after me.'

'But we'd look after you,' said Anna. 'I promise we would.'

'And we wouldn't quarrel or fight,' said Tom.

'And we could stay with Granny Strickland and Granny Lough in the holidays,' said Anna. 'They'd look after us.'

John shook his head. 'I'm afraid I've got to marry Paula,' he said. 'I promised and I do need someone . . . When you grow up you'll understand.'

'More please,' said Anna holding up her plate. 'Me too, please,' said Tom holding up his: whereupon John did an impersonation of an Italian waiter serving spaghetti and the children laughed again.

The next morning John took the children to mass. He sat and knelt and then sat again like the rest of the congregation but did not follow the ceremony or listen to the sermon. His mind was on other things. What should he do with the cottage? The estate agents had told him that a recent murder made a property almost unsaleable. And what should he do with the old Volvo which the police had now returned to him and was parked next to the new one outside his house? A dealer had looked at and offered him its value in scrap. John had turned him down. And what would he do with the furniture which Paula did not want in the house in Lord North Street? It annoyed him that it should prove so difficult to get rid of the goods and chattels of his past life, and he returned home from church in a ruthless, unsentimental mood. As a first step he thought he would tackle the problem of Clare's clothes and pack them into the cardboard boxes which had contained his last consignment of wine. He could then either burn them or give them away.

From the top drawer he took her tights and underclothes; from the second her shirts and blouses; from the third her jerseys and cardigans. It was beneath these that he found three envelopes held together by an elastic band. He picked them up and saw that all were addressed to Clare in a neat, methodical hand. All at once he felt sour in his stomach. Were these letters from Henry? Or from another lover? Perhaps she had betrayed him before, frequently, over many years. He looked again at the envelope on the top of the bundle and saw that it had an Italian stamp. Were they from Henry on a business trip? But the handwriting was not Henry's. Perhaps he had employed someone else to write the address as a subterfuge. John took out the first letter. 'My dear Clare,' it began. He turned the page and looked at the bottom: 'With great affection, Michael'. Michael? Who was Michael? He turned the letter again and saw that it came from the Jesuit College in Rome. It was then that he remembered that Guy's housemaster at Stoneyhurst – the priest as it happened who had married him – was a Jesuit called Father Michael Pearce.

John sat down on the bed with a strange feeling in his legs. He looked again at the first letter. *My dear Clare, I was delighted to get your letter, even though it was a troubled soul which prompted you to write it.* He read on. Clare had clearly written to this priest to say that Henry had made advances which she was tempted to accept. The Jesuit had replied more severely than one might have expected . . . *adultery is unquestionably sinful . . . cancer to the spirit.* Then John saw his own name on the paper. *You do not say much about John: I cannot believe that you would want to hurt and humiliate him.* What had she answered to that? John looked at the next letter. There was more theology. *It isn't certain that if you sleep with Henry Mascall you will go to Hell . . .* That sounded more like a Jesuit. *I am a little confused because you say you love John and yet at times you seem to despise him . . .* What was this? *If you took more interest in John's life and shared his aspirations, perhaps you wouldn't be so bored.* John nodded his assent.

The letters were frustrating because they referred to those Clare had written to the priest. When he had finished the third John went through to the drawing-room, and there at Clare's desk he wrote to Father Michael Pearce.

I have just come across the letters you wrote to Clare. You will have heard by now that she and Henry Mascall were found murdered in our cottage on 17 February. I am naturally most anxious to know what Clare's attitude was towards me when she died. I am afraid that my own affair which you refer to in one of your letters was not invented by Henry Mascall. I was indeed the first to be unfaithful so I have no right to resent her infidelity. All the same I did love her and if you felt it would not betray the confidence she placed in you I would be grateful if you would let me see the letters.

Three weeks later the Jesuit replied from Rome.

Guy wrote to me about Clare's murder. I have never been so affected by such news before – not even by the death of my parents. I almost sent you her letters there and then because although she says some hard things about you she also describes the way she loved you. It may also comfort you to realize how little she cared for Henry Mascall. She never once said she loved him, or that he loved her. I am afraid she felt at a loose end, and I feel as sorry as you must do that we didn't do more to help.

It is interesting that I should say this because it is what one usually says of a suicide. There is in a way a theme of spiritual suicide in these four letters and it is merciful of Almighty God to have left us the evidence that she died repentant.

She was not, strictly speaking, confessing to me so I do not break my vows by enclosing her letters. They are however precious to me and I would be glad to have them back.

With best wishes,
Michael Pearce, S. J.

John put this letter, and the four from Clare, into the pocket of his jacket and waited to read them until later that night when the children were asleep. Then he sat down on the bed he had shared with Clare, worked out the order in which she had written the letters, interspersed her letters with those from the Jesuit and read the correspondence in its proper sequence.

chapter eight

Dear Father Michael,
Happy New Year. I hope you don't mind me writing. Guy gave me your address and said you were very busy and important being an *éminence grise* to Pope Paul, though I can't really see why he should need one – he seems *grise* enough already. I'm writing really because I used to be able to talk to you about God and I haven't found anyone else since. I went to confession before we went away for Christmas and tried to talk to the priest about my problems but he had a heavy Irish accent which always puts me off and there was a huge queue so I took pity on him and confessed 'impure thoughts' in the usual way and got off with a Hail Holy Queen. I felt a bit better afterwards but not much. I'm afraid it hasn't really done the trick, so I thought that since you married us you'd have an interest in how we were getting on so here goes: I'm very much afraid that I'm hurtling towards adultery and I can't seem to stop myself. I thought that if I described the temptation to you you might come up with an antidote.

The 'tempter' in this case is an old friend of John's called Henry Mascall. Perhaps you've met him? It's absurd because Mary – his wife – is my closest friend; in fact we've both known them both since we were married, so it's not a case of a tall, dark and handsome stranger across a crowded room. I wish it was, in a way. Like this it's rather crude and squalid, but the fact is that just before Christmas he rang up and asked me out to lunch in a grand, expensive restaurant. Of course I accepted because he was an old friend and life is pretty dull, but then I found myself washing my hair the night before and choosing my smartest daytime clothes and not bothering to tell John. You see Henry's well known for having love affairs, and an invitation to lunch is as good as a proposition; and I knew it, and I went all the same. I should also confess that I loved that first lunch because somehow it seems quite different *à deux* to *à quatre* and he's famously charming – not just sex appeal but clever and witty. But he makes it quite clear what he wants, without being crude about it, and the truth is that even though I didn't intend to get involved in anything – in fact I thought it was all a bit of a joke – I did love being flattered and 'desired', and when he asked if I'd meet him again I said I would and we agreed we wouldn't tell John or Mary.

That's sin already, I know. A good, modest Catholic mother of two shouldn't conspire like that against her husband and her best friend: but I couldn't resist it. It wasn't the food or the wine or even Henry: it was the excitement of an intrigue. Something to think about while I cooked the children's fish fingers.

We wnt to John's mother for Christmas and to Busey for the New Year. I went to Communion and prayed rather feebly but couldn't stop thinking about Henry and having schoolgirl fantasies about him taking me in his arms. I'm afraid it was a bad case of absence making the heart grow fonder. As soon as we got back yesterday he rang up and asked me out to dinner. I knew I shouldn't – that dinner was much riskier than lunch – but John was up at Hackney doing his politics, the house had been burgled while we were away, so I couldn't resist it. I said yes. Henry had told Mary some far-fetched story about having to take Arabs to the Talk-of-the-Town. We had a lovely dinner in a candlelit restaurant, and on the way home he kissed me in the car, and though I wouldn't let him 'go any further' as we used to say, I did like that kiss more than I've liked anything for years and years. So I'm writing to you as to an agony column. What the Hell do I do now?

With love from
Clare.

PS The children would send their love if they knew I was

writing but I daren't tell them because they might tell John who'd smell a rat. 'Oh what a tangled web we weave . . .'

9 January 1974

My Dear Clare,

I was delighted to get your letter, even though it was a troubled soul which prompted you to write it. My work here is dull administration so I am always glad to be asked for advice on the problems of an individual soul. That, after all, is what we are for. If you were here in Rome or I was there in London I might be able to give you better advice, but I shall do what I can by post.

I seem to remember that I married you about twelve years ago, and I presume from your letter that you haven't been unfaithful to John until now. The problem which even a celibate priest can appreciate is that marriages go stale; that husbands and wives grow to find one another less attractive – even unattractive. The longing for a lover is often an expression of nostalgia for youth. Even priests feel that, but they usually express it through radical theology. The truth is, alas, that our bodies bud, blossom, wither and die just like those plants and animals. The only advantage we have over them is an immortal soul, which in moments of trial such as that you are going through might seem a disadvantage. Otherwise you could have a love affair and if neither wife nor your husband got to know about it, who would suffer?

The answer, as you well know, is that you would suffer because adultery is unquestionably sinful and sin offends God and damages the soul. We all worry so much that smoking will give us lung cancer, and hardly at all about the moral nicotine which gives cancer to the spirit. You could decide to take the risk, but the danger is not just of moral cancer but that I have chosen the wrong analogy; that adultery is like heroin rather than nicotine, a drug which would bring you immediate ecstasy but in the end cause a hundred times more suffering.

You don't say much about John: I cannot believe that you would want to hurt and humiliate him. And what sort of home would it be for your children if you separate? Or live together hating and resenting one another? The Church is often accused of being obsessed with sins of the flesh and repressing people's natural desires: I would not want you to think of the sin which tempts you as one against chastity but rather as one against love – love of your husband, love of your children and love of God.

My advice, then, is that you must stop seeing Henry Mascall alone. Pray to God to help you to see the subtler joys of your life – above all your family life. Pray to Our Lady and to St Joseph to intercede for you. Distract yourself if you can. Try to get out into the country and study the harmony of nature. People say that lax sexual morals are natural, but in truth there is some order and dignity in the way animals treat one another which is often absent in man.

I shall pray for you. With great affection,
Michael.

17 Jan.

Dear Father Michael,

Thank you for writing back. The moment I read you letter I thought I would take your advice and refuse to see him again, but then the telephone rang and my heart missed a beat. I hoped it was him and it was. We're having lunch again tomorrow. So much for my good resolution.

I can see (through a glass darkly!) that everything you say is true, but there are one or two things which you couldn't be expected to know which don't excuse my behaviour but make things a little different. For instance I do love John, and he would be very humiliated if he found out that I'd had an affair, especially with Henry, but he hasn't been faithful to me. I always suspected that he might have had the odd affair and Henry says it's true. He says that John's well known to have affairs and that he's carrying on now with someone called Paula Gerrard. That isn't really an excuse, I know. It's different for men and I don't want to sleep with Henry just to get back at John. At least I don't think I do. I don't believe for a moment that Henry would be faithful to me if I did become his mistress. He's probably got two or three other girlfriends right now. The problem with John is not his roving eye, it's his dullness. I don't think he's dull to everyone. Paula Gerrard obviously sees something in him: but anyone's dull if you know them inside out, even if you love them, and John is so predictable that it gets on my nerves. Did you know that he wants to stand for Parliament for the Labour Party? Typical of him to move left when everyone else is moving right. It might be impressive if he was sincere, but his socialism is an affectation. It always was. He used it to seduce me. That's a bit unfair but I did fall for him originally because he was so idealistic and clever about demolishing the Establishment, as we used to call it. I nearly stopped being a Catholic because of him. Later on I realized that he only loved me *because* I was upper-class. He's really just a straightforward snob. Nothing would upset him more than if I started to put my hair in curlers, talk Cockney, have varicose veins and dish up spam fritters for his tea. Only John doesn't realize it. I thought for a while he was happy leading our kind of *âge mûr doré* life – dinner parties, holidays abroad and buying machines for the garden. Then suddenly he had a relapse – doubtless a sign of the male menopause! He became politically 'active' again. At first I thought it was just an excuse to see some woman, but he was genuinely spending his evenings at meetings of the local Labour Party. But that didn't bring back my old admiration for his radical dash because now it wasn't idealism which inspired him. At best it was just vanity. Most people go into politics because they want to be the centre of attention, don't they? Isn't that the trouble with democracy – that the representatives of the people are necessarily those with character deficiences? Who else would put up with boredom? John suffers from slight *folie de grandeur*. I think a lot of lawyers do. He thinks that just because he's a trained advocate and can win arguments around a dinner table it means he's cleverer than anyone else when in fact I think he's rather stupid. Or maybe he isn't stupid. It's hard for a wife to tell. But he is pedantic, and winning arguments with heavy court-room techniques only puts people off. And his holier-than-thou socialism annoys people too. I know it irritates Henry. In fact I sometimes suspect that he's only taken a fancy to me after all these years to get at John. That isn't very flattering, is it? It makes the sin worse, too, but what's the difference if the abyss is one thousand or ten thousand feet deep?

There are other things about Henry which make it worse still. I'm rather ashamed to admit them, even in a letter, because they might make you despise me, but here goes: the other evening he said quite openly that bored married women were the easiest lays in London. Just like that, meaning that because I'm a bored married woman I'll give in in the end. I said that I wasn't bored and that even if I was I wouldn't sleep with him because even if John had a mistress he wasn't a Catholic and didn't know better whereas I was and did. Henry just laughed. He said that he'd had more Catholic girls than all the others put together. He said that if I didn't sleep with him it would be thanks to middle-class pudeur, not the Grace of God. He named a string of Catholic women who were well known to have lovers so I was rather nonplussed. He also said that the Catholic Church had given up the concept of a 'mortal' sin because it was intellectually untenable. Is that true?

I'm rambling a bit. As you can see the struggle goes on. I agree about nature but there's no point going to the country just at the moment because everything's dead.

Please write again. Be as strict as you like. And tell me about 'mortal' versus 'venial' sin.

With love,
Clare.

25 Jaunary 1974

My dear Clare,
You do not make your admirer sound very attractive. He may be clever and amusing: he also sounds cynical and destructive. It does alarm me that you still see him, knowing that he wants to seduce you and in seducing you humiliate you, your husband and your religion. He is right, in a way, about the Church's view of mortal sin. We are less mechanistic than we used to be: we no longer insist, for example, that if a Catholic leaves his house to buy a Sunday paper with the firm intention of missing mass, and is run over by a bus on his way home, he will inevitably and necessarily go to Hell. But some

sins are still considered much more serious than others and adultery is one of the most serious. It isn't certain that if you sleep with Henry Mascall you will go to Hell: but you will quite consciously be breaking one of the ten commandments and putting at risk the happiness of your husband and children.

I am a little confused because you say you love John and yet at times you seem to despise him. Why are you so unsympathetic towards his political career? You can disagree with him without belittling his motives. There were many Christian socialists before Marx and Lenin. Are you sure it is just vanity which inspires him? Often men in middle-age grasp more than anything for self-respect. It is an impulse to prepare themselves for the Day of Judgement – even in those who do not believe in it. Perhaps John became afraid that earning a lot of money at the Bar and marrying a pretty aristocratic wife was not enough: that he hadn't made the best of the talents given to him by God? He might feel this without believing in God: he might have seen it reflected in your contempt.

Remember, serious sins are often the *thick* end of the wedge. You say yourself that Henry Mascall is consciously taking advantage of your boredom and, perhaps, of your contempt for John. Perhaps the sin starts there. If you took more interest in John's life and shared his aspirations, perhaps you wouldn't be bored. If he didn't sense that you despised him perhaps he wouldn't chase after other women. By the way, you shouldn't take the word of a would-be lover that John is having an affair with another woman. It's the oldest trick in the trade.

I fear that all this sounds rather prudish and severe. I don't want you to think that I am unsympathetic. I know that great temptation brings great suffering, but if you can you should feel exhileration rather than despair. No one smelts a feeble metal or examines a stupid student. If the Devil tempts you it is because he thinks you have a soul worth having, and if God lets you be tempted it is because He knows you can triumph.

With all affection,
Michael.

Dear Father Michael,

It's a losing battle. I feel terribly that God leaves me too much on my own. I went out with Henry last night: another fancy restaurant and then a sleazy nightclub. We danced and he 'touched me up', as they say. It was shaming but I let him and liked it. It's terribly hard to explain to a man and a priest that awful longing one feels for sexual oblivion. The truth is that I would have slept with him last night if he'd tried, even though I still pretend that I won't, but he says he's leaving it to me to say where and when. He won't let me get away with a sudden weakness. It's got to be cold, premeditated sin.

I see what you mean about sins still being serious even if they aren't automatically mortal, but it doesn't make things easier. In the old days you at least knew that death *en flagrant délit* meant Hell-fire for ever. You had to hope you'd survive long enough to repent in a moment of post-coital *tristesse*. Now you feel that a good Guardian Angel could get off with five hundred days in Purgatory. After all, sleeping with Henry wouldn't make me love God any less than I do. In fact I'd probably feel so guilty that I'd love Him more. You see once the Church says that a sin isn't necessarily fatal to one's relationship with God then I'm afraid the floodgates are opened. Look at what happened over birth control. Think of the Catholic women who had baby after baby for fear of Hell if they took the pill. Now we all have IUDs – mini-Auschwitzes, as Henry calls them – and go to Communion without batting an eyelid. If adultery won't necessarily land me in Hell then it makes it awfully tempting to indulge now and pay later.

'I'm sorry if this sounds as if I'm making excuses for last night's sins on the dance floor. Or making excuses in advance for worse to come: but that's a danger too. You feel you've done the dirty deed in your mind so you might as well do it with your body, because doesn't Jesus say somewhere that to think about it is as bad as doing it? Anyway, I'd like you to remind me why adultery is such a bad sin. It isn't irredeemable like murder or abortion. Can't it be classed with birth control? A sort of middle-range sin?

I'm sure that if I respected John more I'd be less likely to risk humiliating him. As a matter of fact since I first wrote to you I've come round a bit to his political point of view. All the people we know are being so absurdly hysterical about the Communists using the workers to get political power, when the truth is that the workers are using the Communists to get more money. I don't think I told you about the awful row I had with John about the cottage. He said we'd have to sell it because he'd be earning less money as an MP. I kicked up a terrible fuss and said it was all to pamper his vanity. I rather regretted it afterwards but I didn't apologize because I can't face his smug, self-righteous face whenever I do.

I agree. I don't really see why he shouldn't be a socialist and perhaps he does feel that he should use his talents to benefit other people. I may be influenced by Henry's cynicism. I think that what irritates me, fundamentally, about John is that he doesn't believe in God, because how can you assume that justice and equality are good if God isn't there to say so? As it is Jesus only said that we were spiritually equal. He rather suggested that we'd always have poor people and that they should grin and bear it because they'd be paid off in the next world. With or without God, the notion of Progress towards a workers' paradise is silly, isn't it? Labour versus Tory is just the age-old quarrel between rich and poor. John, I suspect, has taken the side of the poor and gone all socialist to try and outdo me on the moral plane. His socialism may not be the atheistic Marxist sort but in the context of our relationship it's an anti-Catholic gesture. I wish and pray that he would believe in God, but he would feel that if he did he'd be giving in to me, that he'd lose face, just as I would feel I was giving in to him if I became a socialist. Husbands and wives often hold each other back like that, don't they? They sort of stifle the development of one another's personality. I know that John won't believe in God until I'm dead so I hope that I die first.

The trouble is – I think I said this before – he isn't quite as clever as he thinks he is. I haven't his training, I didn't go to university, but I think in all humility that in many ways I'm cleverer than he is – wiser, anyway. I think a lot of women are and they suffer from seeing their intuitive intelligence outsmarted by their stupid husbands' clever talk. Yet men are such fragile egoists that if the wife shows her husband that she's cleverer and abler and stronger than he is, then she emasculates him. He loses what little he has. I promise you, Father, I know dozens of women who hold themselves back just to bolster up their dull, pompous, insecure husbands.

You say that I shouldn't be bored, but how can I not be bored when I'm stuck at home with the dirty breakfast dishes, the ironing, Women's Hour, the children's tea and at the end of it all a self-important husband expecting a gin and tonic, a hot supper, admiration for the ego-enhancing experiences of his day, commiseration for those which have taken the wind out of his sails? Then up we go: he clips his horrid, horny toenails, trims his corns with a razorblade; powders between his toes with anti-athlete's foot powder and then rolls over for a bit of sex.

Sometimes I feel that if I'd married someone else – Henry, for instance – it would have been different. Certainly when I married John I was much too young to know what I was doing. But now I think that the problem is marriage itself. Henry probably has horny toenails, and he's sure to get athlete's foot from those hotels in Jedda, if not venereal disease from the whores in Beirut. So if I was married to him I'd probably be going out to lunch with John – except he's much too prim to make a pass at the wife of a friend. Certainly I'll tell Anna to wait if she can and marry later than I did. Perhaps, if I'd had a wild youth, I wouldn't be so tempted now. I've never slept with anyone except John and I'm terribly curious to know what it's like with another man.

You asked if I was sure that John was having an affair with Paula Gerrard – that Henry isn't making it up. Yes, I'm pretty sure. He comes home late at night, supposedly from Hackney, but two or three nights a week he doesn't have a bath. That must mean he's had one somewhere else, because he's such a creature of habit.

You also say that you can't see how I can despise and love John at the same time. I don't know but I do. He is and always will be my husband. I would never leave him. He is, in many ways, a better man than Henry and he is often kind. He adores the children and puts up with quite a lot from me. He's sometimes funny – funny-endearing rather than funny-ha ha: if you saw him with his rotovator you'd know what I mean. I also know that he'd never leave me, that he feels very loyal to the family. That's why it's so evil of Henry to make it so clear that he wants to seduce me to humiliate us both. He still insists that I arrange the time and the place. Perhaps I should be glad that he is so evil. The Devil isn't even in disguise.

With love,
Clare.

8 February 1974

My dear Clare,

I can see now that the temptation to have a love affair with Henry Mascall has deep roots in the frustrations of your life. The compulsion is as much psychological as sexual – a need to escape from what you see as the drab confines of your domestic life. I can see this, and I can understand it, but it can never excuse adultery. Indeed rather than suggest other innocent ways through which you might escape from your drudgery – by taking a job, for example, or studying for a degree – I would ask you to think deeply about the value of the life you lead already.

Certainly your dissatisfaction with your role as wife and mother is quite common in the times we live in, but at the risk of irritating you let me suggest that you may have let certain feminist fallacies – similar, perhaps, to the fallacies you criticize in socialism – poison your attitude towards family life. Perhaps you are more intelligent than John: that does not alter your obligations towards him, which are not just to iron his clothes and cook his supper but also to cherish him as you promised when I married you. This may well mean that to some extent you must subordinate your will and personality to his – an idea which I know is repugnant to most women nowadays – but nonetheless it is the traditional teaching of the Church and is well founded in Scripture. In what matters most – the soul – women are or can be as good as men: indeed one woman, Our Lady, soars above all other men in virtue and holiness: but in this life on earth God has given you a subordinate status and the rebellion against this ordering of His creation in modern times is, in my opinion, the cause of much unhappiness.

I say this badly because you have the gift of Faith and through the sacraments the Grace of God, all of which should enable you to see through the vanity of contemporary intellectual fads. Certainly where men are subjugated by other men they have the right to rebel: but if our state of subordination is ordained by God we must learn in humility to accept it. I may feel myself to be an abler and more intelligent man than my superiors here in the Society of Jesus, but God has put them above me and I accept their authority. I try to do with enthusiasm whatever they give me to do. So it should be with a wife. You are married to John so to some extent you must live through him. God's gifts to you of intelligence and perception shouldn't lead you to bemoan the drudgery of domestic life. They should help you to understand that once you are married the ordinary ministrations of a wife and mother become your vocation. Take pride in your home. Do you remember how working-class women used to scrub the front steps of their little terrace houses and then rub on a border with chalk? I often used to think of them when visiting the slovenly homes of dons' wives at Oxford, and wonder which were the better women. I am not saying that you should be all Martha and no Mary, but I do insist that as a Catholic you should not be proud and think yourself too good for a domestic vocation.

You ask me why adultery is a more serious sin than contraception. The only answer I can give is that God suffers whenever we sin but He suffers most when we sin against charity – when it causes pain to others and leads us to harden our hearts. A coil may be a mini-Auschwitz, as your friend puts it, but the putative embryos are invisible, so you need not be evil to destroy them, just as it did not take hard and ruthless airmen to drop bombs on Hiroshima or Dresden. John, Tom and Anna, however, are not invisible, and what you contemplate endangers the happiness of all three. For how long will you be able to hide your infidelity? Will you sleep with John while you sleep with Henry? If he finds out, can you expect John to live with you in the same house? If he did, wouldn't you only despise him more than you do now? So he goes – perhaps to marry another woman – and you either live alone or lure Henry Mascall away from his wife so that two groups of children have broken homes. We talk so much now about human rights, but do not children have the right to be brought up by their own mother and father, living together amicably under the same roof? The fear of the unhappiness you might cause to Tom and Anna should in itself inoculate you against adultery, for Christ had the direst warnings for those who harmed children. You may as well slash at them with a knife as lend your body and your love to another man, for in betraying John and breaking your vows to him you betray them and break the promises implicit in the natural bond between mother and child.

Is this exaggerated? Am I too severe? Would you rather I suggested, as priests have been known to do, that adultery can be 'therapeutic' and might save a marriage that is otherwise doomed? Or belittle the significance of sexual sin as against the greater evil of monopoly capitalism or starvation in the Third World? The truth is, however, that the temptation which faces you is not to starve an Asiatic child or sell goods at excess profit: the temptation is to adultery. You say yourself that Henry Mascall plays the Devil, blatant and undisguised. Sex, alas, has a significance far beyond simple copulation. It is the power behind life; it is, perhaps, the essence of power itself which offers ecstasy to rival the promise of eternal life. You may well dismiss what I say as the ravings of a repressed celibate, but it is not for nothing that the Church has been so wary of sexual desire. The very strength of this instinct which has preserved our species through so many millennia and inspires in its proper place such happiness and beauty, can if misused and perverted wreak great evil and cause much misery. Its imagined delights are the sweet bait in the rat poison. I said, I think, that serious sin is the thick end of the wedge, but the wedge grows thicker still. Evil is indivisible. If you start to follow the Devil you can never know where he will lead you. The worst sins are usually last in the line of one thing leading to another.

I see that I have written these pages of admonition without mentioning God. Never think that He is unconcerned with your suffering. You may imagine for a moment, as Christ did on the Cross, that He has abandoned you, but that is only the last card in the Devil's hand. Believe through doubt and you trump Him. Ask for God's help and He will give it to you. After all, He created you to be His companion in Heaven, but to do that you must grow from a creature of purely physical instinct – a baby at your mother's breast – into a spiritual being, a demi-god. What you suffer now are the growing-pains of your soul. You teach your children to mature: so too God coaxes you through different stages of spiritual growth. When you taught Tom to walk were there not moments when you left him wobbling and uncertain on his own feet? He too must have felt abandoned, but you were there behind him, ready to catch him should he fall. God too is ready to help you, but you must also help yourself. The inert soul does not go to Heaven. When St Paul says that God's Grace is sufficient he does not mean that you can leave it all to Him. It must be possible to choose Evil if Good is to have its value. Even God cannot compel us to love Him because love is by its nature a voluntary emotion.

I said before that you must feel exhilarated, not depressed, that you are tempted. You should feel glad that you have this chance to make a worthwhile sacrifice to God. In the days of the Old Testament they killed a plump calf because that meant most to them. Nowadays, I dare say, one might offer up one's new car or colour television if that was what God wanted; but you He now asks to sacrifice a deeper and more insidious pleasure for His sake so that when it comes to the Last Judgement you can say: 'I may have led a comfortable life with two nice children and a country cottage but for Your sake I stopped seeing Henry Mascall.'

I remember you so vividly, innocent and optimistic under your white veil. I pray constantly to God that your soul may return to the state it was in on your wedding day. Do not be afraid, for as long as you pray to God to save you from sin, you are safe from the Devil in any form.

With great affection,
Michael.

Dear Father Michael,

I got your last letter this morning but I'm afraid it's too late. I had supper with the Mascalls last night. There were several people there – not John, he was up at Hackney. I sat next to Henry and managed to whisper that I'd be alone at the cottage on Saturday night. He said he'd come. The awful thing is that I prayed to God that that would be his answer and I pray now that he'll turn up. My one dread is that he doesn't really fancy me, that it's all a joke – a nasty trick. It would be better, wouldn't it, not to pray at all?

I'm sorry. I feel awful because I know that you've spent hours of your precious time writing those letters and that you've prayed for me when you might have been praying for someone more deserving. Your advice was good advice. I agree with everything you say – even about the role of women – but I'm afraid it's too late. I'm really too far gone for arguments. I definitely agree about not hurting the children and John, and of course I love them more than Henry. It's just that my need for H. now is so urgent that I'm determined to risk a bust-up. As a matter of fact I'm fairly sure it won't come to that. Even if John does find out he won't really care. Wounded pride, perhaps, but I don't think he actually loves me much any more. He's left me for his new career, and he won't want a divorce now that he's an MP (there are lots of Irish Catholics in his constituency!) so the children won't suffer. In fact I feel I can square everyone except God and I can't really bring myself to hold off H. just for someone most people don't believe in anyway. It seems ridiculous. So I've just hung up on Him and I've asked Our Lady and St Joseph to lay off as well, so you can't blame any of them for not helping me.

I did try, by the way – to avoid Henry. Not very hard, though. I read a bit of *The Imitation of Christ*, but found it disgusting – like laying out your own corpse. I can't believe that goodness is meant to be so morbid and dull. I don't want to just hang around waiting to die.

I hope you don't mind but I'd rather you didn't write back.

I may be a wanton woman now, but I'm still capable of feeling ashamed.

    With love,
    Clare.

chapter nine

The next day, a Saturday, John took his children to lunch with Paula at Purves Mews. She had by now filled a cupboard with toys and games to keep them amused; and on this particular occasion had also bought each a little *panier* of French chocolates wrapped in brightly coloured papers. They went to play upstairs while John sat with a drink in the kitchen, half-reading the morning paper, while Paula finished preparing the lunch.

'Have you had any thoughts about how we should do up the house?' she asked, standing at the sink, her back turned to John.

'What was that?' he asked.

'We completed yesterday,' she said. 'They can start decorating on Monday.'

'Good.'

'I know what I want to do in the drawing-room and the hall, but what about your study?'

'I quite like plain white walls.'

'Like your drawing-room? How funny. I always thought that was Clare's lack of imagination.' She laughed. 'Anyway white is no good in London because it shows the dirt.'

John said nothing.

'I always think a sort of underdone roast beef colour is best for a study, or billiard-table green. No, that's too bright. A sort of bottle-green. You should see the library in the French Embassy: that's the colour I mean.'

'Whatever you think,' said John.

She turned to face him. 'It's up to you, of course. It's going to be your study. If you want white walls you can have white walls.'

'I don't really care.'

She wiped her hands on her apron and came to sit next to him. 'What's the matter?' she asked.

'Nothing. Why?'

'You seem depressed. Did you sleep badly?'

'No. I'm all right.'

'You're working too hard,' she said. 'You're taking on too much legal work. You should save your energy for Parliament.'

'I have to earn some money.'

'Not for much longer.'

'And most of what I do in the House of Commons seems a waste of time.'

'Be patient. You'll soon get on to some committee or get a job in the government. Daddy met Harold Lever the other day and from what he said they're certainly aware of your existence.'

John frowned and looked at the paper.

'There is something the matter, isn't there?' said Paula.

'No.'

She stood again. 'Don't tell me if you don't want to, but I know you well enough to be able to tell when there's something wrong.'

Over lunch Paula described the preparations for the wedding. Anna was to be one of four bridesmaids: Tom and a second cousin of Paula's called Hamish Gerrard were to be the two pages. The girls were to wear long green muslin dresses with high, Empire bodices and wreaths of flowers in their hair: the boys were to be dressed in little hussar's uniforms with real shakos and patent leather kneeboots. 'It'll be awfully useful afterwards for fancy dress parties,' Paula said to Tom.

'Will I have a sword?' he asked.

'I'm not sure about that,' said Paula. 'We don't want you to trip up in the aisle.'

'I wouldn't trip up,' said Tom.

'Well we'll see.' She turned to John. 'What will you wear?' she asked.

'I've got a morning coat.'

'What sort?'

'The usual sort.'

'A black coat and striped trousers?'

'Yes.'

'I rather hoped you might get a new one.'

'It isn't very old. I've only worn it half a dozen times.'

She clenched her jaw. 'Maybe, but if you could spare an hour or so next week we could go to Daddy's tailor and he could measure you for a new one – just one colour, a kind of dove-grey.'

John scowled. 'Isn't this wedding getting a little out of control?'

'How do you mean?'

'How many people are going to be invited?'

'It depends on who you want to ask. Mummy's list comes to just over two hundred but I don't suppose they'll all come.'

'Don't you think it's a little tasteless to marry in such style so soon after . . .' He glanced at the children and did not finish his sentence.

'I didn't want a big wedding,' said Paula. 'I'd have been quite happy with a registry office, but I am Mummy and Daddy's only child, and it would be a little selfish of us, wouldn't it, to deny them something they've been looking forward to for years just because you're a widower?'

'Yes. I suppose so.

'Six months is a perfectly respectable period to wait.

'Yes.'

'Particularly when everyone knows that we knew each other before.'

Although he denied it to Paula, John was undoubtedly depressed that day or, to be more exact, he was irritable and withdrawn. He looked at Paula across her kitchen table and found her as pretty as ever: her somewhat bossy manner was not new; her suggestions were always reasonable; and as he watched her he felt the same softness and solicitude as before – but he was distracted from these feelings by some other, imprecise preoccupation, just as if garbled talk from a foreign radio station was interfering with a programme of lyrical music.

After lunch they went once again to see the house in Lord North Street but John could not bring himself even to pretend to care which carpets or curtains should be chosen for which room. Paula became annoyed and said: 'You behave as if you don't want to live here, when I only chose this bloody house because of you.'

'I do want to live here,' John said lamely, 'but you must remember that I've been through this carpet and curtain business before.'

Paula's face went black and she said nothing. Shortly afterwards John left to take the children to tea with some friends: he and Paula kissed one another before they parted.

Alone at home, drinking tea and reading Hansard, John felt the full force of his irritable melancholy. With growing alarm he began to recognize the symptoms of his Ivan Ilychitis, which seemed to him impossible because he had taken the cure – he was a Labour politician, he was helping the poor. Would he be reading this debate on fluoridation if he was not? Then he remembered the letters. It was these which had upset him. He went to Clare's desk and took them out of the drawer as if by holding them he would exorcise their malign influence. He read them again – skipping some passages, re-reading others – trying to assess, reasonably and calmly, why they should have upset him so much.

It was a shock for a start to hear her voice from the grave like this – for as he read the letters he did hear her voice speaking the words she had written. It was also most disagreeable to read between the lines the state of her sexual thrall to Henry Mascall. It was undoubtedly unpleasant to see how little respect she had for him, though in retrospect he should have known this from her attitude towards his political ambitions. Yet he was more annoyed by the way in which, while she explicitly blamed herself for her adultery, he still felt that the onus was left on him. He felt that she had somehow outsmarted him, for though she would not use his infidelity as an excuse for hers, she seemed to believe that he had ceased to love her. Why, if he did not love her, was he suffering now? What right had she to say that he had abandoned her for his career – deserted his lifelong companion, the mother of his children, for senile pensioners in Hackney and a debate on fluoridation? Perhaps he was vain, pompous, pedantic and dull: but why, if she could see that in him, could she not also see that his affection and respect for her were so strong that they were a composite part of his personality?

It was hot. He went to raise one of the tall sash windows which looked out from their drawing-room on to the street below. There entered, with the fresh air, the sounds of the neighbourhood – the surge of traffic at the lights on Holland Park Avenue, the cries of children from the communal gardens beyond the square – and the scent of the clematis which Clare had planted ten years before.

He went back to his armchair and looked again at the letters. That, certainly, was part of what worried him. Over the twelve and a half years of their marriage he and Clare had grown together like the entwined stems of the clematis, and John knew he no longer possessed the elasticity to grow straight again. There was Paula, of course, with her pushing tendrils already feeling for the vacant groove in the twist of old wood. She would grow up beside him, and doubtless cover him so that those who stopped to admire the flowering creeper in future years would never know that it had grown up on the horny old stem of an earlier plant.

He sighed, for he seemed to have reached the melancholy understanding that his love for Paula was like Clare's love for Henry Mascall; that he too had searched for a way 'to let off steam'; that he would never love Paula in the equal, casual, fraternal way that he had loved Clare because he was too old: and he saw ahead of him lifelong protestations of passion to hide the essential superficiality of his love.

The children were brought back by the parents of their friends. John gave them a bath, read them a book and saw them to bed. Mrs Giles came in to baby-sit so that John and Paula could dine with the Barclays. There were six other guests, including Micky Neill and Mary Mascall. Three glasses of whisky put John on form. He teased his host and hostess about their political hysteria before the election. Where were the Commissars? What had happened to the Revolution?

'Oh, it wasn't us,' said Eva Barclay. 'It was silly old Henry.' Whereupon Mary Mascall blushed and there was an embarrassed silence. Then the chatter started up again. They all behaved well. It was a successful evening.

At the door, as they left, Mary and Paula agreed that the four of them should get together some time to see a film or a play.

'Don't the Whips make sure you're in at ten like a good boy?' Micky asked John.

'Not every night,' he replied.

The two women agreed to telephone one another as if it went without saying that they never would. Then the two couples went their different ways. John and Paula returned to Purves Mews, where both being slightly drunk they raucously and noisily made love.

John returned to Holland Park at one in the morning and was up next day in time to give his children their breakfast and then take them to church. The three sat next to one another on a pew near the altar. Above them, on a wooden pedestal, there was a painted plaster statue of Christ pointing to a bleeding heart which protruded from his chest. What, John asked himself, had Clare made of something like that? What, indeed, had she made of any of this mumbo-jumbo? That was something which had surprised him in her letters – that she had taken God and religion so seriously. He had always assumed that she went to mass from habit and brought up the children as Catholics to please her mother. He had never seen or heard her pray, yet clearly she had prayed the whole time. How strange it was that a man could live with a woman for over twelve years and never know what she was thinking. Behind those cool blue eyes she had not only been longing for Henry Mascall; she had also been chatting to God.

How strange, too, that her image of him had been so unlike his image of himself. What was he, he wondered? Her endearing, pedantic bore? Henry's vain and fatuous hypocrite? Paula's masterful, ambitious statesman? Or his own decent, conscientious idealist? A looking glass at least gave an accurate reflection of one's physical appearance, but what mirror was there in which one could examine one's own character and personality? Can one know oneself only through others? And if so, does one not choose to see those who reflect a flattering image? Did he not like Gordon Pratt principally because Gordon believed in his political career? Had he not been drawn to Paula not by her face and figure, not even by her youth, elegance and wealth, but by the admiring reflection in her fine brown eyes of his own personality?

It was this, he now realized, that had most shaken him in reading Clare's letters – the proof that they presented that he was not the person he thought he was, but that like this statue of Christ and his Sacred Heart, he was a different person to different people; and his own appreciation of himself, coloured as it was by self-love, was perhaps the least accurate of all.

A bell was rung at the altar. Tom and Anna knelt and John too went on his knees. The thought that a man or woman could know everyone but himself or herself induced in him once again a philosophical vertigo, for it seemed to remove the foundations on which one built the structure of one's life. Others might be defined by what they did and said; but even here quite disparate motives could dictate the same words and actions. Clare had seen Henry Mascall as the Devil because he had invited her to sleep with him, and had insisted that she choose the time and place. Father Michael concurred with this view, and John certainly thought of him as an evil, loathsome man. But was it not possible – indeed probable – that Henry had seen himself as a decent chap making a friendly gesture to an attractive girl whose husband was screwing around with someone else? Was it not also possible that a sense of propriety, not a wish to humiliate, made him insist that she should show that she knew what she was doing by choosing the time and place?

It was also possible that he, John Strickland, might seem in a certain light just as evil as Henry Mascall. He remembered Ivan Ilych: *Maybe I did not live as I ought to have done?* He remembered his answer: *But how could that be when I did everything properly?* Could he not say the same? Jilly Mascall? A trifling flirtation. Paula? He shifted his weight off his knees and leant his backside against the pew behind. Most successful men had mistresses; and anyway it was different for a man; and at least he had never made an advance to the wife of a friend.

Another bell rang. Tom and Anna lifted their heads and looked up at the altar as the priest raised the host above his head. And that wafer? Had Clare really believed that it was the flesh of Christ and Christ the Son of God? It would be useful, of course, if there was a God, because He at least could see through a man's conceit, and the prejudices of his friends and enemies, to his real personality. He at least could sift the good from the bad in each of his actions. Even I might believe in God, John thought to himself, if He could show me the man I really am.

chapter ten

On Monday 29 July, five days before the wedding, Sir Peter Craxton telephoned John at the House of Commons and asked if he could find time to look in at his chambers some time that week.

'Have the police come up with something?' John asked.

'No, I'm afraid not. It's nothing to do with that. There are a few formalities about the marriage that we ought to go through . . .'

John had a busy week – the tailor had not yet finished his dove-grey morning coat – but the two men agreed to meet at Sir Peter's chambers in Lincoln's Inn on the following Friday morning. When John arrived he found another man present – a balding, bespectacled man – whom Sir Peter introduced as Mr Maitland, the assistant manager of the branch of Coutts Bank which handled Paula's account.

'Do sit down,' said Sir Peter – showing John to a red leather chair which faced his desk, and Mr Maitland to a rather less comfortable one in the corner of the room. 'I called Detective Inspector Thompson just before you came,' he said. 'He was as frank as policemen ever are. They aren't any nearer to finding your wife's murderer.'

'Have they no suspects at all?'

'He says they've followed several leads but none of them have led anywhere. There were no prints, you see. As Thompson said, the murderer was either very lucky or very professional.' Sir Peter settled back in his own chair, which was the most comfortable of all. 'However,' he said, 'we're here to talk about happier matters.'

Behind them Mr Maitland cleared his throat.

'As you probably know,' said Sir Peter in a silken voice, 'Sir Christopher Gerrard is a very wealthy man. What you may not realize quite so clearly is that Paula, upon marriage, becomes a very wealthy woman.'

'I assumed she had some money,' said John.

Sir Peter frowned as if irritated by this interruption. 'It's a little complicated,' he said, 'so let me explain. Paula has until now had no money of her own. She has lived off an allowance from her father. But upon marriage she becomes the beneficiary of a Marriage Settlement Trust set up by Sir Christopher when Paula was born. Now the Trust deed was drawn up with various stipulations which Sir Christopher has regretted since. Paula has been unable to touch either the capital or the income before marriage, so she has until now been a charge to his personal income while the Trust, with its income accruing tax-free year after year, has assets now worth' – he glanced down at a sheet of paper on his desk – 'approximately three and a half million pounds.'

Mr Maitland cleared his throat again.

'I had no idea she would have as much as that,' said John.

'Well I'm glad to be able to give you such an agreeable surprise,' said Sir Peter. 'However, that's not the point of taking up your time this morning. There is provision in the Trust deed – it's a funny document, I didn't draw it up – for payment to be made both to Paula and her prospective husband prior to the marriage up to a limit of ten thousand pounds – that's twenty thousand in all – or more exactly for loans to be made which are then repaid out of the Trust after the marriage. I imagine that whoever drew it up envisaged Paula marrying a pauper who might need the money to buy a morning coat. Be that as it may, the Trust can lend up to ten thousand pounds to you and ten thousand pounds to Paula prior to your marriage.'

John smiled. 'I don't think I shall need ten thousand pounds between now and tomorrow afternoon.'

Sir Peter frowned again. 'I wasn't going to suggest that you did. What Sir Christopher has asked me to do is recover from the Trust any money paid to you or Paula prior to the marriage.'

'I don't quite understand.'

'Sir Christopher feels that the Marriage Settlement Trust should now repay him as far as possible for Paula's allowance.'

'But why, when he gave her a Renoir . . .'

'The Renoir was purchased by the Trust from Sir Christopher. He is, you see, a true financier. He's always short of money because any he has he puts to work.'

'Can't Paula simply repay him once we're married?'

Sir Peter hesitated. 'Yes. Up to a point. But Sir Christopher mustn't appear to be a beneficiary himself . . .'

'Of course not.'

'She can certainly repay him for money she's had in this financial year after the wedding; but the money for the last financial year could come out of these "loans" by the Trustees, making the total forty rather than twenty thousand pounds.'

'I see.'

'What we should like to establish is what sums of money you have received from Sir Christopher through Paula in the two years to the fifth of April.'

'But I haven't received any,' said John.

Sir Peter smiled. 'I understand that there were certain gifts from Miss Gerrard which could now be scheduled as purchases made with the loans from the Trust.'

'Of course, there was the car.'

'Which cost £2,584,' said Mr Maitland.

'Can you think of anything else?' Sir Peter asked John.

John blushed. 'She's bought me some shirts and things.'

'Quite. Miscellaneous items – what, about £200 worth?'

'I've no idea.'

'I can see it's difficult to calculate. We'll say £200.' He noted down the figure. 'You'll probably see now why I didn't ask Paula to come along this morning.'

'Yes I do.'

Sir Peter looked over John's shoulder to Mr Maitland. There's a standing order to a T. E. Clark, isn't there?'

'Yes.'

'That's my children's nanny,' said John.

'And another to A. E. Giles,' said Maitland.

'That's the woman who cleans the house.'

'Is there anything else?' asked Sir Peter.

'Paula has occasionally bought my children some sweets,' said John sarcastically. 'You can put down five or ten pounds for that.'

Sir Peter duly noted the sum with his pencil.

'Nothing else?'

'No.'

Mr Maitland cleared his throat. 'I think you may have forgotten the five thousand pounds Miss Gerrard gave you last February,' he said.

John turned. The man's face was obscured by the light from the window behind him. 'What five thousand pounds?'

Mr Maitland ran his pen down a copy of Paula's bank statement. 'On 15 February,' he said, 'she drew out five thousand pounds in cash.'

'What on earth for?'

'She said it was for you.'

'But why should I want five thousand pounds in cash?'

'I understand that you were somewhat overdrawn.'

'But one doesn't pay off one's overdraft in cash,' said John in an irritable, impatient tone of voice.

'It seemed strange to me,' said Mr Maitland, 'but Miss Gerrard explained that . . . er . . . that you were married and that your wife saw your statements.'

John laughed. 'That's absurd. My wife ran a mile if she saw anything that even looked like a statement.'

'The point,' said Sir Peter, 'is not what you did with the money but whether you received it, because if you did we can reclaim it . . .'

'Of course I didn't,' said John.

Sir Peter sighed. 'It would make things more convenient if you did.'

John turned back to the bank manager. 'Are you sure she drew out five thousand pounds? In cash? On 15 February?'

'Yes, Mr Strickland. I gave it to her myself. I remember her saying that she needn't have brought the bag.'

'What bag?'

'She thought that five thousand in cash would be much more bulky, so she brought this blue canvas bag to put it in.'

John looked at Sir Peter. For a moment their eyes met. Then

279

Sir Peter looked away and said: 'It's not up to us to speculate upon what Paula did with the money. She may have put it on a horse for all we know. But it's quite clear that Mr Strickland didn't receive it so we cannot set it off against his allocation for '73–'74.'

He continued to talk, but John did not listen, and as soon as he could he escaped from Sir Peter's chambers and drove in the Volvo which had cost £2,584 to Purves Mews. Paula was not there. They were due to meet that afternoon for the last time before the wedding, and John thought that she might have already left for lunch with her mother, or have driven down to Prinnet Park with her wedding dress, which like his morning coat had only been ready the day before: but when he went upstairs he saw that it was laid out on the sofa – neatly discarded after the final fitting. The lifeless white garment seemed to him then as much like Clare's shroud as Paula's bridal gown, and as John sat on an armchair in the living-room now filled with bright sunlight he conjured up the images of his two brides – first the one woman, then the other, each innocent, lovely, affectionate: each capable, he now realized, of profound deceit.

He tried to remember the expression on Paula's face when he had stumbled into that same room six months before, two days after she had withdrawn five thousand pounds in a blue canvas bag, the day after Clare had been murdered, to find her alone with Terry Pike. Had there been guilt or fear in her eyes? He remembered only her calming, soothing voice, and her open, blameless expression. Yet he now felt a bottomless mistrust of Paula, and had no doubt but that Terry Pike's hold-all was the same canvas bag, and that it had not contained his pyjamas and toothbrush but five thousand pounds in cash. But why should she pay him five thousand pounds? Was it a parting gift? She would have given it already. A pay-off? For what? He remembered how, at their first lunch together, she had quoted from *Romeo and Juliet*. He rose and went to the bookshelf to find the quotation:

Need and oppression starveth in thy eyes,
Contempt and beggary hang upon thy back,

The world is not thy friend, nor the world's law;
The world affords no law to make thee rich;
Then be not poor, but break it *and take this*.

Romeo was bribing the apothecary to give him poison. But for what could Paula have been paying Terry Pike? What could she want done? And what could have cost such a price?

He went back to the fireplace and then quickly sat down because a suspicion had entered his mind which made his body falter as if for a moment his heart had stopped pumping blood to the brain. He heard the door open below. He sat still and silent. He heard scuffling in the kitchen. Still he said nothing. He heard steps on the stairs. He did not move. Paula came into the living-room and for a moment she did not notice him, so for the first time he saw her features in repose. They were empty. There was no expression. Then she saw him and after a moment of shock the muscles clenched beneath her cheeks to smile and look sweet. 'Goodness you gave me a fright,' she said.

'I'm sorry.'

'What are you doing here?'

'I wanted to see you.'

Her manner too now had all its practised warmth and charm. 'Couldn't you wait until this afternoon?' she asked.

'I've just been with Craxton,' said John.

'What did he want?'

'He explained about your Trust.'

She grinned. 'Isn't it lovely? We're going to be frightfully rich.'

'Your father wants to be repaid as far as possible . . .'

'I know. Typical Daddy.'

'He asked me what money I'd had from you.'

The smile left her face. 'The old fool. He should have asked me. I could have told him.'

'He seemed to think I'd had five thousand pounds in cash.'

She turned to rearrange some flowers in a vase by the fireplace. 'Didn't he mean the Volvo?'

'No. He'd counted that.'

'I don't know what he means, then. I never gave you five thousand pounds in cash.'

'I know,' said John, 'but you apparently told your bank manager . . .'

'Was he there? Mr Maitland?'

'Yes. He said you'd withdrawn five thousand in cash on the fifteenth of February, saying it was for me.'

Paula finished with the flowers and wiping her hands on her skirt turned to face John. 'I'll ring Peter this afternoon and sort it all out.'

'Maitland said you put the money in a blue canvas bag.'

She scowled. 'What business is it of his how I carry my money?'

'It was presumably the same bag which Terry Pike had with him . . .'

'When?'

'That night I found him here.'

Paula sat down on one of the armchairs. 'Yes, well, he was blackmailing me.' She sighed and rubbed her face with her hands.

'About what?'

'You. He said he'd tell Clare. I was afraid.'

'Why?'

She looked at him. 'I knew you'd never leave Clare. I knew that if it was her or me it would be her.'

'So you paid him off?'

'Yes.'

'That night?'

'Yes.'

'Though she was dead?'

'I didn't know.'

'You should have called him back and asked for your money back.'

They sat for some time in silence, as if waiting for jam to set or glue to dry. Eventually John said: 'I don't really believe you.'

'I wish you would,' she replied quite flatly.

'It wouldn't stand up in court.'

'We aren't in a court.'

'I know.'

'Don't think about it. Don't look back.'

'Did you pay him to kill her?'

282

'He didn't kill her. He was somewhere else.'

'I dare say.'

'Think of it as a car crash or leukaemia . . .'

John shook his head. 'I can't.'

'You said that if she died . . .'

'I know.'

'Does it matter . . . now . . . how she died?'

John looked at her. 'Yes.'

'What was done,' said Paula, 'was done because I love you.'

'I know.'

'So it mustn't stop you loving me.' Her eyes now had the sup-
plicating look of someone in extremity.

'It doesn't,' said John, 'but it stops me loving myself. Whenever I look at you now I shall see the reflection of a weak, cold-
hearted egoist . . .'

'But it wasn't you,' she said. 'You didn't know.'

'I didn't know but I'm to blame.' He got to his feet, and said
as if he had just dropped in to see her on his way to another
appointment: 'I must go now.'

'Aren't you hungry? It's past two.'

'No.'

He went down the spiral staircase: Paula followed. At the door
she said: It's off, isn't it? I mean . . . tomorrow?'

'Yes. I'm sorry.'

'We couldn't just go through with it and then sort of go our
own ways?'

He shook his head. 'No. I realize what a business it'll be to
cancel everything, but I couldn't . . . I couldn't go through with
it.'

'Don't worry,' said Paula, biting her lower lip. 'I'll think of
something to say.'

They kissed one another politely on both cheeks and said goodbye like old friends: then John walked away on the cobbles leaving the station-wagon parked outside her door.

chapter eleven

Tom and Anna came home that afternoon to find their father sitting in the kitchen.

'Where's Nanny?' asked Anna.

'She's gone,' said John.

'But I'm meant to try on my dress again.'

'It doesn't matter because I'm not getting married now.'

'Not at all?' asked Tom.

'No.'

'Why not?'

'I thought we could manage on our own.'

'Will we stay in this house?' asked Anna.

'Yes.'

'Good.'

'Are you sure that's all right, Dad?' asked Tom politely. 'The other one is nearer your work, isn't it?'

'Yes, but this is our home.'

'I like it better, I must say, because all my things are here. I didn't really want to move the electric trains just when we'd set them up, I mean, unless you wanted me to.'

'We can leave them now in your room.'

'Aren't we going to Paula's parents' house tonight, then?'

'No. We're going to Norfolk.'

'To Granny's?'

'Yes.'

'When?'

'As soon as we're ready.'

'Why are we going to Granny's?' asked Anna.

'We always do in August.'

'Is it August?'

'Of course it is,' said Tom. 'It started on Thursday.'

They drove up to Busey in the old yellow Volvo and arrived when it was still light. Helen took charge of her two grandchildren and went to feed them in the kitchen while John went out to the front of the house where Eustace was digging weeds out of the lawn with his silver teaspoon. When he saw John he got to his feet and the two men strolled down towards the wicket gate through which the vicars of former times had passed into the churchyard. They did the same and ended their saunter at the hillock of turf which was Clare's grave. A stone had been erected which John had not seen before.

'Are the words all right?' asked Eustace.

'Yes,' said John.

' "Beloved wife" is a bit old-fashioned but it's hard to think of another way to put it.'

'There's no other way.'

The two men stood in silence as the dew settled on the grass.

'So the wedding's off?' said Eustace.

'Yes.'

'Postponed or cancelled?'

'Cancelled.'

Eustace grunted. 'Girl no good?'

'Not quite what I thought she was.'

'You'll find someone else.'

John shook his head. 'I don't think I'll marry again.'

'You should do, for the children.'

'I'll look after them.'

'What about politics?'

'There's talk of an autumn election. If there is, I won't stand again.'

'Not what you thought it was either?'

John smiled. 'No. It is more or less what I expected. I shall go back to it later, when the children are grown up, but one's personal responsibilities come first.'

They turned and walked back towards the house.

'Do you mind,' asked John, 'if I stay here with the children?'

'As long as you like,' said Eustace. 'It was always your home as much as Clare's.'

'I find it strange,' said John, 'that you make vows when you marry to last until you are separated by death, and yet now that Clare is dead I feel no less married to her than I did before.'

'Perhaps marriages are made in Heaven after all,' said Eustace.

'And yet Christ said, didn't He, that there are no husbands and wives in Heaven?'

'We can't expect to understand it all,' said Eustace shaking his head. 'We have to take what we can get and make the most of it.'

'And hope,' said John, 'that He whose understanding matters will understand.'

'Like old Ivan Ilych? Yes. That's about the best we can hope for.'

They reached the terrace and went through the garden door into the house where supper was waiting for them in the kitchen.

Selected Bestsellers

☐	**The Empty Hours**	Ed McBain	£1.25p
☐	**Shanghai**	William Marshall	£1.25p
☐	**Symptoms**	edited by	
		Sigmund Stephen Miller	£2.50p
☐	**Gone with the Wind**	Margaret Mitchell	£2.95p
☐	**Robert Morley's Book of Worries**	Robert Morley	£1.50p
☐	**The Totem**	David Morrell	£1.25p
☐	**The Alternative Holiday Catalogue**	edited by Harriet Peacock	£1.95p
☐	**The Pan Book of Card Games**	Hubert Phillips	£1.50p
☐	**The New Small Garden**	C. E. Lucas Phillips	£2.50p
☐	**Everything Your Doctor Would Tell You If He Had the Time**	Claire Rayner	£4.95p
☐	**A Town Like Alice**	Nevil Shute	£1.50p
☐	**Just Off for the Weekend**	John Slater	£2.50p
☐	**The Deep Well at Noon**	Jessica Stirling	£1.75p
☐	**The Eighth Dwarf**	Ross Thomas	£1.25p
☐	**The Music Makers**	E. V. Thompson	£1.50p
☐	**The Third Wave**	Alvin Toffler	£1.95p
☐	**Auberon Waugh's Yearbook**	Auberon Waugh	£1.95p
☐	**The Flier's Handbook**		£4.95p

All these books are available at your local bookshop or newsagent, or can be ordered direct from the publisher. Indicate the number of copies required and fill in the form below

Name..
(block letters please)
Address..

Send to Pan Books (CS Department), Cavaye Place, London SW10 9PG
Please enclose remittance to the value of the cover price plus:

25p for the first book plus 10p per copy for each additional book ordered to a maximum charge of £1.05 to cover postage and packing Applicable only in the UK

While every effort is made to keep prices low, it is sometimes necessary to increase prices at short notice. Pan Books reserve the right to show on covers and charge new retail prices which may differ from those advertised in the text or elsewhere